NEBULA AWARDS SHOWCASE

2005

THE YEAR'S BEST SF AND FANTASY

Selected by the Science Fiction and
Fantasy Writers of America®

EDITED BY

Jack Dann

A ROC BOOK

ROC
Published by New American Library, a division of
Penguin Group (USA) Inc., 375 Hudson Street,
New York, New York 10014, USA
Penguin Group (Canada), 10 Alcorn Avenue, Toronto,
Ontario M4V 3B2, Canada (a division of Pearson Penguin Canada Inc.)
Penguin Books Ltd., 80 Strand, London WC2R 0RL, England
Penguin Ireland, 25 St. Stephen's Green, Dublin 2,
Ireland (a division of Penguin Books Ltd.)
Penguin Group (Australia), 250 Camberwell Road, Camberwell, Victoria 3124,
Australia (a division of Pearson Australia Group Pty. Ltd.)
Penguin Books India Pvt. Ltd., 11 Community Centre, Panchsheel Park,
New Delhi – 110 017, India
Penguin Group (NZ), cnr Airborne and Rosedale Roads, Albany,
Auckland 1310, New Zealand (a division of Pearson New Zealand Ltd.)
Penguin Books (South Africa) (Pty.) Ltd., 24 Sturdee Avenue,
Rosebank, Johannesburg 2196, South Africa

Penguin Books Ltd., Registered Offices:
80 Strand, London WC2R 0RL, England

First published by Roc, an imprint of New American Library,
a division of Penguin Group (USA) Inc.

First Printing, March 2005
1   3   5   7   9   10   8   6   4   2

Copyright © Science Fiction and Fantasy Writers of America, 2005
Additional copyright notices can be found on p. 328
All rights reserved

Set in Bembo
Designed by Elke Sigal

Ⓡ Registered Trademark—Marca Registrada

Roc trade paperback ISBN: 0-451-46015-4

Printed in the United States of America

IN MEMORY OF PETER MCNAMARA

ACKNOWLEDGMENTS

The author would like to thank the following people for their help and support: Ginjer Buchanan, G. O. Clark, Ellen Datlow, Jane Jewell, Gordon Van Gelder, Janeen Webb, Walter Jon Williams, Sheila Williams, and Eleanor Wood. Special thanks to Jonathan Strahan, Merrilee Heifetz, Pamela Sargent, and George Zebrowski, who walked me through the minefields.

CONTENTS

INTRODUCTION

JACK DANN

started making my bones as a writer in the late 1960s and early 1970s, a time when electricity was in the air, movements were rife, zeitgeists were happening before our very eyes. The world was changing; we were changing. It was the time of sex, drugs, and rock 'n' roll; women's liberation; consciousness raising; the civil rights movement; the anti-war movement; and nestled among all that shifting of season and mind and temper was science fiction's own New Wave movement.

Magazines such as Michael Moorcock's *New Worlds* in England and anthologies such as Robert Silverberg's *New Dimensions* series and Damon Knight's *Orbit* series showcased the brilliant and experimental work of Thomas M. Disch, Samuel R. Delany, Gene Wolfe, M. John Harrison, Kate Wilhelm, Gardner Dozois, George Alec Effinger, Sonya Dorman, Joanna Russ, Carol Emshwiller, R. A. Lafferty, and a host of others. It was a time of literary experimentation in the genre: J. G. Ballard had written his hallucinatory "Vermillion Sands" stories and was writing novels such as *Crash* and what he called "condensed novels," unnerving, wonderfully profane series of stories, which can be found in collections such as *The Atrocity Exhibition* and *Love and Napalm*. Brian Aldiss was writing cutting edge novels such as *Report On Probability A* and his "Acid-Head" war stories, and Samuel R. Delany was writing literary jewel-like novels such as *The Einstein Intersection* and Nebula-winning stories such as "Time Considered as a Helix of Semi-Precious Stones" and "Aye, and Gomorrah."

We were co-opting the tropes and styles and literary tricks of the mainstream and transforming them. John Brunner's *The Sheep Look Up*, for example, was pure Dos Passos, an edgy dystopia set in an ecologically failing future; and some writers such as Brian Aldiss, J. G. Ballard, Samuel R. Delany, James Sallis, and Carol Emshwiller, to name those who first come to mind, *were* being accepted in mainstream venues. But by and large, as brilliant, interesting, experimental, cutting-edge, transformative, and literary as the work was, it didn't have any impact on the larger culture. Science fiction did influence popular culture, but through the media, via *Star Trek* and *Star Wars*.

The literary SF genre was still in the ghetto, where some said it belonged, arguing that the genre's great energy and freedom from convention would not survive in the claustrophobic atmosphere of academic and mainstream fiction. That great energy erupted again in the 1980s with the cyberpunk movement, spearheaded by William Gibson and given voice and coherence by Bruce Sterling's underground critical magazine, *Cheap Truth*.

The science fiction punks were finally influencing the popular culture. Cyberspace entered the lexicon. The future was now.

And now, twenty years after George Orwell's *1984* and three years past the date of Arthur C. Clarke's farseeing *2001,* something odd and strange and wonderfully ironic is happening. The larger culture is busily co-opting the tropes of science fiction and fantasy. The average Joe on the street might not know anything at all about the genre, and probably wouldn't care to; but he does watch television. More specifically, he watches *commercials,* those little magic markers of our culture; and he has been prepared to accept transformation and magic as a matter of course. People eating a specific brand of potato chip become flatlanders, thin enough to fall right through the grates in the street, if they're not careful; Volvo drivers see bearded doppelgangers of themselves everywhere they look, skyscrapers rise up into the sky as actors walk from one office to another, stepping into different cities, different climates; Ford cars drive through impossibly shifting landscapes in one-minute sound and video bytes.

As Terry Pratchett said in a recent interview in the science fiction news magazine *Locus*: "SF has broken out of the ghetto people always used to talk about, but also the tropes of SF are now available for use by everybody else, which is not what anyone expected. For today's SF writers, science fiction is like some big generation ship that's crash-landed on a planet, and in order to build new structures people are taking away bits of it. You can still see the shape of the thing, but everything has been cannibalized for different purposes. Quite a lot of what's out there is still recognizable as science fiction but is recognizable as other things as well."

In the stories and essays that follow, we'll look at this generation ship of science fiction. But before we do, we should take another glance backward because this series of Nebula volumes (which have been appearing since Damon Knight edited the first one in 1965) not only represent the cutting edge of "right now"; they also are weighted with history: the "not now" that our genre rests upon. They are a record of where we came from, what we've done, and what we're doing. As *Locus* predicted, "This series may turn out to be the best record we have of how SF writers have wanted to represent their craft to the world."

In this era of cyberspace and connectivity, when enormous amounts of information are but a double-click away (and even the double-click has just been patented by Microsoft!), we have curiously lost our sense of the history of the genre; and in our rush toward the new and the hot, we've forgotten so many of the writers who have made science fiction what it is today. It is our loss, for the great work stands the test of time.

And so before we journey to the cutting-edge, we should give a nod to some of the classic writers who might not be household names: Clifford Simak, Edgar Pangborn, Keith Roberts, C. M. Kornbluth, Cordwainer Smith, Theodore Sturgeon . . .

The final Nebula Awards ballot for 2004 follows.

I think *all* the stories on the final and preliminary ballots are "SFFWA's choices for the best science fiction and fantasy of the year." Getting onto the ballot is a win in itself. So, herewith, are *all* the winners (I have indicated those that topped the ballot, and you'll also find some selected titles from the 2004 Preliminary Nebula Ballot in the appendixes).

NOVEL

Hidden Empire: The Saga of Seven Suns, Book 1 by Kevin J. Anderson
(Warner Books, July 2002)

Diplomatic Immunity by Lois McMaster Bujold (Baen, May 2002)

The Mount by Carol Emshwiller (Small Beer Press, June 2002)

Light Music by Kathleen Ann Goonan (Eos, June 2002)

The Salt Roads by Nalo Hopkinson (Warner Books, November 2003)

Chindi by Jack McDevitt (Ace, July 2002)

The Speed of Dark by Elizabeth Moon (Ballantine, January 2003)

NOVELLA

"The Potter of Bones" by Eleanor Arnason
(*Asimov's Science Fiction*, September 2002)

"The Empress of Mars" by Kage Baker
(*Asimov's Science Fiction*, July 2003)

"Coraline" by Neil Gaiman
(HarperCollins, July 2002)

"Stories for Men" by John Kessel
(*Asimov's Science Fiction*, October/November 2002)

"Breathmoss" by Ian MacLeod
(*Asimov's Science Fiction*, May 2002)

NOVELETTE

"The Mask of the Rex" by Richard Bowes
(*The Magazine of Fantasy & Science Fiction*, May 2002)

"Of a Sweet Slow Dance in the Wake of Temporary Dogs"
by Adam-Troy Castro (*Imaginings*, Pocket Books 2003)

"OwnzOred" by Cory Doctorow
(*Salon.com*, August 2002)

"The Empire of Ice Cream" by Jeffrey Ford
(*SCI FICTION,* February 26, 2003)
"The Wages of Syntax" by Ray Vukcevich
(*SCI FICTION,* October 16, 2002)

SHORT STORY
"Knapsack Poems" by Eleanor Arnason
(*Asimov's Science Fiction,* May 2002)
"The Brief History of the Dead" by Kevin Brockmeier
(*The New Yorker,* September 8, 2003)
"Goodbye to All That" by Harlan Ellison
(*McSweeney's Mammoth Treasury of Thrilling Tales,* April 2003)
"Grandma" by Carol Emshwiller
(*The Magazine of Fantasy & Science Fiction,* March 2002)
"What I Didn't See" by Karen Joy Fowler
(*SCI FICTION,* July 10, 2002)
"Lambing Season" by Molly Gloss
(*Asimov's Science Fiction,* July 2002)
"The Last of the O-Forms" by James Van Pelt
(*Asimov's Science Fiction,* July 2002)

SCRIPTS
Minority Report by Scott Frank and John Cohen
(Dreamworks, July 2002)
"Where No Fan Has Gone Before" by David A. Goodman
(*Futurama,* April 2002)
Spirited Away by Hayao Miyazaki and Cindy Davis Hewitt and
Donald H. Hewitt
(English screenplay)
(Studio Ghibli and Walt Disney Pictures, September 2002)
Finding Nemo by Andrew Stanton, Bob Peterson, and David Reynolds
(Pixar/Disney, May 2003)
**The Lord of the Rings: The Two Towers by Fran Walsh, Philippa
Bowens, Stephen Sinclair, and Peter Jackson**
(New Line Cinema, December 2002)

GRAND MASTER NEBULA AWARD
ROBERT SILVERBERG

Richard Bowes has published four novels: *Warchild, Goblin Market, Feral Cell,* and *Minions of the Moon,* which won the 1999 Lambda Award. He is also the author of the short story collection *Transfigured Nights and Other Stories.* His novella "Streetcar Dreams" won the 1998 World Fantasy Award for best novella. A short fiction collection, *Streetcar Dreams and Other Midnight Fancies,* is due later this year from PS Publications. Both "The Mask of the Rex" and last year's Nebula nominee "The Ferryman's Wife" are chapters in the mosaic novel *From the Files of the Time Rangers,* which will be published next year by Golden Gryphon Press.

In an interview by Jeffrey Ford—who also appears in this volume—Bowes was asked what books he enjoyed as a child and whether images or ideas from them find their way into his fiction.

"My parents had *The Thurber Carnival.* They used to read me things from it like 'The Night the Ghost Got In' as bedtime stories. And it had pictures, *New Yorker* cartoons that I loved to look at even before I learned to read. I heard all the Hugh Lofting *Doctor Dolittle* books, especially *Doctor Dolittle and The Secret Lake,* which is mostly the firsthand reminiscences of the Great Flood narrated by a pair of ancient giant tortoises. It's never been reprinted maybe because it deals with Biblical events, but it has no religious content. Stevenson's *Child's Garden of Verse,* books of Mother Goose rhymes, got read to me. This primed me. Made me want to read. Otherwise, I doubt that I would have had the motivation.

"When I did, I inherited all these books my uncles and older kids of family friends had. I read *Tanglewood Tales* and Pyle's *Robin Hood* and versions of the King Arthur stories and a lot of Boy's Own Adventure stuff with titles along the lines of *The Motor Car Chums at the Battle of the Somme* ('Golly,' shouted Biff, the stout, jolly Chum, 'If we could attach this Vickers machine gun to the hood, I'll bet we could slaughter those filthy Huns as they're eating breakfast!'). Dave Dawson was a sixteen-year-old World War Two flying ace. I read every novel in the series that I could get my hands on. I reread *Dave Dawson at Dunkirk* recently. The first part of it, anyway. Old loves are best left as memories.

"You ask if images and ideas from these books turn up in my fiction? Are you kidding? In a lot of ways there's nothing else."

"The Mask of the Rex," which follows, is a beautifully wrought story of gods, time, and responsibility.

THE MASK OF THE REX

RICHARD BOWES

PRELUDE

The last days of summer have always been a sweet season on the Maine coast. There's still warmth in the sun, the cricket's song is mellow and the vacationers are mostly gone. Nowhere is that time more golden than on Mount Airey Island.

Late one afternoon in September of 1954, Julia Garde Macauley drove north through the white-shingled coastal towns. In the wake of a terrible loss, she felt abandoned by the gods and had made this journey to confront them.

Then, as she crossed Wenlock Sound Bridge which connects the island with the world, she had a vision. In a fast montage, a man, his face familiar yet changed, stood on crutches in a cottage doorway, plunged into an excited crowd of kids, spoke defiantly on the stairs of a plane.

The images flickered like a TV with a bad picture and Julia thought she saw her husband. When it was over, she realized who it had been. And understood even better the questions she had come to ask.

The village of Penoquot Landing on Mount Airey was all carefully preserved clapboard and widow's walks. Few yachts were still in evidence. Fishing boats and lobster trawlers had full use of the wharves.

Baxter's Grande Hotel on Front Street was in hibernation until next summer. In Baxter's parlors and pavilions over the decades, the legends of this resort and Julia's own family had been woven.

Driving through the gathering dusk, Julia could almost hear drawling voices discussing her recent loss in the same way they did everything having to do with Mount Airey and the rest of the world.

"Great public commotion about that fly-boy she married."

"The day their wedding was announced marked the end of High Society."

"In a single-engine plane in bad weather. As if he never got over the war."

"Or knew he didn't belong where he was."

Robert Macauley, thirty-four years old, had been the junior Senator from New York for a little more than a year and a half.

Beyond the village, Julia turned onto the road her grandfather and Rockefeller had planned and built. *"Olympia Drive, where spectacular views of the mighty Atlantic and piney mainland compete for our attention with the palaces of the great,"* rhapsodized a writer of the prior century. *"Like a necklace of diamonds bestowed upon this island."*

The mansions were largely shut until next year. Some hadn't been opened at all that summer. The Sears Estate had just been sold to the Carmelites as a home for retired nuns.

Where the road swept between the mountain and the sea, Julia turned onto a long driveway and stopped at the locked gates. Atop a rise stood Joyous Garde, all Doric columns and marble terraces. Built at the dawn of America's century, its hundred rooms overlooked the ocean, *"One of the crown jewels of Olympia Drive."*

Joyous Garde had been closed and was, in any case, not planned for convenience or comfort. Julia was expected. She beeped and waited.

Welcoming lights were on in Old Cottage just inside the gates. Itself a substantial affair, the Cottage was built on a human scale. Henry and Martha Eder were the permanent caretakers of the estate and lived here year-round. Henry emerged with a ring of keys and nodded to Julia.

Just then, she caught flickering images of this driveway and what looked at first like a hostile, milling mob.

A familiar voice intoned. "Beyond these wrought iron gates and granite pillars, the most famous private entryway in the United States, and possibly the world, the Macauley family and friends gather in moments of trial and tragedy."

Julia recognized the speaker as Walter Cronkite and realized that what she saw was the press waiting for a story.

Then the gates clanged open. The grainy vision was gone. As Julia rolled through, she glanced up at Mount Airey. It rose behind Joyous Garde covered with dark pines and bright foliage. Martha Eder came out to greet her and Julia found herself lulled by the old woman's Down East voice.

Julia had brought very little luggage. When it was stowed inside, she stood on the front porch of Old Cottage and felt she had come home. The place was wooden-shingled and hung with vines and honeysuckle. Her great-grandfather, George Lowell Stoneham, had built it seventy-five years before. It remained as a guest house and gate house and as an example of a fleeting New England simplicity.

ONE

George Lowell Stoneham was always referred to as one of the discoverers of Mount Airey. The Island, of course, had been found many times. By seals and gulls and migratory birds, by native hunters, by Hudson and Champlain and Scotch-Irish fishermen. But not until after the Civil War was it found by just the right people: wealthy and respectable Bostonians.

Gentlemen, such as the painter Brooks Carr looking for proper subjects, or the Harvard naturalist George Lowell Stoneham trying to lose memories of Antietam, came up the coast by steamer, stayed in the little hotels built for salesmen and schooner captains. They roamed north until they hit Mount Airey.

At first, a few took rooms above Baxter's General Provisions and Boarding House in Penoquot Landing. They painted, explored, captured bugs in specimen bottles. They told their friends, the nicely wealthy of Boston, about it. Brooks Carr rented a house in the village one summer and brought his young family.

To Professor Stoneham went the honor of being the first of these founders to build on the island. In 1875, he bought (after hard bargaining) a chunk of land on the seaward side of Mount Airey and constructed a cabin in a grove of giant white pine that overlooked Mirror Lake.

In the following decades, others also built: plain cabins and studios at first, then cottages. In those days, men and boys swam naked and out of sight at Bachelors' Point on the north end of the island. The women, in sweeping summer hats and dresses that reached to the ground, stopped for tea and scones at Baxter's, which now offered a shady patio in fine weather. There they gossiped about the Saltonstall boy who had married the Pierce girl, then moved to France, and about George Stoneham's daughter Helen and a certain New York financier.

This fillet of land in this cream of a season did not long escape the notice of the truly wealthy. From New York they came, and Philadelphia. They acquired large chunks of property. The structures they caused to rise were still called studios and cottages. But they were mansions on substantial estates. By the 1890s those who could have been anywhere in the world chose to come in August to Mount Airey.

Trails and bridle paths were blazed through the forests and up the slopes of the mountain. In 1892 John D. Rockefeller and Simon Garde constructed a paved road, Olympia Drive, around the twenty-five-mile perimeter of the island.

Hiking parties into the hills, to the quiet glens at the heart of the island, always seemed to find themselves at Mirror Lake with its utterly smooth surface and unfathomable depths. The only work of man visible from the shore, and that just barely, was Stoneham Cabin atop a sheer granite cliff. Julia Garde Macauley didn't know what caused her great-grandfather to build on that exact spot. But she knew it wasn't whim or happenstance. The old tintypes showed a tall man with a beard like a wizard's and eyes that had gazed on Pickett's Charge.

Maybe the decision was like the one Professor Stoneham himself described in his magisterial *Wasps of the Eastern United States:* "In the magic silence of a summer's afternoon, the mud wasp builds her nest. Instinct, honed through the eons, guides her choice."

Perhaps, though, it was something more. A glimpse. A sign. Julia knew for certain that once drawn to the grove, George Stoneham had discovered that it contained one of the twelve portals to an ancient shrine. And that the priest, or the Rex as the priest was called, was an old soldier, Lucius, a Roman centurion who worshipped Lord Apollo.

Lucius had been captured and enslaved during Crassus's invasion of Parthia in the century before Christ. He escaped with the help of his god who then led him to one of the portals of the shrine. The reigning priest at that time was a devoted follower of Dionysius. Lucius found and killed the man, put on the silver mask and became Rex in his place.

Shortly after he built the cabin, George Lowell Stoneham built a cottage for his family at the foot of the mountain. But he spent much time up in the grove. After the death of his wife, he even stayed there, snowbound, for several winters, researching, he said, insect hibernation.

In warmer seasons, ladies in the comfortable new parlors at Baxter's Hotel alluded to the professor's loneliness. Conversation over brandy in the clubrooms of the recently built Bachelors' Point Aquaphiliacs Society dwelt on the "fog of war" that sometimes befell a hero.

There was some truth in all that. But what only Stoneham's daughter Helen knew was that beyond the locked door of the snowbound cabin, two old soldiers talked their days away in Latin. They sat on marble benches overlooking a cypress grove above a still lake in second-century Italy.

Lucius would look out into the summer haze, and come to attention each time a figure appeared, wondering, the professor knew, if this was the agent of his death.

Then on a morning one May, George Lowell Stoneham was discovered sitting in his cabin with a look of peace on his face. A shrapnel splinter, planted in a young soldier's arm during the Wilderness campaign thirty-five years before, had worked its way loose and found his heart.

Professor Stoneham's daughter and only child, Helen, inherited the Mount Airey property. Talk at the Thursday Cotillions in the splendid summer ballroom of Baxter's Grande Hotel had long spun around the daughter, "with old Stoneham's eyes and Simon Garde's millions."

For Helen was the first of the Boston girls to marry New York money. And such money and such a New York man! Garde's hands were on all the late nineteenth-century levers: steel, railroads, shipping. His origins were obscure. Not quite, a few hinted, Anglo Saxon. The euphemism used around the Aquaphiliacs Society was "Eastern."

In the great age of buying and building on Mount Airey, none built better or on a grander scale than Mr. and Mrs. Garde. The old Stoneham property expanded, stretched down to the sea. The new "cottage," Joyous Garde, was sweeping, almost Mediterranean, with its Doric columns and marble terraces, its hundred windows that flamed in the rising sun.

With all this, Helen did not neglect Stoneham Cabin up on the mountain. Over the years, it became quite a rambling affair. The slope on which it was built, the pine grove in which it sat, made its size and shape hard to calculate.

In the earliest years of the century, after the birth of her son, George, it was remarked that Helen Stoneham Garde came up *long before* the season and stayed *well afterwards*. And that she was interested in things Chinese. Not the collections of vases and fans that so many clipper-captain ancestors had brought home, but earthenware jugs, wooden sandals, bows and arrows. And she studied the language. Not high Mandarin, apparently, but some guttural peasant dialect.

Relations with her husband were also a subject for discussion. They were rarely seen together. In 1906, the demented millionaire Harry Thaw shot the philandering architect Stanford White on the rooftop of Madison Square Garden in New York. And the men taking part in the Bachelors' Point Grand Regatta that year joked about how Simon Garde had been sitting two tables away. "As easily it might have been some other irate cuckold with a gun and Stanford White might be building our new yacht club right now."

At the 1912 Charity Ball for the Penoquot Landing Fisherfolk Relief Fund in Baxter's Grande Pavilion, the Gardes made a joint entrance. This was an event rare enough to upstage former President Teddy Roosevelt about to campaign as a Bull Moose.

Simon Garde, famously, mysteriously, died when the French liner *Marseilles* was sunk by a U-boat in 1916. Speculation flourished as to where he was bound and the nature of his mission. When his affairs, financial and otherwise, were untangled, his widow was said to be one of the wealthiest women in the nation.

A true child of New England, Helen Stoneham Garde never took her attention far from the money. Horses were her other interest besides chinoiserie. She bred them and raced them. And they won. Much of her time was spent on the Mount Airey estates. Stories of her reclusivity abounded.

The truth, her granddaughter Julia knew, would have stunned even the most avid of the gossips. For around the turn of the century, Lucius had been replaced. A single arrow in the eye had left the old Rex sprawling on the stone threshold of the shrine. His helmet, his sword, and the matched pair of Colt Naval Revolvers which had been a gift from George Stoneham lay scattered like toys.

A new Rex, or more accurately a Regina, picked the silver mask out of the dust and put it on. This was Ki Mien from north China, a servant of the goddess of forests and woods and a huntress of huge ability.

From a few allusions her grandmother dropped, Julia deduced that Helen Garde and the priestess had, over the next two decades, forged a union. Unknown to any mortal on the Island or in the world, they formed what was called in those days a Boston marriage.

In the years that Helen was occupied with Ki Mien, motorcars came to Mount Airey. Their staunchest supporter was George "Flash" Garde, Simon and Helen's son and only child. "A damned fine looking piece of American beef," as a visiting Englishman remarked.

Whether boy or man, Flash Garde could never drive fast enough. His custom-built Locomobile, all brass and polish and exhaust, was one of the hazards of Olympia Drive. "Racing to the next highball and low lady," it was said at Bachelors' Point. "Such a disappointment to his mother," they sighed at Baxter's.

In fact, his mother seemed unbothered. Perhaps this was because she had, quite early on, arranged his marriage to Cissy Custis, the brightest of the famous Custis sisters. The birth of her granddaughter Julia guaranteed the only succession that really mattered to her.

TWO

I n 1954, on the evening of the last day of summer, Julia had supper in Old Cottage kitchen with the Eders. Mrs. Eder made the same comforting chicken pie she remembered.

The nursery up at Joyous Garde was vast. On its walls were murals of the cat playing the fiddle and the cow jumping the Moon. It contained a puppet theater and a playhouse big enough to walk around in if you were small enough. But some of Julia's strongest memories of Mount Airey centered on Old Cottage.

The most vivid of all began one high summer day in the early 1920s. Her grandmother, as she sometimes did, had taken Julia out of the care of her English nurse and her French governess.

When it was just the two of them, Helen Stoneham Garde raised her right hand and asked, "Do you swear on the head of Ruggles The One-Eared Rabbit not to tell anybody what we will see today?"

Time with her grandmother was always a great adventure. Julia held up the stuffed animal worn featureless with love and promised. Then they went for a walk.

Julia was in a pinafore and sandals and held Ruggles by his remaining ear. The woman of incalculable wealth wore sensible shoes and a plain skirt and carried a picnic basket. Their walk was a long one for somebody with short legs. But finches sang, fledglings chirped on oak branches. Invisible through the leaves, a woodpecker drilled a maple trunk. Red squirrels and jays spread news of their passage.

Up the side of Mount Airey Helen led her grandchild, to the silent white pine grove that overlooked deep, still waters. The Cabin itself was all odd angles, gray shingles and stone under a red roof. It was Julia's first visit to the place.

Years later, when she was able to calculate such things, she realized that the dimensions of Stoneham Cabin did not quite pan out. But only a very persistent visitor would note that something was missing, that one room always remained unexplored.

That first time, on a sunny porch visible from no angle outside the Cabin, Helen Garde set down the basket, unpacked wine and sandwiches along with milk and a pudding for Julia.

Then she stood behind her granddaughter and put her hands on the child's shoulders.

"Julia, I should like you to meet Alcier, whom we call the Rex."

The man in the doorway was big and square-built with dark skin and curly black hair. His voice was low, and, like Mademoiselle Martine, he spoke French, though his was different. He wore sandals and a white shirt and trousers. The priest bowed and said, "I am happy to meet the tiny lady."

He was not frightening at all. On the contrary, morning doves fed out of his hand and he admired Ruggles very much. When they had finished lunch, the Rex asked her grandmother if he could show Julia what lay inside.

The two of them passed through a curtain which the child could feel but couldn't see. She found herself in a round room with doors open in all directions. It was more than a small child could encompass. That first time, she was aware only of a cave opening onto a snowy winter morning and an avenue of trees with the moon above them.

Then Alcier faced her across a fire which flickered in the center of the room even on this warm day. He put on a silver mask that covered his face, with openings for his eyes, nostrils and mouth, and said, *"Just as your grandmother welcomed me to her house, so, as servant of the gods, I welcome you to the Shrine of the Twelve Portals."*

But even as gods spoke through him, Julia could see that Alcier smiled and that his eyes were kind. So she wasn't a bit afraid.

When it was time to say good-bye, the Rex stood on the porch and bowed slightly. A red-tailed hawk came down and sat on his wrist. Because of Alcier's manners, Julia was never frightened of the Rex. Even later when she had seen him wiping his machete clean.

As a small child, Julia didn't know why her grandmother made her promise not to tell anyone about the hawk and the invisible curtain and the nice black man who lived up in the cabin. But she didn't.

Children who tell adults everything are trying to make them as wise as they. Just as children who ask questions already know why the sky is blue and where the lost kitten has gone. What they need is the confirmation that the odd and frightening magic which has turned adults into giants has not completely addled their brains. That Julia didn't need such reassurance she attributed to her grandmother and to Alcier.

On her next visit, she learned to call the place with the flame the Still Room. She found out that it was a shrine, a place of the gods, and that Alcier was a priest, though much different from the ones in the Episcopal church. On the second visit she noticed Alcier's slight limp.

Her grandmother never went inside with them. On Julia's next few visits over several summers, she and Alcier sat on stools in the Still Room and looked out through the twelve doors. The Rex patrolled each of these entrances every day. He had a wife and, over the years, several children whom Julia met. Though she never was told exactly where they lived.

Soon, she had learned the name of what lay beyond each portal: jungle, cypress grove, dark forest, tundra, desert, rock-bound island, marsh, river valley, mountain, cave, plains, sandy shore.

At first she was accompanied up the mountain by her grandmother. Then, in the summer she turned twelve, Julia was allowed to go by herself. By that time, she and Alcier had gone through each of the doors and explored what lay beyond.

The hour of the day, the climate, even, Julia came to realize, the continent varied beyond each portal. All but one, in those years, had a shrine of some kind. This might be a grove or a cave, or a rocky cavern, with a fire burning and, somewhere nearby, a body of water still as a mirror.

The plains, even then, had become a wasteland of slag heaps and railroad sidings. Julia did not remember ever having seen it otherwise.

If she loved Alcier, and she did, it was not because he spared her the truth in his quiet voice and French from the Green Antilles. Early on he showed her the fascinating scar on his left leg and explained that he was an escaped slave, "Like each Rex past and to be."

He told her how he had been brought over the wide waters when he was younger than she, how he had grown up on a plantation in the Sugar Islands. How he had been a house servant, how he had run away and been brought back in chains with his leg torn open.

Julia already knew how one Rex succeeded another. But on that first summer she visited the cabin alone, she and Alcier had a picnic on the wide, empty beach on the Indochina Sea and she finally asked how it had happened.

Before he answered, Alcier drew the silver mask out of the satchel he always carried. Julia noticed that he hardly had to guide it. The mask moved by itself to his face. Then he spoke.

Where I lived, we had a public name for the bringer of wisdom. And a private name known only by those to whom She spoke. When I was very young, She sent me dreams. But after I was taken beyond the sea, it was as if I was lost and She couldn't find me.

Then, after I had escaped and been recaptured and brought back to my owner, She appeared again and told me what to do. When I awoke, I followed Her command.

With the chains that bound my hands, I broke the neck of one who came to feed me. With that one's knife, I killed him who bore the keys. With the machete he dropped, I made the others flee. My left leg carried me well. My right was weak. I did not run as I once had.

In the forest, hunters chased me. But the goddess drew me into a mist and they passed by. Beside a stream, a hare came down to drink. I killed her and drank her blood. That morning, hunters went to my left and to my right. I slipped past them as before.

Then it was past midday. I stood in shadows on the edge of a glade. And all was silent and still. No leaf moved. In the sky directly above me, the sun and a hawk stood still. And I knew gods were at work here. I heard no sounds of hunters. For I was at the heart of the forest.

I saw the lodge made of wood and stone and I knew it was mine for the taking. If I killed the King of this place. I said a prayer to the goddess and let her guide me.

Not a leaf moved, not a bird sang. Then I saw the silver mask and knew the Rex was looking for me. My heart thumped. I commanded it to be still. The head turned one way then another. But slowly. The Rex was complacent, maybe, expecting to find and kill me easily. Or old and tired.

My goddess protected me. Made me invisible. Balanced on my good leg and my bad, I stood still as the Rex crossed the glade. I studied the wrinkled throat that hung below the mask. And knew I would have one chance. Just out of range of my knife, the priest hesitated for an instant. And I lunged. One great stride. I stumbled on my bad leg. But my arm carried true. The knife went into the throat. And I found it was a woman and that I was King in her place.

The shrine has existed as long as the gods. Along one of the paths someday will come the one who succeeds me, he told her. *When the gods wish, that one will do away with me.*

The Rex could speak of his own death the same way he might about a change of the seasons. But sometime after that, on a visit to the Still Room, Julia noticed derricks and steel tanks on the rocky island. When she asked Alcier about the destruction of another shrine, he seemed to wince, shook his head and said nothing.

THREE

A t night in Old Cottage, years later, Julia looked out the windows into the dark. And saw Mount Airey by daylight. The cabin and the grove were gone. The bare ground they had stood on was cracked and eroded. She told Mrs. Eder that she was going to visit Stoneham Cabin next morning.

Falling asleep, Julia remembered the resort as it had been. As a child, she had learned to swim at Bachelors' Point and heard the story of Mount Airey being spun. Men tamed and in trunks, women liberated in one-piece suits, swam together now and talked of the useful Mr. Coolidge and, later, the traitorous Franklin Delano Roosevelt.

When she was fifteen, her father died in an accident. Nothing but the kindest condolences were offered. But Julia, outside an open door, heard someone say, "Ironic, Flash Garde's being cut down by a speeding taxi."

"In front of the Stork Club, though, accompanied by a young lady described as a 'hostess.' He would have wanted it that way." She heard them all laugh.

By then, cocktail hour had replaced afternoon tea at Baxter's. In tennis whites, men sat with their legs crossed, women with their feet planted firmly on the ground. Scandal was no longer whispered. Julia knew that her mother's remarriage less than two months after her father's death would have been fully discussed. As would the decision of this mother she hardly ever saw to stay in Europe.

Julia's grandmother attended her son's funeral and shed not a tear. Her attitude was called stoic by some. Unfeeling by others. No one at Baxter's or Bachelors' Point had the slightest idea that the greatest love of Helen Garde's life had, over their twenty years together, given her hints of these events yet to come.

After her father's death and her mother's remarriage, Julia visited the Rex. From behind the silver mask, Alcier spoke. *"The gods find you well. You will wed happily with their blessings,"* he said. *"The divine ones will shield your children."*

Much as she adored Alcier, Julia thought of this as fortuneteller stuff. She began, in the way of the young, to consider the Rex and the Shrine of the Twelve Portals as being among the toys of childhood.

That fall, she went to Radcliffe as her grandmother wished. There, the thousand and one things of a wealthy young woman's life drove thoughts of the gods to the back of her mind. They didn't even reemerge on a sunny day on Brattle Street in her senior year.

Julia and her friend Grace Shipton were headed for tennis lessons. At the curb, a young man helped a co-ed from Vassar into the seat of an MG

Midget. He looked up and smiled what would become a well-known smile. And looked again, surprised. It was the first time he had laid eyes on the woman he would marry.

Before this moment, Julia had experienced a girl's tender thoughts and serious flirtations. Then her eyes met those of the young man in the camel hair jacket. She didn't notice the boy who watched them, so she didn't see his mischievous smile or feel the arrow. But in a moment of radiance her heart was riven.

When Julia asked Grace who the young man was, something in her voice made the Shipton heiress look at her. "That's Robert Macauley," came the answer. "The son of that lace curtain thug who's governor of New York."

Julia Garde and the young Macauley were locked in each other's hearts. All that afternoon she could think of nothing else. Then came the telegram that read, "Sorry to intrude. But I can't live without you."

"Until this happened, I never believed in this," she told him the next afternoon when they were alone and wrapped in each others' arms.

Robert proposed a few days later. "The neighbors will burn shamrocks on your front lawn," he said when Julia accepted.

She laughed, but knew that might be true. And didn't care.

Polite society studied Helen Stoneham Garde's face for the anger and outrage she must feel. The heiress to her fortune had met and proposed to marry an Irishman, *a Catholic, A DEMOCRAT!*

But when Julia approached her grandmother in the study at Joyous Garde and broke the news, Helen betrayed nothing. Her eyes were as blue as the wide Atlantic that lay beyond the French doors. And as unknowable.

"You will make a fine-looking couple," she said. "And you will be very happy."

"You knew."

"Indirectly. You will come to understand. The wedding should be small and private. Making it more public would serve no immediate purpose."

"Best political instincts I've encountered in a Republican," the governor of the Empire State remarked on hearing this. "Be seen at Mass," he told his son. "Raise the children in the Church. With the Garde money behind you, there'll be no need to muck about with concrete contracts."

"There will be a war and he will be a fighter pilot," Helen told Julia after she had met Robert. Before her granddaughter could ask how she knew, she said impatiently, "All but the fools know a war is coming. And young men who drive sports cars always become pilots."

It was as she said. Robert was in Naval Flight Training at Pensacola a month after Pearl Harbor. The couple's song was, "They Can't Take That Away from Me."

Their son Timothy was not yet three and their daughter Helen was just born when Robert Macauley sailed from San Francisco on the aircraft carrier

Constellation. Julia saw him off, then found herself part of the great, shifting mass of soldiers and sailors home on leave, women returning after saying good-bye to husbands, sons, boyfriends.

On a crowded train, with sailors sleeping in the luggage racks, she and a Filipino nurse cried about their men in the South Pacific. She talked with a woman, barely forty, who had four sons in the army.

Julia felt lost and empty. She reread *The Metamorphoses* and *The Odyssey* and thought a lot about Alcier and the Still Room. It had been two years since she had visited Mount Airey. She felt herself drawn there all that winter.

Early in spring, she left her children in the care of nurses and her grandmother and went by train from New York to Boston and from Boston to Bangor. She arrived in the morning and Mr. Eder met her at the station. They drove past houses with victory gardens and V's in the windows if family members were in the service.

A sentry post had been established on the mainland end of Wenlock Sound Bridge. The Army Signal Corps had taken over Bachelors' Point for the duration of the war.

The bar at Baxter's was an officers' club. On Olympia Drive, some of the great houses had been taken for the duration. Staff cars, jeeps, canvas-topped trucks stood in the circular drives.

It was just after the thaw. Joyous Garde stood empty. Patches of snow survived on shady corners of the terraces. The statues looked as if they still regretted their lack of clothes.

Julia found a pair of rubber boots that fit and set off immediately for Stoneham Cabin. In summer, Mount Airey was nature in harness, all bicycle paths and hiking parties. In Mud Time, dry beds ran with icy water, flights of birds decorated a gray sky, lake-sized puddles had appeared, the slopes lay leafless and open.

Julia saw the stranger as she approached the cabin. But this was her land and she did not hesitate. Sallow-faced, clean-shaven with the shadow of a beard, he was expecting her. When she stepped onto the porch, he came to attention. She knew that sometime in the recent past he had murdered Alcier.

"Corporal John Smalley, Her Britannic Majesty's London Fusiliers," he said. "Anxious to serve you, my lady."

In the Still Room, when they entered, Julia looked around, saw wreckage in the desert shrine, smashed tanks on the sand. Dead animals lay around the oasis and she guessed the water was poisoned.

The murderer put on the silver mask and spoke. His voice rang. Julia felt a chill.

"It's by the will of the gods that I'm here today. By way of a nasty scrap in the hills. Caught dead to rights and every one of us to die. Officers down. No great moment. But the sergeant major was gone. A spent round ricocheted off my Worsley helmet and I was on me back looking up.

I lay still but I could hear screams and thought it was up and done with and I would dance on hot coals for as long as it took. For cheating and philandering and the cove I stabbed in Cheapside. And I prayed as I'd never done.

Then He appeared. Old Jehovah as I thought, all fiery eyes and smoke behind his head. Then He spoke and it seems it was Mars himself. I noticed he wore a helmet and carried a flaming sword. He told me I was under His protection and nothing would happen to me.

Good as His word. No one saw when I rose up and took my Enfield. He led the way all through the night, talking in my ear. About the shrine and the priest that lives here.

A runaway slave it always is who kills the old priest and takes over. And I choked at that. Not the killing, But Britons never will be slaves and all.

Lord Mars told me enlistment in Her Majesty's Army came close enough. New thinking, new blood was what was needed. Led me to a hill shrine before dawn. Left me to my own devices.

The shrine's that one through that portal behind your ladyship. A grove with the trees all cut short by the wind and a circle of stone and a deep pool. When I was past the circle and beside the pool, the wind's sound was cut off and it was dead still.

A path led down to the pool and on it was a couple of stones and a twig resting on them. And I knew not to disturb that. So I went to ground. Oiled my Enfield. Waited. Took a day or two. But I was patient. Ate my iron rations and drank water from the pool.

When he came, it was at dusk and he knew something was up. A formidable old bugger he was. But. . . .

He trailed off. Removed the mask. "You knew him. Since you were a little girl, I hear."

Julia's eyes burned. "He had a wife and children."

"I've kept them safe. He'd put a sum aside for them from shrine offerings and I saw they had that. Got my own bit of bother and strife tucked away. We know in this job we aren't the first. And won't be the last. Living on a loan of time so to speak."

He pointed to the ruined shrines. "The gods have gotten wise that things will not always go their way."

The corporal told her about defense works and traps he was building. Like a tenant telling the landlady about improvements he is making, thought Julia. She knew that was the way it would be between them and that she would always miss her noble Alcier.

Just before she left, Smalley asked, "I wonder if I could see your son, m'lady. Sometime when it's convenient."

Julia said nothing. She visited her grandmother, eighty and erect, living in Taos in a spare and beautiful house. Her companion was a woman from the Pueblo, small, silent and observant.

"Timothy is the whole point of our involvement," said the old woman.

She sat at a table covered with breeding charts and photos of colts. "You and I are the precursors."

"He's just a child."

"As were you when you were taken to the shrine. Think of how you loved Alcier. He would have wanted you to do this. And you shall have your rewards. Just as I have."

"And they are?"

"At this point in your life, you would despise them if I told you. In time, they will seem more than sufficient."

Julia knew that she would do as the Rex had asked. But that summer Robert was stationed in Hawaii. So she went out to be with him instead of going to Mount Airey. The next August, she gave birth to Cecilia, her second daughter.

The year after that, Robert was in a naval hospital in California, injured in a crash landing on a carrier flight deck. His shoulder was smashed but healed nicely. A three-inch gash ran from his left ear to his jaw. It threw his smile slightly off-kilter.

He seemed distant, even in bed. Tempered like a knife. And daring. As if he too sensed death and destiny and the will of the gods.

When the war was over Robert had a Navy Cross, a trademark smile, and a scar worth, as he put it, "Fifty thousand votes while they still remember."

Over his own father's objections, the young Macauley ran for Congress from the West Side of Manhattan. The incumbent, one of the old man's allies, was enmeshed in a corruption scandal. Robert won the primary and the election. His lovely wife and three young children were features of his campaign.

Julia paid a couple of fast visits to the cabin. On one of them the Corporal told her, "I know it's a kid will be my undoing. But it will be a little girl." On another he said, "The gods would take it as a great favor if you let me speak to your son."

Thus it was that one lovely morning the following summer, Julia left her two little daughters in the huge nursery at Joyous Garde and brought Timothy to Stoneham Cabin. As if it were part of a ritual, she had Mrs. Eder pack lunch. Julia stuck a carton of the Luckies she knew the Corporal favored into the basket and started up the hill. Her son, age seven and startlingly like the father he rarely saw, darted around, firing a toy gun at imaginary enemies.

The corporal, tanned and wiry, sat on the back porch, smoking and cleaning his rifle. Tim stared at him, wide-eyed. "Are you a commando?" he asked after the introductions were made and he'd learned that their guest was English.

"Them's Navy," Smalley said. "And I'm a soldier of the Queen. Or King as it is."

Julia stared down at Mirror Lake. Except when Smalley spoke, she could imagine that Alcier was still there. Something even more intense than this must have happened to her grandmother after the death of Ki Mien.

"Have you killed anybody?"

"Killing's never a nice thing, lad. Sometimes a necessity. But never nice," Smalley said. "Now what do you say that we ask your mother if I can show you around?"

Later, on their way back to the cottage, Timothy was awestruck. "He showed me traps he had set! In a jungle! He told me I was going to be a great leader!"

As her grandmother had with her, Julia demanded his silence. Timothy agreed and kept his word. In fact, he rarely mentioned the cabin and the shrine. Julia wondered if Smalley had warned him not to. Then and later, she was struck by how easily her son accepted being the chosen of the gods.

Fashion had passed Mount Airey by. That summer, the aging bucks at Bachelors' Point drawled on about how Dewey was about to thrash Truman. And how the Rockefellers had donated their estate to the National Parks Service.

"What else now that the Irish have gotten onto the island?"

"And not even through the back door."

That summer, Helen Stoneham Garde stayed in New Mexico. But Joyous Garde jumped. "Prominent Democrats from the four corners of the nation come to be bedazzled," as Congressman Macauley murmured to his wife.

Labor leaders smoked cigars in the oak and leather splendor of Simon Garde's study. Glowing young Prairie Populists drank with entrenched Carolina Dixiecrats. The talk swirled around money and influence, around next year's national elections and Joe Kennedy's boy down in Massachusetts.

Above them, young Macauley with his lovely wife stood on the curve of the pink and marble stairs. Julia had grown interested in this game. It reminded her of her grandmother's breeding charts and racehorses.

The following summer, Helen Stoneham Garde returned to her estate. Afternoons at Baxter's were drowsy now and dowager-ridden.

"Carried in a litter like royalty."

"Up the mountain to the cabin."

"Returned there to die it seems."

"Her granddaughter and grandson-in-law will have everything." Shudders ran around the room.

On an afternoon of warm August sun and a gentle sea breeze, Julia sat opposite her grandmother on the back porch of Stoneham Cabin, "Only the rich can keep fragments of the past alive," Helen told her. "To the uneducated eye, great wealth can be mistaken for magic."

Below them, a party had picnicked next to Mirror Lake a bit earlier. Hikers had passed through. But at the moment, the shore was deserted, the surface undisturbed. The Rex was not in evidence.

Helen's eye remained penetrating, her speech clear. "A peaceful death," she said, "is one of the gifts of the gods."

Julia wished she had thought to ask her grandmother more questions about how their lives had been altered by the shrine. She realized that her own introduction to it at so young an age had occurred because Helen could not stand dealing with the man who had murdered the one closest to her.

The two sat in a long silence. Then the old woman said, "My dearest child, I thought these might be of interest," and indicated a leather folder on the table.

Julia opened it and found several photos. She stared, amazed at the tree-lined Cambridge Street and the young couple agape at their first glimpse of each other. She couldn't take in all the details at once: the deliveryman hopping from his cart, the elderly gent out for a stroll, the boy who walked slightly behind what must have been his parents. Small, perhaps foreign in his sandals, he alone saw the tall, dark-haired young man, the tall blond young woman, stare at each other in wonder.

"You knew before . . . ," Julia said, looking up. She didn't dare breathe. Her grandmother still smiled slightly. Her eyes were wide. Beside her stood a figure in a silver mask. Tall and graceful. Not Corporal Smalley. Not at all. He wore only a winged helmet and sandals. Hermes, Lord Mercury, touched Helen with the silver caduceus staff he carried.

Julia caught her breath. Her grandmother slumped slightly. Helen Stoneham Garde's eyes were blank. Her life was over. The figure was gone.

FOUR

First day of Autumn," Martha Eder said when Julia came down the Old Cottage stairs the morning after her return. A picnic basket had been packed. Julia had not brought cigarettes for Smalley, had reason to think they weren't necessary.

The air was crisp but the sun was warm enough that all Julia needed was a light jacket. As she set out, Henry Eder interrupted his repair of a window frame. "I can go with you, see if anything needs doing." When she declined, he nodded and went back to his work.

Grief was a private matter to Mainers. Besides, even after three quarters of a century, Julia's family were still "summer folk" and thus unfathomable.

The walk up Mount Airey was magnificent. Julia had rarely seen it this late in the year. Red and gold leaves framed green pine. Activity in the trees and undergrowth was almost frantic. A fox, intent on the hunt, crossed her path.

After her grandmother's death, she had returned to the cabin only on the occasions when she brought Tim. In the last few years, she hadn't been back at all.

She remembered a day when she and Robert sat in the study of their Georgetown mansion and Timothy knocked on the door. Just shy of twelve, he wore his Saint Anthony's Priory uniform of blazer and short pants. In 1951, the American upper class kept its boys in shorts for as long as possible. A subtle means of segregating them from the masses.

Representative Robert Macauley (D-NY) was maneuvering for a Senate nomination in what promised to be a tough year for Democrats. He looked up from the speech he was reviewing. Julia, busy with a guest list, watched them both.

Timothy said, "What I would like for my birthday this year is a crewcut. Lots of the kids have them. And I want long pants when I'm not in this stupid monkey suit. And this summer I want to be allowed to go up to the cabin on Mount Airey by myself."

Julia caught the amusement and look of calculation in her husband's eyes. Did his kid in short pants gain him more votes from women who thought it was adorable than he lost from men who thought it was snooty?

"In matters like this, we defer to the upper chamber," he said with a quick, lopsided smile and nodded to Julia.

She felt all the pangs of a mother whose child is growing up. But she negotiated briskly. The first demand was a throwaway as she and her son both knew.

"No crewcut. None of the boys at your school have them. The brothers don't approve." The brothers made her Protestant skin crawl. But they were most useful at times like this.

"Long pants outside school? Please!" he asked. "Billy Chervot and his brothers all get to wear blue jeans!" Next year would be Timothy's last with the brothers. Then he'd be at Choate and out in the world.

"Perhaps. For informal occasions."

"Jeans!"

"We shall see." He would be wearing them, she knew, obviously beloved, worn ones. On a drizzly morning in Maine. His hair would be short. He'd have spent that summer in a crewcut.

Julia had studied every detail of a certain photo. She estimated Tim's age at around fifteen. The shot showed him as he approached Stoneham Cabin. He wore his father's old naval flight jacket, still too big for him, though he had already gotten tall.

"Mount Airey?" the eleven-year-old Tim asked.

She heard herself saying. "Yes. That should be fine. Check in with Mrs. Eder when you're going. And tell her when you come back. Be sure to let me know if anything up there needs to be done."

Her son left the room smiling. "What's the big deal about that damned cabin?" her husband asked.

Julia shrugged. "The Wasps of the Eastern United States," she said and they both laughed. The title of her grandfather's tome was a joke between them. It referred to things no outsider could ever understand or would want to.

Julia returned to her list. She had memorized every detail of the photo of their son. He had tears in his eyes. The sight made her afraid for them all.

Her husband held out a page of notes. "Take a look. I'm extending an olive branch to Mrs. Roosevelt. Her husband and my dad disagreed." He grinned. Franklin Roosevelt, patrician reformer, and Timothy Macauley, machine politician, had famously loathed each other.

Julia stared at her husband's handwriting. Whatever the words said would work. The third photo in the leather folder her grandmother had given her showed FDR's widow on a platform with Robert. Julia recognized a victory night.

She could trace a kind of tale with the photos. She met her husband. He triumphed. Their son went for comfort to the Rex. A story was told. Or, as in *The Iliad,* part of one.

That day in the study in Georgetown, she looked at Robert Macauley, in the reading glasses he never wore publicly, and felt overwhelming tenderness. Julia could call up every detail of the photo of their meeting.

Only the boy in the background looked directly at the couple who stared into each other's eyes. He smiled. His hand was raised. Something gold caught the sun. A ring? A tiny bow? Had Robert and she been hit with Eros's arrow? All she knew was that the love she felt was very real.

How clever they were, the gods, to give mortals just enough of a glimpse of their workings to fascinate. But never to let them know everything.

That summer, her son went up Mount Airey alone. It bothered Julia as one more sign he was passing out of her control. "The gods won't want to lose this one, m'lady," Smalley had told her.

Over the next few years, Timothy entered puberty, went away to school, had secrets. His distance increased. When the family spent time at Joyous Garde, Tim would go to the cabin often and report to her in privacy. Mundane matters like "Smalley says the back eaves need to be reshingled." Or vast, disturbing ones like, "That jungle portal is unpassable now. Smalley says soon ours will be the only one left."

Then came a lovely day in late August 1954. Sun streamed through the windows of Joyous Garde, sailboats bounced on the water. In the ballroom, staff moved furniture. A distant phone rang. A reception was to be held that evening. Senator Macauley would be flying in from Buffalo that afternoon.

Julia's secretary, her face frozen and wide-eyed, held out a telephone and couldn't speak. Against all advice, trusting in the good fortune which had carried him so far, her husband had taken off in the face of a sudden Great Lakes storm. Thunder, lightning, and hail had swept the region. Radio contact with Robert Macauley's one-engine plane had been lost.

The crash site wasn't found until late that night. The death wasn't confirmed until the next morning. When Julia looked for him, Timothy was gone. The day was cloudy with a chill drizzle. She stood on the porch of Old Cottage a bit later when he returned. His eyes red. Dressed as he was in the photo.

As they fell into each others' arms, Julia caught a glimpse that was gone in an instant. Her son, as in the photo she had studied so often, approached Stoneham Cabin. This time, she saw his grief turn to surprise and a look of stunned betrayal. Timothy didn't notice.

The two hugged and sobbed in private sorrow before they turned toward Joyous Garde and the round of public mourning. As they did, he said, "You go up there from now on. I never want to go back."

FINALE

Julia approached the grove and cabin on that first morning of Fall. She was aware that it lay within her power to destroy this place. Julia had left a sealed letter to be shown to Timothy if she failed to return. Though she knew that was most unlikely to happen.

A young woman, casual in slacks and a blouse, stood on the porch. In one hand she held the silver mask. "I'm Linda Martin," she said. "Here by the will of the gods."

Julia recognized Linda as contemporary and smart. "An escaped slave?" she asked.

"In a modern sense, perhaps." The other woman shrugged and smiled. "A slave of circumstances."

"I've had what seem to be visions," Julia said as she stepped onto the porch. "About my son and about this property."

"Those are my daughter's doing, I'm afraid. Sally is nine." Linda was apologetic yet proud. "I've asked her not to. They aren't prophecy. More like possibility."

"They felt like a promise. And a threat."

"Please forgive her. She has a major crush on your son. Knows everything he has done. Or might ever do. He was very disappointed last month when he was in pain and wanted to talk to the corporal. And found us."

"Please forgive Tim. One's first Rex makes a lasting impression." Julia was surprised at how much she sounded like her grandmother.

The living room of Stoneham Cabin still smelled of pine. The scent reminded Julia of Alcier and her first visit. As before, a door opened where no door had been. She and Linda passed through an invisible veil and the light from the twelve portals mingled and blended in the Still Room.

"Sally, this is Julia Garde Macauley. Timothy's mother."

The child who sat beyond the flame was beautiful. She wore a blue tunic adorned with a silver boy riding a dolphin. She bowed slightly. "Hello, Mrs. Macauley. Please explain to Timothy that the Corporal knew what happened was Fate and not me."

Julia remembered Smalley saying, "It's a child will be my undoing." She smiled and nodded.

Linda held out the mask which found its way to Sally's face.

"This is something I dreamed about your son."

What Julia saw was outdoors and in winter. It was men mostly. White mostly. Solemn. Formally dressed. A funeral? No. A man in judicial robes held a book. He was older, but Julia recognized an ally of her husband's, a young Congressman from Oregon. This was the future.

"A future," said the voice from behind the mask. Julia froze. The child was uncanny.

Another man, seen from behind, had his hand raised as he took the oath of office. An inauguration. Even with his back turned, she knew her son.

"And I've seen this. Like a nightmare." Flames rose. The cabin and the grove burned.

"I don't want that. This is our home." She was a child and afraid.

Later, Linda and Julia sat across a table on the rear porch and sipped wine. The foliage below made Mirror Lake appear to be ringed with fire.

"It seems that the gods stood aside and let my husband die. Now they want Tim."

"Even the gods can't escape Destiny," Linda said. "They struggle to change it by degrees."

She looked deep into her glass. "I have Sally half the year. At the cusps of the four seasons. The rest of the time she is with the Great Mother. Once her abilities were understood, that was as good an arrangement as I could manage. Each time she's changed a little more."

Another mother who must share her child, Julia thought. We have much to talk about. How well the Immortals know how to bind us to their plans. She would always resent that. But she was too deeply involved not to comply. Foreknowledge was an addiction.

A voice sang, clear as mountain air. At first Julia thought the words were in English and that the song came from indoors. Then she realized the language was ancient Greek and that she heard it inside her head.

The song was about Persephone, carried off to the Underworld, about Ganymede abducted by Zeus. The voice had an impossible purity. Hypnotic, heartbreaking, it sang about Time flowing like a stream and children taken by the gods.

James Van Pelt teaches English at Fruita Monument High School and Mesa State College in western Colorado. He graduated from Metro State College in Denver in 1978 and earned a Master's Degree in Creative Writing from the University of California in Davis in 1990. His first published short story appeared in 1990. His stories have appeared in *Asimov's, Analog, Weird Tales, Realms of Fantasy, Talebones, The Third Alternative, On Spec, Alfred Hitchcock's Mystery Magazine, Dark Terrors,* and SciFi.com. He is also the author of the short story collection, *Strangers and Beggars,* which was named a "Best Book for Young Adults" by The American Library Association.

When asked what his long-term writing goals were, he said: "I feel a little like that guy in the old *Tales from the Crypt* comic who was trying to blow the ultimate jazz riff on his saxophone. He kept trying and trying and trying, until one day he finally did it. I don't remember what happened to him, but it was cosmic. I'm like that with my writing. I'm trying to write the ultimate string of sentences that will result in something cosmic. I know, it's an unreachable goal, but maybe along the way I'll write some decent riffs."

And when asked about teaching: "When I teach science fiction, one of my basic arguments is that SF as a literature is based on the idea that the world can and will be different. It exists in a state of flux. Mainstream lit has a tendency to ignore change and argue that whatever condition exists in the novel is universal and timeless. I disagree. I believe SF prepares us for change by positing that change is always inevitable."

James Van Pelt explores the familiar, the strange, and the many degrees of change in this rich and disturbing story.

THE LAST OF THE O-FORMS

JAMES VAN PELT

Beyond the big rig's open window, the Mississippi river lands rolled darkly by. Boggy areas caught the moon low on the horizon like a silver coin, flickering through black-treed hummocks, or strained by split-rail fence, mile after mile. The air smelled damp and dead-fish mossy, heavy as a wet towel, but it was better than the animal enclosures on a hot afternoon when the sun pounded the awnings and the exhibits huddled in weak shade. Traveling at night was the way to go. Trevin counted the distance in minutes. They'd blow through Roxie soon, then hit Hamburg, McNair, and Harriston in quick secession. In Fayette, there was a nice diner where they could get breakfast, but it meant turning off the highway and they'd hit the worst of Vicksburg's morning traffic if they stopped. No, the thing to do was to keep driving, driving to the next town, where he could save the show.

He reached across the seat to the grocery sack between him and Caprice. She was asleep, her baby-blonde head resting against the door, her small hands holding a Greek edition of the *Odyssey* open on her lap. If she were awake, she could glance at the map and tell him exactly how many miles they had left to Mayersville, how long to the minute at this speed it would take, and how much diesel, to the ounce, they'd have left in their tanks. Her little-girl eyes would pin him to the wall. "Why can't you figure this out on your own?" they'd ask. He thought about hiding her phone book so she'd have nothing to sit on and couldn't look out the window. That would show her. She might look two years old, but she was really twelve, and had the soul of a middle-aged tax attorney.

At the sack's bottom, beneath an empty donut box, he found the beef jerky. It tasted mostly of pepper, but underneath it had a tingly, metallic flavor he tried not to think about. Who knew what it might have been made from? He doubted there were any original-form cows, the o-cows, left to slaughter.

After a long curve, a city limit sign loomed out of the dark. Trevin stepped on the brakes, then geared down. Roxie cops were infamous for speed traps, and there wasn't enough bribe money in the kitty to make a ticket go away. In his rearview mirror, the other truck and a car with Hardy the handyman and his crew of roustabouts closed ranks.

Roxie's traffic signal blinked yellow over an empty intersection, while the closed shops stood mute under a handful of streetlights. After the four-block-long downtown, another mile of beat-up houses and trailers lined the road, where broken washing machines and pickups on cinder blocks dotted moonlit front yards. Something barked at him from behind a chain link fence. Trevin slowed for a closer look. Professional curiosity. It looked like an o-dog under a porch light, an original-form animal, an old one, if his stiff-gaited walk was an indicator. Weren't many of *those* left anymore. Not since the mutagen hit. Trevin wondered if the owners keeping an o-dog in the backyard had troubles with their neighbors, if there was jealousy.

A toddler voice said, "If we don't clear $2,600 in Mayersville, we'll have to sell a truck, Daddy."

"Don't call me Daddy, *ever.*" He took a long curve silently. Two-laned highways often had no shoulder, and concentration was required to keep safe. "I didn't know you were awake. Besides, a thousand will do it."

Caprice closed her book. In the darkness of the cab, Trevin couldn't see her eyes, but he knew that they were polar-ice blue. She said, "A thousand for diesel, sure, but we're weeks behind on payroll. The roustabouts won't stand for another delay, not after what you promised in Gulfport. The extension on the quarterly taxes is past, and I can't keep the feds off like the other creditors by pledging extra payments for a couple months. We've got food for most of the animals for ten days or so, but we have to buy fresh meat for the tigerzelle and the crocomouse or they'll die. We stay afloat with $2,600, but just barely."

Trevin scowled. It had been years since he'd found her little-girl voice and little-girl pronunciation to be cute, and almost everything she said was sarcastic or critical. It was like living with a pint-sized advocate for his own self-doubt. "So we need a house of . . ." He wrinkled his forehead. "$2,600 divided by four and a half bucks. . . ."

"Five hundred and seventy-eight. That'll leave you an extra dollar for a cup of coffee," Caprice said. "We haven't had a take that big since Ferriday last fall, and that was because Oktoberfest in Natchez closed early. Thank God for Louisiana liquor laws! We ought to admit the show's washed up, cut the inventory loose, sell the gear, and pay off the help."

She turned on the goosenecked reading light that arced from the dashboard and opened her book.

"If we can hold on until Rosedale . . ." He remembered Rosedale when they last came through, seven years ago. The city had recruited him.

Sent letters and e-mails. They'd met him in New Orleans with a commit-
tee, including a brunette beauty who squeezed his leg under the table when
they went out to dinner.

"We can't," Caprice said.

Trevin recalled the hand on his leg feeling good and warm. He'd almost jumped from the table, his face flushed. "The soybean festival draws
them in. Everything's made out of soybeans. Soybean pie. Soybean beer.
Soybean ice cream." He chuckled. "We cleaned up there. I got to ride
down Main Street with the Rosedale Soybean Queen."

"We're dead. Take your pulse." She didn't look up.

The Rosedale Soybean Queen had been friendly too, and oh so grateful that he'd brought the zoo to town. He wondered if she still lived there.
He could look her up. "Yeah, if we make the soybean festival, we'll do fine.
One good show and we're sailing again. I'll repaint the trucks. Folks love us
when we come into town, music playing. World's greatest traveling novelty
zoo! You remember when *Newsweek* did that story? God, that was a day!"
He glanced out the window again. The moon rested on the horizon now,
pacing them, big as a beachball, like a burnished hubcap rolling with them
in the night, rolling up the Mississippi twenty miles to the west. He could
smell the river flowing to the sea. How could she doubt that they would
make it big? I'll show her, he thought. Wipe that smirk off her little-girl
face. I'll show her in Mayersville and then Rosedale. Money'll be falling off
the tables. We'll have to store it in sacks. She'll see. Grinning, he dug deep
for another piece of beef jerky, and he didn't think at all what it tasted like
this time.

Trevin pulled the truck into Mayersville at half past ten, keeping his
eyes peeled for their posters and flyers. He'd sent a box of them up two
weeks earlier, and if the boy he'd hired had done his job, they should have
been plastered everywhere, but he only saw one, and it was torn nearly in
half. There were several banners welcoming softball teams to the South-
Central Spring Time Regional Softball Tourney, and the hotels sported
NO VACANCY signs, so the crowds were there. He turned the music on,
and it blared from the loudspeakers on top of the truck. Zoo's in town, he
thought. Come see the zoo! But other than a couple of geezers sitting in
front of the barbershop, who watched them coolly as they passed, no one
seemed to note their arrival.

"They can't play ball *all* day, eh, Caprice. They've got to do something
in between games."

She grunted. Her laptop was open on the seat beside her, and she was
double-entering receipts and bills into the ledger.

The fairgrounds were on the north edge of town, next to the ball
fields. A park attendant met them at the gates, then climbed onto the running board so his head was just below the window.

"There's a hundred dollar occupancy fee," he said, his face hidden beneath a wide-brimmed straw hat that looked like it had been around the world a few times.

Trevin drummed his fingers on the steering wheel and stayed calm. "We paid for the site up front."

The attendant shrugged. "It's a hundred dollars or you find some other place to plant yourself."

Caprice, on her knees, leaned across Trevin. She deepened her voice in her best Trevin impersonation. "Do we make that check out to Mayersville City Parks or to Issaquena County?"

Startled, the attendant looked up before Caprice could duck out of sight, his sixty-year-old face as dusty as his hat. "Cash. No checks."

"That's what I thought," she said to Trevin as she moved back from the window. "Give him twenty. There better be the portable potties and the electrical hookups we ordered."

Trevin flicked the bill to him, and the attendant caught it neatly in flight as he stepped off the running board. "Hey, mister," he said. "How old's your little girl?"

"A million and ten, asshole," said Trevin, dropping the clutch to move the big rig forward. "I've *told* you to stay out of sight. We'll get into all kinds of trouble if the locals find out I've got a mutant keeping the books. They have labor laws, you know. Why'd you tell me to give him any money anyway? We could have bought a day or two of meat with that."

Caprice stayed on her knees to look out her window. "He's really a janitor. Never piss off the janitor. Hey, they cleaned this place up a bit! There was a patch of woods between us and the river last time."

Trevin leaned on the wheel. Turning the truck was tough at anything less than highway speed. "Would you want trees and brush next to where *you* were playing softball? You chase a foul shot into the undergrowth and never come back. . . ."

Beyond the fair grounds, the land sloped down to the levee, and past that flowed the Mississippi, less than a hundred yards away, a great, muddy plain marked with lines of sullen grey foam drifting under the mid-morning sun. A black barge so distant that he couldn't hear it chugged upstream. Trevin noted with approval the endless stretch of ten-foot-tall chain-link fence between them and the river. Who knew what god-awful thing might come crawling out of there?

As always, it took most of the day to set up. The big animals, stinking of hot fur and unwashed cage bottoms in their eight-foot-high enclosures, came out of the semi-trailers first. Looking lethargic and sick, the tigerzelle, a long-legged, hoofed animal sporting almost no neck below an impressive face filled with saber-like teeth, barely looked up as its cage was lowered to the soggy ground. It hooted softly. Trevin checked its water. "Get a tarp over it right away," he said to handyman Harper, a big, grouchy man who wore old rock concert T-shirts inside out. Trevin added, "That trailer had to be a hundred and twenty degrees inside." Looking at the animal fondly, Trevin remembered when he'd acquired it from a farm in Illinois, one of the first American mutababies, before the mutagen was recognized and named, before it became a plague. The tigerzelle's sister was almost as bizarre: heavy legs, scaly skin, and a long, thin head, like a whippet, but the farmer had already killed it by the time Trevin arrived. Their mother, as ordinary a cow as you'd ever see, looked at its children with dull confusion. "What the *hell's* wrong with my cow?" asked the farmer several times, until they started dickering for the price. Once Trevin had paid him, the man said, "If 'n I get any other weird-lookin' animal, you want I should give you a call?"

Trevin smelled profit. Charging twenty dollars per customer, he cleared ten thousand a week in June and July, showing the tigerzelle from the back of his pickup. He thought, I may not be too smart, but I do know how to make a buck. By the end of the summer, Dr. Trevin's Traveling Zoological Extravaganza was born. That was the year Caprice rode beside him in a child's car seat, her momma dead in childbirth. In August, they were going north from Senetobia to Memphis, and, at eleven months old, Caprice said her first words: "Isn't eighty over the speed limit?" Even then, there was a biting, sardonic tone to her voice. Trevin nearly wrecked the truck.

The crocomouse snarled and bit at the bars as it came out, its furry snout banging against the metal. It threw its two hundred pounds against the door and almost tipped the cage out of the handlers' grip. "Keep your hands away," snapped Harper to his crew, "or you'll be taping a pencil to a stub to write your mommas!"

Then the rest of the animals were unloaded: a porcumander, the warped child of a bullfrog that waved its wet, thorny hide at every shadow; the unigoose, about the size of a wild turkey atop four tiny legs, shedding ragged feathers by the handful below the pearl-like glinting horn, and each of the other mutababies, the unrecognizable progeny of cats and squirrels and horses and monkeys and seals and every other animal Trevin could gather to the zoo. Big cages, little ones, aquariums, terrariums, little corrals, bird cages, tethering poles—all came out for display.

By sunset, the last animal had been arranged and fed. Circus flags fluttered from the semi-trailer truck tops. The loudspeakers perched atop their posts.

The park attendant wandered through the cages, his hands pushed deep into his pockets, as casual and friendly as if he hadn't tried to rip them off earlier in the day. "Y'all best stay in your trucks once the sun sets if you're camping here."

Suspicious, Trevin asked, "Why's that?"

The man raised his chin toward the river, which was glowing red like a bloody stain in the setting sun. "Water level was up a couple days ago, over the fences. The levee held, but any sorta teethy mutoid might be floppin' around on our side now. It's got so you can't step in a puddle without somethin' takin' a bite outta ya! Civil Defense volunteers walk the banks every day, lookin' for the more cantankerous critters, but it's a big old river. You got a gun?"

Trevin shrugged. "Baseball bat. Maybe we'll get lucky and add something to the zoo. You expecting crowds for the softball tournament?"

"Thirty-two teams. We shipped in extra bleachers."

Trevin nodded. If he started the music early in the morning, maybe he'd attract folks waiting for games. Nothing like a little amusement before the heat set in. After a couple of minutes, the park attendant left. Trevin was glad to see him walk away. He had the distinct impression that the man was looking for something to steal.

After dinner, Caprice clambered into the upper bunk, her short legs barely giving her enough of a reach to make it. Trevin kicked his blanket aside. Even though it was after ten, it was still over ninety degrees, and there wasn't a hint of a breeze. Most of the animals had settled in their cages. Only the tigerzelle made noise, one long warbling hoot after another, a soft, melodic call that hardly fit its ferocious appearance.

"You lay low tomorrow. I'm not kidding," said Trevin after he'd turned off the light. "I don't want you driving people off."

Caprice sniffed loudly. "It's pretty ironic that I can't show myself at a mutoid zoo. I'm tired of hiding away like a freak. Another fifty years and there won't be any of your kind left anyway. Might as well accept the inevitable. I'm the future. They should be able to deal with that."

Trevin put his hands behind his head and stared up at her bunk. Through the screen he'd fitted over the windows, he could hear the Mississippi lapping against the bank. An animal screeched in the distance, its call a cross between a whistle and a bad cough. He tried to imagine what would make a sound like that. Finally he said, "People don't like human mutoids, at least ones that look human."

"Why's that?" she asked, all the sarcasm and bitterness suddenly gone. "I'm not a bad person, if they'd get to know me. We could discuss books, or philosophy. I'm a *mind,* not just a body."

The animal cried out again in the dark, over and over, until in mid-screech, it stopped. A heavy thrashing sound followed by splashes marked the creature's end. "I guess it makes them sad, Caprice."

"Do I make *you* sad?" In the truck cab's dim interior, she sounded exactly like a two-year-old. He remembered when she *was* a little girl, before he knew that she wasn't normal, that she'd never "grow up," that her DNA showed that she wasn't human. Before she started talking uppity and making him feel stupid with her baby-doll eyes. Before he'd forbidden her to call him

Dad. He'd thought she looked a little like her mother then. He still caught echoes of her when Caprice combed her hair, or when she fell asleep and her lips parted to take a breath, just like her mother. The air caught in his throat thinking of those times.

"No, Caprice. You don't make me sad."

Hours later, long after Caprice had gone to sleep, Trevin drifted off into a series of dreams where he was being smothered by steaming Turkish towels, and when he threw the towels off, his creditors surrounded him. They carried payment-overdue notices, and none of them were human.

Trevin was up before dawn to feed the animals. Half the trick of keeping the zoo running was in figuring out what the creatures ate. Just because the parent had been, say, an o-form horse didn't mean hay was going to do the trick. Caprice kept extensive charts for him: the animal's weight, how much food it consumed, what vitamin supplements seemed most helpful. There were practicalities to running a zoo. He dumped a bucket of corn on the cob into the pigahump's cage. It snorted, then lumbered out of the doghouse it stayed in, not looking much like a pig, or any other animal Trevin knew. Eyes like saucers, it gazed at him gratefully before burying its face in the trough.

He moved down the rows. Mealworms in one cage. Grain in the next. Bones from the butcher. Dog food. Spoiled fish. Bread. Cereal. Old vegetables. Oats. The tigerzelle tasted the rump roast he tossed in, its delicate tongue, so like a cat's, lapping at the meat before it tore a small chunk off to chew delicately. It cooed in contentment.

At the end of the row, closest to the river, two cages were knocked off their display stands and smashed. Black blood and bits of meat clung to the twisted bars, and both animals the cages had contained, blind, leathery birdlike creatures, were gone. Trevin sighed and walked around the cages, inspecting the ground. In a muddy patch, a single webbed print a foot across, marked with four deep claw indents, showed the culprit. A couple of partial prints led up from the river. Trevin put his finger in the track, which was a half-inch deep. The ground was wet but firm. It took a hard press to push just his fingertip a half-inch. He wondered at the weight of the creature, and made a note to himself that tonight they'd have to store the smaller cages in the truck, which would mean more work. He sighed again.

By eight, the softball fields across the park had filled. Players warmed up outside the fences, while games took place. Tents to house teams or for food booths sprang up. Trevin smiled and turned on the music. Banners hung from the trucks. DR. TREVIN'S TRAVELING ZOOLOGICAL EXTRAVAGANZA. SEE NATURE'S ODDITIES! EDUCATIONAL! ENTERTAINING! By noon, there had been fifteen paying customers.

Leaving Hardy in charge of tickets, Trevin loaded a box with handbills, hung a staple gun to his belt, then marched to the ballfields, handing out flyers. The sun beat down like a humid furnace, and only the players in the field weren't under tents or umbrellas. Several folks offered him a beer—he took one—but his flyers, wrinkly with humidity, vanished under chairs or behind coolers. "We're doing a first day of the tournament special," he said. "Two bucks each, or three for you and a friend." His shirt clung to his back. "We'll be open after sunset, when it's cooler. These are displays not to be missed, folks!"

A woman in her twenties, her cheeks sun-reddened, her blonde hair tied back, said, "I don't need to *pay* to see a reminder, damn it!" She crumpled the paper and dropped it. One of her teammates, sitting on the ground, a beer between his knees, said, "Give him a break, Doris. He's just trying to make a living."

Trevin said, "We were in *Newsweek*. You might have read about us."

"Maybe we'll come over later, fella," said the player on the ground.

Doris popped a can open. "It might snow this afternoon, too."

"Maybe it will," said Trevin congenially. He headed toward town, on the other side of the fairgrounds. The sun pressured his scalp with prickly fire. By the time he'd gone a hundred yards, he wished he'd worn a hat, but it was too hot to go back.

He stapled a flyer to the first telephone pole he came to. "Yep," he said to himself. "A little publicity and we'll rake it in!" The sidewalk shimmered in white heat waves as he marched from pole to pole, past the hardware, past the liquor store, past the Baptist Church—SUFFER THE CHILDREN read the marquee—past the pool hall, and the auto supply shop. He went inside every store and asked the owner to post his sign. Most did. Behind Main Street stood several blocks of homes. Trevin turned up one street and down the next, stapling flyers, noting with approval the wire mesh over the windows. "Can't be too careful, nowadays," he said, his head swimming in the heat. The beer seemed to be evaporating through his skin all at once, and he felt sticky with it. The sun pulsed against his back. The magic number is five-seventy-eight, he thought. It beat within him like a song. Call it six hundred. Six hundred folks, come to the zoo, come to the zoo, come to the *zoo!*

When he finally made his way back to the fairgrounds, the sun was on its way down. Trevin dragged his feet, but the flyers were gone.

Evening fell. Trevin waited at the ticket counter in his zoo-master's uniform, a broad-shouldered red suit with gold epaulets. The change box popped open with jingly joy; the roll of tickets was ready. Circus music played softly from the loudspeakers as fireflies flickered in the darkness above the river. Funny, he thought, how the mutagen affected only the bigger vertebrate animals, not mice-sized mammals or little lizards, not small fish or bugs or plants. What would a bug mutate *into* anyway? They look alien to begin with. He chuckled to himself, his walking-up-the-sidewalk song still echoing: six hundred folks, come to the zoo, come to the zoo, come to the *zoo*.

Every car that passed on the highway, Trevin watched, waiting for it to slow for the turn into the fairgrounds.

From sunset until midnight, only twenty customers bought admissions; most of them were ball players who'd discovered that there wasn't much night-life in Mayersville. Clouds had moved in, and distant lightning flickered within their steel-wool depths.

Trevin spun the roll of tickets back and forth on its spool. An old farmer couple wearing overalls, their clothes stained with rich, Mississippi soil, shuffled past on their way out. "You got some strange animals here, mister," said the old man. His wife nodded. "But nothing stranger than what I've found wandering in my fields for the last few years. Gettin' so I don't remember what o-form normal looks like."

"Too close to the river," said his wife. "That's our place right over there." She pointed at a small farm house under a lone light, just beyond the last ball field. Trevin wondered if they ever retrieved home-run balls off their porch.

The thin pile of bills in the cash box rustled under Trevin's fingers. The money should be falling off the tables, he thought. We should be drowning in it. The old couple stood beside him, looking back into the zoo. They reminded him of his parents, not in their appearance, but in their solid patience. They weren't going anywhere fast.

He had no reason to talk to them, but there was nothing else left to do. "I was here a few years ago. Did really well. What's happened?"

The wife held her husband's hand. She said, "This town's dyin', mister. Dyin' from the bottom up. They closed the elementary school last fall. No elementary-age kids. If you want to see a *real* zoo display, go down to Issaquena County Hospital pediatrics. The penalty of parenthood. Not that many folks are having babies, though."

"Or whatever you want to call them," added the old man. "Your zoo's depressin'."

"I'd heard you had somethin' special, though," said the woman shyly.

"Did you see the crocomouse?" asked Trevin. "There's quite a story about that one. And the tigerzelle. Have you seen that one?"

"Saw 'em," she said, looking disappointed.

The old couple climbed into their pickup, and it rattled into life after a half-dozen starter-grinding tries.

"I found a buyer in Vicksburg for the truck," said Caprice.

Trevin whirled. She stood in the shadows beside the ticket counter, a notebook jammed under her arm. "I told you to stay out of view."

"Who's going to see me? You can't get customers even on a discount!" She gazed at the vacant lot. "We don't have to deliver it. He's coming to town next week on other business. I can do the whole transaction, transfer the deed, take the money, all of it, over the Internet."

One taillight out, the farmer's pickup turned from the fairgrounds and onto the dirt road that led to their house, which wasn't more than two hundred yards away. "What would we do with the animals?" He felt like weeping.

"Let the safe ones go. Kill the dangerous ones."

Trevin rubbed his eyes. She stamped her foot. "Look, this is no time for sentimentality! The zoo's a bust. You're going to lose the whole thing soon anyway. If you're too stubborn to give it all up, sell this truck now and you get a few extra weeks, maybe a whole season if we economize."

Trevin looked away from her. The fireflies still flickered above the river. "I'll have to make some decisions," he said heavily.

She held out the notebook. "I've already made them. This is what will fit in one semi-trailer. I already let Hardy and the roustabouts go with a severance check, postdated."

"What about the gear, cages?"

"The county dump is north of here."

Was that a note of triumph he detected in her voice? Trevin took the notebook. She dropped her hands to her side, chin up, staring at him. The zoo's lights cast long shadows across her face. I could kick her, he thought, and for a second his leg trembled with the idea of it.

He tucked the notebook under his arm. "Go to bed."

Caprice opened her mouth, then clamped it shut on whatever she might have said. She turned away.

Long after she'd vanished into the cab, Trevin sat on the stool, elbow on his knee, chin in his hand, watching insects circle the lights. The tigerzelle squatted on its haunches, alert, looking toward the river. Trevin remembered a ghastly cartoon he'd seen once. A couple of crones sat on the seat of a wagon full of bodies. The one holding the reins turned to the other and said, "You know, once the plague is over, we're out of a job."

The tigerzelle rose to its feet, focusing on the river. It paced intently in its cage, never turning its head from the darkness. Trevin straightened. What did it see out there? For a long moment, the tableau remained the same: insects swirled around the lights, which buzzed softly, highlighting the cages; shining metal against the enveloping spring night, the pacing tigerzelle, the ticket counter's polished wood against Trevin's hand, and the Mississippi's pungent murmuring in the background.

Beyond the cages, from the river, a piece of blackness detached itself from the night. Trevin blinked in fascinated paralysis, all the hairs dancing on the back of his neck. The short-armed creature stood taller than a man, surveyed the zoo, then dropped to all fours like a bear, except that its skin gleamed with salamander wetness. Its triangular head sniffed at the ground, moving over the moist dirt as if following a scent. When it reached the first cage, a small one that held the weaselsnake, the river creature lifted its forelegs off the ground, grasping the cage in web-fingered claws. In an instant, the cage was unrecognizable, and the weaselsnake was gone.

"Hey!" Trevin yelled, shaking off his stupor. The creature looked at him. Reaching under the ticket counter, Trevin grabbed the baseball bat and advanced. The monster turned away to pick up the next cage. Trevin's face flushed. "No, no, no, damn it!" He stepped forward again, stepped again, and suddenly he was running, bat held overhead. "Get away! Get away!" He brought the bat down on the animal's shoulder with a meaty whump.

It shrieked.

Trevin fell back, dropping the bat to cover his ears. It shrieked again, loud as a train whistle. For a dozen heartbeats, it stood above him, claws extended, then it seemed to lose interest and moved to the next cage, dismantling it with one jerk on the bars.

His ears ringing, Trevin snatched the bat off the ground and waded in, swinging. On its rear legs, the monster bared its teeth, dozens of glinting needles in the triangular jaw. Trevin nailed the creature in the side. It folded with surprising flexibility, backing away, claws distended, snarling in a deafening roar. Trevin swung. Missed. The monster swiped at his leg, ripping his pants and almost jerking his feet out from under him.

The thing moved clumsily, backing down the hill toward the levee fence as Trevin swung again. Missed. It howled, tried to circle around him. Trevin scuttled sideways, careful of his balance on the slick dirt. If he should fall! The thing charged, mouth open, but pulled back like a threatened dog when Trevin raised the bat. He breathed in short gasps, poked the bat's end at it, always shepherding it away from the zoo. Behind him, a police siren sounded, and car engines roared, but he didn't dare look around. He could only stalk and keep his bat at the ready.

After a long series of feints, its back to the fence, the nightmare stopped, hunched its back, and began to rise just as Trevin brought the bat down in a two-handed, over-the-head chop. Through the bat, he felt the skull crunch, and the creature dropped into a shuddery mass in the mud. Trevin, his pulse pounding, swayed for a moment, then sat beside the beast.

Up the hill, under the zoo's lights, people shouted into the darkness. Were they ball players? Town people? A police cruiser's lights blinked blue then red, and three or four cars, headlights on, were parked near the trucks. Obviously they couldn't see him, but he was too tired to call. Ignoring the wet ground, he lay back.

The dead creature smelled of blood and river mud. Trevin rested a foot on it, almost sorry that it was dead. If he could have captured it, what an addition it would have made to the zoo! Gradually, the heavy beat in his chest calmed. The mud felt soft and warm. Overhead, the clouds thinned a bit, scudding across the full moon.

At the zoo, there was talking. Trevin craned his head around to see. People jostled about, and flashlights cut through the air. They started down the hill. Trevin sighed. He hadn't saved the zoo, not really. Tomorrow would come and they'd leave one of the trucks behind. In a couple of months, it would all be gone, the other truck, the animals—he was most sorry about the tigerzelle—the pulling into town with music blaring and flags flapping and people lined up to see the menagerie. No more reason to wear the zoo-master's uniform with its beautiful gold epaulets. *Newsweek* would never interview him again. It was all gone. If he could only sink into the mud and disappear, then he wouldn't have to watch the dissolving of his own life.

He sat up so that they wouldn't think he was dead; waved a hand when the first flashlight found him. Mud dripped from his jacket. The policemen arrived first.

"God almighty, that's a big one!" The cop trained his light on the river creature.

"Told you the fences warn't no good," said the other.

Everyone stayed back except the police. The first cop turned the corpse over. Lying on its back, its little arms flopped to the side, it didn't look nearly as big or intimidating. More folk arrived: some townies he didn't recognize, the old couple from the farmhouse across the ball fields, and finally, Caprice, the flashlight looking almost too big for her to carry.

The first cop knelt next to the creature, shoved his hat up off his forehead, then said low enough that Trevin guessed that only the other cop could hear him, "Hey, doesn't this look like the Andersons' kid? They said they'd smothered him."

"He wasn't half that big, but I think you're right." The other cop threw a coat over the creature's face, then stood for a long time looking down at it. "Don't say anything to them, all right? Maggie Anderson is my wife's cousin."

"Nothing here to see, people," announced the first cop in a much louder voice. "This is a dead 'un. Y'all can head back home."

But the crowd's attention wasn't on them anymore. The flashlights turned on Caprice.

"It's a baby girl!" someone said, and they moved closer.

Caprice shined her flashlight from one face to the other. Then, desperation on her face, she ran clumsily to Trevin, burying her face in his chest.

"What are we going to do?" she whispered.

"Quiet. Play along." Trevin stroked the back of her head, then stood. A sharp twinge in his leg told him he'd pulled something. The world was all bright lights, and he couldn't cover his eyes. He squinted against them.

"Is that your girl, mister?" someone said.

Trevin gripped her closer. Her little hands fisted in his coat.

"I haven't seen a child in ten years," said another voice. The flashlights moved in closer.

The old farmer woman stepped into the circle, her face suddenly illuminated. "Can I hold your little girl, son? Can I just hold her?" She extended her arms, her hands quivering.

"I'll give you fifty bucks if you let me hold her," said a voice behind the lights.

Trevin turned slowly, lights all around, until he faced the old woman again. A picture formed in his mind, dim at first but growing clearer by the second. One semi-trailer truck, the trailer set up like a child's room—no, like a nursery! Winnie-the-Pooh wallpaper. A crib. One of those musical rotating things, what cha' call ums—a mobile! A little rocking chair. Kid's music. And they'd go from town to town. The banner would say THE LAST O-FORM GIRL CHILD, and he would *charge* them, yes he would, and they would line *up*. The money would fall off the table!

Trevin pushed Caprice away from him, her hands clinging to his coat. "It's okay, darling. The nice woman just wants to hold you for a bit. I'll be right here."

Caprice looked at him, despair clear in her face. Could she already see the truck with the nursery? Could she picture the banner and the unending procession of little towns?

The old woman took Caprice in her arms like a precious vase. "That's all right, little girl. That's all right." She faced Trevin, tears on her cheeks. "She's just like the granddaughter I always wanted! Does she talk yet? I haven't heard a baby's voice in forever. Does she talk?"

"Go ahead, Caprice dear. Say something to the nice lady."

Caprice locked eyes with him. Even by flashlight, he could see the polar blue. He could hear her sardonic voice night after night as they drove across country. "It's not financially feasible to continue," she'd say in her two-year-old voice. "We should admit the inevitable."

She looked at him, lip trembling. She brought her fist up to her face. No one moved. Trevin couldn't even hear them breathing.

Caprice put her thumb in her mouth. "Daddy," she said around it. "Scared, Daddy!"

Trevin flinched, then forced a smile. "That's a good girl."

"Daddy, *scared*."

Up the hill, the tigerzelle hooted, and, just beyond the fence, barely visible by flashlight, the Mississippi gurgled and wept.

MOVEMENTS IN SCIENCE FICTION AND FANTASY: A SYMPOSIUM

INTRODUCTION

Jack Dann

In *Nebula Awards 31* (1997), editor Pamela Sargent wrote: "Science fiction and fantasy are genres that continue to attract a varied and diverse number of writers with very different literary goals. For any one commentator to have a coherent view of the field or to assess the relative importance of individual works is difficult at best. I have instead asked several knowledgeable and gifted writers to point out certain signposts, or to comment on the particular fictional territories they have recently explored."

As I did when I edited *Nebula Awards 32* in 1998, I have followed Sargent's tradition . . . but this time with a bit of a twist. When I began editing this volume, I felt a bit like a latter-day Rip Van Winkle. I had isolated myself from the real world to finish my James Dean novel *The Rebel*; and when I finally turned off the laptop, stood up and stretched old, creaking muscles, shook off the dust and cobwebs, and looked blinking into the sunlight, I found that there had been quite a few changes in our genre's quad.

I discovered that in the few years that I had sequestered myself away from the genre, a number of movements had started . . . simultaneously, it seemed. If they weren't full-fledged movements, they certainly *looked* like movements.

What the hell are "The New Weird," "The Romantic Underground," "The New Space Opera," and the "The Interstitial Movement"?

To find out, I asked the writers associated with these varied literatures to please explain. And I asked Bruce Sterling—the great explainer of what's going on at the cutting edge—to provide an overview. As I did in *Nebula Awards 32*, I promised to print whatever the authors wrote; and, as a result, the essays in this symposium run the gamut from detailed explanation to postmodern irony and humor.

Bruce Sterling is one of the most important writers to emerge in the '70s. To quote Gardner Dozois, "He had almost as much to do (as writer, critic, propagandist, aesthetic theorist, and tireless polemicist) with the shaping and evolution of SF in the eighties and nineties as Michael Moorcock did with the shaping of SF in the sixties; it is not for nothing that many of his peers refer to him, half ruefully, half admiringly, as 'Chairman Bruce.'" His novels include *Involution Ocean, The Artificial Kid, Schismatrix, Islands in the Net, Heavy Weather, Holy Fire, The Difference Engine* (with Wiliam Gibson), *Zeitgeist, Distraction,* and *The Zenith Angle.* His nonfiction includes *The Hacker Crackdown: Law and Disorder on the Electric Frontier* and *Tomorrow Now: Envisioning the Next Fifty Years.* He edited the definitive cyberpunk anthology *Mirrorshades,* and his short stories can be found in his collections *Crystal Express, Globalhead,* and *A Good Old-Fashioned Future.* He won the Hugo Award in 1997. Sterling lives in Austin, Texas, where he wrote the entry on science fiction for the *Encyclopedia Britannica* and new introductions for two books by Jules Verne.

The *Bookseller* called China Miéville's first novel, *King Rat,* "an absolutely brilliant and imaginative debut novel." Arthur C. Clarke Award winner Tricia Sullivan called Miéville "a bona-fide wizard, a powerful hybrid strain of magician, scientist, and poet." He is certainly *the* hot, new writer of the new millennium. (Have we all agreed to call the "2000s" the "naughts," or the "naughties"?) Miéville's novels include *Perdido Street Station, The Scar,* and *Iron Council,* which won the Arthur C. Clarke Award, the British Fantasy Award, and the Kurt Lasswitz Award.

Paul McAuley was a research scientist at Oxford University and UCLA and lectured at St. Andrews University. His first novel, *Four Hundred Billion Stars,* won the Philip K. Dick Memorial Award. He has also won the Arthur C. Clarke Award, the John W. Campbell Award for Best Novel, the British Fantasy Award, and the Sidewise Award. His other novels include *Secret Harmonies, Eternal Light, Child of the River, Ancients of Days, Shrine of Stars, Red Dust, Pasquale's Angel, Fairyland, Ship of Fools, Making History, The Secret of Life, Whole Wide World, Little Machines,* and *White Devils.* Some of his short stories can be found in his collections *The King of the Hill and Other Stories* and *The Invisible Country.*

To quote multiple award–winning author Michael Swanwick: "I am no keeper of the lists, but anybody's roster of those central to the radical hard SF thing would have to include Iain Banks, Greg Egan (who's Australian, but included as a courtesy), Stephen Baxter—and Paul J. McAuley. In many ways, Paul is the exemplar of the movement. He can do it all— space, hard science, adventure, and excitement. . . ."

World Fantasy and Mythopoeic Award winner Ellen Kushner is the author of the novels *The Enchanted Kingdom* (with Judith Mitchell), *Thomas the Rhymer, Swordspoint,* and *The Fall of the Kings* (with Delia Sherman). She has edited the anthologies *Basilisk* and *The Horns of Elfland* (with Donald G. Keller and Delia Sherman). She is also the writer and host of the national public radio series *Sound & Spirit.*

Jeff VanderMeer was born in Pennsylvania in 1968, but spent much of his childhood in the Fiji Islands. Although he has pursued careers in editing and publishing, he is primarily a fiction writer. His work has appeared in ten languages in sixteen countries in publications such as *Asimov's, Amazing Stories, Weird Tales, Interzone, Nebula Awards 30, Best New Horror 7, The Year's Best Fantastical Fiction, Dark Voices 5, Dark Terrors,* and *The Year's Best Dark Fantasy 2001.* He has won the Rhysling Award, Fear Magazine's Best Short Story Award, the World Fantasy Award, and a Florida Individual Artist Fellowship for excellence in fiction. His nonfiction has appeared in publications such as *SF Eye; Tangent; The St. James Guide to Gothic, Ghost, and Horror Writers; Nova Express; The New York Review of Science Fiction; Magill's Guide to Science Fiction & Fantasy Literature;* and publications from Gale Research. His books include *The Book of Lost Places; Veniss Underground; Dradin, In Love; Dradin, in Love and Other Stories; The Early History of Ambergris; The Exchange; City of Saints and Madmen: The Book of Ambergris;* and *Why Should I Cut Your Throat when I Can Just Ask You for the Money?,* a collection of nonfiction. VanderMeer's publishing house, *Ministry of Whimsy,* has published such notables as Pulitzer Prize winner Richard Eberhart and National Book Award winner Donald Justice.

DEEP IN THE HEART OF THE STATE OF THE ART

Bruce Sterling

As a commercial enterprise, science fiction today is dominated by tie-in books from movies, television, and computer-gaming. Chain bookstores and Amazon continue their now-traditional havoc, while book publishing in general has become the meager handmaiden of media consolidation.

SF writers love to complain about this dire turmoil, since it basically makes their lives unlivable, but they deserve and cherish their grievances, which are far from new. It could well be argued that science fiction improves radically when its writers know their cause is beyond hope.

Whenever SF makes no commercial sense, the people who care about it become frantically devoted. The small press is thriving in 2004. It's as if the living spirit of the SF genre has jumped right back into its original Arkham House bomb shelter. The material from established SF lines has become pitifully gray and formulaic—even fantasy can't fantasize any more—but the underground boils over with unnumbered gangs and cliques. There are so many—these New Wave Fabulist New Weird New Space Opera Interstitialist Overclocker Rat Bastard Rosebud Wristleteers, so many of them, I say, that they have to swap their personnel just to write a manifesto.

The dawn of the twenty-first century sees science fiction still wrapped in its confused, oxymoronic struggle between science and fiction. The graying humanists and cyberpunks of the 1980s have found their favorite easy chairs by now, while handing on that unresolved struggle to yet another generation.

The humanists gamely continue their long march through the institutions of SF. The literate spec-fic wing of the '80s never directly seized power, but boy could those cats ever teach. The humanists proved to be wizards of the humanities—they practically *all* teach something or other: Clarion, writers workshops, universities, state arts bureaus, plus the tireless industry scutwork of nominating for and divvying up the Nebulas.

To teach has its rewards. The earnest efforts of John Kessel, humanist ideologue and pedagogue, gave the world Andy Duncan, the star New Fabulist. Karen Joy Fowler was the mentor for Kelly Link, and found a woman whose skills and moxie bid fair to eclipse those of the headmistress. Kelly Link is the very model of a GenX genre modernist. That stuff that she is writing, editing, and self-publishing in her self-founded small press . . . Well, this superb material is beyond my meager ability to critically delineate.

SF's literary wing always resented the boundaries between genre SF and mainstream literature. From the generous ambitions of humanist SF rose modern Interstitialism, an SF movement so advanced that it has a Web site, tax-free foundation status, and a considered critical position in the graphic arts.

Interstitialists seek to work directly in the cracks between genres, feeling that this is somehow usefully subversive. And it is, kinda, but, well, what if they won? What's the victory condition? Interstitialism is very postmodern, in that it calls old definitions into question without bothering to invent plausible new ones.

In his delightful essay of 2002, "The Squandered Promise of Science Fiction," Jonathan Lethem grew loudly appalled that SF writers somehow preferred to slum with squalid, insular fandom, when the likes of Pynchon, DeLillo, Barthelme, Coover, Jeanette Winterson, and Steve Erickson were becoming ascendant literary powers and Booker Prize candidates. Could that possibly be just and fair?

Lethem's considered position makes sense. Lethem likes SF not for its geeky science—mere "technojargon," in his vocabulary—but for the latitude SF offers for Kafkaesque literary conceits. Jonathan Lethem was unrivalled in his deft treatment of oddities such as talking kangaroos and criminals turned into concrete blocks—but to what grand end? Wouldn't it be more sensible to just settle down and write some fine, relatively conventional novels about race relations, and life in Brooklyn, and small-time gangsters with speech defects? And lo, Jonathan Lethem fulfilled his promise, to much acclaim. The relief within SF was palpable, for his friends rejoiced for him, while the backward natives were scarcely aware that he had abandoned the field.

Cyberpunks in the early twenty-first century have their own internal contradictions to trip over. Cyberpunks are literateurs mostly by accident. When not feverishly typing on Internet-linked keyboards, they spend their spare time with Linux programmers, and computer gamers, and special-effects mavens, and industrial designers, and cops, and foreigners, and criminals.

Cyberpunk's core problem is that cyberpunks are lethally close to the white heat of technological advance. Therefore, in the year 2004, a dark epoch full of colorful terrorists and megacorporate globalist moguls, cyberpunks are basically forced to exist hip-deep in their own extrapolations.

It's now a nothing deal for William Gibson to write a "nowpunk" book like *Pattern Recognition,* a classic off-the-wall cyberpunk novel effort-lessly recast as a highly plausible work in the present day. John Shirley runs a futurist, trend-spotting Web site. Rudy Rucker programs, Marc Laidlaw writes computer games, while Sterling pontificates in a glossy magazine opinion column.

If (like all good cyberpunks) you are truly fascinated by the glamorous spectacle of technology impacting society—then why would you want to write yet another novel, a literary effort burdened with plot, characters, and denouement, where some guy ends up kissing some girl? Logically, wouldn't you be much better off in the real-life company of genuine scientists, engineers, venture capitalists, government R&D wonks, futurist pundits, social activists, DARPA, NASA, European Union industrial-policy junketeers, and so forth? Why write twinkly, imaginative science fiction stories for *Asimov's* and *Fantasy and Science Fiction* when you could be writing somber, nonfic-tional, heavy-lidded technosocial commentary for the likes of *Wired, Technology Review, I.D., Metropolis, Fortune, Time,* and *Newsweek?*

This may not pose a fatal temptation for all SF writers, but it's enough to prove that cyberpunk science fiction could never make literature do what it wanted. Cyberpunks made repeated rushes at the electronic frontier and then witnessed society genuinely transforming. The frontier shifted under their feet, it became civilization. Respectability does not so much beckon as envelop.

Cyberpunk's modern successors are not science fiction people doing cyber, but cyber people doing science fiction—Neal Stephenson, program-mer turned novelist, Cory Doctorow, programmer turned novelist, Charles Stross, programmer turned novelist. (And maybe Benjamin Rosenbaum, programmer turned artsy, Calvino-esque short story writer.)

Cyberpunk's successors, best known as "Overclockers," do not merely talk technojargon; since they are natives of a technosociety, Overclockers actually *think* technojargon. The living heartwood of cyberpunk today isn't found in books or magazines but in Web sites: boingboing.net, worldchanging.com. Although SF people do go there, those are by no means literary sites. These Web sites are, in one ungainly word, techno-countercultural.

In the oxymoronic world of science fiction, the term "new" signifies revivalism. New Weird is weird. New Space Opera is space opera. New Wave in the 1960s was a wave, and New Wave Fabulism is fabulism. The New Fabulism can be pretty good fabulism, but it's not hugely different in character from many earlier fabulisms, like, say, Southern Gothic, or South American magic realism, or Eastern European fantastyka, or anything ever written by James Blaylock or Howard Waldrop. There is much to be said in its favor, too. After the genre's tropes have been extensively stressed by Stross and Doctorow, guys who can twist the English language till it kinks like barbed wire, some easygoing fabulism comes as a massive relief.

Whenever Britain does well in science fiction, science fiction is healthy: that is a principle. China Miéville's work is a bound-breaking melange of horror, and fantasy, and SF. It's also British, and radically left-wing, and totally contemporary, and yet is eagerly read on every shore the genre reaches. Critical and popular justice is finally being done to the splendid M. John Harrison, the only writer on the planet who could be New Wave, New Weird, and New Space Opera, all at once, authentically, and without even needing to be new.

Science fiction's new core problems in 2004 are its old problems. They are the problems science fiction writers have been wrestling with since 1926 and probably since Mary Shelley. We wrestle to reconcile science and literature. That is a grave, sublime, mighty, worthy, cultural challenge. We have never succeeded, ever. We aren't even close.

When we do that successfully, then we will win. When we win, then the world will become science-fictional, in its soul, in its heart, and in its brain. Then we will find our true fulfillment. The world will belong to us. We will have remade it whole and entire, in the shape of our hearts' desire.

Then, and only then, will we cease to exist.

NEW WEIRD

China Miéville

A Europe is haunting the spectral—the Europe of New Weird. Out of British decay it comes to the Americas, the New Worlds of the Old World cross-breeding with the Old Weird of the New World. Bastard of continents, of High Art and Low Culture, of the Oneiric and Quotidian, the Numinous and the most Profane,

New Weird is the pulp wing of Surrealism. It is an exorcist, come to lay the unquiet of degraded "fantasy," hermetic idiot spirits that do not know they are dead, traditions of dead generations that weigh like the most unimaginative nightmares on the brains of the living. Uncanny, rise up: you have nothing to lose but this bane.

—From *The New Weird Manifesto*

'm sorry. Did I say that out loud?

That's quite enough of that. Everyone involved in the New Weird project/experiment/classification/thing has stressed time and again that we're not proposing a manifesto. "Nothing could be more unenlightening or useless," Michael Cisco has said. And he's right of course.

(Only . . . sometimes, I wonder if we protest too much. Sometimes in my most ornery spirit, I find bad thoughts in my head. They whisper to me that perhaps now as we're all abasing ourselves to say how unprogrammatic and open-minded we are, perhaps precisely now, a manifesto's exactly what's needed. Here's to *not* enlightening but insisting. Don't tell a soul.)

On 29 April 2003, M. John Harrison asked, on an internet bulletin board: "The New Weird. Who does it? What is it? Is it even anything?" Thus are monsters unleashed. The misbegotten thing slouched off across the information superhighway, and a year, several books' worth of postings, and a fair bit of ill-tempered debate later, it's not clear that we're any wiser. But even if that's the case—and that's moot—it doesn't mean the questions weren't worth asking.

Fantastic literature's in astoundingly good shape right now. The quality's as high as it's ever been, and—which doesn't always follow—we're being noticed. Particularly in Britain, the arena I know best, SF/F/H is getting reviewed and discussed in the mainstream, its ideas and tropes are being ripped off by "literary" writers (I'm as cynical as the next genre geek about these brief bursts of trendiness, but there's no reason we shouldn't enjoy it while it's going on). There's been talk of—whisper it—a renaissance.

It was in an attempt to get to grips with some of the specifics of this boom that the nebulous, fuzzy-as-hell but still useful concept of New Weird—a moment rather than a movement, though that itself's a blurry distinction—got thrown up.

New Weird is not a marketing plan. It is not a prescription—though it would be disingenuous to deny that it embeds certain notions of what the fantastic can do particularly well. It is not a statement of what should, to the exclusion of other things, be read—some of my favorite books, as they (nearly) say, are not new, or are not weird, or are neither. It is not

a gang—some of the writers associated with it would be cheerfully unin-
terested or even actively antipathetic to the notion. It is an act of making
sense, of pointing at a perceived phenomenon in world, and arguably particularly British, speculative fiction: the explosion of the high-quality literary fantastic, accompanied by a certain uncanny baroque, a grotesque, a
vivid real-of-the-unreal, uniting otherwise variegated authors.

There've been countless discussions of New Weird, including illuminat-
ing musings on its taxonomy and genre, like Michael Cisco's excellent recent column (http://www.themodernword.com/columns/cisco_001.html),
which open-mindedly draws the scope of New Weird broader than others
might, but teaches us a great deal by so doing. There have been serious,
thoughtful criticisms of the whole enterprise, like Nick Mamatas's
(http://www.livejournal.com/users/nihilistic_kid/395922.html), that those of
us persuaded that there's something to the category have had to engage
with. There've also, though, been a whole host of unconvincing blather
about the Bad Practice of Pigeonholing and Labelling and How It Con-
strains Writers, and so on. I'd argue, by contrast, that the human mind is a
machine to organize and make connections. Any act of naming is precisely
an argument, an intervention. It's a claim about one set or other of those
connections, a claim that's not a neutral observation, but that in the very
moment of seeing can organize and make visible.

It's down to the namer to argue the point that this or that label is
useful—that it is good to think with. The very *Sturm und Drang* which
greeted Harrison's playful provocation suggests that New Weird is at least
that—which suggests in turn that there's something going on. It's not every
literary pronouncement would spawn hundreds of thousands of words of
debate. (In fact as an experiment, I hereby announce the existence of the
Crypto-Thalassophiles. The core writers of this movement are Anita
Brookner, Paul Coelho, Tricia Sullivan and, ooh, say, Caryl Phillips. Let's see
if anything comes of it.)

The fact is that many of the newer writers, and some of the more established ones—Harrison himself, of course, Al Reynolds, Steve Cockayne,
Steph Swainston, Justina Robson, Liz Williams, K.J. Bishop, and way too
many others to mention—though enormously and obviously heteroge-
neous, nonetheless share something. Something New, and, um, Weird. (It
can be a diverting parlour game to debate and assign people membership or
not of the category.) Above all, they've all got a disrespect for traditional
boundaries, both between genre and mainstream, and between the subdivi-
sions of genre itself. Like the Old Weird of Lovecraft and Clark Ashton
Smith, these are writers who pinch blithely from fantasy, from SF, from horror, and mix it up however they're moved.

We all know what the clichés of the fantastic are, and New Weird
(among other mo(ve)ments) has had enough of them. Its is a more grotesque

unreal. But what subversions or inversions or conversions it attempts it does so lovingly. Because as soon as the fantastic becomes a cliché, it's no longer fantastic. And it's against that internal betrayal that New Weird militates. New Weird is a *return* to the radical fantastic.

Key texts of New Weird achieve this with a particularly "generic" love of the fantastic itself. This is political fiction that does not, as so many "literary" writers do, make the mistake of thinking that the politics of the fantastic inhere solely and simplistically in allegory and metaphor. For me, and I think for the best New Weird, the fantastic will of course resonate with certain "meanings" in the real world (we can't help but process metaphors wherever we look), but it is also and crucially *its own end*. In this model, what distinguishes New Weird from some Magic Realism, say, or from certain varieties of postmodernist writing, is that it surrenders to the weird itself.

Postmodernoid fourth-wall breaking—the writer and reader colluding in the knowledge that what's being written/read is a *text*—is sometimes seen as the most sophisticated stuff out there, because it knows, unlike "naïve" fiction, what it is. It can also, however, offer the reader a too-easy get-out clause, a hide: Michael Moorcock has brilliantly excoriated "the joke which specifically indicates to the reader that the story is not really 'true' . . . to make the experience described comfortingly unreal." By contrast, a (New) surrender to the Weird isn't an act of untheoretical naivety, but is a deliberate engagement. We know—of course we know—that this is "just fiction," but in loving, debasedly loving, the weird, in literalizing, not metaphorizing, the impossible, we perform an act of *radical forgetting*. I am the Weird's Bitch. We know the fantastic will always-already be metaphorical, but it also has its own integrity.

As Steph Swainston pointed out in the original New Weird thread on Harrison's board (that huge, canonical, and astoundingly fascinating conversation subsequently lost to server shenanigans, of which [archivists please take note] I possess what may be the only hard copy in the world), New Weird is secular and political. It's my opinion that the surge in the unescapist, engaged fantastic, with its sense of limitless potentiality and the delighted bursting of boundaries, is an expression of a similar opening up of potentiality in "real life," in politics. Neoliberalism collapsed the social imagination, stunting the horizons of the possible. With the crisis of the Washington Consensus and the rude grass-roots democracies of the movements for global justice, millions of people are remembering what it is to imagine. That's why New Weird is post-Seattle fiction.

This is emphatically not to suggest that all the authors share a particular political (or (non-)religious) viewpoint, but to stress that the fiction *itself* is messy, problematic and problematising—it's a reaction against moralism and consolatory mythicism.

Etc etc etc. That's the trouble with trying to counter clichés—the counterclichés cliché quicker than shit off a shovel, and with that comes domestication. Either you lose any subversive gloss at all—the hip-hop which now sells us jeans and cheese once fought the power—or, what's perhaps worse, a horrible zombie gloss of radicalism is retained while you shuffle into the corridors of establishment, rotting. (Think of the later Dali's craven court-jestering for lucre and the faint patina of radical chic. Compare that to *Un Chien Andalou*. Sad, isn't it?) New Weird—along with the other mo(ve)ments of which it's some kind of cousin, the Ratbastards, the Interstitial Arts, the New Space Opera and others—reflected a major cultural shakeup. Soon, though, if not already, those groups will have their epigones, and will probably be the very fantasy mainstream they were railing against. At which point, doubtless, some new punkass radicals will come along and subvert us all, by writing about hobbits.

There's not much we can do about this future history, only try to go unquietly into the un–good night of respectability. Personally, I don't think I'm going to say too much about New Weird any more. As a great person once (nearly) said in a different context, "It is more pleasant and useful to go through the 'experience of New Weird' than to write about it."

THE NEW SPACE OPERA

Paul McAuley

Many writers, from Isaac Asimov and Leigh Brackett to David Brin and Samuel R. Delany, have upgraded the epically baroque stage sets of pulp space opera to suit their own individually conceived dramas, but what has been tagged by *Locus* as the New Space Opera (NSO) has the yeasty tang of a collective enterprise, bubbling with energy, optimism, and the kind of internalized self-critical dialogue necessary to any vital genre movement. Characterized by an infusion of hard science, left-wing political attitudes, and an outsider's perspective, NSO is perceived to be something of a British phenomenon, but is inspired by decidedly American sources. It has borrowed from Larry Niven's Known Space the idea that the galaxy is a kind of vast archaeological site from which wonders and secret histories may be mined and in which, as in Fred Saberhagen's Berserker series, ancient dangers inimical to the spread of intelligence may also lurk; and it populates its stories with a promiscuously colorful brew of human and posthuman cultures that, as in John Varley's Eight Worlds sequence, and Bruce Sterling's *Schismatrix*, have adapted to extra-planetary life by use of genetic engineering and ingenious exploitation of radical technologies that are often, cyberpunk-style, incorporated into the human body.

Unlike pulp space opera, which is notoriously light on science of any kind and either cheerfully or ignorantly bends the metrical frame of the universe to suit its stories, NSO is notable for imaginative exploration of cutting-edge ideas from cosmology, quantum theory, information technology, theories of consciousness, and much else. It is also imbued with an ebullient multiculturalism: there are few centralized governments in NSO, no autarchs or high emperors, no great palace-planets or plucky princesses, no fleets of warships commanded by implacable admirals. Or, if they are present, it's as the butt of satirical exercises that demonstrate how easily the adaptable small mammals of the new can outsmart the saurian monsters of the old. In novels as diverse as Iain M. Banks's *Consider Phlebas,* Charles Stross's *Singularity Sky,* or (here I'm extrapolating from the first part of a two-volume series, but it's an easy reach) Peter F. Hamilton's Commonwealth Saga, monolithic empires rubbing up against the swarming diversity of NSO Cultures, Commonwealths and Confederations always come off worst, just as, in good old-fashioned Campbellian science fiction, witty, adaptable and infinitely ingenious humans always worked their way to the top of the Galactic heap. And while the spaceships may be as vast as ever, they're usually privately owned, and their captains and pilots have more in common with Harrison Ford's cynical but fundamentally decent Han Solo than with the Hornblower-style space cadets of military space opera, except that they're as often as not female, and usually possess a couple of malfunctioning cybernetic implants (or may even, as in M. John Harrison's *Light,* or Justina Robson's *Natural History,* be inextricably coeval with their ships). Most heroes of NSO are *reluctant* heroes, reflexive individualists (true children of the free market era of Thatcher and Reagan) who are more interested in turning a quick profit than in maintaining the status quo. If they do happen to save the universe, it's usually more by accident than design.

It's hard to assign a common vector to the buzzing, blooming multiplicity of NSO, but most writers of the form are engaged with at least one of two major themes. The first, inspired by recent radical revisions of cosmology, is that of explicating secret histories of the universe—extending the epic interstellar sweep of space opera into deep time. Often, as in my own *Eternal Light,* M. John Harrison's *Light,* Robert Reed's *Marrow,* or Justina Robson's *Natural History,* humans are merely the latest intelligent species to trespass on a galaxy littered with the ruins and abandoned wonders of earlier intelligent species. Sometimes, as in Alastair Reynolds's Inhibitor series, the ruins are patrolled by ruthless exterminators of upstart species; or, as in Peter F. Hamilton's Night's Dawn trilogy, ancient technology sets a warped version of humanity against itself. Sometimes, the ruins are inhabited. Godlike ancient ones preside over a plurality of worlds in Ken MacLeod's Engines of Light trilogy. In Stephen Baxter's Xeelee series, humanity escapes the leash of more powerful intelligent species only to become entangled in a war that encompasses the entire universe from big-bang birth to the extended *diminuendo* of heat-death.

The second theme is one that is increasingly engaging much serious science fiction: Vernor Vinge's Singularity, the tipping point where either humanity, its machines, or a fusion of both achieve an enlightenment that wrenches history into a completely new and theoretically unknowable form. Greg Egan, notably in *Diaspora* and *Schild's Ladder,* confronts the Singularity head-on with bold, intricate and intellectually rigorous speculation. In Vernor Vinge's *A Fire Upon the Deep* and *A Deepness in the Sky,* the galaxy is divided into zones where thought moves at different speeds, so that the Singularity (and faster-than-light travel) is possible only in the outermost reaches, where angels dwell. Charles Stross's *Singularity Sky* maps a patchwork of interstellar empires established after post-Singularity intelligences scattered human communities across the sky. Ken MacLeod's *Newton's Wake,* in which ordinary humans expand into a universe reengineered by posthuman intelligences, fuses the theme of a junkyard galaxy and the Singularity into a seamless whole. It occurs to me that most NSO fictions are, in various guises, stories about the Singularity. After all, the godlike ancient ones whose abandoned toys are rediscovered by human explorers have often vanished into their own equivalent of the Singularity, and many of the large-scale adventures of NSO drive knowingly or unknowingly towards the furious, all-consuming light of a Singularity-like transcendental Becoming where the known fuses with the unknown and something new and terrifying and wonderful is born. Like all the best science fiction narratives, they are breathless ascents that end with leaps into the transfiguring unknown.

As soon as a critical apparatus is assembled to deal with a new movement within any genre, that movement has almost certainly passed its peak. As with the New Wave and cyberpunk, NSO has advanced science fiction's boundaries and gleefully refurbished its tropes, but now finds its core values dissipating into the main body of the genre. Its radical ideas are becoming part of the genre's toolbox. Perhaps it's telling that in both Charles Stross's *Singularity Sky* and Ken MacLeod's *Newton's Wake,* the Singularity isn't an end to history after all, but a narrative device that remakes the Galaxy into a place congenial for classic space opera adventures. Having eaten its ancestors, its ancestors have in turn eaten NSO. The revolution is dead: long live the revolution!

THE INTERSTITIAL ARTS FOUNDATION

Ellen Kushner

In the early 1990s, in the last remaining coffeehouse in Harvard Square, a musician friend of mine ran a Sunday afternoon concert series. Warren Senders is a musician originally trained in jazz who then went to India to study Hindustani singing. The concert series Warren produced included the Really Eclectic String Quartet playing Jimi Hendrix and Balkan tunes (but no Mozart), and an Indian singing about Hindu legends with electric guitar.

Warren called the series "Interstitial Music." At every show he explained that he was featuring music that falls in the interstices of recognized categories, that can't be defined as quite one thing or another. It's hard to market, it's hard to explain to people in one sentence. . . . We loved it all.

Fast forward a couple of years. We're in my livingroom, fellow-novelists Delia Sherman, Terri Windling, and I, drinking something or other, munching biscuits, and gently moaning about how hard it is to reach our audience. When our work is published in genre, it is well-received—except by those who are utterly baffled by the fact that it fails to follow the rhetoric of strict genre fantasy, who complain bitterly. When we submit it out of genre, we're told it contains too many nonrealistic elements—code for "it has Fantasy Cooties." We also wax indignant on behalf of our favorite science fiction writers whose quirky, brilliant short stories fly under the radar of literary critics, and, more importantly, of the reading public. Terri brings up her concerns as a painter working with fantastical and mythic images that fall uncomfortably between "fine art" and traditional illustration. . . . I think about the music I'm playing on *Sound & Spirit*, stuff everyone responds to but none of my listeners can find in the carefully ordered bins in the record store.

This is too much, we said. We're living in an age of category, of ghettoization—the Balkanization of Art! We should do something.

"Guys?" I said. "Would you mind if I just phoned Warren and asked if he's free this afternoon? He coined the phrase 'Interstitial Music'—maybe it's time to start talking about 'Interstitial Art'!"

We met. We talked. We schemed. In the fall of 2002, we took action. By then we'd met up with writer and academic Heinz Insu Fenkl, whose theory of meta-fantasy and understanding of the reading and writing processes seemed to tie in with ours so well that when he became the director of the Creative Writing department at a State University of New York, he instituted a summer program, ISIS: the Interstitial Studies Institute at SUNY, New Paltz. As Heinz points out in an online essay, "The word 'interstice' comes from the Latin roots *inter* (between) and *sistere* (to stand). . . . It generally refers to a space between things: a chink in a fence, a gap in the clouds, a DMZ between nations at war, the potentially infinite space between two musical notes, a form of writing that defies genre classification." (http://www.artistswithoutborders.org/why/index.html)

We held our first symposium at SUNY/New Paltz in June, 2003, and determined to create a Web site, to publish anthologies with Small Beer Press, and work on how to insinuate the notion of art without borders into the broader world; to reach out to librarians and bookstore owners and others who guard the gates between the work and the readers.

In 2004, novelist and educator Midori Snyder orchestrated the creation of a Web site with over 100 pages of material by a dozen or so contributors (linked to a discussion board), and we became a genuine Foundation with 501c3 status in 2004. Our Mission Statement includes these words:

> Rigid categorization by critics and educators is an unsatisfactory method for understanding the border-crossing works to be found in all areas of the arts today: . . . We are . . . claiming a place in a wider artistic and academic community. The mission of the Interstitial Arts Foundation is to give all border-crossing artists and art scholars a forum and a focus for their efforts. Rather than creating a new genre with new borders, we support the free movement of artists across the borders of their choice. (http://www.ArtistsWithoutBorders.org)

In his essay "What's in the Wind" Gregory Frost offered another metaphor, that of cross-pollination: "I think a whole lot of our genetically modified products," Frost writes, "have escaped from the fantasy orchard and blown onto that really big field across the barrier; for some while now, we within the orchard have been trying to describe to ourselves all that cross-pollinated mutant stuff. [. . .] However, winds blow from more than one direction. While the huge literary field was being contaminated by fantasy, so, too, was the genre orchard being sprinkled with stuff coming the other way." (*New York Review of Science Fiction*, August 2003)

Borne on the wind, Interstitial Art is incredibly hard to explain and define, precisely because it's all about the indefinable, the ever-shifting borders that current commerce and public fashion force upon the distribution and consumption of that most intangible of "products," creative art.

This drives some people crazy. They want rules, clear definitions—to have a real movement with recognized leaders . . . but that's the antithesis of life and work on the border.

As I travel around the country, I meet many like-minded souls. At a talk at the Brooklyn Public Library, I watch librarians nodding energetically whenever Delia utters the magic words, "resisting categorization." In an independent bookstore in Kalamazoo, we see a wall of recommended reading that practically defines the Interstitial credo, with Michael Chabon's "literary" *The Amazing Adventures of Kavalier and Clay* right next to Sarah Smith's "mystery" novels. When I get all excited about this, the bookstore person says, "Yeah, we do get people in here asking, 'Where's the Gay Books section?' and we tell them, 'We don't like to ghettoize.'"

We want more, more, more things like that to happen everywhere, in ways we haven't even thought of yet. Whatever fueled our initial passion, we're all coming to realize just how critical it is, right now, in a world increasingly segregated by the dark forces of marketing and promotion, to give people the freedom of the in-between places. Obviously, we're getting support from other artists who feel their work isn't adequately represented. But the people the IAF ultimately serves are the consumers of art (among whom we also count ourselves!): the readers and listeners and audiences whom popular culture mainly denies the rich world of the interstices.

We feel for those poor reviewers who spend half their ink trying to describe what something *isn't*, when they should have the liberty to approach a work on its own terms. A webzine review of Neal Stephenson's latest begins:

> We need the categories, of course. Some writers may dream of breaking free of the genre ghetto and have wild dreams of bookstores simply divided down the middle . . . Readers would go quietly mad, of course. . . .

But concludes:

> [Stephenson's] Baroque Cycle defies categories. It has elements of every genre, from swashbuckling romance to gee-whiz science to historical fiction to spy thriller to modern fantasy and high-tone literature. . . . Yet it's hard to accurately finger why these books encompass this paradox. . . . (http://www.bookslut.com/specific_floozy/2004_05_002063.php)

I can tell her why: "It's interstitial."

The Interstitial Arts Foundation is not just about books and writing, and it's certainly not just about science fiction and fantasy, though to some people, it may look like we're just a bunch of pissed off genre writers. As Terri wrote me, "Of *course* we're promoting the kind of things we write. We believe in it. That's why we write it. Duh."

There is another branch of IA, the academic. Writer and scholar Theodora Goss explains that the academic side of IA is "trying to examine interstitial texts, which are often left out of academic discourse because they fall outside the categories by which conferences and journals are organized, and to create theories about interstitial arts"—theories in plural, she stresses. Just as crucial, Goss adds, is "trying to think of innovative ways to teach texts, ways that cross the usual academic borders."

On the IAF's academic discussion board, highly trained experts argue about the exact definition of the term "genre". . . . But for me, it all comes down to more personal things: When public radio colleagues read my novels, published in genre with genre covers, they return the books to me saying, "I don't usually read This Kind of Thing . . . but *this* was *good!*" When I was on a panel at an sf con this year, asked to list the best fantasy I'd read lately, of a room of nearly 200 fans—all interested enough in modern fantasy to be there instead of across the hall listening to something else—when I asked who had read Elizabeth Knox (*The Vintner's Luck, Black Oxen, Daylight*) or Chitra Banerjee Divakaruni (*Mistress of Spices*), both published as "Mainstream Literature," only one or two hands were waveringly raised.

The Interstitial Arts Foundation is not meant to be a movement in the strictest sense; rather, it seeks to express support for what's already moving in the arts: we're simply trying to give a local habitation and a name to a mindset that already exists, and has existed all along. We're not setting up in opposition to the New Weird or Slipstream or anything else—we call ourselves an "umbrella organization" but maybe a better image would be a *holding tank* full of nourishment for all the innovative work being created with no place in the world of categories. It's work that may or may not achieve liftoff on its own, succeeding through intrinsic virtue and word-of-mouth (and maybe even ultimately spawning its very own category). With the difficult word "Interstitial" we hope to create a vocabulary that makes this possible: for critics, for reviewers, for scholars, and most importantly for readers and audiences.

We are in effect a place for the disaffected of many stripes to hang out—a place for non-joiners not to join, but to stand up and be counted.

THE ROMANTIC UNDERGROUND: AN EXPLORATION OF A NONEXISTENT AND SELF-DENYING NONMOVEMENT

Jeff VanderMeer

With apologies to my friends and colleagues in the various real "movements," "umbrellas," and "committees" mentioned in this essay, all of whom I regard with affection and respect.

Although the phrase "the romantic underground" is often attributed to Shelley and his minor poem "The Assignation of Lapels" (1819), the Romantic Underground actually began as an offshoot of the Decadent Movement in France.[1] The first text identified with the Romantic Underground was Gustave Flaubert's *The Temptation of St. Anthony* (1874), since claimed by the Symbolists.

Flaubert vehemently denied that his book was a Romantic Underground text; in fact, he denied the existence of the movement altogether. This has been a recurring refrain in the development of the Romantic Underground: every author identified as an adherent of the movement has denied this fact. No text has long remained part of the Romantic Underground because no living author has allowed it to for very long. (In some cases, another movement has made a better case in claiming a particular text, as well.)

Some of the authors "outed" as "Romantic Underground-nistas" in those early years included Remy de Gourmont, Oscar Wilde, August Strindberg, Emile Zola, Alfred Kubin, Andre Breton, and Ronald Firbank. Some have even claimed that Breton himself formed the surrealists as an offshoot of the Romantic Underground, not as a reaction to Dada, Futurism, and the proto-magic realists.

Regardless, the enduring properties of the Romantic Underground remain a lack of membership by those authors cited and a general lack of identifying characteristics. At first, reading between the lines of critical texts from the period—some from the infamous *Yellow Book*—the Romantic Underground apparently formed a "loose umbrella" around certain authors, attempting to provide a critical and imaginative landscape in which creativity could have free, albeit vague, reign. Authors being skittish at best, most apparently saw the umbrella as more of a trap and escaped without their names ever being connected to rumors of a vast but secret literary organization dedicated to the antithesis of anything popular, tidy, or, indeed, logical.

---

[1] The author is unable to confirm or deny whether any actual "RU" research has been done for this essay.

Chroniclers of the Romantic Underground lost track of it during the 1920s and most of the 1930s, when the group may have decided to form "literary guerilla cells of single individuals, with no communication between any two cells." It is supposed that Jorge Luis Borges joined the movement in the 1940s, but only a reference to "the underground romantic with his hopeless beret" in his short story "The Immortal" (1962) suggests any active participation. Fellow South Americans Pablo Neruda and Gabriel Garcia Marquez may have joined the movement in the 1960s and 1970s, but, again, both deny the existence of the movement and any participation in it—thus seeming to substantiate the rumors, since this behavior is all too indicative of Romantic Underground members.

During the science fiction New Wave movement of the 1960s, the Romantic Underground again came to the fore, with many literary critics, including Brian Stableford and Colin Wilson, claiming that the New Wave was nothing more or less than an especially visible cell of the Romantic Underground. *New Worlds* contributor Rachel Pollack, however, called this "Bullshit" at the time, while *NW* editor Michael Moorcock later wrote in his book *Wizardry and Wild Romance* (1986) that "there was nothing romantic or underground about the New Wave. We had no time for sentimental tripe nor did we want to remain part of some invisible subculture. We were very much in the public eye."[2]

In the 1980s, writers such as Rikki Ducornet, Angela Carter, Edward Whittemore, and Alasdair Gray all denied being part of the Romantic Underground movement. At this point, noted critic John Clute, in a footnote to a review of Iain M. Banks' Culture novel *Consider Phlebas* (*Interzone*, 1987), wrote, "The sole criteria of the so-called Romantic Underground movement? The conscription of idiosyncratic writers dragged without their consent to the renunciation block, where they proceed to deny entrapment in anything as clandestine and formless."

In this respect, the Romantic Underground seems to mirror the Slipstream list put forth by Texas technophile Bruce Sterling.[3] Sterling published his list in a magazine called *SF Eye* (July 1989). For several years, publishers, some writers, and fewer readers mouthed the word "slipstream" whenever confronted by any text that did not fit a tidy definition of "genre fiction." It seems clear today that Sterling, depending on his mood, meant his term

---

[2]However, Moorcock added almost a decade later, "I refer you to Capek's subtle RUR (Romantic Underground Revival) in which he introduced the word 'robot' to the world. Also the 'Apocalypse' movement of the 30s and 40s. The Welsh 'Coven of 12' which included Henry Treece, Ruthven Todd, Dylan Thomas, and was connected to the so-called Wenlock Coven of which Alan Garner was probably the most prominent member. All have equally denied the existence of the RU while exhibiting many familiar characteristics of membership. 'RU RU if so Y?' as the familiar text message reads."

[3]Sterling was also part of a cheerfully dysfunctional literary movement called "cyberpunk" that falls outside of the scope of this essay. All that survives of this movement today is the pairing of advanced technology and dark sunglasses with badly woven sweaters, as exemplified by the Matrix movies.

"slipstream" more as a joke or the approximation of a joke, given the Catholic qualities of the list. In many respects, Sterling may thus be considered an agent of chaos—or, perhaps, a Romantic Underground mole ordered by the RU elites to create misdirection and mischief, all with the purpose of directing attention away from the RU. Sterling's repeated denial of this accusation only makes his actions all the more suspicious.

Still, the ultimate effect of Sterling's coined term—competition from a movement just as ill-defined, composed of writers who refused to call their work "Slipstream" in the same way earlier generations refuted "Romantic Underground"—appears to have irritated the invisible elites of the RU's command and control. For many years, throughout the 1990s, in fact, no further word was heard from the Romantic Underground.

For example, the Splatterpunk movement raised not a single hackle in the form of an implied reference to the Romantic Underground or even a non-consecutive footnote number in a *New York Review of SF* article (which might have suggested the suppression of a reference to the Romantic Underground). It is possible, of course, that the blood-and-alcohol-soaked Splatterpunks—with a "no limits" slogan that apparently meant "no limits to the badly written material we'll champion"—were not seen as a threat by the "shadow cabinet" (as I have come to think of the Romantic Movement's hidden elites).

However, in this new century, hints of the Romantic Movement have again come into the light—a glimmer of an old coin at the bottom of a fountain pool; the suggestion of a shadow watching from a vine-entangled forest. More specifically, the Interstitial Movement, which has taken up the task of defining the indefinable, appears to have some of the characteristics of the Romantic Underground movement. Could the Interstitial Movement be a new and subversive way of leveraging the Romantic Underground into the public eye while leaving its shadow cabinet once again unknown?

At first glance, it would appear that this could be the case. Certainly the Interstitial Movement, much like the Romantic Underground movement in the 1890s, believes in forming an "umbrella" for a motley assortment of idiosyncratic writers, most of whom have nothing in common, some of whom are not in fact interstitial at all, and many of whom do not identify themselves as interstitial, even though "pegged" as such by the Interstitial Arts Foundation.[4] This would be a typical Romantic Underground tactic. Similarly, the Interstitial strategy of continuing to insist that "we are not a movement" would appear to mirror the Romantic Underground's propensity for general denial.

However, a closer examination of the Interstitial reveals too many

---

[4]Certainly, the IAF's inclusion of a contingent of mythopoetic writers raises questions. Can a group with its own National Public Radio outlet, pop culture guru (Joseph Campbell), and a convention sponsored by Krispy Kreme Donuts really be considered to "cross borders" in an edgy way?

clashes with the presumed agenda of the Romantic Underground. First of all, no Romantic Underground movement writer—or Surrealist movement writer, for that matter—would tolerate for one moment the presence of so many writers of an easily definable nature; writers whose work is identifiable as belonging to one genre and, while often excellent, does not in fact "cross boundaries" (the clarion call of the Interstitial). Nor do the Interstitial writers graze far from the pastures of genre itself, whereas the Romantic Underground has always included members of the literary mainstream who could smugly and steadfastly deny their involvement in the movement.

Finally, it would take any Romantic Underground writer every bit of self-control he or she possessed to say, definitively, "I am an Interstitial writer," since the very essence/core of a Romantic Underground writer cries out for disassociation with any formal group of any kind. And yet, most "Interstitial" writers blithely bleat out their allegiance at the slightest provocation, or wear bright buttons proclaiming this fact. (Most damning, however, may be a certain lack of cohesion within the Interstitial Arts Foundation, completely at odds with the almost sinister, yet beautiful, organization and knack for secrecy the Romantic Underground movement has demonstrated for over one hundred years.)

Another movement put forward in recent years comes from the United Kingdom—the New Weird, espoused by China Miéville and, to some extent, M. John Harrison. An oddity in the brave new world of computers and the Internet, the New Weird is unaffected by modern communication and modern "online communities," for, as has been repeatedly stated, this movement is a uniquely *British* phenomenon.[5] It cannot be found elsewhere; it's something in the soil, akin to the inability in Florida to grow any but grapes for the sweetest of wines.

The New Weird also preaches a return to the pre-postmodern world. This is an earnest world in which irony does not exist, a world in which John Barth and his ilk took up carpentry rather than writing, Barth's hugely idiosyncratic novels consigned to the trashcan of *might have been*. In this world—ironically enough—the *Argentine* writer Jorge Luis Borges has often been heralded as the godfather, since his work predates the formal postmodern experimentation that was based in part on his stories.

Although the irony inherent in a movement that abhors irony indicates the presence of individual RU cells, the New Weird does not represent the new clandestine rise of the Romantic Underground. For one thing, the Romantic Underground would never insist on its members hailing from one particular country or group of countries. This would be too limiting to an international organization that relies on literally thousands of writer-members

[5]Except when it's not.

from over one hundred nations to maintain the strict secrecy that allows it to continue to deny that it has ever existed.

Further, no Romantic Underground writer would ever deny him- or herself the right to employ postmodern technique where appropriate. Would an artist be taken seriously if he or she said that a particular type of brush, a particular color of paint, a particular thickness of canvas would never again be used in the service of art? As a very secret self-denying organization, the Romantic Underground does not have the luxury of denying itself every tool at its disposal.

Therefore, I reluctantly tip my hat to the cleverness of the Romantic Underground movement. It appears once again to have relegated itself to single-author cells, none of which are in communication with any other, similar cells. Although writers such as Angela Carter, Edward Whittemore, and Vladimir Nabokov, as well as such contemporary authors as Edward Carey, Peter Carey, A.S. Byatt, Thomas Pynchon, Martin Amis, Ursula K. LeGuin, Jack Dann, M. John Harrison (a double-agent), Kelly Link (another double-agent, working for both the Interstitial and RU), Paul Di Filippo, Zoran Zivkovic, Gene Wolfe, Jeffrey Ford, K.J. Bishop, Michael Cisco, Stepan Chapman, Rhys Hughes, Liz Williams, Ian R. MacLeod, and myself have at one time or another been associated with the Romantic Underground movement—depending on the tone or theme or style of a particular book—none of us has ever admitted belonging to such a movement (either while living or after death). The Romantic Underground, it would appear, retains its crafty self-denying ability even one hundred years after its non-formation and the non-creation of its non-rules. In short, dear reader, the Romantic Underground, like many so-called movements, *does not exist*.[6]

---

[6]That said, it is worth noting the recent discovery of a new journal by Angela Carter. This journal may finally cut through the fog of denials to the core of the Romantic Underground movement. In the journal, Carter scrawled a list of points that seem uncannily like the recipe for the perfect literary movement. Could this be the manifesto of the Romantic Underground-nistas? It reads as follows:

1   It should focus on individual works.
2   It should include no works that do not fit its manifesto or mission statement.
3   It should appeal to both the heart and the head, inciting passion and thought in equal measure.
4   It should be blind to gender, race, and nationality.
5   It should separate commerce from art and only operate at the level of art.
6   It should encourage creativity and experimentation.
7   It should partake equally of high and low culture.
8   It should partake equally of high and low literature.
9   It should do no harm to any writer.
10 It should be both humble and arrogant, as appropriate.
11 It should deny its own existence at all times.
12 It should exist in the soul and spirit, heart and brain, of one individual writer at a time.
13 It should express the bittersweet confluence of seriousness and humor, honesty and deception, that we all experience in life.

CAROL EMSHWILLER

Carol Emshwiller is the author of the novels *Carmen Dog*, *Leaping Man Hill*, *Ledoyt*, and *The Mount*. Her short story collections include *Joy In Our Cause*, *The Start of the End of It All*, and *Report to the Men's Club and Other Stories*. She has won the World Fantasy Award, the James Tiptree, Jr. Award, the Philip K. Dick Award, the Nebula Award, and the SF Chronicle Award. Ursula K. Le Guin has called her "a wild mixture of Italo Calvino (intellectual games) and Grace Paley (perfect honesty) and Fay Weldon (outrageous wit) and Jorge Luis Borges (pure luminosity), but no—her voice is perfectly her own. She isn't like anybody."

Carol Emshwiller writes:

"Born in Ann Arbor Michigan. My dad was a professor of linguistics there. I grew up in France and Ann Arbor. I was a dreadful student, just squeaking through with Cs and a few Ds. I can just barely spell CAT. And I'm such a slow reader. I often wonder why I'm in this job . . . in the teaching of writing and needing to read all the time. But even though I was a bad student, I always did love to read.

"I was a housewife with three children in the main, big middle part of my life. I struggled for every little moment of writing time I could get. It's hard living with another artist. Especially one whose art brings in the money and whose experience of painting is so different from writing. My husband wondered why I couldn't write with kids hanging all over me. He could do his illustrations with kids sitting on stools behind him watching or cavorting in his studio.

"My young adult novel, *Mr. Boots*, will come out from Penguin/Firebird next year. Also they'll reissue *The Mount* as a young adult novel. Tachyon Publications will put out my fifth book of short stories, *I Live with You and You Don't Know It*, sometime next year. We don't have a title for it yet. Small Beer Press is reissuing *Carmen Dog*."

Emshwiller on writing:

"I've seldom liked a story that was just itself, even a (so called) good story. I don't know what resonance is, exactly, but I feel it when I read it and I get goose bumps when I find it and I get goose bumps when I write it.

"Usually that's my reason for writing. That's what turns me

on about a story idea—that it means more than it says. As I start writing, I can tell by the first paragraph whether I should go on with it. If I get that trembly feeling I know I'm hitting something more than just the story idea."

GRANDMA

CAROL EMSHWILLER

Grandma used to be a woman of action. She wore tights. She had big boobs, but a teeny weeny bra. Her waist used to be twenty-four inches. Before she got so hunched over she could do way more than a hundred of everything, pushups, sit-ups, chinning . . . . She had naturally curly hair. Now it's dry and fine and she's a little bit bald. She wears a babushka all the time and never takes her teeth out when I'm around or lets me see where she keeps them, though of course I know. She won't say how old she is. She says the books about her are all wrong, but, she says, that's her own fault. For a long while she lied about her age and other things, too.

She used to be on every search and rescue team all across these mountains. I think she might still be able to rescue people. Small ones. Her set of weights is in the basement. She has a punching bag. She used to kick it, too, but I don't know if she still can do that. I hear her thumping and grunting around down there—even now when she needs a cane for walking. And talk about getting up off the couch!

I go down to that gym myself sometimes and try to lift those weights. I punch at her punching bag. (I can't reach it except by standing on a box. When I try to kick it, I always fall over.)

Back in the olden days Grandma wasn't as shy as she is now. How could she be and do all she did? But now she doesn't want to be a bother. She says she never wanted to be a bother, just help out is all.

She doesn't expect any of us to follow in her footsteps. She used to, but not anymore. We're a big disappointment. She doesn't say so, but we have to be. By now she's given up on all of us. Everybody has.

It started . . . *we* started with the idea of selective breeding. Everybody wanted more like Grandma: strong, fast thinking, fast acting, and with the *desire* . . . that's the most important thing . . . a desire for her kind of life, a life of several hours in the gym every single day. Grandma loved it. She says (and says and says), "I'd turn on some banjo music and make it all into a dance."

Back when Grandma was young, offspring weren't even thought of since who was there around good enough for her to marry? Besides, everybody thought she'd last forever. How could somebody like her get old? is what they thought.

She had three . . . "husbands" they called them (donors more like it), first a triathlon champion, then a prize fighter, then a ballet dancer.

There's this old wives tale of skipping generations, so, after nothing good happened with her children, Grandma (and everybody else) thought, surely it would be us grandchildren. But we're a motley crew. Nobody pays any attention to us anymore.

I'm the runt. I'm small for my age, my foot turns in, my teeth stick out, I have a lazy eye . . . . There's lots of work to be done on me. Grandma's paying for all of it though she knows I'll never amount to much of anything. I wear a dozen different kinds of braces, teeth, feet, a patch over my good eye. My grandfather, the ballet dancer!

Sometimes I wonder why Grandma does all this for me, a puny, limping, limp-haired girl? What I think is, I'm her *real* baby at last. They didn't let her have any time off to look after her own children—not ever until now when she's too old for rescuing people. She not only was on all the search and rescue teams, she was a dozen search and rescue teams all by herself, and often she had to rescue the search and rescue teams.

Not only that, she also rescued animals. She always said the planet would die without its creatures. You'd see her leaping over mountains with a deer under each arm. She moved bears from camp grounds to where they wouldn't cause trouble. You'd see her with handfuls of rattlesnakes gathered from golf courses and carports, flying them off to places where people would be safe from them and they'd be safe from people.

She even tried to rescue the climate, pulling and pushing at the clouds. Holding back floods. Reraveling the ozone. She carried huge sacks of water to the trees of one great dying forest. In the long run there was only failure. Even after all those rescues, always only failure. The bears came back. The rattlesnakes came back.

Grandma gets to thinking all her good deeds went wrong. Lots of times she had to let go and save . . . maybe five babies and drop three. I mean even Grandma only had two arms. She expected more of herself. I always say, "You did save lots of people. You kept that forest alive ten years longer than expected. And me. *I'm* saved." That always makes her laugh, and I *am* saved. She says, "I guess my one good eye can see well enough to look after you, you rapscallion."

She took me in after my parents died. (She couldn't save them. There are some things you just can't do anything about no matter who you are, like drunken drivers. Besides, you can't be everywhere.)

When she took me to care for, she was already feeble. We needed each other. She'd never be able to get along without me. I'm the saver of the saver.

How did we end up this way, way out here in the country with me her only helper? Did she scare everybody else off with her neediness? Or maybe people couldn't stand to see how far down she's come from what she used to be. And I suppose she has gotten difficult, but I'm used to her. I hardly notice. But she's so busy trying not to be a bother she's a bother. I have to read her mind. When she holds her arms around herself, I get her old red sweatshirt with her emblem on the front. When she says, "*Oh* dear," I get her a cup of green tea. When she's on the couch and struggles and leans forward on her cane, trembling, I pull her up. She likes quiet. She likes for me to sit by her, lean against her, and listen to the birds along with her. Or listen to her stories. We don't have a radio or TV set. They conked out a long time ago and no one thought to get us new ones, but we don't need them. We never wanted them in the first place.

Grandma sits me down beside her, the lettuce planted, the mulberries picked, sometimes a mulberry pie already made (I helped), and we just sit. "I had a grandma," she'll say, "though I know, to look at me, it doesn't seem like I could have. I'm older than most grandmas ever get to be, but we all had grandmas, even me. Picture that: Every single person in the world with a grandma." Then she giggles. She still has her girlish giggle. She says, "Mother didn't know what to make of me. I was opening her jars for her before I was three years old. Mother. . . . Even *that* was a long time ago."

When she's in a sad mood she says everything went wrong. People she had just rescued died a week later of something that Grandma couldn't have helped. Hantavirus or some such that they got from vacuuming a closed room, though sometimes Grandma had just warned them not to do that. (Grandma believes in prevention as much as in rescuing.)

I've rescued things. Lots of them. Nothing went wrong either. I rescued a junco with a broken wing. After rains I've rescued stranded worms from the wet driveway and put them back in our vegetable garden. I didn't let Grandma cut the suckers off our fruit trees. I rescued mice from sticky traps. I fed a litter of feral kittens and got fleas and worms from them. Maybe this rescuing is the one part of Grandma I inherited.

Who's to say which is more worthwhile, pushing atom bombs far out into space or one of these little things? Well, I do know which is more important, but if I were the junco I'd like being rescued.

Sometimes Grandma goes out, though rarely. She gets to feeling it's a necessity. She wears sunglasses and a big floppy hat and scarves that hide her wrinkled-up face and neck. She still rides a bicycle. She's so wobbly it's scary to see her trying to balance herself down the road. I can't look. She likes to bring back ice-cream for me, maybe get me a comic book and a licorice stick to chew on as I read it. I suppose in town they just take her for a crazy lady, which I guess she is.

When visitors come to take a look at her I always say she isn't home, but where else would a very, very, very old lady be but mostly home? If she knew people had come she'd have hobbled out to see them and probably scared them half to death. But they probably wouldn't have believed it was her, anyway. Only the president of the Town and Country Bank—she rescued him a long time ago—I let him in. He'll sit with her for a while. He's old but of course not as old as she is. And he likes her for herself. They talked all through his rescue and really got to know each other back then. They talked about tomato plants and wildflowers and birds. When she rescued him they were flying up with the wild geese. (They still talk about all those geese they flew with and how exciting that was with all the honking and the sound of wings flapping right beside them. I get goose bumps—geese bumps?—just hearing them talk about it.) She should have married somebody like him, potbelly, pock-marked face and all. Maybe we'd have turned out better.

I guess you could say I'm the one that killed her—*caused* her death, anyway. I don't know what got into me. Lots of times I don't know what gets into me and lots of times I kind of run away for a couple of hours. Grandma knows about it. She doesn't mind. Sometimes she even tells me, "Go on. Get out of here for a while." But this time I put on her old tights and one of the teeny tiny bras. I don't have breasts yet so I stuffed the cups with Kleenex. I knew I couldn't do any of the things Grandma did, I just thought it would be fun to pretend for a little while.

I started out toward the hill. It's a long walk but you get to go through a batch of piñons. But first you have to go up an arroyo. Grandma's cape dragged over the rocks and sand behind me. It was heavy, too. To look at the satiny red outside you'd think it would be light, but it has a felt lining. "Warm and waterproof," Grandma said. I could hardly walk. How did she ever manage to fly around in it?

I didn't get very far before I found a jackrabbit lying in the middle of the arroyo half dead (but half alive, too), all bit and torn. I'll bet I'm the one that scared off whatever it was that did that. That rabbit was a goner if I didn't rescue it. I was a little afraid because wounded rabbits bite. Grandma's cape was just the right thing to wrap it in so it wouldn't.

Those jackrabbits weigh a lot. And with the added weight of the cape. . . .

Well, all I did was sprain my ankle. I mean I wasn't really hurt. I always have the knife Grandma gave me. I cut some strips off the cape and bound myself up good and tight. It isn't as if Grandma has a lot of capes. This is her only one. I felt bad about cutting it. I put the rabbit across my shoulders. It was slow going but I wasn't leaving the rabbit for whatever it was to finish eating it. It began to be twilight. Grandma knows I can't see well in twilight. The trouble is, though she used to see like an eagle, Grandma can't see very well anymore either.

She tried to fly, as she used to do. She *did* fly. For my sake. She skimmed along just barely above the sage and bitterbrush, her feet snagging at the taller ones. That was all the lift she could get. I could see, by the way she leaned and flopped like a dolphin, that she was trying to get higher. She was calling, "Sweetheart. Sweetheart. Where are yoooooowwww?" Her voice was almost as loud as it used to be. It echoed all across the mountains.

"Grandma, go back. I'll be all right." My voice can be loud, too.

She heard me. Her ears are still as sharp as a mule's.

The way she flew was kind of like she rides a bicycle. All wobbly. Veering off from side to side, up and down, too. I knew she would crack up. And she looked funny flying around in her print dress. She only has one costume and I was wearing it.

"Grandma, go back. Please go back."

She wasn't at all like she used to be. A little fall like that from just a few feet up would never have hurt her a couple of years ago. Or even last year. Even if, as she did, she landed on her head.

I covered her with sand and brush as best I could. No doubt whatever was about to eat the rabbit would come gnaw on her. She wouldn't mind. She always said she wanted to give herself back to the land. She used to quote, I don't know from where, "All to the soil, nothing to the grave." Getting eaten is sort of like going to the soil.

I don't dare tell people what happened—that it was all my fault—that I got myself in trouble sort of on purpose, trying to be like her, trying to rescue something.

But I'm not as sad as you might think. I knew she would die pretty soon anyway and this is a better way than in bed looking at the ceiling, maybe in pain. If that had happened, she wouldn't have complained. She'd not have said a word, trying not to be a bother. Nobody would have known about the pain except me. I would have had to grit my teeth against her pain the whole time.

I haven't told anybody partly because I'm waiting to figure things out. I'm here all by myself, but I'm good at looking after things. There are those who check on us every weekend—people who are paid to do it. I wave at them. "All okay." I mouth it. The president of the Town and Country Bank came out once. I told him Grandma wasn't feeling well. It wasn't *exactly* a lie. How long can this go on? He'll be the one who finds out first— if anybody does. Maybe they won't.

I'm nursing my jackrabbit. We're friends now. He's getting better fast. Pretty soon I'll let him go off to be a rabbit. But he might rather stay here with me.

I'm wearing Grandma's costume most of the time now. I sleep in it. It makes me feel safe. I'm doing my own little rescues as usual. (The vegetable garden is full of happy weeds. I keep the bird feeder going. I leave scraps out for the skunk.) Those count—almost as much as Grandma's rescues did. Anyway, I know the weeds think so.

The Grand Master Nebula Award is given to a living writer for a lifetime of achievement, and Robert Silverberg certainly deserves this honor, for he has had a profound effect on the genre, both as an author and as an editor.

One of SF's most honored writers, he has won five Hugo awards, five Nebula awards, the Jupiter award, the Prix Apollo, the Prix Utopia, and the Locus award. His work is complex, richly textured, and elegant; and, as Isaac Asimov said, "Where Silverberg goes today, Science Fiction will follow tomorrow."

His novels (of which there are almost three hundred!) include *Thorns*, *Hawksbill Station*, *The Masks of Time*, *Nightwings*, *The Man in the Maze*, *To Live Again*, *Tower of Glass*, *The World Inside*, *The Book of Skulls*, *Dying Inside*, *Shadrach in the Furnace*, *Lord Valentine's Castle*, *Majipoor Chronicles*, *Valentine Pontifex*, *Gilgamesh the King*, *Tom O'Bedlam*, *Hot Sky at Midnight*, *The Mountains of Majipoor*, *Sorcerors of Majipoor*, *Lord Prestimion*, *King of Dreams*, *The Longest Way Home*, and *Roma Eterna*. Among his many short story collections are *The Collected Stories of Robert Silverberg*, *The Best of Robert Silverberg*, *Sundance and Other Science Fiction Stories*, *Unfamiliar Territory*, *Edge of Light: The Robert Silverberg Omnibus*, *Sailing To Byzantium*, *In Another Country and Other Short Novels*, *Other Dimensions*, and the classic *Born With the Dead*.

He has also edited well over a hundred anthologies. His original anthologies include the seminal New Dimensions series, which spanned the period from 1971 to 1980, and, along with Damon Knight's Orbit series and Terry Carr's Universe series, defined the field. He also edited the high profile benchmark *Legends* anthologies. His reprint anthologies include the brilliant *The Mirror of Infinity*, the *Alpha* series, *Dark Stars*, *Great Science Fiction of the Twentieth Century*, *The New Atlantis*, *Science Fiction Hall of Fame, Volume 1*, and *The Arbor House Treasury of Modern Science Fiction*, to name a very few.

Silverberg's stylish, focused, and brilliant novels of the early 1970s had a profound effect on an entire generation of writers . . . my generation.

Harlan Ellison, another author whose work has had a

profound impact on the field, said it best: "From 1970 to 1974, a time of upheaval and metamorphosis in America, Silverberg's work reflected the angst and mortal dreads of the world around him. Massive changes over a decade had altered his view of his species, and of himself; and the work dealt more impressively than that of any other writer of the time with the great questions we had begun to ask ourselves. *Downward to the Earth, The World Inside, Tower of Glass, Son of Man, A Time of Changes, Dying Inside,* and *The Stochastic Man*— among a flood of others—became deeply troubling icons for a generation of readers learning not only to live decently in their own skins, but who were at last coming to realize they were part of a human chain, each link of which was commanded to ask for whom the bell tolls."

And Silverberg's later books have affected later generations . . .

This, from author Catherine Asaro, the president of the Science Fiction and Fantasy Writers of America:

"In graduate school, I found myself in need of a respite from the grind of writing my doctoral thesis. Wandering through the bookstore, I discovered shelf after shelf of books—all science fiction and fantasy. I was like a kid running free from school, both in revisiting old friends and in discovering new authors who had expanded the genre. A few works have particularly stayed in my mind in the quarter of a century since, books that made science fiction and fantasy come alive for me again.

"One of those books is *Lord Valentine's Castle* by Robert Silverberg. . . .

"When I hear the name Silverberg, though, I will always think first of how his work helped me recapture that radiant sense of wonder I had thought I lost in my youth. At the time I read *Lord Valentine's Castle*, I would have never dreamed that a few decades later, I would have the pleasure to name Robert Silverberg as the Damon Knight Memorial Grand Master Award for the Science Fiction and Fantasy Writers of America."

The Grand Master Nebula Award was presented to Robert Silverberg April 18, 2004, at the Westin Seattle in Seattle, Washington, where the 2004 Nebula Awards banquet was held.

In this volume Barry N. Malzberg discusses Robert Silver-berg and his work. Malzberg is the author of more than ninety books and three hundred short stories. His books include *The Falling Astronauts, Beyond Apollo, Underlay, Galaxies, Chorale, The Remaking of Sigmund Freud, Herovit's World, The Men In-side, Guernica Night, The Cross of Fire,* and the darkly brilliant critique of the genre, *The Engines of the Night*. He is a former editor of both *Amazing* and *Fantastic,* a multiple Nebula and Hugo nominee, and winner of the very first John W. Campbell Memorial Award for Best Novel.

In addition, it's my pleasure to present a bit of vintage Robert Silverberg: the sleek and disturbing "Sundance."

THE STOCHASTIC WRITER

BARRY N. MALZBERG

Here was the idea: write science fiction, yes, rigorous, well-plotted, logically extrapolative science fiction but bring to it the full range of modern literary technique. Write it as Nabokov or Phillip Roth, Malamud or John Cheever would have written science fiction, as if Fred Pohl had come to them at a Milford Conference and had whispered, "I'll guarantee acceptance at our highest word rate, just do the best you can." As if Betty Ballantine or Lawrence Ashmead had sent an open appeal to the faculty at Iowa and Stanford Creative Writing Workshops: "I don't care how you write or what you write as long as I don't have to argue with the Board about it being science fiction." This was sometime around 1960. "I just got bored with being a hack," Robert Silverberg told me a decade later, "I just wanted to try something different." So he tried something different. *Up The Line. Thorns.* "The Feast of St. Dionysius." *Born with the Dead.* "Good News from the Vatican." Oh boy, those were different.

Well, okay. Alfred Bester, another Grand Master (1987), was trying the same thing in the 1970s, so was Theodore Sturgeon in that decade (no Grand Master for Sturgeon, he died in 1985, a few years too soon), and the Kuttners, Catherine and Henry, were lighting it up in the 1940s all the way through John Campbell's *Astounding.* (No Grand Master for the Kuttners either, Henry was dead in 1958 before the SFWA was born and Catherine never published a line of science fiction after his death.) Sturgeon, Bester, the Kuttners: fierce and in the fire long before our New Wave. But Silverberg's work in its grace, deliberativeness and great aggregation was not so much their successor as proof of a proposal: You really could do this stuff to the highest level of literary intent and it would be *better* science fiction precisely because of that.

A revelation! Of course there were others who started at about the same time (whereas Silverberg had already had one career) who were doing this as well. Ballard, Aldiss, Gene Wolfe, Ursula K. LeGuin, and maybe the merciless Raphael Aloysius Lafferty. But no one this prolific. The man was not only at the front of a movement, he was through fecundity virtually a movement himself.

So then and not a year too soon (a few years too late in fact) a celebration. Like Wallace Shawn's Designated Mourner I perch as Designated Celebrant. This had better cajole humility, for our newest Grand Master is indeed his own celebration. He needs no sounding brass, tinkling cymbal, not from me anyway.

But let me, as Allan Tate said of an Emily Dickinson poem, consider the situation.

An essay about our Grand Master, not about me, of course. But let me nonetheless note that I wrote Silverberg's profile for the Special Issue (4/74) of *Fantasy & Science Fiction* dedicated to him and a year later the introduction to the Pocket Books collection *The Best of Robert Silverberg*. Nice rounding effect, surely. In the magazine essay I proclaimed the author's height to be five feet seven inches and his condition as the best living writer in English. Both judgments discombobulated their ever-poised subject and so in the Introduction to the collection I had another go, estimating his height at a fraction under six feet (he has subsequently informed me that he is actually five feet ten inches tall) and adding less grandiloquently that Silverberg could be termed *one* of the ten best living writers in the language, thus grouping him with the aforementioned Malamud, Roth, Nabokov, etc. This latter correction made him blush only a shade less brightly but I have nonetheless always regretted; my first judgment was closer to correct. Nabokov published *Transparent Things* that year and Malamud's *Dubin's Lives* lay ahead of him but neither was worth a Mass. *Born with the Dead* is worth a Mass. (Roth did become indisputably great but that took another twenty years.)

And another personal note: in 1984 our Grand Master introduced me in Brooklyn to his mother, Helen. She was—like my own mother, two years deceased then—a retired schoolteacher who over a period of at least twenty years had coincidentally lived less than a mile from my own dear Mom. I said to Helen in the most bemused fashion, "Your son has always been ahead of me and I don't mean just chronologically. He is in fact the Stations of my Cross. I am a science fiction writer from Brooklyn, he is *the* science fiction writer from Brooklyn. My first science fiction story was a 1,200-word squib in the August 1967 *Galaxy*, your son had the lead novella ("Hawksbill Station") in that issue. I through luck and circumstance sell a couple of novels to Random House, he sells Random House *Born with the Dead*. I sell a 1,000-word story to the gorgeous new *Omni* and two months later he sells them a novelette and then another and then another and then another. I publish a few okay science fiction novels, he publishes twenty masterpieces. I take my mother into a backdate magazine store on Nostrand

Avenue in 1980 and she says to the proprietor 'My son writes science fiction' and the proprietor says, 'The mother of another science fiction writer comes in here for his magazines all the time. She is so proud of him.' (My mother was not proud of me.) I might say that this was kind of humiliating except that he gives me honor by being my friend. He is not only ahead of me, he is ahead of us all."

Certainly true in 1984 and had already been so for almost twenty years. The accomplishment is so astonishing that the Grand Master conveyed is obiter dicta. Had he not gotten his right soon, right quick, the award would have been an embarrassment to any other recipient.

The acclaimed masterpieces—*Dying Inside, The Book of Skulls, Tower of Glass*—are indisputable of course but—ah, Fast Eddie Felsen, patron saint of the circumstantially challenged!—my deepest caritas is for the Silverberg novels at least as good which, because of his sheer prolificacy, never attracted the attention they deserved. *The Second Trip* (Bester's *Demolished Man* turned another way and ignited), *The Stochastic Man,* probably the best of all science fiction novels of politics, and the fierce and riotous *Up the Line*—the time travel novel about the man who pursued, won and bedded his remote ancestress—is as stylistically poised, rococo, savagely baroque as anything by Bester and also over-the-top humorous, a comic novel to stand with Voltaire's or those of Peter de Vries. Grand Masters get their due but not necessarily all of their works.

Silverberg himself has dated the true beginning of his more intense and literary work to 1962 with the short story "To See the Invisible Man," a riff out of Borges which was the first story written for Fred Pohl's magazines under an unusual contractual arrangement which gave Silverberg, story by story, utter creative freedom. (The arrangement: Pohl would buy the story submitted although he could then terminate the agreement. Silverberg found this to be utterly liberating, he could write to stylistic or subjectual limit, absolved of rejection.) "To See the Invisible Man," a narrative of social cruelty and alienation unusual for its elegance and restraint in the penumbra of a brutal theme, was more than commendable but its skill and force are in fact well foreshadowed in some of the earlier work. What Silverberg called his yard-goods period in the 1955–1960 period was yard goods only to him. "Birds of a Feather" (carnival time in the spaceways), "Warm Man" (more alienation), "The Iron Chancellor" (a house which could have been wired by Gallegher and locked by Kuttner), are considerable. Yard goods there were also, assigned space-filler for the Ziff-Davis magazines, but the early Ace Doubles show real craft and are better than most of the work surrounding them. (In an introduction written in 1978 for a reissue of those Ace Doubles Silverberg noted without inflection how many readers there were who felt that these were his best work, work before he had gone into the valleys of pretension, and he dedicated one of those reissues to such readers.)

Conventional wisdom, an oxymoron if one ever existed, gives us an "early" (pre-1967), transcendent "middle" (1967–1978) and somewhat lesser "late" (to the present) Silverberg but conventional wisdom is like payback. Conventional wisdom with its glass eye, cane, and small, blurry features stumbles through the servants' entrance and falls down the stairs. From that "late" period came the novellas "In Another Country," "The Secret Sharer," "Sailing to Byzantium," came "Hot Sky at Midnight," came "Blindsight," which was one of the brilliant dozen stories done for *Playboy,* and these are not only at the level of "middle" Silverberg but in some cases ("Another Country" in the 3/89 *Asimov* and published by Tor the most serious culprit) perhaps beyond. Unlike so many of us our Grand Master got larger as he went on.

An early (1974) collection of mine is dedicated to "Robert Silverberg, the best one." He's the best two and three as well. All the dozens, all the variegate colors, all of the fire. I wrote when he was writing, I published in some of the places he published contemporaneously. These are my greatest accomplishment by proxy.

SUNDANCE

ROBERT SILVERBERG

Today you liquidated about 50,000 Eaters in Sector A, and now you are spending an uneasy night. You and Herndon flew east at dawn, with the green-gold sunrise at your backs, and sprayed the neural pellets over a thousand hectares along the Forked River. You flew on into the prairie beyond the river, where the Eaters have already been wiped out, and had lunch sprawled on that thick, soft carpet of grass where the first settlement is expected to rise. Herndon picked some juiceflowers, and you enjoyed half an hour of mild hallucinations. Then, as you headed toward the copter to begin an afternoon of further pellet spraying, he said suddenly, "Tom, how would you feel about this if it turned out that the Eaters weren't just animal pests? That they were *people*, say, with a language and rites and a history and all?"

You thought of how it had been for your own people.

"They aren't," you said.

"Suppose they were. Suppose the Eaters—"

"They aren't. Drop it."

Herndon has this streak of cruelty in him that leads him to ask such questions. He goes for the vulnerabilities; it amuses him. All night now his casual remark has echoed in your mind. Suppose the Eaters . . . Suppose the Eaters . . . Suppose . . . Suppose . . .

You sleep for a while, and dream, and in your dreams you swim through rivers of blood.

Foolishness. A feverish fantasy. You know how important it is to exterminate the Eaters fast, before the settlers get here. They're just animals, and not even harmless animals at that; ecology-wreckers is what they are, devourers of oxygen-liberating plants, and they have to go. A few have been saved for zoological study. The rest must be destroyed. Ritual extirpation of undesirable beings, the old, old story. But let's not complicate our job with moral qualms, you tell yourself. Let's not dream of rivers of blood.

The Eaters don't even *have* blood, none that could flow in rivers, any-way. What they have is, well, a kind of lymph that permeates every tissue and transmits nourishment along the interfaces. Waste products go out the same way, osmotically. In terms of process, it's structurally analogous to your own kind of circulatory system, except there's no network of blood vessels hooked to a master pump. The life-stuff just oozes through their bodies, as though they were amoebas or sponges or some other low-phylum form. Yet they're definitely high phylum in nervous system, digestive setup, limb-and-organ template, etc. Odd, you think. The thing about aliens is that they're alien, you tell yourself, not for the first time.

The beauty of their biology for you and your companions is that it lets you exterminate them so neatly.

You fly over the grazing grounds and drop the neural pellets. The Eaters find and ingest them. Within an hour the poison has reached all sectors of the body. Life ceases; a rapid breakdown of cellular matter follows, the Eater literally falling apart molecule by molecule the instant that nutrition is cut off; the lymph-like stuff works like acid; a universal lysis occurs; flesh and even the bones, which are cartilaginous, dissolve. In two hours, a puddle on the ground. In four, nothing at all left. Considering how many millions of Eaters you've scheduled for extermination here, it's sweet of the bodies to be self-disposing. Otherwise what a charnel house this would become!

Suppose the Eaters . . .

Damn Herndon. You almost feel like getting a memory-editing in the morning. Scrape his stupid speculations out of your head. If you dared. If you dared.

In the morning he does not dare. Memory-editing frightens him; he will try to shake free of his new-found guilt without it. The Eaters, he ex-plains to himself, are mindless herbivores, the unfortunate victims of human expansionism, but not really deserving of passionate defense. Their exter-mination is not tragic; it's just too bad. If Earthmen are to have this world, the Eaters must relinquish it. There's a difference, he tells himself, between the elimination of the Plains Indians from the American prairie in the nineteenth century and the destruction of the bison on that same prairie. One feels a little wistful about the slaughter of the thundering herds; one regrets the butchering of millions of the noble brown woolly beasts, yes. But one feels outrage, not mere wistful regret, at what was done to the Sioux. There's a difference. Reserve your passions for the proper cause.

He walks from his bubble at the edge of the camp toward the center of things. The flagstone path is moist and glistening. The morning fog has not yet lifted, and every tree is bowed, the long, notched leaves heavy with droplets of water. He pauses, crouching, to observe a spider analog spinning its asymmetrical web. As he watches, a small amphibian, delicately shaded turquoise, glides as inconspicuously as possible over the mossy ground. Not inconspicuously enough; he gently lifts the little creature and puts it on the back of his hand. The gills flutter in anguish, and the amphibian's sides quiver. Slowly, cunningly, its color changes until it matches the coppery tone of the hand. The camouflage is excellent. He lowers his hand and the amphibian scurries into a puddle. He walks on.

He is forty years old, shorter than most of the other members of the expedition, with wide shoulders, a heavy chest, dark glossy hair, a blunt, spreading nose. He is a biologist. This is his third career, for he has failed as an anthropologist and as a developer of real estate. His name is Tom Two Ribbons. He has been married twice but has had no children. His great-grandfather died of alcoholism; his grandfather was addicted to hallucinogens; his father had compulsively visited cheap memory-editing parlors. Tom Two Ribbons is conscious that he is failing a family tradition, but he has not yet found his own mode of self-destruction.

In the main building he discovers Herndon, Julia, Ellen, Schwartz, Chang, Michaelson, and Nichols. They are eating breakfast; the others are already at work. Ellen rises and comes to him and kisses him. Her short soft yellow hair tickles his cheeks. "I love you," she whispers. She has spent the night in Michaelson's bubble. "I love you," he tells her, and draws a quick vertical line of affection between her small pale breasts. He winks at Michaelson, who nods, touches the tops of two fingers to his lips, and blows them a kiss. We are all good friends here, Tom Two Ribbons thinks.

"Who drops pellets today?" he asks.

"Mike and Chang," says Julia. "Sector C."

Schwartz says, "Eleven more days and we ought to have the whole peninsula clear. Then we can move inland."

"If our pellet supply holds up," Chang points out.

Herndon says, "Did you sleep well, Tom?"

"No," says Tom. He sits down and taps out his breakfast requisition. In the west, the fog is beginning to burn off the mountains. Something throbs in the back of his neck. He has been on this world nine weeks now, and in time it has undergone its only change of season, shading from dry weather to foggy. The mists will remain for many months. Before the plains parch again, the Eaters will be gone and the settlers will begin to arrive. His food slides down the chute and he seizes it. Ellen sits beside him. She is a little more than half his age; this is her first voyage; she is their keeper of records, but she is also skilled at editing. "You look troubled," Ellen tells him. "Can I help you?"

"No. Thank you."

"I hate it when you get gloomy."

"It's a racial trait," says Tom Two Ribbons.

"I doubt that very much."

"The truth is that maybe my personality reconstruct is wearing thin. The trauma level was so close to the surface. I'm just a walking veneer, you know."

Ellen laughs prettily. She wears only a sprayon halfwrap. Her skin looks damp; she and Michaelson have had a swim at dawn. Tom Two Ribbons is thinking of asking her to marry him, when this job is over. He has not been married since the collapse of the real estate business. The therapist suggested divorce as part of the reconstruct. He sometimes wonders where Terry has gone and whom she lives with now. Ellen says, "You seem pretty stable to me, Tom."

"Thank you," he says. She is young. She does not know.

"If it's just a passing gloom I can edit it out in one quick snip."

"Thank you," he says. "No."

"I forgot. You don't like editing."

"My father—"

"Yes?"

"In fifty years he pared himself down to a thread," Tom Two Ribbons says. "He had his ancestors edited away, his whole heritage, his religion, his wife, his sons, finally his name. Then he sat and smiled all day. Thank you, no editing."

"Where are you working today?" Ellen asks.

"In the compound, running tests."

"Want company? I'm off all morning."

"Thank you, no," he says, too quickly. She looks hurt. He tries to remedy his unintended cruelty by touching her arm lightly and saying, "Maybe this afternoon, all right? I need to commune a while. Yes?"

"Yes," she says, and smiles, and shapes a kiss with her lips.

After breakfast he goes to the compound. It covers a thousand hectares east of the base; they have bordered it with neural-field projectors at intervals of eighty meters, and this is a sufficient fence to keep the captive population of two hundred Eaters from straying. When all the others have been exterminated, this study group will remain. At the southwest corner of the compound stands a lab bubble from which the experiments are run: metabolic, psychological, physiological, ecological. A stream crosses the compound diagonally. There is a low ridge of grassy hills at its eastern edge. Five distinct copses of tightly clustered knifeblade trees are separated by patches of dense savanna. Sheltered beneath the grass are the oxygen-plants, almost completely hidden except for the photosynthetic spikes that jut to heights of three or four meters at regular intervals, and for the lemon-colored respiratory bodies, chest high, that make the grassland sweet and dizzying with exhaled gases. Through the fields move the Eaters in a straggling herd, nibbling delicately at the respiratory bodies.

Tom Two Ribbons spies the herd beside the stream and goes toward it. He stumbles over an oxygen-plant hidden in the grass but deftly recovers his balance and, seizing the puckered orifice of the respiratory body, inhales deeply. His despair lifts. He approaches the Eaters. They are spherical, bulky, slow-moving creatures, covered by masses of coarse orange fur. Saucer-like eyes protrude above narrow rubbery lips. Their legs are thin and scaly, like a chicken's, and their arms are short and held close to their bodies. They regard him with bland lack of curiosity. "Good morning, brothers!" is the way he greets them this time, and he wonders why.

I noticed something strange today. Perhaps I simply sniffed too much oxygen in the fields; maybe I was succumbing to a suggestion Herndon planted; or possibly it's the family masochism cropping out. But while I was observing the Eaters in the compound, it seemed to me, for the first time, that they are behaving intelligently, that they were functioning in a ritualized way.

I followed them around for three hours. During that time they uncovered half a dozen outcroppings of oxygen-plants. In each case they went through a stylized pattern of action before starting to munch. They:

Formed a straggly circle around the plants.

Looked toward the sun.

Looked toward their neighbors on left and right around the circle.

Made fuzzy neighing sounds *only* after having done the foregoing.

Looked toward the sun again.

Moved in and ate.

If this wasn't a prayer of thanksgiving, a saying of grace, then what was it? And if they're advanced enough spiritually to say grace, are we not therefore committing genocide here? Do chimpanzees say grace? Christ, we wouldn't even wipe out chimps the way we're cleaning out the Eaters! Of course, chimps don't interfere with human crops, and some kind of co-existence would be possible, whereas Eaters and human agriculturalists simply can't function on the same planet. Nevertheless, there's a moral issue here. The liquidation effort is predicated on the assumption that the intelligence level of the Eaters is about on a par with that of oysters, or, at best sheep. Our consciences stay clear because our poison is quick and painless and because the Eaters thoughtfully dissolve upon dying, sparing us the mess of incinerating millions of corpses. But if they pray—

I won't say anything to the others just yet. I want more evidence, hard, objective. Films, tapes, record cubes. Then we'll see. What if I can show that we're exterminating intelligent beings? My family knows a little about genocide, after all, having been on the receiving end just a few centuries back. I doubt that I could halt what's going on here. But at the very least I could withdraw from the operation. Head back to Earth and stir up public outcries.

I hope I'm imagining this.

I'm not imagining a thing. They gather in circles; they look to the sun; they neigh and pray. They're only balls of jelly on chicken-legs, but they give thanks for their food. Those big round eyes now seem to stare accusingly at me. Our tame herd there knows what's going on: that we have descended from the stars to eradicate their kind, and that they alone will be spared. They have no way of fighting back or even of communicating their displeasure, but they know. And hate us. Jesus, we have killed two million of them since we got here, and in a metaphorical way I'm stained with blood, and what will I do, what can I do?

I must move very carefully, or I'll end up drugged and edited.

I can't let myself seem like a crank, a quack, an agitator. I can't stand up and *denounce!* I have to find allies. Herndon, first. He surely is on to the truth; he's the one who nudged me to it, that day we dropped pellets. And I thought he was merely being vicious in his usual way!

I'll talk to him tonight.

He says, "I've been thinking about that suggestion you made. About the Eaters. Perhaps we haven't made sufficiently close psychological studies. I mean, if they really are intelligent—"

Herndon blinks. He is a tall man with glossy dark hair, a heavy beard, sharp cheekbones. "Who says they are, Tom?"

"You did. On the far side of the Forked River, you said—"

"It was just a speculative hypothesis. To make conversation."

"No, I think it was more than that. You really believed it."

Herndon looks troubled. "Tom, I don't know what you're trying to start, but don't start it. If I for a moment believed we were killing intelligent creatures, I'd run for an editor so fast I'd start an implosion wave."

"Why did you ask me that thing, then?" Tom Two Ribbons says.

"Idle chatter."

"Amusing yourself by kindling guilts in somebody else? You're a bastard, Herndon. I mean it."

"Well, look, Tom, if I had any idea that you'd get so worked up about a hypothetical suggestion—" Herndon shakes his head. "The Eaters aren't intelligent beings. Obviously. Otherwise we wouldn't be under orders to liquidate them."

"Obviously," says Tom Two Ribbons.

Ellen said, "No, I don't know what Tom's up to. But I'm pretty sure he needs a rest. It's only a year and a half since his personality reconstruct, and he had a pretty bad breakdown back then."

Michaelson consulted a chart. "He's refused three times in a row to make his pellet-dropping run. Claiming he can't take time away from his research. Hell, we can fill in for him, but it's the idea that he's ducking chores that bothers me."

"What kind of research is he doing?" Nichols wanted to know.

"Not biological," said Julia. "He's with the Eaters in the compound all the time, but I don't see him making any tests on them. He just watches them."

"And talks to them," Chang observed.

"And talks, yes," Julia said.

"About what?" Nichols asked.

"Who knows?"

Everyone looked at Ellen. "You're closest to him," Michaelson said. "Can't you bring him out of it?"

"I've got to know what he's in, first," Ellen said. "He isn't saying a thing."

You know that you must be very careful, for they outnumber you, and their concern for your mental welfare can be deadly. Already they realize you are disturbed, and Ellen has begun to probe for the source of the disturbance. Last night you lay in her arms and she questioned you, obliquely, skillfully, and you knew what she is trying to find out. When the moons appeared she suggested that you and she stroll in the compound, among the sleeping Eaters. You declined, but she sees that you have become involved with the creatures.

You have done probing of your own—subtly, you hope. And you are aware that you can do nothing to save the Eaters. An irrevocable commitment has been made. It is 1876 all over again; these are the bison, they are the Sioux, and they must be destroyed, for the railroad is on its way. If you speak out here, your friends will calm you and pacify you and edit you, for they do not see what you see. If you return to Earth to agitate, you will be mocked and recommended for another reconstruct. You can do nothing. You can do nothing.

You cannot save, but perhaps you can record.

Go out into the prairie. Live with the Eaters; make yourself their friend; learn their ways. Set it down, a full account of their culture, so that at least that much will not be lost. You know the techniques of field anthropology. As was done for your people in the old days, do now for the Eaters.

He finds Michaelson. "Can you spare me for a few weeks?" he asks.

"Spare you, Tom? What do you mean?"

"I've got some field studies to do. I'd like to leave the base and work with Eaters in the wild."

"What's wrong with the ones in the compound?"

"It's the last chance with wild ones, Mike. I've got to go."

"Alone, or with Ellen?"

"Alone."

Michaelson nods slowly. "All right, Tom. Whatever you want. Go. I won't hold you here."

I dance in the prairie under the green-gold sun. About me the Eaters gather. I am stripped; sweat makes my skin glisten; my heart pounds. I talk to them with my feet, and they understand.

They understand.

They have a language of soft sounds. They have a god. They know love and awe and rapture. They have rites. They have names. They have a history. Of all this I am convinced.

I dance on thick grass.

How can I reach them? With my feet, with my hands, with my grunts, with my sweat. They gather by the hundreds, by the thousands, and I dance. I must not stop. They cluster about me and make their sounds. I am a conduit for strange forces. My great-grandfather should see me now! Sitting on his porch in Wyoming, the firewater in his hand, his brain rotting—see me now, old one! See the dance of Tom Two Ribbons! I talk to these strange ones with my feet under a sun that is the wrong color. I dance. I dance.

"Listen to me," I say. "I am your friend, I alone, the only one you can trust. Trust me, talk to me, teach me. Let me preserve your ways, for soon the destruction will come."

I dance, and the sun climbs, and the Eaters murmur.

There is the chief. I dance toward him, back, toward, I bow, I point to the sun, I imagine the being that lives in that ball of flame, I imitate the sounds of these people, I kneel, I rise, I dance. Tom Two Ribbons dances for you.

I summon skills my ancestors forgot. I feel the power flowing in me. As they danced in the days of the bison, I dance now, beyond the Forked River.

I dance, and now the Eaters dance too. Slowly, uncertainly, they move toward me, they shift their weight, lift leg and leg, sway about. "Yes, like that!" I cry. "Dance!"

We dance together as the sun reaches noon height.

Now their eyes are no longer accusing. I see warmth and kinship. I am their brother, their redskinned tribesman, he who dances with them. No longer do they seem clumsy to me. There is a strange ponderous grace in their movements. They dance. They dance. They caper about me. Closer, closer, closer!

We move in holy frenzy.

They sing, now, a blurred hymn of joy. They throw forth their arms, unclench their little claws. In unison they shift weight, left foot forward, right, left, right. Dance, brothers, dance, dance, dance! They press against me. Their flesh quivers; their smell is a sweet one. They gently thrust me across the field, to a part of the meadow where the grass is deep and un-trampled. Still dancing, we seek for the oxygen-plants, and find clumps of them beneath the grass, and they make their prayer and seize them with their awkward arms, separating the respiratory bodies from the photosynthetic spikes. The plants, in anguish, release floods of oxygen. My mind reels. I laugh and sing. The Eaters are nibbling the lemon-colored perforated globes, nibbling the stalks as well. They thrust their plants at me. It is a reli-gious ceremony, I see. Take from us, eat with us, join with us, this is the body, this is the blood, take, eat, join. I bend forward and put a lemon-colored globe to my lips. I do not bite; I nibble, as they do, my teeth slicing away the skin of the globe. Juice spurts into my mouth, while oxygen drenches my nostrils. The Eaters sing hosannas. I should be in full paint for this, paint of my forefathers, feathers too, meeting their religion in the re-galia of what should have been mine. Take, eat, join. The juice of the oxygen-plant flows in my veins. I embrace my brother. I sing, and as my voice leaves my lips it becomes an arch that glistens like new steel, and I pitch my song lower, and the arch turns to tarnished silver. The Eaters crowd close. The scent of their bodies is fiery red to me. Their soft cries are puffs of steam. The sun is very warm; its rays are tiny jagged pings of puck-ered sound, close to the top of my range of hearing, plink! plink! plink! The thick grass hums to me, deep and rich, and the wind hurls points of flame along the prairie. I devour another oxygen-plant, and then a third. My brothers laugh and shout. They tell me of their gods, the god of warmth, the god of food, the god of pleasure, the god of death, the god of holiness, the god of wrongness, and the others. They recite for me the names of their kings, and I bear their voices as splashes of green mold on the clean sheet of the sky. They instruct me in their holy rites. I must remember this, I tell myself, for when it is gone it will never come again. I continue to dance. They continue to dance. The color of the hills becomes rough and coarse, like abrasive gas. Take, eat, join. Dance. They are so gentle!

I hear the drone of the copter, suddenly.

It hovers far overhead. I am unable to see who flies in it. "No," I scream. "Not here! Not these people! Listen to me! This is Tom Two Ribbons! Can't you hear me? I'm doing a field study here! You have no right—!"

My voice makes spirals of blue moss edged with red sparks. They drift upward and are scattered by the breeze.

I yell, I shout, I bellow. I dance and shake my fists. From the wings of the copter the jointed arms of the pellet-distributors unfold. The gleaming spigots extend and whirl. The neural pellets rain down into the meadow, each tracing a blazing track that lingers in the sky. The sound of the copter becomes a furry carpet stretching to the horizon, and my shrill voice is lost in it.

The Eaters drift away from me, seeking the pellets, scratching at the roots of the grass to find them. Still dancing, I leap into their midst, striking the pellets from their hands, hurling them into the stream, crushing them to powder. The Eaters growl black needles at me. They turn away and search for more pellets. The copter turns and flies off, leaving a trail of dense oily sound. My brothers are gobbling the pellets eagerly.

There is no way to prevent it.

Joy consumes them and they topple and lie still. Occasionally a limb twitches; then even this stops. They begin to dissolve. Thousands of them melt on the prairie, sinking into shapelessness, losing their spherical forms, flattening, ebbing into the ground. The bonds of the molecules will no longer hold. It is the twilight of protoplasm. They perish. They vanish. For hours I walk the prairie. Now I inhale oxygen; now I eat a lemon-colored globe. Sunset begins with the ringing of leaden chimes. Black clouds make brazen trumpet calls in the east and the deepening wind is a swirl of coaly bristles. Silence comes. Night falls. I dance. I am alone.

The copter comes again, and they find you, and you do not resist as they gather you in. You are beyond bitterness. Quietly you explain what you have done and what you have learned, and why it is wrong to exterminate these people. You describe the plant you have eaten and the way it affects your senses, and as you talk of the blessed synesthesia, the texture of the wind and the sound of the clouds and the timbre of the sunlight, they nod and smile and tell you not to worry, that everything will be all right soon, and they touch something cold to your forearm, so cold that it is a whir and a buzz and the deintoxicant sinks into your vein and soon the ecstasy drains away, leaving only the exhaustion and the grief.

He says, "We never learn a thing, do we? We export all our horrors to the stars. Wipe out the Armenians, wipe out the Jews, wipe out the Tasmanians, wipe out the Indians, wipe out everyone who's in the way, and then come out here and do the same damned murderous thing. You weren't with me out there. You didn't dance with them. You didn't see what a rich, complex culture the Eaters have. Let me tell you about their tribal structure. It's dense: seven levels of matrimonial relationships, to begin with, and an exogamy factor that requires—"

Softly Ellen says, "Tom, darling, nobody's going to harm the Eaters."

"And the religion," he goes on. "Nine gods, each one an aspect of *the* god. Holiness and wrongness both worshipped. They have hymns, prayers, a theology. And we, the emissaries of the god of wrongness—"

"We're not exterminating them," Michaelson says. "Won't you understand that, Tom? This is all a fantasy of yours. You've been under the influence of drugs, but now we're clearing you out. You'll be clean in a little while. You'll have perspective again."

"A fantasy?" he says bitterly. "A drug dream? I stood out in the prairie and saw you drop pellets. And I watched them die and melt away. I didn't dream that."

"How can we convince you?" Chang asks earnestly. "What will make you believe? Shall we fly over the Eater country with you and show how many millions there are?"

"But how many millions have been destroyed?" he demands.

They insist that he is wrong. Ellen tells him again that no one has ever desired to harm the Eaters. "This is a scientific expedition, Tom. We're here to *study* them. It's a violation of all we stand for to injure intelligent life-forms."

"You admit that they're intelligent?"

"Of course. That's never been in doubt."

"Then why drop the pellets?" he asks. "Why slaughter them?"

"None of that has happened, Tom," Ellen says. She takes his hand between her cool palms. "Believe us. Believe us."

He says bitterly, "If you want me to believe you, why don't you do the job properly? Get out the editing machine and go to work on me. You can't simply *talk* me into rejecting the evidence of my own eyes."

"You were under drugs all the time," Michaelson says.

"I've never taken drugs! Except for what I ate in the meadow, when I danced—and that came after I had watched the massacre going on for weeks and weeks. Are you saying that it's a retroactive delusion?"

"No, Tom," Schwartz says. "You've had this delusion all along. It's part of your therapy, your reconstruct. You came here programmed with it."

"Impossible," he says.

Ellen kisses his fevered forehead. "It was done to reconcile you to mankind, you see. You had this terrible resentment of the displacement of your people in the nineteenth century. You were unable to forgive the industrial society for scattering the Sioux, and you were terribly full of hate. Your therapist thought that if you could be made to participate in an imaginary modern extermination, if you could come to see it as a necessary operation, you'd be purged of your resentment and able to take your place in society as—"

He thrusts her away. "Don't talk idiocy! If you knew the first thing about reconstruct therapy, you'd realize that no reputable therapist could be so shallow. There are no one-to-one correlations in reconstructs. No, don't touch me. Keep away. Keep away."

He will not let them persuade him that this is merely a drug-born dream. It is no fantasy, he tells himself, and it is no therapy. He rises. He goes out. They do not follow him. He takes a copter and seeks his brothers.

Again I dance. The sun is much hotter today. The Eaters are more numerous. Today I wear paint, today I wear feathers. My body shines with my sweat. They dance with me, and they have a frenzy in them that I have never seen before. We pound the trampled meadow with our feet. We clutch for the sun with our hands. We sing, we shout, we cry. We will dance until we fall.

This is no fantasy. These people are real, and they are intelligent, and they are doomed. This I know.

We dance. Despite the doom, we dance.

My great-grandfather comes and dances with us. He too is real. His nose is like a hawk's, not blunt like mine, and he wears the big headdress, and his muscles are like cords under his brown skin. He sings, he shouts, he cries.

Others of my family join us.

We eat the oxygen-plants together. We embrace the Eaters. We know, all of us, what it is to be hunted.

The clouds make music and the wind takes on texture and the sun's warmth has color.

We dance. We dance. Our limbs know no weariness.

The sun grows and fills the whole sky, and I see no Eaters now, only my own people, my father's fathers across the centuries, thousands of gleaming skins, thousands of hawk's noses, and we eat the plants, and we find sharp sticks and thrust them into our flesh, and the sweet blood flows and dries in the blaze of the sun, and we dance, and we dance, and some of us fall from weariness, and we dance, and the prairie is a sea of bobbing head-dresses, an ocean of feathers, and we dance, and my heart makes thunder, and my knees become water, and the sun's fire engulfs me, and I dance, and I fall, and I dance, and I fall, and I fall, and I fall.

Again they find you and bring you back. They give you the cool snout on your arm to take the oxygen-plant drug from your veins, and then they give you something else so you will rest. You rest and you are very calm. Ellen kisses you and you stroke her soft skin, and then the others come in and they talk to you, saying soothing things, but you do not listen, for you are searching for realities. It is not an easy search. It is like falling through many trapdoors, looking for the one room whose floor is not hinged. Everything that has happened on this planet is your therapy, you tell yourself, designed to reconcile an embittered aborigine to the white man's conquest; nothing is really being exterminated here. You reject that and fall through and realize that this must be the therapy of your friends; they carry the weight of accumulated centuries of guilts and have come here to shed that load, and you are here to ease them of their burden, to draw their sins into yourself and give them forgiveness. Again you fall through, and see that the Eaters are mere animals who threaten the ecology and must be removed; the culture you imagined for them is your hallucination, kindled out of old churnings. You try to withdraw your objections to this necessary extermination, but you fall through again and discover that there is no extermination except in your mind, which is troubled and disordered by your obsession with the crime against your ancestors, and you sit up, for you wish to apologize to these friends of yours, these innocent scientists whom you have called murderers. And you fall through.

Molly Gloss is a fourth-generation Oregonian who lives in Portland, Oregon. She is the author of *Outside the Gates,* a fantasy novel for young adults, and more than two dozen short stories, essays, and book reviews, which have appeared in numerous magazines and anthologies. Her novel *The Jump-Off Creek* was a finalist for the PEN/Faulkner Award for American Fiction, and a winner of both the Pacific Northwest Booksellers Award and the Oregon Book Award. In 1996 she was a recipient of a Whiting Writers Award. *The Dazzle of Day* was named a New York Times Notable Book and was awarded the PEN Center West Fiction Prize. *Kirkus Reviews* called her fourth novel, *Wild Life,* "a masterpiece." It won the James Tiptree Jr. Award and was chosen as the 2002 selection for "If All Seattle Read the Same Book."

About her writing, she says:

"When I first began writing, I was writing western short stories. Then I looked around and realized I had nowhere to send them. I wrote them because I grew up reading western fiction and western literature of all kinds, but there were no short fiction markets for westerns. By that time, Louis L'Amour owned the book market, as far as I could tell. There were no Western movies, no Western TV series—it was just a dead field.

"But I'd begun to read science fiction, and I realized that I could probably write science fiction that would allow me to explore some of the same questions. You can put people on unpopulated landscapes and give them pioneer-like situations—it just maybe wouldn't be on this planet. That worked like a charm. I wrote a number of science fiction short stories, all of which got published pretty rapidly. All of them had rural farm or ranch kinds of settings and questions I enjoyed exploring."

LAMBING SEASON

MOLLY GLOSS

From May to September, Delia took the Churro sheep and two dogs and went up on Joe-Johns Mountain to live. She had that country pretty much to herself all summer. Ken Owen sent one of his Mexican hands up every other week with a load of groceries, but otherwise she was alone, alone with the sheep and the dogs. She liked the solitude. Liked the silence. Some sheepherders she knew talked a blue streak to the dogs, the rocks, the porcupines, they sang songs and played the radio, read their magazines out loud, but Delia let the silence settle into her, and, by early summer, she had begun to hear the ticking of the dry grasses as a language she could almost translate. The dogs were named Jesus and Alice. "Away to me, Jesus," she said when they were moving the sheep. "Go bye, Alice." From May to September these words spoken in command of the dogs were almost the only times she heard her own voice; that, and when the Mexican brought the groceries, a polite exchange in Spanish about the weather, the health of the dogs, the fecundity of the ewes.

The Churros were a very old breed. The O-Bar Ranch had a federal allotment up on the mountain, which was all rimrock and sparse grasses well suited to the Churros, who were fiercely protective of their lambs and had a long-stapled top coat that could take the weather. They did well on the thin grass of the mountain where other sheep would lose flesh and give up their lambs to the coyotes. The Mexican was an old man. He said he remembered Churros from his childhood in the Oaxaca highlands, the rams with their four horns, two curving up, two down. "Buen' carne," he told Delia. Uncommonly fine meat.

The wind blew out of the southwest in the early part of the season, a wind that smelled of juniper and sage and pollen; in the later months, it blew straight from the east, a dry wind smelling of dust and smoke, bringing down showers of parched leaves and seedheads of yarrow and bittercress. Thunderstorms came frequently out of the east, enormous cloudscapes with hearts of livid magenta and glaucous green. At those times, if she was camped on a ridge, she'd get out of her bed and walk downhill to find a draw where she could feel safer, but if she were camped in a low place, she would stay with the sheep while a war passed over their heads, spectacular jagged flares of lightning, skull-rumbling cannonades of thunder. It was maybe bred into the bones of Churros, a knowledge and a tolerance of mountain weather, for they shifted together and waited out the thunder with surprising composure; they stood forbearingly while rain beat down in hard blinding bursts.

Sheepherding was simple work, although Delia knew some herders who made it hard, dogging the sheep every minute, keeping them in a tight group, moving all the time. She let the sheep herd themselves, do what they wanted, make their own decisions. If the band began to separate, she would whistle or yell, and often the strays would turn around and rejoin the main group. Only if they were badly scattered did she send out the dogs. Mostly she just kept an eye on the sheep, made sure they got good feed, that the band didn't split, that they stayed in the boundaries of the O-Bar allotment. She studied the sheep for the language of their bodies, and tried to handle them just as close to their nature as possible. When she put out salt for them, she scattered it on rocks and stumps as if she were hiding Easter eggs, because she saw how they enjoyed the search.

The spring grass made their manure wet, so she kept the wool cut away from the ewes' tail area with a pair of sharp, short-bladed shears. She dosed the sheep with wormer, trimmed their feet, inspected their teeth, treated ewes for mastitis. She combed the burrs from the dogs' coats and inspected them for ticks. *You're such good dogs,* she told them with her hands. *I'm very very proud of you.*

She had some old binoculars, 7 x 32s, and in the long quiet days, she watched bands of wild horses miles off in the distance, ragged looking mares with dorsal stripes and black legs. She read the back issues of the local newspapers, looking in the obits for names she recognized. She read spine-broken paperback novels and played solitaire and scoured the ground for arrowheads and rocks she would later sell to rockhounds. She studied the parched brown grass, which was full of grasshoppers and beetles and crickets and ants. But most of her day was spent just walking. The sheep sometimes bedded quite a ways from her trailer and she had to get out to them before sunrise when the coyotes would make their kills. She was usually up by three or four and walking out to the sheep in darkness. Sometimes she returned to the camp for lunch, but always she was out with the sheep again until sundown, when the coyotes were likely to return, and then she walked home after dark to water and feed the dogs, eat supper, climb into bed.

In her first years on Joe-Johns, she had often walked three or four miles away from the band just to see what was over a hill, or to study the intricate architecture of a sheepherder's monument. Stacking up flat stones in the form of an obelisk was a common herders' pastime, their monuments all over that sheep country, and though Delia had never felt an impulse to start one herself, she admired the ones other people had built. She sometimes walked miles out of her way just to look at a rockpile up close.

She had a mental map of the allotment, divided into ten pastures. Every few days, when the sheep had moved on to a new pasture, she moved her camp. She towed the trailer with an old Dodge pickup, over the rocks and creekbeds, the sloughs and dry meadows, to the new place. For a while afterward, after the engine was shut off and while the heavy old body of the truck was settling onto its tires, she would be deaf, her head filled with a dull roaring white noise.

She had about eight hundred ewes, as well as their lambs, many of them twins or triplets. The ferocity of the Churro ewes in defending their offspring was sometimes a problem for the dogs, but in the balance of things, she knew that it kept her losses small. Many coyotes lived on Joe-Johns, and sometimes a cougar or bear would come up from the salt pan desert on the north side of the mountain, looking for better country to own. These animals considered the sheep to be fair game, which Delia understood to be their right; and also her right, hers and the dogs', to take the side of the sheep. Sheep were smarter than people commonly believed and the Churros smarter than other sheep she had tended, but by mid-summer the coyotes always passed the word among themselves, buen' carne, and Delia and the dogs then had a job to work, keeping the sheep out of harm's way.

She carried a .32 caliber Colt pistol in an old-fashioned holster worn on her belt. *If you're a coyot' you'd better be careful of this woman,* she said with her body, with the way she stood and the way she walked when she was wearing the pistol. That gun and holster had once belonged to her mother's mother, a woman who had come West on her own and homesteaded for a while, down in the Sprague River Canyon. Delia's grandmother had liked to tell the story: how a concerned neighbor, a bachelor with an interest in marriageable females, had pressed the gun upon her, back when the Klamaths were at war with the army of General Joel Palmer; and how she never had used it for anything but shooting rabbits.

In July, a coyote killed a lamb while Delia was camped no more than two hundred feet away from the bedded sheep. It was dusk, and she was sitting on the steps of the trailer reading a two-gun western, leaning close over the pages in the failing light, and the dogs were dozing at her feet. She heard the small sound, a strange high faint squeal she did not recognize and then did recognize, and she jumped up and fumbled for the gun, yelling at the coyote, at the dogs, her yell startling the entire band to its feet but the ewes making their charge too late, Delia firing too late, and none of it doing any good beyond a release of fear and anger.

A lion might well have taken the lamb entire; she had known of lion kills where the only evidence was blood on the grass and a dribble of entrails in the beam of a flashlight. But a coyote is small and will kill with a bite to the throat and then perhaps eat just the liver and heart, though a mother coyote will take all she can carry in her stomach, bolt it down and carry it home to her pups. Delia's grandmother's pistol had scared this one off before it could even take a bite, and the lamb was twitching and whole on the grass, bleeding only from its neck. The mother ewe stood over it, crying in a distraught and pitiful way, but there was nothing to be done, and, in a few minutes, the lamb was dead.

There wasn't much point in chasing after the coyote, and anyway, the whole band was now a skittish jumble of anxiety and confusion; it was hours before the mother ewe gave up her grieving, before Delia and the dogs had the band calm and bedded down again, almost midnight. By then, the dead lamb had stiffened on the ground, and she dragged it over by the truck and skinned it and let the dogs have the meat, which went against her nature, but was about the only way to keep the coyote from coming back for the carcass.

While the dogs worked on the lamb, she stood with both hands pressed to her tired back, looking out at the sheep, the mottled pattern of their whiteness almost opalescent across the black landscape, and the stars thick and bright above the faint outline of the rock ridges, stood there a moment before turning toward the trailer, toward bed, and afterward, she would think how the coyote and the sorrowing ewe and the dark of the July moon and the kink in her back, how all of that came together and was the reason that she was standing there watching the sky, was the reason that she saw the brief, brilliantly green flash in the southwest and then the sulfur yellow streak breaking across the night, southwest to due west on a descending arc onto Lame Man Bench. It was a broad bright ribbon, rainbow-wide, a cyanotic contrail. It was not a meteor, she had seen hundreds of meteors. She stood and looked at it.

Things to do with the sky, with distance, you could lose perspective; it was hard to judge even a lightning strike, whether it had touched down on a particular hill or the next hill or the valley between. So she knew this thing falling out of the sky might have come down miles to the west of Lame Man, not onto Lame Man at all, which was two miles away, at least two miles, and getting there would be all ridges and rocks, no way to cover the ground in the truck. She thought about it. She had moved camp earlier in the day, which was always troublesome work, and it had been a blistering hot day, and now the excitement with the coyote. She was very tired, the tiredness like a weight against her breastbone. She didn't know what this thing was, falling out of the sky. Maybe if she walked over there she would find just a dead satellite or a broken weather balloon and not dead or broken people. The contrail thinned slowly while she stood there looking at it, became a wide streak of yellowy cloud against the blackness, with the field of stars glimmering dimly behind it.

After a while, she went into the truck and got a water bottle and filled it, and also took the first aid kit out of the trailer and a couple of spare batteries for the flashlight and a handful of extra cartridges for the pistol, and stuffed these things into a backpack and looped her arms into the straps and started up the rise away from the dark camp, the bedded sheep. The dogs left off their gnawing of the dead lamb and trailed her anxiously, wanting to follow, or not wanting her to leave the sheep. "Stay by," she said to them sharply, and they went back and stood with the band and watched her go. *That coyot', he's done with us tonight:* This is what she told the dogs with her body, walking away, and she believed it was probably true.

Now that she'd decided to go, she walked fast. This was her sixth year on the mountain, and, by this time, she knew the country pretty well. She didn't use the flashlight. Without it, she became accustomed to the starlit darkness, able to see the stones and pick out a path. The air was cool, but full of the smell of heat rising off the rocks and the parched earth. She heard nothing but her own breathing and the gritting of her boots on the pebbly dirt. A little owl circled once in silence and then went off toward a line of cottonwood trees standing in black silhouette to the northeast.

Lame Man Bench was a great upthrust block of basalt grown over with scraggly juniper forest. As she climbed among the trees, the smell of something like ozone or sulfur grew very strong, and the air became thick, burdened with dust. Threads of the yellow contrail hung in the limbs of the trees. She went on across the top of the bench and onto slabs of shelving rock that gave a view to the west. Down in the steep-sided draw below her there was a big wing-shaped piece of metal resting on the ground, which she at first thought had been torn from an airplane, but then realized was a whole thing, not broken, and she quit looking for the rest of the wreckage. She squatted down and looked at it. Yellow dust settled slowly out of the sky, pollinating her hair, her shoulders, the toes of her boots, faintly dulling the oily black shine of the wing, the thing shaped like a wing.

While she was squatting there looking down at it, something came out from the sloped underside of it, a coyote she thought at first, and then it wasn't a coyote but a dog built like a greyhound or a whippet, deep-chested, long legged, very light-boned and frail-looking. She waited for somebody else, a man, to crawl out after his dog, but nobody did. The dog squatted to pee and then moved off a short distance and sat on its haunches and considered things. Delia considered, too. She considered that the dog might have been sent up alone. The Russians had sent up a dog in their little sputnik, she remembered. She considered that a skinny almost hairless dog with frail bones would be dead in short order if left alone in this country. And she considered that there might be a man inside the wing, dead or too hurt to climb out. She thought how much trouble it would be, getting down this steep rock bluff in the darkness to rescue a useless dog and a dead man.

After a while, she stood and started picking her way into the draw. The dog by this time was smelling the ground, making a slow and careful circuit around the black wing. Delia kept expecting the dog to look up and bark, but it went on with its intent inspection of the ground as if it was stone deaf, as if Delia's boots making a racket on the loose gravel was not an announcement that someone was coming down. She thought of the old Dodge truck, how it always left her ears ringing, and wondered if maybe it was the same with this dog and its wing-shaped sputnik, although the wing had fallen soundless across the sky.

When she had come about half way down the hill, she lost footing and slid down six or eight feet before she got her heels dug in and found a handful of willow scrub to hang onto. A glimpse of this movement—rocks sliding to the bottom, or the dust she raised—must have startled the dog, for it leaped backward suddenly and then reared up. They looked at each other in silence, Delia and the dog, Delia standing leaning into the steep slope a dozen yards above the bottom of the draw, and the dog standing next to the sputnik, standing all the way up on its hind legs like a bear or a man and no longer seeming to be a dog but a person with a long narrow muzzle and a narrow chest, turned-out knees, delicate dog-like feet. Its genitals were more cat-like than dog, a male set but very small and neat and contained. Dog's eyes, though, dark and small and shining below an anxious brow, so that she was reminded of Jesus and Alice, the way they had looked at her when she had left them alone with the sheep. She had years of acquaintance with dogs and she knew enough to look away, break off her stare. Also, after a moment, she remembered the old pistol and holster at her belt. In cowboy pictures, a man would unbuckle his gunbelt and let it down on the ground as a gesture of peaceful intent, but it seemed to her this might only bring attention to the gun, to the true intent of a gun, which is always killing. *This woman is nobody at all to be scared of,* she told the dog with her body, standing very still along the steep hillside, holding onto the scrub willow with her hands, looking vaguely to the left of him, where the smooth curve of the wing rose up and gathered a veneer of yellow dust.

The dog, the dog person, opened his jaws and yawned the way a dog will do to relieve nervousness, and then they were both silent and still for a minute. When finally he turned and stepped toward the wing, it was an unexpected, delicate movement, exactly the way a ballet dancer steps along on his toes, knees turned out, lifting his long thin legs; and then he dropped down on all-fours and seemed to become almost a dog again. He went back to his business of smelling the ground intently, though every little while he looked up to see if Delia was still standing along the rock slope. It was a steep place to stand. When her knees finally gave out, she sat down very carefully where she was, which didn't spook him. He had become used to her by then, and his brief, sliding glance just said, *That woman up there is nobody at all to be scared of.*

What he was after, or wanting to know, was a mystery to her. She kept expecting him to gather up rocks, like all those men who'd gone to the moon, but he only smelled the ground, making a wide slow circuit around the wing the way Alice always circled round the trailer every morning, nose down, reading the dirt like a book. And when he seemed satisfied with what he'd learned, he stood up again and looked back at Delia, a last look delivered across his shoulder before he dropped down and disappeared under the edge of the wing, a grave and inquiring look, the kind of look a dog or a man will give you before going off on his own business, a look that says, *You be okay if I go?* If he had been a dog, and if Delia had been close enough to do it, she'd have scratched the smooth head, felt the hard bone beneath, moved her hands around the soft ears. *Sure, okay, you go on now, Mr. Dog:* This is what she would have said with her hands. Then he crawled into the darkness under the slope of the wing, where she figured there must be a door, a hatch letting into the body of the machine, and after a while he flew off into the dark of the July moon.

In the weeks afterward, on nights when the moon had set or hadn't yet risen, she looked for the flash and streak of something breaking across the darkness out of the southwest. She saw him come and go to that draw on the west side of Lame Man Bench twice more in the first month. Both times, she left her grandmother's gun in the trailer and walked over there and sat in the dark on the rock slab above the draw and watched him for a couple of hours. He may have been waiting for her, or he knew her smell, because both times he reared up and looked at her just about as soon as she sat down. But then he went on with his business. *That woman is nobody to be scared of,* he said with his body, with the way he went on smelling the ground, widening his circle and widening it, sometimes taking a clod or a sprig into his mouth and tasting it, the way a mild-mannered dog will do when he's investigating something and not paying any attention to the person he's with.

Delia had about decided that the draw behind Lame Man Bench was one of his regular stops, like the ten campsites she used over and over again when she was herding on Joe-Johns Mountain; but after those three times in the first month, she didn't see him again.

At the end of September, she brought the sheep down to the O-Bar. After the lambs had been shipped out she took her band of dry ewes over onto the Nelson prairie for the fall, and in mid-November, when the snow had settled in, she brought them to the feed lots. That was all the work the ranch had for her until lambing season. Jesus and Alice belonged to the O-Bar. They stood in the yard and watched her go.

In town, she rented the same room as the year before, and, as before, spent most of a year's wages on getting drunk and standing other herders to rounds of drink. She gave up looking into the sky.

In March, she went back out to the ranch. In bitter weather, they built jugs and mothering-up pens, and trucked the pregnant ewes from Green, where they'd been feeding on wheat stubble. Some ewes lambed in the trailer on the way in, and after every haul, there was a surge of lambs born. Delia had the night shift, where she was paired with Roy Joyce, a fellow who raised sugar beets over in the valley and came out for the lambing season every year. In the black, freezing cold middle of the night, eight and ten ewes would be lambing at a time. Triplets, twins, big singles, a few quads, ewes with lambs born dead, ewes too sick or confused to mother. She and Roy would skin a dead lamb and feed the carcass to the ranch dogs and wrap the fleece around a bummer lamb, which was intended to fool the bereaved ewe into taking the orphan as her own, and sometimes it worked that way. All the mothering-up pens swiftly filled, and the jugs filled, and still some ewes with new lambs stood out in the cold field waiting for a room to open up.

You couldn't pull the stuck lambs with gloves on, you had to reach into the womb with your fingers to turn the lamb, or tie cord around the feet, or grasp the feet barehanded, so Delia's hands were always cold and wet, then cracked and bleeding. The ranch had brought in some old converted school buses to house the lambing crew, and she would fall into a bunk at daybreak and then not be able to sleep, shivering in the unheated bus with the gray daylight pouring in the windows and the endless daytime clamor out at the lambing sheds. All the lambers had sore throats, colds, nagging coughs. Roy Joyce looked like hell, deep bags as blue as bruises under his eyes, and Delia figured she looked about the same, though she hadn't seen a mirror, not even to draw a brush through her hair, since the start of the season.

By the end of the second week, only a handful of ewes hadn't lambed. The nights became quieter. The weather cleared, and the thin skiff of snow melted off the grass. On the dark of the moon, Delia was standing outside the mothering-up pens drinking coffee from a thermos. She put her head back and held the warmth of the coffee in her mouth a moment, and, as she was swallowing it down, lowering her chin, she caught the tail end of a green flash and a thin yellow line breaking across the sky, so far off anybody else would have thought it was a meteor, but it was bright, and dropping from southwest to due west, maybe right onto Lame Man Bench. She stood and looked at it. She was so very goddamned tired and had a sore throat that wouldn't clear, and she could barely get her fingers to fold around the thermos, they were so split and tender.

She told Roy she felt sick as a horse, and did he think he could handle things if she drove herself into town to the Urgent Care clinic, and she took one of the ranch trucks and drove up the road a short way and then turned onto the rutted track that went up to Joe-Johns.

The night was utterly clear and you could see things a long way off. She was still an hour's drive from the Churros' summer range when she began to see a yellow-orange glimmer behind the black ridgeline, a faint nimbus like the ones that marked distant range fires on summer nights.

She had to leave the truck at the bottom of the bench and climb up the last mile or so on foot, had to get a flashlight out of the glove box and try to find an uphill path with it because the fluttery reddish lightshow was finished by then, and a thick pall of smoke overcast the sky and blotted out the stars. Her eyes itched and burned, and tears ran from them, but the smoke calmed her sore throat. She went up slowly, breathing through her mouth.

The wing had burned a skid path through the scraggly junipers along the top of the bench and had come apart into about a hundred pieces. She wandered through the burnt trees and the scattered wreckage, shining her flashlight into the smoky darkness, not expecting to find what she was looking for, but there he was, lying apart from the scattered pieces of metal, out on the smooth slab rock at the edge of the draw. He was panting shallowly and his close coat of short brown hair was matted with blood. He lay in such a way that she immediately knew his back was broken. When he saw Delia coming up, his brow furrowed with worry. A sick or a wounded dog will bite, she knew that, but she squatted next to him. *It's just me,* she told him, by shining the light not in his face but in hers. Then she spoke to him. "Okay," she said. "I'm here now," without thinking too much about what the words meant, or whether they meant anything at all, and she didn't remember until afterward that he was very likely deaf anyway. He sighed and shifted his look from her to the middle distance, where she supposed he was focused on approaching death.

Near at hand, he didn't resemble a dog all that much, only in the long shape of his head, the folded-over ears, the round darkness of his eyes. He lay on the ground flat on his side like a dog that's been run over and is dying by the side of the road, but a man will lie like that too when he's dying. He had small-fingered nail-less hands where a dog would have had toes and front feet. Delia offered him a sip from her water bottle, but he didn't seem to want it, so she just sat with him quietly, holding one of his hands, which was smooth as lambskin against the cracked and roughened flesh of her palm. The batteries in the flashlight gave out, and sitting there in the cold darkness she found his head and stroked it, moving her sore fingers lightly over the bone of his skull, and around the soft ears, the loose jowls. Maybe it wasn't any particular comfort to him, but she was comforted by doing it. *Sure, okay, you can go on.*

She heard him sigh, and then sigh again, and each time wondered if it would turn out to be his death. She had used to wonder what a coyote, or especially a dog, would make of this doggish man, and now while she was listening, waiting to hear if he would breathe again, she began to wish she'd brought Alice or Jesus with her, though not out of that old curiosity. When her husband had died six years before, at the very moment he took his last breath, the dog she'd had then had barked wildly and raced back and forth from the front to the rear door of the house as if he'd heard or seen something invisible to her. People said it was her husband's soul going out the door or his angel coming in. She didn't know what it was the dog had seen or heard or smelled, but she wished she knew. And now she wished she had a dog with her to bear witness.

She went on petting him even after he had died, after she was sure he was dead, went on petting him until his body was cool, and then she got up stiffly from the bloody ground and gathered rocks and piled them onto him, a couple of feet high, so that he wouldn't be found or dug up. She didn't know what to do about the wreckage, so she didn't do anything with it at all.

In May, when she brought the Churro sheep back to Joe-Johns Mountain, the pieces of the wrecked wing had already eroded, were small and smooth-edged like the bits of sea glass you find on a beach, and she figured that this must be what it was meant to do: to break apart into pieces too small for anybody to notice, and then to quickly wear away. But the stones she'd piled over his body seemed like the start of something, so she began the slow work of raising them higher into a sheepherder's monument. She gathered up all the smooth eroded bits of wing, too, and laid them in a series of widening circles around the base of the monument. She went on piling up stones through the summer and into September, until it reached fifteen feet. Mornings, standing with the sheep miles away, she would look for it through the binoculars and think about ways to raise it higher, and she would wonder what was buried under all the other monuments sheepherders had raised in that country. At night, she studied the sky, but nobody came for him.

In November, when she finished with the sheep and went into town, she asked around and found a guy who knew about star-gazing and telescopes. He loaned her some books and sent her to a certain pawnshop, and she gave most of a year's wages for a 14 x 75 telescope with a reflective lens. On clear, moonless nights, she met the astronomy guy out at the Little League baseball field, and she sat on a fold-up canvas stool with her eye against the telescope's finder while he told her what she was seeing: Jupiter's moons, the Pelican Nebula, the Andromeda Galaxy. The telescope had a tripod mount, and he showed her how to make a little jerry-built device so she could mount her old 7 x 32 binoculars on the tripod too. She used the binoculars for their wider view of star clusters and small constellations. She was indifferent to most discomforts, could sit quietly in one position for hours at a time, teeth rattling with the cold, staring into the immense vault of the sky until she became numb and stiff, barely able to stand and walk back home. Astronomy, she discovered, was a work of patience, but the sheep had taught her patience, or it was already in her nature before she ever took up with them.

Cory Doctorow is the author of *Someone Comes to Town, Someone Leaves Town* (forthcoming from Tor Books), *Eastern Standard Tribe,* and *Down and Out in the Magic Kingdom,* as well as the short story collection *A Place So Foreign.* His short fiction has appeared in magazines and online publications such as *Asimov's, Realms of Fantasy, Interzone, Science Fiction Age,* and *scifi.com.* His nonfiction has appeared in many publications including *The Globe and Mail, Wired, Mindjack,* and *O'Reilly Network.* He wrote a regular column for *Science Fiction Age,* reviewing internet sites, and is the author (with Karl Shroeder) of *The Complete Idiot's Guide to Writing Science Fiction.* He is a recipient of the John W. Campbell Award. He lives in London, where he works for the Electronic Frontier Foundation (eff.org), a civil liberties group, and he is the co-editor of *boingboing.net* and a contributing writer to *Wired Magazine.* He cofounded OpenCola, an open source P2P software company.

Cory Doctorow writes:

"There are certain recurring themes in my work; garbage and Disney appear in almost everything I write. I'm obsessed with both. Throughout my life, I've been exposed to people who are doing novel things with trash: my buddy Darren, who clears CDN$100K/yr pulling discarded computer parts out of Dumpsters; my neighbor Roger Wood, who makes breathtaking assemblage sculptures out of crap he finds at yard sales and flea-markets; my friend Murray, a handyman who makes everything from wheelbarrows to sheds out of scraps . . . The list goes on and on. I live in a humongous warehouse, and it's full to the brim with crap from yard sales and thrifts.

"Disney's a little harder to explain. My grandparents are snowbirds, spending their winters in Fort Lauderdale, Florida, and I grew up spending Christmas breaks with them. Those trips always included a pilgrimage to Walt Disney World (because what the hell else are you going to do when your grand-kids come to stay with you at your seniors-only retirement condo?). The Disney organization fascinates me: internally, the theme parks operate like socialist utopias, while externally, Disney is known as a rights-grabbing litigious bully."

OwnzOreD

CORY DOCTOROW

Ten years in the Valley, and all Murray Swain had to show for it was a spare tire, a bald patch, and a life that was friendless and empty and maggoty-rotten. His only ever California friend, Liam, had dwindled from a tubbaguts programmer-shaped potato to a living skeleton on his death-bed the year before, herpes blooms run riot over his skin and bones in the absence of any immunoresponse. The memorial service featured a framed photo of Liam at his graduation; his body was donated for medical science.

Liam's death really screwed things up for Murray. He'd gone into one of those clinical depression spirals that eventually afflicted all the aging bright young coders he'd known during his life in tech. He'd get misty in the morning over his second cup of coffee and by the midafternoon blood-sugar crash, he'd be weeping silently in his cubicle, clattering nonsensically at the keys to disguise the disgusting snuffling noises he made. His waste-basket overflowed with spent tissues and a rumor circulated among the evening cleaning-staff that he was a compulsive masturbator. The impossibility of the rumor was immediately apparent to all the other coders on his floor who, pr0n-hounds that they were, had explored the limits and extent of the censoring proxy that sat at the headwaters of the office network. Nevertheless, it was gleefully repeated in the collegial fratmosphere of his workplace and wags kept dumping their collections of conference-snarfed hotel-sized bottles of hand-lotion on his desk.

The number of bugs per line in Murray's code was 500 percent that of the overall company average. The QA people sometimes just sent his code back to him (From: qamanager@globalsemi.com To: mswain@globalsemi .com Subject: Your code . . . Body: . . . sucks) rather than trying to get it to build and run. Three weeks after Liam died, Murray's team leader pulled his commit privileges on the CVS repository, which meant that he had to grovel with one of the other coders when he wanted to add his work to the project.

Two months after Liam died, Murray was put on probation.

Three months after Liam died, Murray was given two weeks' leave and an e-mail from HR with contact info for an in-plan shrink who could counsel him. The shrink recommended Cognitive Therapy, which he explained in detail, though all Murray remembered ten minutes after the session was that he'd have to do it every week for years, and the name reminded him of Cognitive Dissonance, which was the name of Liam's favorite stupid Orange County garage band.

Murray returned to Global Semiconductor's Mountain View headquarters after three more sessions with the shrink. He badged in at the front door, at the elevator, and on his floor, sat at his desk and badged in again on his PC. From: tvanya@globalsemi.com To: mswain@globalsemi.com Subject: Welcome back! Come see me . . . Body: . . . when you get in.

Tomas Vanya was Murray's team lead, and rated a glass office with a door. The blinds were closed, which meant: dead Murray walking. Murray closed the door behind him and sighed a huge heave of nauseated relief. He'd washed out of Silicon Valley and he could go home to Vancouver and live in his parents' basement and go salmon fishing on weekends with his high-school drinking buds. He didn't exactly love Global Semi, but shit, they were number three in a hot, competitive sector where Moore's Law drove the cost of microprocessors relentlessly downwards as their speed rocketed relentlessly skyward. They had four billion in the bank, a healthy share price, and his options were above water, unlike the poor fucks at Motorola, number four and falling. He'd washed out of the nearly-best, what the fuck, beat spending his prime years in Hongcouver writing government-standard code for the Ministry of Unbelievable Dullness.

Even the number-two chair in Tomas Vanya's office kicked major ergonomic azz. Murray settled into it and popped some of the controls experimentally until the ess of his spine was cushioned and pinioned into chiropractically correct form. Tomas unbagged a Fourbucks Morning Harvest muffin and a venti coconut Frappucino and slid them across his multi-tiered Swedish Disposable Moderne desque.

"A little welcome-back present, Murray," Tomas said. Murray listened for the sound of a minimum-wage security guard clearing out his desk during this exit-interview-cum-breakfast-banquet. He wondered if Global Semi would forward-vest his options and mentally calculated the strike price minus the current price times the number of shares times the conversion rate to Canadian Pesos and thought he could maybe put down 25 percent on a two bedroom in New Westminster.

"Dee-licious and noo-tritious," Murray said and slurped at the frappe.

"So," Tomas said. "So."

Here it comes, Murray thought, and sucked up a brain-freezing mouthful of frou-frou West Coast caffeine delivery system. G0nz0red. Fi0red. Sh17canned. Thinking in leet-hacker crap made it all seem more distant.

"It's really great to see you again," Tomas said. "You're a really important part of the team here, you know?"

Murray restrained himself from rolling his eyes. He was fired, so why draw it out? There'd been enough lay-offs at Global Semi, enough boom and bust and bust and bust that it was a routine, they all knew how it went.

But though Murray was on an Air Canada jet headed for Vangroover, Tomas wasn't even on the damned script. "You're sharp and seasoned. You can communicate effectively. Most techies can't write worth a damn, but you're good. It's rare."

Ah, the soothing sensation of smoke between one's buttocks. It was true that Murray liked to write, but there wasn't any money in it, no glory either. If you were going to be a writer in the tech world, you'd have to be—

"You've had a couple weeks off to reassess things, and we've been reassessing, too. Coding, hell, most people don't do it for very long. Especially assembler, Jesus, if you're still writing assembler after five years, there's something, you know, *wrong*. You end up in management or you move horizontally. Or you lose it." Tomas realized that he'd said the wrong thing and blushed.

Aw, shit.

"Horizontal movement. That's the great thing about a company this size. There's always somewhere you can go when you burn out on one task."

No, no, no.

"The Honorable Computing initiative is ready for documentation, Murray. We need a tech writer who can really *nail it*."

A tech writer. Why not just break his goddamned fingers and poke his eyes out? Never write another line of code, never make the machine buck and hum and make his will real in the abstract beauty of silicon? Tech writers were coders' janitors, documenting the plainly self-evident logic of APIs and code-structures, niggling over punctuation and grammar and frigging stylebooks, like any of it *mattered*—human beings could parse English, even if it wasn't well-formed, even if you had a comma-splice or a dangling participle.

"It's a twelve month secondment, a change of pace for you and a chance for us to evaluate your other strengths. You go to four weeks' vacation and we accelerate your vesting and start you with a new grant at the same strike price, over 24 months."

Murray did the math in his head, numbers dancing. Four weeks' vacation—that was three years ahead of schedule, not that anyone that senior ever used his vacation days, but you could bank them for retirement or, ahem, exit strategy. The forward vesting meant that he could walk out and fly back to Canada in three weeks if he hated it and put *30* percent down on a two-bedroom in New West.

And the door was closed and the blinds were drawn and the implication was clear. Take this job or shove it.

He took the job.

A month later he was balls-deep in the documentation project and feeling, you know, not horrible. The Honorable Computing initiative was your basic Bond-villain world-domination horseshit, of course, but it was technically sweet and it kept him from misting over and bawling. And they had cute girls on the documentation floor, liberal arts/electrical engineering double-majors with abs you could bounce a quarter off of who were doing time before being promoted up to join the first cohort of senior female coders to put their mark on the Valley.

He worked late most nights, only marking the passing of five PM by his instinctive upwards glance as all those fine, firm rear ends walked past his desk on their way out of the office. Then he went into night mode, working by the glow of his display and the emergency lights until the custodians came in and chased him out with their vacuum cleaners.

One night, he was struggling to understand the use-cases for Honorable Computing when the overhead lights flicked on, shrinking his pupils to painful pinpricks. The cleaners clattered in and began to pointedly empty the wastebins. He took the hint, grabbed his shoulderbag and staggered for the exit, badging out as he went.

His car was one of the last ones in the lot, a hybrid Toyota with a lot of dashboard geek-toys like a GPS and a back-seat DVD player, though no one ever rode in Murray's back seat. He'd bought it three months before Liam died, cashing in some shares and trading in the giant gas-guzzling SUV he'd never once taken off-road.

As he aimed his remote at it and initiated the cryptographic handshake—i.e., unlocked the doors—he spotted the guy leaning against the car. Murray's thumb jabbed at the locking button on the remote, but it was too late: the guy had the door open and he was sliding into the passenger seat.

In the process of hitting the remote's panic button, Murray managed to pop the trunk and start the engine, but eventually his thumb mashed the right button and the car's lights strobed and the horn blared. He backed slowly towards the office doors, just as the guy found the dome-light control and lit up the car's interior and Murray got a good look at him.

It was Liam.

Murray stabbed at the remote some more and killed the panic button. Jesus, who was going to respond at this hour in some abandoned industrial park in the middle of the Valley anyway? The limp-dick security guard? He squinted at the face in the car.

Liam. Still Liam. Not the skeletal Liam he'd last seen rotted and intu-
bated on a bed at San Jose General. Not the porcine Liam he'd laughed
with over a million late-night El Torito burritos. A fit, healthy, *young* Liam,
the Liam he'd met the day they both started at Global Semi at adjacent
desks, Liam fresh out of Cal Tech and fit from his weekly lot-hockey game
and his weekend dirtbike rides in the hills. Liam-prime, or maybe Liam's
younger brother or something.

Liam rolled down the window and struck a match on the passenger-
side door, then took a Marlboro Red from a pack in his shirt pocket and lit
it. Murray walked cautiously to the car, his thumb working on his cellphone, punching in the numbers 9-1-1 and hovering over "SEND." He got
close enough to see the scratch the match-head had left on the side-panel
and muttered *"fuck"* with feeling.

"Hey dirtbag, you kiss your mother with that mouth?" Liam said. It
was Liam.

"You kiss *your* mother after I'm through with her mouth?" Murray
said, the rote of old times. He gulped for air.

Liam popped the door and got out. He was ripped, bullish chest and
cartoonish wasp-waist, rock-hard abs through a silvery club-shirt and
bulging thighs. A body like that, it's a full-time job, or so Murray had con-
cluded after many failed get-fit initiatives involving gyms and retreats and
expensive home equipment and humiliating early-morning jogs through
the sidewalk-free streets of Shallow Alto.

"Who the fuck are you?" Murray said, looking into the familiar eyes,
the familiar smile-lines and the deep wrinkle between Liam's eyes from his
concentration face. Though the night was cool, Murray felt runnels of
sweat tracing his spine, trickling down between his buttocks.

"You know the answer, so why ask? The question isn't who, it's *how*.
Let's drive around a little and I'll tell you all about it."

Liam clapped a strong hand on his forearm and gave it a companion-
able squeeze. It felt good and real and human.

"You can't smoke in my car," Murray said.

"Don't worry," Liam said. "I won't exhale."

Murray shook his head and went around to the driver's side. By the
time he started the engine, Liam had his seatbelt on and was poking ran-
domly at the on-board controls. "This is pretty rad. You told me about it, I
remember, but it sounded stupid at the time. Really rad." He brought up
the MP3 player and scrolled through Murray's library, adding tracks to a
mix, cranking up the opening crash of an old, old, old punk Beastie Boys
song. "The speakers are for shit, though!" he hollered over the music.

Murray cranked the volume down as he bounced over the speed bumps,
badged out of the lot, and headed for the hills, stabbing at the GPS to bring
up some roadmaps that included the private roads way up in the highlands.

"So, do I get two other ghosts tonight, Marley, or are you the only one?"

Liam found the sunroof control and flicked his smoke out into the road. "Ghost, huh? I'm meat, dude, same as you. Not back from the dead, just back from the *mostly dead.*" He did the last like Billy Crystal as Miracle Max in "The Princess Bride," one of their faves. "I'll tell you all about it, but I want to catch up on your shit first. What are you working on?"

"They've got me writing docs," Murray said, grateful of the car's darkness covering his blush.

"Awwww," Liam said. "You're shitting me."

"I kinda lost it," Murray said. "Couldn't code. About six months ago. After."

"Ah," Liam said.

"So I'm writing docs. It's a sideways promotion and the work's not bad. I'm writing up Honorable Computing."

"What?"

"Sorry, it was after your time. It's a big deal. All the semiconductor companies are in on it: Intel, AMD, even Motorola and Hitachi. And Microsoft—they're hardcore for it."

"So what is it?"

Murray turned onto a gravel road, following the tracery on the glowing GPS screen as much as the narrow road, spiraling up and up over the sparse lights of Silicon Valley. He and Liam had had a million bullshit sessions about tech, what was vaporware and what was killer, and now they were having one again, just like old times. Only Liam was dead. Well, if it was time for Murray to lose his shit, what better way than in the hills, great tunes on the stereo, all alone in the night? .

Murray was warming up to the subject. He'd wanted someone he could really chew this over with since he got reassigned, he'd wanted Liam there to key off his observations. "OK, so, the Turing Machine, right? Turing's Universal Machine. The building-block of modern computation. In Turing's day, you had all these specialized machines: a machine for solving quadratics, a machine for calculating derivatives, and so on. Turing came up with the idea of a machine that could configure itself to be any specialized machine, using symbolic logic: software. Included in the machines that you can simulate in a Turing Machine is another Turing Machine, like Java or VMWare. With me?"

"With you." .

"So this gives rise to a kind of existential crisis. When your software is executing, how does it know what its execution environment is? Maybe it's running on a Global Semi Itanium clone at 1.6 gigahertz, or maybe it's running on a model of that chip, simulated on a Motorola G5 RISC processor."

"Got it."

"Now, forget about that for a sec and think about Hollywood. The coked-up Hollyweird fatcats hate Turing Machines. I mean, they want to release their stuff over the Internet, but they want to deliver it to you in a lockbox. You get to listen to it, you get to watch it, but only if they say so, and only if you've paid. You can buy it over and over again, but you can never own it. It's scrambled—encrypted—and they only send you the keys when you satisfy a license server that you've paid up. The keys are delivered to a secure app that you can't fuxor with, and the app locks you out of the video card and the sound card and the drive while it's decrypting the stream and showing it to you, and then it locks everything up again once you're done and hands control back over to you."

Liam snorted. "It is to laugh."

"Yeah, I know. It's bullshit. It's Turing Machines, right? When the software executes on your computer, it has to rely on your computer's feedback to confirm that the video card and the sound card are locked up, that you're not just feeding the cleartext stream back to the drive and then to 10,000,000 pals online. But the 'computer' it's executing on could be simulated inside another computer, one that you've modified to your heart's content. The 'video card' is a simulation; the 'sound card' is a simulation. The computer is a brain in a bottle, it's in the Matrix, it can't trust its senses because you're in control, it's a Turing Machine nested inside another Turing Machine."

"Like Descartes."

"What?"

"You gotta read your classics, bro. I've been catching up over the past six months or so, doing a *lot* of reading. Mostly free e-books from the Gutenberg Project. Descartes' 'Meditations' are some heavy shiznit. Descartes starts by saying that he wants to figure out some stuff about the world, but he can't, right, because in order to say stuff about the world, he needs to trust his senses, but his senses are wrong all the time. When he dreams, his senses deliver full-on THX all-digital IMAX, but none of it's really *there*. How does he know when he's dreaming or when he's awake? How does he know when he's experiencing something or imagining it? How does he know he's not a brain in a jar?"

"So, how does he know?" Murray asked, taking them over a reservoir on a switchback road, moonlight glittering over the still water, occulted by fringed silhouettes of tall California pines.

"Well, that's where he pulls some religion out of his ass. Here's how it goes: God is good, because part of the definition of God is goodness. God made the world. God made me. God made my senses. God made my senses *so that I could experience the goodness of his world*. Why would God give me bum senses? QED, I can trust my senses."

"It *is* like Descartes," Murray said, accelerating up a new hill.

"Yeah?" Liam said. "Who's God, then?"

"Crypto," Murray said. "Really good, standards-defined crypto. Public ciphersystems whose details are published and understood. AES, RSA, good crypto. There's a signing key for each chip fab—ours is in some secret biometrics-and-machineguns bunker under some desert. That key is used to sign *another* key that's embedded in a tamper-resistant chip—"

Liam snorted again.

"No, really. Not tamper-*proof*, obviously, but tamper-*resistant*—you'd need a tunneling microscope or a vat of Freon to extract the keys from the chip. And every chip has its own keys, so you'd need to do this for every chip, which doesn't, you know, *scale*. So there's this chip full of secrets, they call the Fritz chip, for Fritz Hollings, the Senator from Disney, the guy who's trying to ban computers so that Hollywood won't go broke. The Fritz chip wakes up when you switch on the machine, and it uses its secret key to sign the operating system—well, the boot-loader and the operating system and the drivers and stuff—so now you've got a bunch of cryptographic signatures that reflect the software and hardware configuration of your box. When you want to download Police Academy *n*, your computer sends all these keys to Hollywood central, *attesting* to the operating environment of your computer. Hollywood decides on the fly if it wants to trust that config, and if it does, it encrypts the movie, using the keys you've sent. That means that you can only unscramble the movie when you're running that Fritz chip, on that CPU, with that version of the OS and that video driver and so on."

"Got it: so if the OS and the CPU and so on are all 'Honorable' "— Liam described quote-marks with his index fingers—"then you can be sure that the execution environment is what the software expects it to be, that it's not a brain in a vat. Hollywood movies are safe from Napsterization."

They bottomed out on the shore of the reservoir and Murray pulled over. "You've got it."

"So basically, whatever Hollywood says, goes. You can't fake an interface, you can't make any uses that they don't authorize. You know that these guys sued to make the VCR illegal, right? You can't wrap up an old app in a compatibility layer and make it work with a new app. You say Microsoft loves this? No fucking wonder, dude—they can write software that won't run on a computer running Oracle software. It's your basic Bond-villain—"

"—world-domination horseshit. Yeah, I know."

Liam got out of the car and lit up another butt, kicked loose stones into the reservoir. Murray joined him, looking out over the still water.

"Ring Minus One," Liam said, and skipped a rock over the oily-black surface of the water, getting four long bounces out of it.

"Yeah," Murray said. Ring Zero, the first registers in the processor, was where your computer checked to figure out how to start itself up. Compromise Ring Zero and you can make the computer do anything—load an alternate operating system, turn the whole box into a brain-in-a-jar, executing in an unknown environment. Ring Minus One, well, that was like God-code, space on another, virtual processor that was unalterable, owned by some remote party, by LoCal and its entertainment giants. Software was released without any copy-prevention tech because everyone knew that copy-prevention tech *didn't work*. Nevertheless, Hollywood was always chewing the scenery and hollering, they just didn't believe that the hairfaces and ponytails didn't have some seekrit tech that would keep their movies safe from copying until the heat death of the universe or the expiry of copyright, whichever came last.

"You run this stuff," Liam said, carefully, thinking it through, like he'd done before he got sick, murdered by his need to feed speedballs to his golden, tracked-out arm. "You run it and while you're watching a movie, Hollywood 0wnz your box." Murray heard the zero and the zee in 0wnz. Hacker-speak for having total control. No one wants to be 0wnz0red by some teenaged script-kiddie who's found some fresh exploit and turned it loose on your computer.

"In a nutsac. Gimme a butt."

Liam shook one out of the pack and passed it to Murray, along with a box of Mexican strike-anywhere matches. "You're back on these things?" Liam said, a note of surprise in his voice.

"Not really. Special occasion, you being back from the dead and all. I've always heard that these things'd kill me, but apparently being killed isn't so bad—you look great."

"Artful segue, dude. You must be burning up with curiosity."

"Not really," Murray said. "Figgered I'm hallucinating. I haven't hallucinated up until now, but back when I was really down, you know, clinical, I had all kinds of voices muttering in my head, telling me that I'd fucked up, it was all fucked up, crash the car into the median and do the world a favor, whatever. You get a little better from that stuff by changing jobs, but maybe not all the way better. Maybe I'm going to fill my pockets with rocks and jump in the lake. It's the next logical step, right?"

Liam studied his face. Murray tried to stay deadpan, but he felt the old sadness that came with the admission, the admission of guilt and weakness, felt the tears pricking his eyes. "Hear me out first, OK?" Liam said.

"By all means. It'd be rude not to hear you out after you came all the way here from the kingdom of the dead."

"Mostly dead. Mostly. Ever think about how all the really good shit in your body—metabolism, immunoresponse, cognition—it's all in Ring Minus One? Not user-accessible? I mean, why is it that something like wiggling your toes is under your volitional control, but your memory isn't?"

"Well, that's complicated stuff—heartbeat, breathing, immunoresponse, memory. You don't want to forget to breathe, right?"

Liam hissed a laugh. "Horse-sheeit," he drawled. "How complicated is moving your arm? How many muscle-movements in a smile? How many muscle-movements in a heartbeat? How complicated is writing code versus immunoresponse? Why when you're holding your breath can't you hold it until you don't want to hold it anymore? Why do you have to be a fucking Jedi Master to stop your heart at will?"

"But the interactions—"

"More horseshit. Yeah, the interactions between brain chemistry and body and cognition and metabolism are all complicated. I was a speed-freak, I know all about it. But it's not any more complicated than any of the other complex interactions you master every day—wind and attack and spin when someone tosses you a ball; speed and acceleration and vectors when you change lanes; don't even get me started on what goes on when you season a soup. No, your body just isn't *that* complicated—it's just hubris that makes us so certain that our meat-sacks are transcendently complex.

"We're simple, but all the good stuff is 0wned by your autonomic systems. They're like conditional operators left behind by a sloppy coder: while x is true, do y. We've only had the vaguest idea what x is, but we've got a handle on y, you betcha. Burning fat, for example." He prodded Murray's gut-overhang with a long finger. Self-consciously, Murray tugged his JavaOne gimme jacket tighter.

"For forty years now, doctors have been telling us that the way to keep fit is to exercise more and eat less. That's great fucking advice, as can be demonstrated by the number of trim, fit residents of Northern California that can be found waddling around any shopping mall off Interstate 101. Look at exercise, Jesus, what could be stupider? Exercise doesn't burn fat, exercise just satisfies the condition in which your body is prepared to burn fat off. It's like a computer that won't boot unless you restart it twice, switch off the monitor, open the CD drive and stand on one foot. If you're a luser, you do all this shit every time you want to boot your box, but if you're a leet hax0r like you and me, you just figure out what's wrong with the computer and *fix it*. You don't sacrifice a chicken twice a day, you 0wn the box, so you make it dance to your tune.

"But your meat, it's not under your control. You know you have to exercise for 20 minutes before you start burning any fat at all? In other words, the first twenty minutes are just a goddamned waste of time. It's sacrificing a chicken to your metabolism. Eat less, exercise more is a giant chicken-sacrifice, so I say screw it. I say, you should be super-user in your own body. You should be leet as you want to be. Every cell in your body should be end-user modifiable."

Liam held his hands out before them, then stretched and stretched and stretched the fingers, so that each one bent over double. "Triple jointed, metabolically secure, cognitively large and *in charge*. I 0wn, dude."

Liam fished the last cig out of the pack, crumpled it and tucked it into a pocket. "Last one," he said. "Wanna share?"

"Sure," Murray said, dazedly. "Yeah," he said, taking the smoke and bringing it to his lips. The tip, he realized too late, was dripping with saliva. He made a face and handed it back to Liam. "Aaagh! You juiced the filter!"

"Sorry," Liam said, "talking gets my spit going. Where was I? Oh, yeah, I 0wn. Want to know how it happened?"

"Does it also explain how you ended up not dead?"

"Mostly dead. Indeed it does."

Murray walked back to the car and lay back on the hood, staring at the thin star-cover and the softly swaying pine-tops. He heard Liam begin to pace, heard the cadence of Liam's thinking stride, the walk he fell into when he was on a roll.

"Are you sitting comfortably?" Liam said. "Then I shall begin."

The palliatives on the ward were abysmal whiners, but they were still better than the goddamned church volunteers who came by to patch-adams at them. Liam was glad of the days when the dementia was strong, morphine days when the sun rose and set in a slow blink and then it was bedtime again.

Lucky for him, then, that lucid days were fewer and farther between. Unlucky for him that his lucid days, when they came, were filled with the G-Men.

The G-Men had come to him in the late days of his tenure on the palliative ward. They'd wheeled him into a private consultation room and given him a cigarette that stung the sores on his lips, tongue and throat. He coughed gratefully.

"You must be the Fed," Liam said. "No one else could green-light indoor smoking in California." Liam had worked for the Fed before. Work in the Valley and you end up working for the Fed, because when the cyclic five-year bust arrives, the only venture capital that's liquid in the U.S. is military research green—khaki money. He'd been seconded twice to biometrics-and-machineguns bunkers where he'd worked on need-to-know integration projects for Global Semi's customers in the Military-Industrial Simplex.

The military and the alphabet soup of Fed cops gave birth to the Valley. After WWII, all those shipbuilder engineers and all those radar engineers and all those radio engineers and the tame academics at Cal Tech and Cal and Stanford sorta congealed, did a bunch of startups and built a bunch of crap their buds in the Forces would buy.

Khaki money stunted the Valley. Generals didn't need to lobby in Congress for bigger appropriations. They just took home black budgets that were silently erased from the books, aerosolized cash that they misted over the eggheads along Highway 101. Two generations later, the Valley was filled with techno-determinists, swaggering nerd squillionaires who were steadfastly convinced that the money would flow forever and ever amen.

Then came Hollywood, the puny $35 billion David that slew the

$600 billion Goliath of tech. They bought Congresscritters, had their business-models declared fundamental to the American way of life, extended copyright ad [inifinitum | nauseam] and generally kicked the shit out of tech in DC. They'd been playing this game since 1908, when they sued to keep the player piano off the market, and they punched well above their weight in the legislative ring. As the copyright police began to crush tech companies throughout the Valley, khaki money took on the sweet appeal of nostalgia, strings-free cash for babykiller projects that no one was going to get sued over.

The Feds that took Liam aside that day could have been pulled from a fiftieth anniversary revival of "Nerds and Generals." Clean-cut, stone-faced, prominent wedding-bands. The Feds had never cared for Liam's jokes, though it was his trackmarks and not his punchlines that eventually accounted for his security clearance being yanked. These two did not crack a smile as Liam wheezed out his pathetic joke.

Instead, they introduced themselves gravely. Col. Gonzalez—an MD, with caduceus insignia next to his silver birds—and Special Agent Fredericks. Grateful for his attention, they had an offer to make him.

"It's experimental, and the risks are high. We won't kid you about that."

"I appreciate that," Liam wheezed. "I like to live dangerously. Give me another smoke, willya?"

Col. Gonzalez lit another Marlboro Red with his brass Zippo and passed him a sheaf of papers. "You can review these here, once we're done. I'm afraid I'll have to take them with me when we go, though."

Liam paged through the docs, passing over the bio stuff and nodding his head over the circuit diagrams and schematics. "I give up," he said. "What does it all do?"

"It's an interface between your autonomic processes and a microcontroller."

Liam thought about that for a moment. "I'm in," he said.

Special Agent Fredericks' thin lips compressed a hair and his eyes gave the hintiest hint of a roll. But Col. Gonzalez nodded to himself. "All right. Here's the protocol: tomorrow, we give you a bug. It's a controlled mutagen that prepares your brainstem so that it emits and receives weak electromagnetic fields that can be manipulated with an external microcontroller. In subjects with effective immunoresponse, the bug takes less than one percent of the time—"

"But if you're dying of AIDS, that's not a problem," Liam said and smiled until some of the sores at the corners of his mouth cracked and released a thin gruel of pus. "Lucky fucking me."

"You grasp the essentials," the Colonel said. "There's no surgery involved. The interface regulates immunoresponse in the region of the insult to prevent rejection. The controller has a serial connector that connects to a PC that instructs it in respect of the governance of most bodily functions."

Liam smiled slantwise and butted out. "God, I'd hate to see the project you developed this shit for. Zombie soldiers, right? You can tell me, I've got clearance."

Special Agent Fredericks shook his head. "Not for three years, you haven't. And you never had clearance to get the answer to that question. But once you sign here and here and here, you'll *almost* have clearance to get *some* of the answers." He passed a clipboard to Liam.

Liam signed, and signed, and signed. "Autonomic processes, right?"

Col. Gonzalez nodded. "Correct."

"Including, say, immunoresponse?"

"Yes, we've had very promising results in respect of the immune system. It was one of the first apps we wrote. Modifies the genome to produce virus-hardened cells and kick-starts production of new cells."

"Yeah, until some virus out-evolves it," Liam said. He knew how to debug vaporware.

"We issue a patch," the Colonel said.

"I write good patches," Liam said.

"We know," Special Agent Fredericks said, and gently prized the clipboard from his fingers.

The techs came first, to wire Liam up. The new bug in his system broadened his already-exhaustive survey of the ways in which the human body can hurt. He squeezed his eyes tight against the morphine rush and lazily considered the possibility of rerouting pain to a sort of dull tickle.

The techs were familiar Valley-dwellers, portly and bedecked with multitools and cellular gear and wireless PDAs. They handled him like spoiled meat, with gloves and wrinkled noses, and talked shop over his head to one another.

Colonel Gonzalez supervised, occasionally stepping away to liaise with the hospital's ineffectual medical staff.

A week of this—a week of feeling like his spine was working its way out of his asshole, a week of rough latex hands and hacker jargon—and he was wheeled into a semi-private room, surrounded by *louche* oatmeal-colored commodity PCs—no keyboards or mice, lest he get the urge to tinker.

The other bed was occupied by Joey, another Silicon Valley needle-freak, a heroin addict who'd been a design engineer for Apple, figuring out how to cram commodity hardware into stylish gumdrop boxen. Joey and Liam croaked conversation between themselves when they were both lucid and alone. Liam always knew when Joey was awake by the wet hacking coughs he wrenched out of his pneumonia-riddled lungs. Alone together, ignored by the mad scientists who were hacking their bodies, they struck up a weak and hallucinogenic camaraderie.

"I'm not going to sleep," Joey said, in one timeless twilight.

"So don't sleep, shit," Liam said.

"No, I mean, ever. Sleep, it's like a third of your life, 20, 30 years. What's it good for? It resets a bunch of switches, gives your brain a chance to sort through its buffers, a little oxygenation for your tissues. That stuff can all take place while you're doing whatever you feel like doing, hiking in the hills or getting laid. Make 'em into cron jobs and nice them down to the point where they just grab any idle cycles and do their work incrementally."

"You're crazy. I like to sleep," Liam said.

"Not me. I've slept enough in this joint, been on the nod enough, I never want to sleep another minute. We're getting another chance, I'm not wasting a minute of it." Despite the braveness of his words, he sounded like he was half-asleep already.

"Well, that'll make *them* happy. All part of a good super-soldier, you know."

"Now who's crazy?"

"You don't believe it? They're just getting our junkie asses back online so they can learn enough from us to field some mean, lean, heavily modified fighting-machines."

"And then they snuff us. You told me that this morning. Yesterday? I still don't believe it. Even if you're right about why they're doing this, they're still going to want us around so they can monitor the long-term effects."

"I hope you're right."

"You know I am."

Liam stared into the ceiling until he heard Joey's wet snores, then he closed his eyes and waited for the fever dreams.

Joey went critical the next day. One minute, he was snoring away in bed while Liam watched a daytime soap with headphones. The next minute, there were twenty people in the room: nurses, doctors, techs, even Col. Gonzalez. Joey was doing the floppy dance in the next bed, the OD dance that Liam had seen once or twice, danced once or twice on an Emergency Room floor, his heart pounding the crystal meth mambo.

Someone backhanded Liam's TV and it slid away on its articulated arm and yanked the headphones off his head, ripping open the scabs on the slowly healing sores on his ears. Liam stifled a yelp and listened to the splashing sounds of all those people standing ankle-deep in something pink and bad-smelling, and Liam realized it was watery blood and he pitched forward and his empty stomach spasmed, trying to send up some bile or mucus, clicking on empty.

Colonel Gonzales snapped out some orders and two techs abandoned their fretting over one of the computers, yanked free a tangle of roll-up, rubberized keyboards and trackballs and USB cables, piled them on the side of Liam's gurney, snapped up the guard rails and wheeled him out of the room.

They crashed through a series of doors before hitting a badgepoint. One tech thought he'd left his badge back in the room on its lanyard (he hadn't—he'd dropped it on the gurney and Liam had slipped it under the sheets), the other one wasn't sure if his was in one of his many pockets. As they frisked themselves, Liam stole his skeletal hand out from under the covers, a hand all tracked out with collapsed IV veins and yellowing fingernails, a claw of a hand.

The claw shook as Liam guided it to a keyboard, stole it under the covers, rolled it under the loose meat of his thigh.

"Need to know?" Liam said, spitting the words at Col. Gonzalez. "If I don't need to know what happened to Joey, who the fuck does?"

"You're not a medical professional, Liam. You're also not cleared. What happened to Joey was an isolated incident, nothing to worry about."

"Horseshit! You can tell me what happened to Joey or not, but I'll find out, you goddamned betcha."

The Colonel sighed and wiped his palms on his thighs. He looked like shit, his brush-cut glistening with sweat and scalp-oil, his eyes bagged and his youthful face made old with exhaustion lines. It had been two hours since Joey had gone critical—two hours of lying still with the keyboard nestled under his thigh, on the gurney in the locked room, until they came for him again. "I have a lot of work to do yet, Liam. I came to see you as a courtesy, but I'm afraid that the courtesy is at a close." He stood.

"Hey!" Liam croaked after him. "Gimme a fucking cigarette, will you?"

Once the Colonel was gone, Liam had the run of the room. They'd mopped it out and disinfected it and sent Joey's corpse to an Area 51 black ops morgue for gruesome autopsy, and there was only half as much hardware remaining, all of it plugged back into the hard pucker of skin on the back of Liam's neck.

Cautiously, Liam turned himself so that the toes of one foot touched the ground. Knuckling his toes, he pushed off towards the computers, the gurney's wheels squeaking. Painfully, arthritically, he inched to the boxes, then plugged in and unrolled the keyboard.

He hit the spacebar and got rid of the screen-saver, brought up a login prompt. He'd been stealthily shoulder-surfing the techs for weeks now, and had half a dozen logins in his brain. He tapped out the login/pass combination and he was in.

The machine was networked to a CVS repository in some bunker, so the first thing he did was login to the server and download all the day's commits, then he dug out the READMEs. While everything was downloading, he logged into the tech's e-mail account and found Col. Gonzalez's account of Joey's demise.

It was encrypted with the group's shared key as well as the tech's key, but he'd shoulder-surfed both, and after three tries, he had cleartext on the screen.

Hydrostatic shock. The membranes of all of Joey's cells had ruptured simultaneously, so that he'd essentially burst like a bag of semi-liquid Jell-O. Preliminary indications were that the antiviral cellular modifications had gone awry due to some idiosyncrasy of Joey's "platform"—his physiology, in other words—and that the "fortified" cell-membranes had given way disastrously and simultaneously.

A ghoulish giggle escaped Liam's lips. Venture capitalists liked to talk about "liquidity events"—times in the life of a portfolio company when the investors get to cash out: acquisition and IPO, basically. Liam had always joked that the VCs needed adult diapers to cope with their liquidity events, but now he had a better one. Joey had experienced the ultimate liquidity event.

The giggle threatened to rise into a squeal as he contemplated a liquidity event of his own, so he swallowed it and got into the READMEs and the source code.

He wasn't a biotech, wasn't a medical professional, but neither were the coders who'd been working on the mods that were executing on his "platform" at that very moment. In their comments and data-structures and READMEs, they'd gone to great pains to convert medical jargon to geekspeak, so that Liam was actually able to follow most of it.

One thing he immediately gleaned is that his interface was modifying his cells to be virus-hardened as slowly as possible. They wanted a controlled experiment, data on every stage of the recovery—if a recovery was indeed in the cards.

Liam didn't want to wait. He didn't even have to change the code—he just edited a variable in the config file and respawned the process. Where before he'd been running at a pace that would reverse the course of HIV in his body in a space of three weeks, now he was set to be done in three *hours*. What the fuck—how many chances was he going to get to screw around after they figured out that he'd been tinkering?

Manufacturing the curative made him famished. His body was burning a lot of calories, and after a couple hours he felt like he could eat the ass out of a dead bear. Whatever was happening was happening, though! He felt the sores on his body dry up and start to slough off. He was hungry enough that he actually caught himself peeling off the scabby cornflakes and eating them. It grossed him out, but he was *hungry*.

His only visitor that night was a nurse, who made enough noise with her trolley on the way down the hall that he had time to balance the keyboard on top of the monitor and knuckle the bed back into position. The nurse was pleased to hear that he had an appetite and obligingly brought him a couple of supper-trays—the kitchen had sent up one for poor Joey, she explained.

Once Liam was satisfied that she was gone, he returned to his task with a renewed sense of urgency. No techs and no docs and no Colonel for six hours now—there must be a shitload of paperwork and fingerpointing over Joey, but who knew how long it would last?

He stuffed his face, nailing about three thousand calories over the next two hours, poking through the code. Here was a routine for stimulating the growth of large muscle-groups. Here was one for regenerating fine nerves. The enhanced reflexes sounded like a low-cal option, too, so he executed it. It was all betaware, but as between a liquidity event, a slow death on the palliative ward and a chance at a quick cure, what the fuck, he'd take his chances.

He was chuckling now, going through the code, learning the programmers' style and personality from their comments and variable names. He was so damned hungry, and the muscles in his back and limbs and ass and gut all felt like they were home to nests of termites.

He needed more food. He gingerly peeled off the surgical tape holding on controller and its cable. Experimentally, he stood. His inner ear twirled rollercoaster for a minute or two, but then it settled down and he was actually erect—upright—well, both, he could cut glass with that boner, it was the first one he'd had in a year—and *walking*!

He stole out into the hallway, experiencing a frisson of delight and then the burning ritual humiliation of any person who finds himself in a public place wearing a hospital gown. His bony ass was hanging out of the back, the cool air of the dim ward raising goose-pimples on it.

He stepped into the next room. It was dusky-dark, the twilight of a hospital nighttime, and the two occupants were snoring in contratime. Each had his (her? it was too dark to tell) own nightstand, piled high with helium balloons, Care Bears, flowers and baskets of nuts, dried fruits and chocolates. Saliva flooded Liam's mouth. He tiptoed across to each nightstand and held up the hem of his gown, then grinched the food into the pocket it made.

Stealthily, he stole his way down the length of the ward, emptying fruitbaskets, boxes of candy and chocolate, leftover dinner trays. By the time he returned to his room, he could hardly stand. He dumped the food out on the bed and began to shovel it into his face, going back through the code, looking for obvious bugs, memory leaks, buffer overruns. He found several and recompiled the apps, accelerating the pace of growth in his muscles. He could actually feel himself bulking up, feel the tone creeping back into his flesh.

He'd read the notes in the READMEs on waste heat and the potential to denature enzymes, so he stripped naked and soaked towels in a quiet trickle of ice-water in the small sink. He kept taking breaks from his work to wring out the steaming towels he wrapped around his body and wet them down again.

The next time he rose, his legs were springy. He parted the slats of the blinds and saw the sun rising over the distant ocean and knew it was time to hit the road, jack.

He tore loose the controller and its cable and shut down the computer. He undid the thumbscrews on the back of the case and slid it away, then tugged at the sled for the hard-disk until it sprang free. He ducked back out into the hall and quickly worked his way through the rooms until he found one with a change of men's clothes neatly folded on the chair—ill-fitting tan chinos and a blue Oxford shirt, the NoCal yuppie uniform. He found a pair of too-small penny-loafers too and jammed his feet into the toes. He dressed in his room and went through the wallet that was stuck in the pants pocket. A couple hundred bucks' worth of cash, some worthless plastic, a picture of a heavyset wife and three chubby kids. He dumped all the crap out, kept the cash, snatched up the drive-sled and booted, badging out with the tech's badge.

"How long have you been on the road, then?" Murray asked. His mouth tasted like an ashtray and he had a mild case of the shakes.

"Four months. I've been breaking into cars mostly. Stealing laptops and selling them for cash. I've got a box at the rooming-house with the hard-drive installed, and I've been using an e-gold account to buy little things online to help me out."

"Help you out with *what*?"

"Hacking—duh. First thing I did was reverse-engineer the interface bug. I wanted a safe virus I could grow arbitrary payloads for in my body. I embedded the antiviral hardening agent in the vector. It's a sexually trans-missible *wellness,* dude. I've been barebacking my way through the skanki-est crack-hoes in the Tenderloin, playing Patient Zero, infecting everyone with the Cure."

Murray sat up and his head swam. "You did what?"

"I cured AIDS. It's going around, it's catching, you might already be a winner."

"Jesus, Liam, what the fuck do you know about medicine? For all you know, your cure is worse than the disease—for all you know, we're all go-ing to have a—'liquidity event' any day now!"

"No chance of that happening, bro. I isolated the cause of that early on. This medical stuff is just *not that complicated*—once you get over the new jar-gon, it's nothing you can't learn as you go with a little judicious googling. Trust me. You're soaking in it."

It took Murray a moment to parse that. "You infected *me*?"

"The works—I've viralized all the best stuff. Metabolic controllers, until further notice, you're on a five-cheeseburger-a-day diet; increased dendrite density; muscle-builders. At-will pain-dampeners. You'll need those—I gave you the interface, too."

A spasm shot up Murray's back, then down again.

"It was on the cigarette butt. You're cancer-immune, by the by. I'm extra contagious tonight." Liam turned down his collar to show Murray the taped lump there, the dangling cable that disappeared down his shirt, connecting to the palmtop strapped to his belt.

Murray arched his back and mewled through locked jaws.

Liam caught his head before it slammed into the Toyota's hood. "Breathe," he hissed. "Relax. You're only feeling the pain because you're choosing not to ignore it. Try to ignore it, you'll see. It kicks azz."

"I needed an accomplice. A partner in crime. I'm underground, see? No credit-card, no ID. I can't rent a car or hop a plane. I needed to recruit someone I could trust. Naturally, I thought of you."

"I'm flattered," Murray sarcased around a mouthful of double-bacon cheeseburger with extra mayo.

"You should be, asshole," Liam said. They were at Murray's one-bedroom techno-monastic condo: shit sofa, hyper-ergonomic chairs, dusty home theatre, computers everywhere. Liam drove them there, singing into the wind that whipped down from the sunroof, following the GPS's sterile eurobabe voice as it guided them back to the anonymous shitbox building where Murray had located his carcass for eight years.

"Liam, you're a pal, really, my best friend ever, I couldn't be happier that you're alive, but if I could get up I would fucking *kill you*. You *raped me,* asshole. Used my body without my permission."

"You see it that way now, but give it a couple weeks, it'll, ah, grow on you. Trust me. It's rad. So, call in sick for the next week—you're going to need some time to get used to the mods."

"And if I don't?"

"Do whatever you want, buddy, but I don't think you're going to be in any shape to go to work this week—maybe not next week either. Tell them it's a personal crisis. Take some vacation days. Tell 'em you're going to a fat-farm. You must have a shitload of holidays saved up."

"I do," Murray said. "I don't know why I should use them, though."

"Oh, this is the best vacation of all, the Journey Thru Innerspace. You're going to love it."

Murray hadn't counted on the coding.

Liam tunneled into his box at the rooming house and dumped its drive to one of the old laptops lying around Murray's apartment. He set the laptop next to Murray while he drove to Fry's Electronics to get the cabling and components he needed to make the emitter/receiver for the interface. They'd always had a running joke that you can build *anything* from parts at Fry's, but when Liam invoked it, Murray barely cracked a smile. He was stepping through the code in a debugger, reading the comments Liam had left behind as he'd deciphered its form and function.

He was back in it. There was a runtime that simulated the platform and as he tweaked the code, he ran it on the simulator and checked out how his body would react if he executed it for real. Once he got a couple of liquidity events, he saw that Liam was right, they just weren't that hard to avoid.

The API was great, there were function calls for just about everything. He delved into the cognitive stuff right off, since it was the area that was rawest, that Liam had devoted the least effort to. At-will serotonin production. Mnemonic perfection. Endorphin production, adrenalin. Zen master on a disk. Who needs meditation and biofeedback when you can do it all in code?

Out of habit, he was documenting as he went along, writing proper tutorials for the API, putting together a table of the different kinds of interaction he got with different mods. Good, clear docs, ready for printing, able to be slotted in as online help in the developer toolkit. Inspired by Joey, he began work on a routine that would replace all the maintenance chores that the platform did in sleep-mode, along with a subroutine that suppressed melatonin and all the other circadian chemicals that induced sleep.

Liam returned from Fry's with bags full of cabling and soldering guns and breadboards. He draped a black pillowcase over a patch of living-room floor and laid everything out on it, wires and strippers and crimpers and components and a soldering gun, and went to work methodically, stripping and crimping and twisting. He'd taken out his own connector for reference and he was comparing them both, using a white LED torch on a headband to show him the pinouts on the custom end.

"So I'm thinking that I'll clone the controller and stick it on my head first to make sure it works. You wear my wire and I'll burn the new one in for a couple days and then we can swap. OK?"

"Sure," Murray said, "whatever." His fingers rattled on the keys.

"Got you one of these," Liam said and held up a bulky Korean palmtop. "Runs Linux. You can cross-compile the SDK and all the libraries for it; the compiler's on the drive. Good if you want to run an interactive app—" an application that changed its instructions based on output from the platform—"and it's stinking cool, too. I fucking *love* gear."

"Gear's good," Murray agreed. "Cheap as hell and faster every time I turn around."

"Well, until Honorable Computing comes along," Liam said. "That'll put a nail in the old coffin."

"You're overreacting."

"Naw. Just being realistic. Open up a shell, OK? See at the top, how it says 'tty'? The kernel thinks it's communicating with a printer. Your shell window is a simulation of a printer, so the kernel knows how to talk to it— it's got plenty of compatibility layers between it and you. If the guy who wrote the code doesn't want you to interface with it, you can't. No emulation, that's not 'honorable.' Your box is 0wned."

Murray looked up from his keyboard. "So what do you want me to do about it, dead man?"

"Mostly dead," Liam said. "Just think about it, OK? How much money you got in your savings account?"

"Nice segue. Not enough."

"Not enough for what?"

"Not enough for sharing any of it with you."

"Come on, dude, I'm going back underground. I need fifty grand to get out of the country—Canada, then buy a fake passport and head to London. Once I'm in the EU, I'm in good shape. I learned German last week, this week I'm doing French. The dendrite density shit is the shit."

"Man und zooperman," Murray said. "If you're zo zooper, go and earn a buck or two, OK?"

"Come on, you know I'm good for it. Once this stuff is ready to go—"

"What stuff?"

"The codebase! Haven't you figured it out yet? It's a startup! We go into business in some former-Soviet Stan in Asia or some African kleptocracy. We infect the locals with the Cure, then the interface, and then we sell 'em the software. It's *viral marketing,* gettit?"

"Leaving aside CIA assassins, if only for the moment, there's one gigantic flaw in your plan, dead man."

"I'm all aflutter with anticipation."

"There's no fucking revenue opportunity. The platform spreads for free—it's already out there, you've seeded it with your magic undead supercock. The hardware is commodity hardware, no margin and no money. The controller can be built out of spare parts from Fry's—next gen, we'll make it WiFi, so that we're using commodity wireless chipsets and you can control the device from a distance—"

"—yeah, and that's why we're selling the software!" Liam hopped from foot to foot in a personal folk-dance celebrating his sublime cleverness.

"In Buttfuckistan or Kleptomalia. Where being a warez d00d is an honorable trade. We release our libraries and binaries and APIs and fifteen minutes later, they're burning CDs in every *souk* and selling them for ten cents a throw."

"Nope, that's not gonna happen."

"Why not?"

"We're gonna deploy on Honorable hardware."

"I am not hearing this." Murray closed the lid of his laptop and tore into a slice of double-cheese meat-lover's deep-dish pizza. "You are not telling me this."

"You are. I am. It's only temporary. The interface isn't Honorable, so anyone who reverse-engineers it can make his own apps. We're just getting ours while the getting is good. All the good stuff—say, pain-control and universal antiviral hardening—we'll make for free, viralize it. Once our stuff is in the market, the whole world's going to change, anyway. There'll be apps for happiness, cures for every disease, hibernation, limb-regeneration, whatever. Anything any human body has ever done, ever, you'll be able to do at-will. You think there's going to be anything recognizable as an economy once we're ubiquitous?"

Every morning, upon rising, Murray looked down at his toes and thought, "Hello toes." It had been ten years since he'd had regular acquaintance with anything south of his gut. But his gut was gone, tight as a drum-head. He was free from scars and age-marks and unsightly moles and his beard wouldn't grow in again until he asked it to. When he thought about it, he could feel the dull ache of the new teeth coming in underneath the ones that had grown discolored and chipped, the back molar with all the ugly amalgam fillings, but if he chose to ignore it, the pain simply went away.

He flexed the muscles, great and small, all around his body. His fat index was low enough to see the definition of each of those superbly toned slabs of flexible contained energy—he looked like an anatomy lesson, and it was all he could do not to stare at himself in the mirror all day.

But he couldn't do that—not today, anyway. He was needed back at the office. He was already in the shitter at work over his "unexpected trip to a heath-farm," and if he left it any longer, he'd be out on his toned ass. He hadn't even been able to go out for new clothes—Liam had every liquid cent he could lay hands on, as well as his credit-cards.

He found a pair of ancient, threadbare jeans and a couple of medium t-shirts that clung to the pecs that had grown up underneath his formerly sagging man-boobs and left for the office.

He drew stares on the way to his desk. The documentation department hummed with hormonal female energy, and half a dozen of his co-workers found cause to cruise past his desk before he took his morning break. As he greedily scarfed up a box of warm Krispy Kremes, his cellphone rang.

"Yeah?" he said. The caller-ID was the number of the international GSM phone he'd bought for Liam.

"They're after us," Liam said. "I was at the Surrey border-crossing and the Canadian immigration guy had my pic!"

Murray's heart pounded. He concentrated for a moment, then his heart calmed, a jolt of serotonin lifting his spirits. "Did you get away?"

"Of course I got away. Jesus, you think that the CIA gives you a phone call? I took off cross-country, went over the fence for the duty-free and headed for the brush. They shot me in the fucking leg—I had to dig the bullet out with my multitool. I'm sending in ass-loads of T-cells and knitting it as fast as I can."

Panic crept up Murray's esophagus, and he tamped it down. It broke out in his knees, he tamped it down. His balance swam, he stabilized it. He focused his eyes with an effort. "They *shot* you?"

"I think they were trying to wing me. Look, I burned all the source in 4,096-bit GPG ciphertext onto a couple of CDs, then zeroed out my drive. You've got to do the same, it's only a matter of time until they run my back-trail to you. The code is our only bargaining chip."

"I'm at work—the backups are at home, I just can't."

"Leave, asshole, like *now*! Go—get in your car and *drive*. Go home and start scrubbing the drives. I left a bottle of industrial paint-stripper behind and a bulk eraser. Unscrew every drive-casing, smash the platters and dump them in a tub with all the stripper, then put the tub onto the bulk-eraser—that should do it. Keep one copy, ciphertext only, and make the key a good one. Are you going?"

"I'm badging out of the lot, shit, shit, shit. What the fuck did you do to me?"

"Don't, OK? Just don't. I've got my own problems. I've got to go now. I'll call you later once I get somewhere."

He thought hard on the way back to his condo, as he whipped down the off-peak emptiness of Highway 101. Being a coder was all about doing things in the correct order: first a; then b; then, if c equals d, e; otherwise, f.

First, get home. Then set the stateful operation of his body for maximal efficiency: reset his metabolism, increase the pace of dendrite densification. Manufacture viralized antiviral in all his serum. Lots of serotonin and at-will endorphin. Hard times ahead.

Next, encipher and back up the data to a removable. Did he have any CD blanks at home? With eidetic clarity, he saw the half-spent spool of generic blanks on the second shelf of the media totem.

Then trash the disks, pack a bag and hit the road. Where to?

He pulled into his driveway, hammered the elevator button a dozen times, then bolted for the stairs. Five flights later, he slammed his key into the lock and went into motion, executing the plan. The password gave him pause—generating a 4,096 bit key that he could remember was going to be damned hard, but then he closed his eyes and recalled, with perfect clarity, the first five pages of documentation he'd written for the API. His fingers rattled on the keys at speed, zero typos.

He was just dumping the last of the platters into the acid bath when they broke his door down. Half a dozen big guys in martian riot-gear, out-sized science-fiction black-ops guns. One flipped up his visor and pointed to a badge clipped to a D-ring on his tactical vest.

"Police," he barked. "Hands where I can see them."

The serotonin flooded the murky grey recesses of Murray's brain and he was able to smile nonchalantly as he straightened from his work, hands held loosely away from his sides. The cop pulled a zap-strap from a holster at his belt and bound his wrists tight. He snapped on a pair of latex gloves and untaped the interface on the back of Murray's neck, then slapped a bandage over it.

"Am I under arrest?"

"You're not cleared to know that," the cop said.

"Special Agent Fredericks, right?" Murray said. "Liam told me about you."

"Dig yourself in deeper, that's right. No one wants to hear from you. Not yet, anyway." He took a bag off his belt, then, in a quick motion, slid it over Murray's head, cinching it tight at the throat, but not so tight he couldn't breathe. The fabric passed air, but not light, and Murray was plunged into total darkness. "There's a gag that goes with the hood. If you play nice, we won't have to use it."

"I'm nice, I'm nice," Murray said.

"Bag it all and get it back to the house. You and you, take him down the back way."

Murray felt the bodies moving near him, then thick zap-straps cinching his arms, knees, thighs and ankles. He tottered and tipped backwards, twisting his head to avoid smacking it, but before he hit the ground, he'd be roughly scooped up into a fireman's carry, resting on bulky body-armor.

As they carried him out, he heard his cellphone ring. Someone plucked it off his belt and answered it. Special Agent Fredericks said, "Hello, Liam."

Machineguns-and-biometrics bunkers have their own special signature scent, scrubbed air and coffee farts and ozone. They cut his clothes off and dis-infected him, then took him through two air-showers to remove particulate that the jets of icy pungent Lysol hadn't taken care of. He was dumped on a soft pallet, still in the dark.

"You know why you're here," Special Agent Fredericks said from somewhere behind him.

"Why don't you refresh me?" He was calm and cool, heart normal. The cramped muscles bound by the plastic straps eased loose, relaxing under him.

"We found two CDs of encrypted data on your premises. We can crack them, given time, but it will reflect well on you if you assist us in our inquiries."

"Given about a billion years. No one can brute-force a 4,096-bit GPG cipher. It's what you use in your own communications. I've worked on military projects, you know that. If you could factor out the products of large primes, you wouldn't depend on them for your own security. I'm not getting out of here ever, no matter how much I cooperate."

"You've got an awfully low opinion of your country, sir." Murray thought he detected a note of real anger in the Fed's voice and tried not to take satisfaction in it.

"Why? Because I don't believe you've got magic technology hidden away up your asses?"

"No, sir, because you think you won't get just treatment at our hands."

"Am I under arrest?"

"You're not cleared for that information."

"We're at an impasse, Special Agent Fredericks. You don't trust me and I don't have any reason to trust you."

"You have every reason to trust me," the voice said, very close in now.

"Why?"

The hood over his tag was tugged to one side and he heard a sawing sound as a knife hacked through the fabric at the base of his skull. Gloved fingers worked at the familiar interfacing spots there. "Because," the voice hissed in his ear, "because I am *not* stimulating the pain center of your brain. Because I am not cutting off the blood-supply to your extremities. Because I am not draining your brain of all the serotonin there or leaving you in a vegetative state. Because I can do all of these things and I'm not."

Murray tamped his adrenals, counteracted their effect, relaxed back into his bonds. "You think you could outrace me? I could stop my heart right now, long before you could do any of those things." Thinking: I am a total bad-azz, I am. But I don't want to die.

"Tell him," Liam said.

"Liam?" Murray tried to twist his head toward the voice, but strong hands held it in place.

"Tell him," Liam said again. "We'll get a deal. They don't want us dead, they just want us under control. Tell him, OK?"

Murray's adrenals were firing at max now, he was sweating uncontrol-lably. His limbs twitched hard against his bonds, the plastic straps cutting into them, the pain surfacing despite his efforts. It hit him. His wonderful body was 0wnz0red by the Feds.

"Tell me, and you have my word that no harm will come to you. You'll get all the resources you want. You can code as much as you want."

Murray began to recite his key, all five pages of it, through the muffling hood.

Liam was fully clothed, no visual restraints. As Murray chafed feeling back into his hands and feet, Liam crossed the locked office with its grey in-dustrial carpeting and tossed him a set of khakis and a pair of boxers. Mur-ray dressed silently, then turned his accusing glare on Liam.

"How far did you get?"

"I didn't even make it out of the state. They caught me in Sebastopol, took me off the Greyhound in cuffs with six guns on me all the time."

"The disks?"

"They needed to be sure that you got rid of all the backups, that there wasn't anything stashed online or in a safe-deposit box, that they had the only copy. It was their idea."

"Did you really get shot?"

"I really got shot."

"I hope it really fucking hurt."

"It really fucking hurt."

"Well, good."

The door opened and Special Agent Fredericks appeared with a big brown bag of Frappuccinos and muffins. He passed them around.

"My people tell me that you write excellent documentation, Mr. Swain."

"What can I say? It's a gift."

"And they tell me that you two have written some remarkable code."

"Another gift."

"We always need good coders here."

"What's the job pay? How are the bennies? How much vacation?"

"As much as you want, excellent, as long as you want, provided we ap-prove the destinations first. Once you're cleared."

"It's not enough," Murray said, upending twenty ounces of West Coast frou-frou caffeine delivery system on the carpeting.

"Come on, Murray," Liam said. "Don't be that way."

Special Agent Fredericks fished in the bag and produced another nov-elty coffee beverage and handed it to Murray. "Make this one last, it's all that's left."

"With all due respect," Murray said, feeling a swell of righteousness in his chest, in his thighs, in his groin, "go fuck yourself. You don't 0wn me."

"They do, Murray. They 0wn both our asses," Liam said, staring into the puddle of coffee slurry on the carpet.

Murray crossed the room as fast as he could and smacked Liam, open palm, across the cheek.

"That will do," Special Agent Fredericks said, with surprising mildness.

"He needed smacking," Murray said, without rancor, and sat back down.

"Liam, why don't you wait for us in the hallway?"

"You came around," Liam said. "Everyone does. These guys 0wn."

"I didn't ask to share a room with you, Liam. I'm not glad I am. I'd rather not be reminded of that fact, so shut your fucking mouth before I shut it for you."

"What do you want, an apology? I'm sorry. I'm sorry I infected you, I'm sorry I helped them catch you. I'm sorry I fuxored your life. What can I say?"

"You can shut up anytime now."

"Well, this is going to be a *swell* living-arrangement."

The room was labeled "Officers' Quarters," and it had two good, firm queen-sized mattresses, premium cable, two identical stainless-steel dressers, and two good ergonomic chairs. There were junction boxes beside each desk with locked covers that Murray supposed housed Ethernet ports. All the comforts of home.

Murray lay on his bed and pulled the blankets over his head. Though he didn't need to sleep, he chose to.

For two weeks, Murray sat at his assigned desk, in his assigned cube, and zoned out on the screen-saver. He refused to touch the keyboard, refused to touch the mouse. Liam had the adjacent desk for a week, then they moved him to another office, so that Murray had solitude in which to contemplate the whirling star-field. He'd have a cup of coffee at 10:30 and started to feel a little sniffly in the back of his nose. He ate in the commissary at his own table. If anyone sat down at his table, he stood up and left. They didn't sit at his table. At 2PM, they'd send in a box of warm Krispy Kremes, and by 3PM, his blood-sugar would be crashing and he'd be sobbing over his key-board. He refused to adjust his serotonin levels.

On the third Monday, he turned up at his desk at 9AM as usual and found a clipboard on his chair with a ball-point tied to it.

Discharge papers. Non-disclosure agreements. Cross-your-heart swears on pain of death. A modest pension. Post-It "sign here" tabs had been stuck on here, here and here.

The junkie couldn't have been more than fifteen years old. She was death-camp skinny, tracked out, sitting cross-legged on a cardboard box on the sidewalk, sunning herself in the thin Mission noonlight. "Wanna buy a laptop? Two hundred bucks."

Murray stopped. "Where'd you get it?"

"I stole it," she said. "Out of a convertible. It looks real nice. One-fifty."

"Two hundred," Murray said. "But you've got to do me a favor."

"Three hundred, and you wear a condom."

"Not that kind of favor. You know the Radio Shack on Mission at 24th? Give them this parts list and come back here. Here's a $100 down-payment."

He kept his eyes peeled for the minders he'd occasionally spotted shadowing him when he went out for groceries, but they were nowhere to be seen. Maybe he'd lost them in the traffic on the 101. By the time the girl got back with the parts he'd need to make his interface, he was sweating bullets, but once he had the laptop open and began to rekey the entire codebase, the eidetic rush of perfect memory dispelled all his nervousness, leaving him cool and calm as the sun set over the Mission.

From the sky, Africa was green and lush, but once the plane touched down in Mogadishu, all Murray saw was sere brown plains and blowing dust. He sprang up from his seat, laundering the sleep toxins in his brain and the fatigue toxins in his legs and ass as he did.

He was the first off the jetway and the first at the Customs desk.

"Do you have any commercial or work-related goods, sir?"

"No sir," Murray said, willing himself calm.

"But you have a laptop computer," the Customs man said, eyeballing his case.

"Oh, yeah. That. Can't ever get away from work, you know how it is."

"I certainly hope you find time to relax, sir." The Customs man stamped the passport he'd bought in New York.

"When you love your work, it can be relaxing."

"Enjoy your stay in Somalia, sir."

We are indeed living in a media age, and those who are not aficionados of science fiction and fantasy mostly know of the genres through film and television. Many of the hottest, highest grossing films are genre related. Case in point is *The Lord of the Rings* film trilogy. (This year's Nebula Award winner for Best Script was *The Two Towers*.) Serious made-for-television films such as *Angels in America* and teenage television series such as *Charmed, Buffy the Vampire Slayer,* and spin-offs such as *Angel* have become as mainstream as *The Sopranos* and *Sex and the City*.

Even when SFWA was not awarding a Nebula in the category of film, as it does now, it has been traditional to include a survey of the year's most important science fiction and fantasy films in each volume.

Lucius Shepard, who is the film reviewer for *The Magazine of Fantasy & Science Fiction* and *ElectricStory,* analyses the genre films of 2003. Here is Shepard as his best: acerbic, funny, and brilliantly insightful.

Shepard has been called "an outrageously talented writer" by Iain Banks, "a dark genius" by Bob Shacochis, and "the rarest of writers, a true artist" by the *Washington Post*. Indeed, Shepard has produced brilliant work, which includes stories such as "R & R," "The Jaguar Hunter," "The Man Who Painted the Dragon Griaule," "Black Coral," "Beast of the Heartland," and "Shades." His novels include *Green Eyes, Life During Wartime, The Scalehunter's Beautiful Daughter, The Father of Stones, The Golden, The Last Time; A Handbook for American Prayer, Valentine,* and *Louisiana Breakdown;* and his short story collections include *The Jaguar Hunter, Kalimantan, The Ends of the Earth, Sports and Music,* and *Barnacle Bill the Spacer and Other Stories*. Shepard has won the Clarion Award, the Locus Award, the John W. Campbell Award for Best New Writer, the Science Fiction Chronicle Award, the World Fantasy Award, the Sturgeon Award, the Rhysling Award, the International Horror Guild Award, the Hugo Award, and the Nebula Award.

FILM: THE YEAR IN REVIEW

LUCIUS SHEPARD

If you went to the movies in 2003 looking for a formulaic science fiction or fantasy film with nary a whit of originality or panache, something bright and brainless to munch your popcorn by, then boy, were you in luck. Of the thirty-three genre films given a relatively wide release in the U.S. (including ten horror movies; six sequels; four comic book flicks; three remakes; a spattering of genre-ish comedies like *Bruce Almighty, The Haunted Mansion, Pirates of the Carribbean,* and *Elf;* the inescapable Stephen King adaptation; and a partridge in a pear tree), only a handful could be said to possess the least drop of entertainment value. *House of a Thousand Corpses, House of the Dead* (in case your taste for cadaverous real estate has not been assuaged by the previously listed movie), *Underworld, Gothika, Final Destination 2, Freddy vs. Jason, The Core, The Haunted Mansion, Jeepers Creepers 2,* and etc. It's a list that might well cause one to shudder, albeit not in fear, but rather in astonishment that so many tired concepts could have been greenlighted and thereafter executed with such appalling clumsiness. While sitting in a theater seat, waiting for one or another of these emblems of cultural decline to begin (and, God help me, I saw most of them), I found myself praying that the advertisements would never end, that instead of a movie, I would be exposed to two hours or thereabouts of anthropomorphic soft drinks and popcorn boxes with skinny legs and candy bars with lipstick mouths waltzing around, lip-synching inane jingles concerning the paradise of flavor that awaited me at the concession stand, because I suspected the dramatic potential therein would far outstrip that promised by *Dreamcatcher, The League of Extraordinary Gentlemen,* and their ilk.

I suppose that 2003 may be considered notable in cinematic history since it marked the conclusion (or, in two cases, the collapse) of three major genre film trilogies: *The Lord of the Rings, The Matrix,* and *The Terminator.* The third Terminator film, *Rise of the Machines,* featuring a female machine villain and once again starring the soon-to-be Governor of California, proved to be a by-the-numbers explosion-fest that moved as stiffly as did its titular figure, lumbering along on its predictable course like an ancient incontinent rhino looking for a place to do its business before fading into extinction, or, as the case may be, Republican politics. The *Matrix* trilogy, which started life as an idea for a comic book, was summed up in two 2003 films, *The Matrix: Reloaded* and *The Matrix: Revolutions,* the first of which was so stunningly inferior to the original, so full of self-congratulatory pomposity—this no doubt due to the ludicrous praise heaped upon its creators, the Wachowski Brothers—it caused people to stay away in droves from the third. What began as a surprisingly effective and innovative entertainment that somehow overcame the dimwitted presence of Keanu Reeves devolved in its sequels into—on one level—an exercise in marketing strategy and—on another—a video game larded with tendentious philosophizing that might have been better served by the title *The Passion of the Neo-Christ.* The final battle for the underground city of Zion was spectacular, but by the time it arrived, the audience generally felt toward the franchise as they would toward a game played too often, one whose gimmicks they either already knew or could anticipate.

Winner of eleven Oscars, including Best Picture and Best Director, *The Return of the King* was without question the most significant genre film of the year. Whether it was, indeed, the best film of the year will be impossible to determine until the extended version is released on DVD, for it's the twelve-hour-long rendering of Tolkien's seminal work that will be subject to the judgment of time, not the significantly shorter theatrical release. Whatever else may be said of *LotR,* the trilogy has gone into the culture, standing as an unparalleled technical achievement, and any criticism of the project will be seen as a paltry dust raised by its vast passage. Nevertheless, it should be mentioned that while the set pieces in the theatrical release of *The Return of the King* are beautifully realized, matters of character are either given short shrift or no shrift at all—and thus the overall effect upon the viewer is less that of a movie than of a tour through a Tolkien theme park. Instead of creating small moments that might have humanized the finale and made it seem less a highlight package of the novel, director Peter Jackson seems in a hurry to get from Frodo's encounter with Shelob to the next big wow, and the connective tissue for the most part consists of redundant scenes featuring snatches of Tolkien's signature faux-Shakespearean dialogue. When Legolas, for instance, standing on a battlement with Aragorn on the evening before they intend to engage the hosts of Mordor, is given to intone, "There is a sleepless malice in the West," the only appropriate response I could think of, considering the circumstance, was, "Wow!! You think?" That said, *The Return of the King* is hands-down the best high fantasy film ever made. Whether this makes it a great film or the winner of a beauty contest for hippos is, as mentioned, yet to be determined.

The best of the comic book adaptations, a serviceable *X-Men 2,* could not compensate for the abuses visited upon us by *Daredevil, The Hulk,* and Alan Moore's *League of Extraordinary Gentlemen,* this last being perhaps the most execrable movie in recent memory, featuring Sean Connery doing a fair-to-middling Sean Connery impression and some of the least convincing CGI ever. Based on Frank Miller's "Elektra Saga," one of the better comic book narratives of the 80s, *Daredevil* doesn't stand a chance in the incompetent hands of director Mark Steven Johnson. Johnson is Ed Wood with a budget and his looks-like-a-movie-but-isn't plays like an episode of *Celebrity Mismatch,* that show in which just for yucks we put together two Hollywood stars (Jennifer Garner and the less talented half of Bennifer*) and see how little chemistry they can generate while surrounded by pertinently placed popular brands of candy, soft drinks, and toothpaste. In sum, it's an idiotic, overstuffed jumble of story lines held together by vacuous characters and ineptly conceived scenes, all dressed up in the usual post-*Matrix* camera tricks and larded with spasmodic bouts of brainless violence and lapses into sophomoric humor.

While it might have been predicted that *Daredevil* would arrirve still-born, *Hulk* proved a major disappointment. Directed by Ang Lee (*Crouching Tiger, Hidden Dragon*) and starring Jennifer Connelly and Eric Bana, both quality actors, it seemed to promise a comic book adaptation done with panache and intelligence, something that we haven't seen since Tim Burton abandoned the Batman franchise. Lee did manage to do an excellent job of adapting the physical format of comics to a kinetic medium. Many of the scenes are enhanced by split-screen effects designed to give the frames the look of comic-book pages and these effects are themselves enhanced by a variety of digital zooms, wipes, and dissolves. Images are spun, split, letter-boxed, shunted to one side, etc., and the overall effect is like opening a comic book whose pages then come to life—though sometimes confusing, on the whole it's a stimulating and beautifully managed device. Unfortunately, Lee had no such empathy for the materials of the Hulk's story. While there is nothing intrinsically wrong in beginning an action picture with forty minutes of character development, if you're hoping to please an action audience—any audience, for that matter—you'd best make said development dramatic. The exchanges of dialogue between Bana and Connelly that dominate the first third of *Hulk* are marked by a flatness that makes the Mojave look like a mountain range. The interjection of a minor-league villain, a smarmy corporate pirate played with an Oil Can Harry-ish lack of shading by Josh Lucas, does absolutely nothing in the way of striking a spark, even though it's his unrelenting no-goodness that eventually pushes Bruce's badass button. By the time Bana morphed into the Grumpy

---

* Bennifer is what the tabloids call Ben Affleck and Jennifer Lopez.

Green Giant, I had begun to wonder whether Jennifer Connelly's moist-eyed somnolence was a directorial choice or the result of a mild flu; to hope that the mountain-bike-riding Bruce would hit the mother of all gopher holes, take a spill, and subsequently lay green-fisted waste to all the little forest creatures; and to speculate that Ang Lee had decided to do a Zen thing and film the first superhero movie in which the central figure was never seen.

Science fiction fared even worse than fantasy and comic book heroes in last year's films. Apart from the two *Matrix* movies, we had *The Core,* an on-the-cheap disaster movie in which a cast of indie actors—Stanley Tucci, Aaron Eckhardt, Hilary Swank—cram into what looks like a giant unlabeled Coke can and attempts to save humankind by seeding nuclear bombs throughout the earth's core. Kind of *Boys Don't Cry* meets *Armageddon.* Though it was amusing to watch these better-than-average attempts to establish character while enunciating snatches of ineptly written gearhead dialog, the only sensible reason to see *The Core* was if you were a critic or else chose a theater in which to hide from the police. Then there was *Paycheck,* yet another unimaginative adaptation of a Phillip K. Dick story concerned with the nature of memory, this one directed by the once-great-but-now-moribund John Woo and starring Jennifer's ex, Ben. Obviously expected to do big things, given a Christmas release, it keeled over and died at the box office, a fate it richly deserved. Lastly, there's that Stephen King adaptation, a tale of alien possession and invasion that plays like a season of abysmal *X-Files* episodes jammed into two hours plus, and essentially consists of action sequences larded with clumsy passages of exposition, a number of which entail various characters explaining things not to other people, but to themselves, and containing what seems like one those repackaged albums sold only at K-Mart, *King's Greatest Tropes.* You got your Native American magic (the dreamcatcher, a ritual object whose function is never satisfactorily explained); you got your telepathy; you got your aliens; you got your other aliens; you got your boyhood chums gifted with psychic powers granted them by a mentally challenged lad whom they rescued from bullies. Not in the least scary, it stands among the worst films ever made from King material, ranking a notch or two above abominations such as *Silver Bullet* and King's own directorial effort, *Maximum Overdrive.*

Implausible as it may seem, apart from the Tolkien trilogy, the year's more interesting genre films were horror movies (two falling into the sub-genre of comedy-horror). Though only *Bubba Ho-Tep* bore the stamp of originality as regards its materials, *28 Days Later, Pirates of the Caribbean,* and *Darkness* made their mark by either making gentle fun of genre tropes or lending them a contemporary gloss. Based on one of Joe Lansdale's trademark gonzo takes on Texican mythology, *Bubba Ho-tep* supposes that Elvis Presley (Bruce Campbell) did not die in a bathroom at Graceland, but lived on into his seventies and now survives in a seedy and abusively neglectful East Texas nursing home. Through flashbacks and a voiceover, we learn that years before, grown weary of fame, the real Elvis traded places with the world's best Elvis imitator. The two men wrote a contract establishing that the real Elvis could reclaim his rightful status whenever he wished, but when the contract was destroyed, Elvis became trapped in his new role. After his replacement's ignominious death, he makes his way through the world earning a livelihood by imitating himself until he breaks his hip in a fall from the stage. Now, afflicted with a penile cancer and forced to go about on a walker, paunchy, his trademark sideburns and pompadour gone gray, he divided his time between hobbling about the halls of the nursing home, clad in robe and pajamas, and watching his old movies. The other residents of the home are equally deracinated, living joylessly and without hope. Among them is one John F. Kennedy (Ossie Davis), who claims to be the former president of the United States transformed into an Afro-American by means of surgery and skin dye at the behest of his mortal enemy, Lyndon Baines Johnson. It appears that Elvis does not believe the old man is JFK, but he treats him with the respect due a president (that due a good one, at any rate), and this allows them to join forces against an Egyptian mummy (deposited in the area of the rest home thanks to a traffic accident) who writes hieroglyphic graffiti on bathroom stalls and sucks out the souls of the residents. As Elvis, Cambell gives an unexpectedly moving performance. Instead of delivering an impression of the septuagenarian Elvis, still sporting big hair and wraparound glasses, he offers a nicely observed portrait of a man who, though reduced by age and disappointment, is possessed by a shadow of the macho self-parodying persona he adopted along his road to fame and is intent upon reclaiming his dignity and pride.

The zombie flick, *28 Days Later,* directed by Danny Boyle, re-establishes the prime directive for horror movies, that they should be scary, a commandment that has fallen into neglect in Hollywood . . . or else screenwriters and directors there have forgotten how to construct suspense. Boyle's update of Romero's *Night of the Living Dead* tells the tale from the point of view of a London bike messenger who wakes from a 28-day-long coma to find the city apparently deserted, wreckage everywhere, newspapers lying about with the banner headlines that trumpet EVACUATION. Soon he learns that the population of the city has been infected with a kind of super-rabies (the Rage) and transformed into zombies, but not the torpid, sluggish zombies of the Romero film—these zombies are adrenalized, ultra-quick killers. Though the film plays out as one might expect (hardy bands of survivors, a journey across dangerous territory) and has a disappointing ending, its high-octane suspense is undeniable. A 2002 picture that saw light in the States last year, *Darkness,* starring Anna Paquin and Lena Olin, directed by Jaume Balagueró, who a couple of years previously gave us *Los Sin Nombre,* the excellent film version of Ramsey Campbell's *The Nameless,* is another in the recent series of outstanding dark suspense films to derive from Spain. It owes much to King's *The Shining,* but achieves its own identity thanks to Balagueró's slick direction and use of special effects, and—again—his ability to generate suspense. Gore Verbinski's remake of Japan's *The Ring,* although less sinister and suspenseful than the original, nevertheless provided a decent fright and was notable for Naomi Watts' solid performance. For a movie based on an amusement park ride, *Pirates of the Caribbean,* another type of zombie flick, entertains well enough and is noteworthy for Johnny Depp's performance as a less-than-macho pirate and clever direction by, again, Gore Verbinski. It's utterly forgettable and shallow, yet it's the sort of movie one is forced to grade on a curve due to low expectation. If you're in the mood for good-looking fluff, this fills the bill.

Though it was one of the less original of the recent spate of good Asian horror movies, *The Eye,* a Japanese film by the Pang Brothers, received a wide U.S. release. Despite being creepy and having good production values, the picture was weighted down by the staleness of its storyline—that of a girl who receives a corneal transplant and begins to see strange things. Among the most impressive of the Asian entries last year was Takeshi Kitano's *Zatoichi,* a film dealing with Japan's legendary blind swordsman and his assistance of two geishas in wreaking vengeance upon the murderers of their family. It's only marginally a genre picture (if you really stretch the margins), but by examining the connection between the sounds of the world and the workings of Zatoichi's consciousness, Kitano achieves a feeling such as is evoked by the best fantasy, making it seem that we are channeling an inhuman—or ultrahuman—presence, an effect enhanced by Keiichi Suzuki's trancey, tribal music.

Equally impressive, yet completely different in feeling, is Takashi Miike's *Gozu (Audition),* a movie occupying a position in the cinematic landscape that might be described as post-Lynchian—it throws a young low-level yakuza, Minami, into conflict with a group of peculiar suburb-dwellers and a cow-headed demon (Gozu himself). As the movie begins, Minami is directed by the gang boss to kill his immediate superior, Ozaki, who has been behaving erratically, the inciting incident being his announcement that a chihuahua has been sent to murder them all. Though he's not eager to kill his friend and mentor, Minami is on his way to carry out the order, with Ozaki in the back seat, when he slams on the brakes and accidentally breaks Ozaki's neck. Soon thereafter the body disappears from the car and Minami becomes stranded in a suburb among a group of people who appear to be insane, including an American sake vendor who reads his lines from cue cards, a transvestite shop owner, and an autistic innkeeper and his lactating daughter. Before long, a beautiful woman emerges from the back seat of Minami's car—she appears to know secrets about Minami that he has only confided to Ozaki. From this point on, the film descends more deeply into the grotesque and, perhaps, into Minami's subconscious, a journey that proves in turn disturbing and hilarious. The movie is difficult to categorize, but if you considered *Twin Peaks* to have genre elements, then *Gozu* should satisfy your definition of dark fantasy.

Films like *Jeepers Creepers 2* (so much worse than its pedestrian original, it should have been called *Jeepers*), *Freddy vs. Jason,* the remakes of *Willard* and *The Texas Chainsaw Massacre,* and the rest of the 2003 list barely deserve mention here, let alone even a cursory examination. *Underworld,* purporting to be a story about an eternal war between werewolves and vampires, but primarily devoted to the display of fun leathers, more fashion statement than movie, merits notice simply because of its awfulness; and *Gothika,* in which a psychiatrist wakes to find herself committed to a haunted asylum, proved that winning an Oscar has done little for Halle Berry's career. It was, as stated, a very bad year. As the millennium begins, it's clear that worn-out stories with increasingly ridiculous pyrotechnics and CGI effects constitute Hollywood's notion of what makes a good genre film, and that the cutting edge of the genre can be found in Europe and Asia. It is to be hoped that Hollywood will expand its conception of science fiction to include other than disasters, monsters, and Phillip K. Dick–related material, and that instead of remaking foreign dark suspense films, the studios will seek to reinvigorate the creative process with a few fresh ideas of their own. We dare not hope for this too much, but early signs are promising as to the quality of upcoming domestic genre films and it's already apparent that 2004 will be a better year than 2003. Sad to say, it could scarcely be worse.

Eleanor Arnason has been called "one of the often-unsung Grand Dames of Feminist Science Fiction." She is the author of five published novels and many poems and short stories. She has received both the James Tiptree, Jr. award for "gender-bending SF" and the Mythopoeic Society's Mythopoeic Fantasy Award for the novel *A Woman of the Iron People,* as well as the Minnesota Book Award for *Ring of Swords.* Her earlier novels are *The Sword Smith, To the Resurrection Station,* and *Daughter of the Bear King.* Her short stories have appeared in *Orbit, New Improved Sun, Tales of the Unanticipated, Xanadu, A Room of One's Own, New Women of Wonder, The Norton Book of SF,* and other places.

KNAPSACK POEMS

ELEANOR ARNASON

Within this person of eight bodies, thirty-two eyes, and the usual number of orifices and limbs, resides a spirit as restless as gossamer on wind. In youth, I dreamed of fame as a merchant-traveler. In later years, realizing that many of my parts were prone to motion sickness, I thought of scholarship or accounting. But I lacked the Great Determination that is necessary for both trades. My abilities are spontaneous and brief, flaring and vanishing like a falling star. For me to spend my life adding numbers or looking through dusty documents would be like "lighting a great hall with a single lantern bug" or "watering a great garden with a drop of dew."

Finally, after consulting the care-givers in my crèche, I decided to become a traveling poet. It's a strenuous living and does not pay well, but it suits me.

Climbing through the mountains west of Ibri, I heard a *wishik* call, then saw the animal, its wings like white petals, perched on a bare branch.

> "Is that tree flowering
> So late in autumn?
> Ridiculous idea!
> I long for dinner."

One of my bodies recited the poem. Another wrote it down, while still others ranged ahead, looking for signs of habitation. As a precaution, I carried cudgels as well as pens and paper. One can never be sure what will appear in the country west of Ibri. The great poet Raging Fountain died there of a combination of diarrhea and malicious ghosts. Other writers, hardly less famous, have been killed by monsters or bandits, or, surviving these, met their end at the hands of dissatisfied patrons.

The Bane of Poets died before my birth. Its[1] ghost or ghosts offered

Raging Fountain the fatal bowl of porridge. But other patrons still remain "on steep slopes and in stony dales."

> "Dire the telling
> Of patrons in Ibri:
> Bone-breaker lurks
> High on a mountain.
> Skull-smasher waits
> In a shadowy valley.
> Better than these
> The country has only
> Grasper, Bad-bargain,
> And Hoarder-of-Food."

Why go to such a place, you may be wondering? Beyond Ibri's spiny mountains lie the wide fields of Greater and Lesser Ib, prosperous lands well-known for patronage of the arts.

Late in the afternoon, I realized I would find no refuge for the night. Dark snow-clouds hid the hills in front of me. Behind me, low in the south, the sun shed pale light. My shadows, long and many-limbed, danced ahead of me on the rutted road.

My most poetic self spoke:

> "The north is blocked
> By clouds like boulders.
> A winter sun
> Casts shadows in my way."

Several of my other selves frowned. My scribe wrote the poem down with evident reluctance.

"Too obvious," muttered a cudgel-carrier.

Another self agreed. "Too much like Raging Fountain in his/her mode of melancholy complaint."

Far ahead, a part of me cried alarm. I suspended the critical discussion and hurried forward in a clump, my clubs raised and ready for use.

Soon, not even breathless, I stopped at a place I knew by reputation: the Tooth River. Wide and shallow, it ran around pointed stones, well-exposed

---

[1]Goxhat units, or "persons" as the goxhat say, comprise four to sixteen bodies and two or three sexes. The Bane of Poets was unusual in being entirely neuter, which meant it could not reproduce. According to legend, it was reproductive frustration and fear of death that made The Bane so dangerous to poets.

Why poets? They produce two kinds of children, those of body and those of mind, and grasp in their pincers the gift of undying fame.

this time of year and as sharp as the teeth of predators. On the far side of the river were bare slopes that led toward cloudy mountains. On the near side of the river, low cliffs cast their shadows over a broad shore. My best scout was there, next to a bundle of cloth. The scout glanced up, saw the rest of me, and—with deft fingers—undid the blanket folds.

Two tiny forms lay curled at the blanket's center. A child of one year, holding itself in its arms.

"Alive?" I asked myself.

The scout crouched closer. "One body is and looks robust. The other body—" my scout touched it gently "—is cold."

Standing among myself, I groaned and sighed. There was no problem understanding what had happened. A person had given birth. Either the child had been unusually small, or the other parts had died. For some reason, the parent had been traveling alone. Maybe he/she/it had been a petty merchant or a farmer driven off the land by poverty. If not these, then a wandering thief or someone outlawed for heinous crimes. A person with few resources. In any case, he/she/it had carried the child to this bitter place, where the child's next-to-last part expired.

Imagine standing on the river's icy edge, holding a child who had become a single body. The parent could not bear to raise an infant so incomplete! What parent could? One did no kindness by raising such a cripple to be a monster among ordinary people.

Setting the painful burden down, the parent crossed the river.

I groaned a second time. My most poetic self said:

"Two bodies are not enough;
One body is nothing."

The rest of me hummed agreement. The poet added a second piece of ancient wisdom:

"Live in a group
Or die."

I hummed a second time.

The scout lifted the child from its blanket. "It's female."

The baby woke and cried, waving her four arms, kicking her four legs, and urinating. My scout held her as far away as possible. Beyond doubt, she was a fine, loud, active mite! But incomplete. "Why did you wake her?" asked a cudgel-carrier. "She should be left to die in peace."

"No," said the scout. "She will come with me."

"Me! What do you mean by me?" my other parts cried.

There is neither art nor wisdom in a noisy argument. Therefore, I will not describe the discussion that followed as night fell. Snowflakes drifted from the sky—slowly at first, then more and more thickly. I spoke with the rudeness people reserve for themselves in privacy; and the answers I gave myself were sharp indeed. Words like pointed stones, like the boulders in Tooth River, flew back and forth. Ah! The wounds I inflicted and suffered! Is anything worse than internal dispute?

The scout would not back down. She had fallen in love with the baby, as defective as it was. The cudgel-bearers, sturdy males, were outraged. The poet and the scribe, refined neuters, were repulsed. The rest of me was female and a bit more tender.

I had reached the age when fertile eggs were increasingly unlikely. In spite of my best efforts, I had gained neither fame nor money. What respectable goxhat would mate with a vagabond like me? What crèche would offer to care for my offspring? Surely this fragment of a child was better than nothing.

"No!" said my males and neuters. "This is not a person! One body alone can never know togetherness or integration!"

But my female selves edged slowly toward the scout's opinion. Defective the child certainly was. Still, she was alive and goxhat, her darling little limbs waving fiercely and her darling mouth making noises that would shame a monster.

Most likely, she would die. The rest of her had. Better that she die in someone's arms, warm and comfortable, than in the toothy mouth of a prowling predator. The scout rewrapped the child in the blanket.

It was too late to ford the river. I made camp under a cliff, huddling together for warmth, my arms around myself, the baby in the middle of the heap I made.

When morning came, the sky was clear. Snow sparkled everywhere. I rose, brushed myself off, gathered my gear, and crossed the river. The water was low, as I expected this time of year, but ice-cold. My feet were numb by the time I reached the far side. My teeth chattered on every side like castanets. The baby, awakened by the noise, began to cry. The scout gave her a sweet cake. That stopped the crying for a while.

At mid-day, I came in sight of a keep. My hearts lifted with hope. Alas! Approaching it, I saw the walls were broken.

The ruination was recent. I walked through one of the gaps and found a courtyard, full of snowy heaps. My scouts spread out and investigated. The snow hid bodies, as I expected. Their eyes were gone, but most of the rest remained, preserved by cold and the season's lack of bugs.

"This happened a day or two ago," my scouts said. "Before the last snow, but not by much. *Wishik* found them and took what they could, but didn't have time—before the storm—to find other predators and lead them here. This is why the bodies are still intact. The *wishik* can pluck out eyes, but skin is too thick for them to penetrate. They need the help of other animals, such as *hirg*." One of the scouts crouched by a body and brushed its rusty back hair. "I won't be able to bury these. There are too many."

"How many goxhat are here?" asked my scribe, taking notes.

"It's difficult to say for certain. Three or four, I suspect, all good-sized. A parent and children would be my guess."

I entered the keep building and found more bodies. Not many. Most of the inhabitants had fallen in the courtyard. There was a nursery with scattered toys, but no children.

"Ah! Ah!" I cried, reflecting on the briefness of life and the frequency with which one encounters violence and sorrow.

My poet said:

> "Broken halls
> and scattered wooden words.
> How will the children
> learn to read and write?"[2]

Finally I found a room with no bodies or toys, nothing to remind me of mortality. I lit a fire and settled for the night. The baby fussed. My scout cleaned her, then held her against a nursing bud—for comfort only; the scout had no milk. The baby sucked. I ate my meager rations. Darkness fell. My thirty-two eyes reflected firelight. After a while, a ghost arrived. Glancing up, I saw it in the doorway. It looked quite ordinary: three goxhat bodies with rusty hair.

"Who are you?" one of my scouts asked.

"The former owner of this keep, or parts of her. My name was Content-in-Solitude; and I lived here with three children, all lusty and numerous.—Don't worry."

My cudgel-carriers had risen, cudgels in hand.

"I'm a good ghost. I'm still in this world because my death was so recent and traumatic. As soon as I've gathered myself together, and my children have done the same, we'll be off to a better place.[3]

"I stopped here to tell you our names, so they will be remembered."

---

[2]This translation is approximate. Like humans, goxhat use wooden blocks to teach their children writing. However, their languages are ideogrammic, and the blocks are inscribed with entire words. Their children build sentences shaped like walls, towers, barns and other buildings. Another translation of the poem would be:

> Broken walls.
> Broken sentences.
> Ignorant offspring.
> Alas!

[3] According to the goxhat, when a person dies, his/her/its goodness becomes a single ghost known as "The Harmonious Breath" or "The Collective Spirit." This departs the world for a better place. But a person's badness remains as a turbulent and malicious mob, attacking itself and anyone else who happens along.

"Content-in-Solitude," muttered my scribe, writing.

"My children were Virtue, Vigor, and Ferric Oxide. Fine offspring! They should have outlived me. Our killer is Bent Foot, a bandit in these mountains. He took my grandchildren to raise as his own, since his female parts—all dead now—produced nothing satisfactory. Mutant children with twisted feet and nasty dispositions! No good will come of them; and their ghosts will make these mountains worse than ever. Tell my story, so others may be warned."

"Yes," my poet said in agreement. The rest of me hummed.

For a moment, the three bodies remained in the doorway. Then they drew together and merged into one. "You see! It's happening! I am becoming a single ghost! Well, then. I'd better be off to find the rest of me, and my children, and a better home for all of us."

The rest of the night was uneventful. I slept well, gathered around the fire, warmed by its embers and my bodies' heat. If I had dreams, I don't remember them. At dawn, I woke. By sunrise, I was ready to leave. Going out of the building, I discovered three *hirg* in the courtyard: huge predators with shaggy, dull-brown fur. *Wishik* fluttered around them as they tore into the bodies of Content and her children. I took one look, then retreated, leaving the keep by another route.

That day passed in quiet travel. My poet spoke no poetry. The rest of me was equally silent, brooding on the ruined keep and its ghost.

I found no keep to shelter me that night or the next or the next. Instead, I camped out. My scout fed the baby on thin porridge. It ate and kept the food down, but was becoming increasingly fretful and would not sleep unless the scout held it to a nursing bud. Sucking on the dry knob of flesh, it fell asleep.

"I don't mind," said the scout. "Though I'm beginning to worry. The child needs proper food."

"Better to leave it by the way," a male said. "Death by cold isn't a bad ending."

"Nor death by dehydration," my other male added.

The scout looked stubborn and held the child close.

Four days after I left the ruined keep, I came to another building, this one solid and undamaged.

My scribe said, "I know the lord here by reputation. She is entirely female and friendly to the womanly aspects of a person. The neuter parts she tolerates. But she doesn't like males. Her name is The Testicle Straightener."

My cudgel-carriers shuddered. The scribe and poet looked aloof, as they inevitably did in such situations. Clear-eyed and rational, free from sexual urges, they found the rest of me a bit odd.

The scout carrying the baby said, "The child needs good food and warmth and a bath. For that matter, so do I."

Gathering myself together, I strode to the gate and knocked. After several moments, it swung open. Soldiers looked out. There were two of them: one tall and grey, the other squat and brown. Their bodies filled the entrance, holding spears and axes. Their eyes gleamed green and yellow.

"I am a wandering poet, seeking shelter for the night. I bring news from the south, which your lord might find useful."

The eyes peered closely, then the soldiers parted—grey to the left, brown to the right—and let me in.

Beyond the gate was a snowy courtyard. This one held no bodies. Instead, the snow was trampled and urine-marked. A living place! Though empty at the moment, except for the two soldiers who guarded the gate.

I waited in an anxious cluster. At length, a servant arrived and looked me over. "You need a bath and clean clothes. Our lord is fastidious and dislikes guests who stink. Come with me."

I followed the servant into the keep and down a flight of stairs. Metal lamps were fastened to the walls. Most were dark, but a few shone, casting a dim light. The servant had three sturdy bodies, all covered with black hair.

Down and down. The air grew warm and moist. A faint, distinctive aroma filled it.

"There are hot springs in this part of Ibri," the servant said. "This keep was built on top of one; and there is a pool in the basement, which always steams and smells."

Now I recognized the aroma: rotten eggs.

We came to a large room, paved with stone and covered by a broad, barrel vault. Metal lanterns hung from the ceiling on chains. As was the case with the lamps on the stairway, most were dark. But a few flickered dimly. I could see the bathing pool: round and carved from bedrock. Steps went down into it. Wisps of steam rose.

"Undress," said the servant. "I'll bring soap and towels."

I complied eagerly. Only my scout hesitated, holding the baby.

"I'll help you with the mite," said my scribe, standing knee-deep in hot water.

The scout handed the baby over and undressed.

Soon I was frolicking in the pool, diving and spouting. Cries of joy rang in the damp, warm room. Is anything better than a hot bath after a journey?

The scout took the baby back and moved to the far side of the pool. When the servant returned, the scout sank down, holding the baby closely, hiding it in shadow. Wise mite, it did not cry!

The rest of me got busy, scrubbing shoulders and backs. Ah, the pleasure of warm lather!

Now and then, I gave a little yip of happiness. The servant watched with satisfaction, his/her/its arms piled high with towels.

On the far side of the pool, my best scout crouched, nursing the babe on a dry bud and watching the servant with hooded eyes.

At last, I climbed out, dried off, and dressed. In the confusion—there was a lot of me—the scout managed to keep the baby concealed. Why, I did not know, but the scout was prudent and usually had a good reason for every action, though parts of me still doubted the wisdom of keeping the baby. There would be time to talk all of this over, when the servant was gone.

He/she/it led me up a new set of stairs. The climb was long. The servant entertained me with the following story.

The keep had a pulley system, which had been built by an ingenious traveling plumber. This lifted buckets of hot water from the spring to a tank on top of the keep. From there the water descended through metal pipes, carried by the downward propensity that is innate in water. The pipes heated every room.

"What powers the pulley system?" my scribe asked, notebook in hand.

"A treadmill," said the servant.

"And what powers the treadmill?"

"Criminals and other people who have offended the lord. No keep in Ibri is more comfortable," the servant continued with pride. "This is what happens when a lord is largely or entirely female. As the old proverb says, male bodies give a person forcefulness. Neuter bodies give thoughtfulness and clarity of vision. But nurture and comfort come from a person's female selves."

Maybe, I thought. But were the people in the treadmill comfortable?

The servant continued the story. The plumber had gone east to Ib and built other heated buildings: palaces, public baths, hotels, hospitals, and crèches. In payment for this work, several of the local lords mated with the plumber; and the local crèches vied to raise the plumber's children, who were numerous and healthy.

"A fine story, with a happy ending," I said, thinking of my fragment of a child, nursing on the scout's dry bud. Envy, the curse of all artists and artisans, roiled in my hearts. Why had I never won the right to lay fertile eggs? Why were my purses empty? Why did I have to struggle to protect my testes and to stay off treadmills, while this plumber—surely not a better person than I—enjoyed fame, honor, and fertility?

The guest room was large and handsome, with a modern wonder next to it: a defecating closet. Inside the closet, water came from the wall in two metal pipes, which ended in faucets. "Hot and cold," said the servant, pointing. Below the faucets was a metal basin, decorated with reliefs of frolicking goxhat. Two empty buckets stood next to the basin.

The servant said, "If you need to wash something, your hands or feet or any other part, fill the basin with water. Use the buckets to empty the basin; and after you use the defecating throne, empty the buckets down it. This reduces the smell and gets rid of the dirty water. As I said, our lord is fastidious; and we have learned from her example. The plumber helped, by providing us with so much water.

"I'll wait in the hall. When you're ready to meet the lord, I'll guide you to her."

"Thank you," said my scribe, always courteous.

I changed into clean clothing, the last I had, and put bardic crowns on my heads[4]. Each crown came from a different contest, though all were minor. I had never won a really big contest. Woven of fine wool, with brightly colored tassels hanging down, the crowns gave me an appearance of dignity. My nimble-fingered scouts unpacked my instruments: a set of chimes, a pair of castanets and a bagpipe. Now I was ready to meet the lord.

All except my best scout, who climbed into the middle of a wide soft bed, child in arms.

"Why did you hide the mite?" asked my scholar.

"This keep seems full of rigid thinkers, overly satisfied with themselves and their behavior. If they saw the child they would demand an explanation. 'Why do you keep it? Can't you see how fragmentary it is? Can't you see that it's barely alive? Don't you know how to cut your losses?' I don't want to argue or explain."

"What is meant by 'I'?" my male parts asked. "What is meant by 'you'?"

"This is no time for an argument," said the poet.

All of me except the scout went to meet the keep's famous lord.

The Straightener sat at one end of a large hall: an elderly goxhat with frosted hair. Four parts of her remained, all sturdy, though missing a few pieces here and there: a foot, a hand, an eye or finger. Along the edges of the hall sat her retainers on long benches: powerful males, females, and neuters, adorned with iron and gold.

"Great your fame,
Gold-despoiler,
Bold straightener of scrota,
Wise lord of Ibri.

"Hearing of it,
I've crossed high mountains,
Anxious to praise
Your princely virtues."

My poet stopped. Straightener leaned forward. "Well? Go on! I want to hear about my princely virtues."

---

[4] Actually, cerebral bulges. The goxhat don't have heads as humans understand the word.

"Give me a day to speak with your retainers and get exact details of your many achievements," the poet said. "Then I will be able to praise you properly."

The goxhat leaned back. "Never heard of me, have you? Drat! I was hoping for undying fame."

"I will give it to you," my poet said calmly.

"Very well," the lord said. "I'll give you a day, and if I like what you compose, I'll leave your male parts alone."

All of me thanked her. Then I told the hall about my stay at the ruined keep. The retainers listened intently. When I had finished, the lord said, "My long-time neighbor! Dead by murder! Well, death comes to all of us. When I was born, I had twenty parts. A truly large number! That is what I'm famous for, as well as my dislike of men, which is mere envy. My male bodies died in childhood, and my neuter parts did not survive early adulthood. By thirty, I was down to ten bodies, all female. The neuters were not much of a loss. Supercilious twits, I always thought. But I miss my male parts. They were so feisty and full of piss! When travelers come here, I set them difficult tasks. If they fail, I have my soldiers hold them, while I unfold their delicate, coiled testicles. No permanent damage is done, but the screaming makes me briefly happy."

My male bodies looked uneasy and shifted back and forth on their feet, as if ready to run. But the two neuters remained calm. My poet thanked the lord a second time, sounding confident. Then I split up and went in all directions through the hall, seeking information.

The drinking went on till dawn, and the lord's retainers were happy to tell me stories about the Straightener. She had a female love of comfort and fondness for children, but could not be called tender in any other way. Rather, she was a fierce leader in battle and a strict ruler, as exact as a balance or a straight-edge.

"She'll lead us against Bent Foot," one drunk soldier said. "We'll kill him and bring the children here. The stolen children, at least. I don't know about Bent Foot's spawn. It might be better for them to die. Not my problem. I let the lord make all the decisions, except whether or not I'm going to fart."

Finally, I went up to my room. My scout lay asleep, the baby in her arms. My male parts began to pace nervously. The rest of me settled to compose a poem.

As the sky brightened, the world outside began to wake and make noise. Most of the noise could be ignored, but there was a *wishik* under the eaves directly outside my room's window. Its shrill, repeating cry drove my poet to distraction. I could not concentrate on the poem.

Desperate, I threw things at the animal: buttons from my sewing kit, spare pens, an antique paperweight I found in the room. Nothing worked.

The *wishik* fluttered away briefly, then returned and resumed its irritating cry.

At last my scout woke. I explained the problem. She nodded and listened to the *wishik* for a while. Then she fastened a string to an arrow and shot the arrow out the window. It hit the *wishik*. The animal gave a final cry. Grabbing the string, my scout pulled the beast inside.

"Why did I do that?" I asked.

"Because I didn't want the body to fall in the courtyard."

"Why not?"

Before she could answer, the body at her feet expanded and changed its shape. Instead of the body of a dead *wishik,* I saw a grey goxhat body, pierced by the scout's arrow, dead.

My males swore. The rest of me exclaimed in surprise.

My scout said, "This is part of a wizard, no doubt employed by the keep's lord, who must really want to unroll my testicles, since she is willing to be unfair and play tricks. The *wishik* cry was magical, designed to bother me so much than I could not concentrate on my composition. If this body had fallen to the ground, the rest of the wizard would have seen it and known the trick had failed. As things are, I may have time to finish the poem." The scout looked at the rest of me severely. "Get to work."

My poet went back to composing, my scribe to writing. The poem went smoothly now. As the stanzas grew in number, I grew increasingly happy and pleased. Soon I noticed the pleasure was sexual. This sometimes happened, though usually when a poem was erotic. The god of poetry and the god of sex are siblings, though they share only one parent, who is called the All-Mother-Father.

Even though the poem was not erotic, my male and female parts became increasingly excited. Ah! I was rubbing against myself. Ah! I was making soft noises! The poet and scribe could not feel this sexual pleasure, of course, but the sight of the rest of me tumbling on the rug was distracting. Yes, neuters are clear-eyed and rational, but they are also curious; and nothing arouses their curiosity more than sex. They stopped working on the poem and watched as I fondled myself.[5]

Only the scout remained detached from sensuality and went into the defecating closet. Coming out with a bucket of cold water, the scout poured it over my amorous bodies.

I sprang apart, yelling with shock.

"This is more magic," the scout said. "I did not know a spell inciting lust could be worked at such a distance, but evidently it can. Every part of me that is male or female, go in the bathroom! Wash in cold water till the

---

[5] The goxhat believe masturbation is natural and ordinary. But reproduction within a person—inbreeding, as they call it—is unnatural and a horrible disgrace. It rarely happens. Most goxhat are not intrafertile, for reasons too complicated to explain here.

idea of sex becomes uninteresting! As for my neuter parts—" The scout glared. "Get back to the poem!"

"Why has one part of me escaped the spell?" I asked the scout.

"I did not think I could lactate without laying an egg first, but the child's attempts to nurse have caused my body to produce milk. As a rule, nursing mothers are not interested in sex, and this has proved true of me. Because of this, and the child's stubborn nursing, there is a chance of finishing the poem. I owe this child a debt of gratitude."

"Maybe," grumbled my male parts. The poet and scribe said, "I shall see."

The poem was done by sunset. That evening I recited it in the lord's hall. If I do say so myself, it was a splendid achievement. The *wishik's* cry was in it, as was the rocking up-and-down rhythm of a sexually excited goxhat. The second gave the poem energy and an emphatic beat. As for the first, every line ended with one of the two sounds in the *wishik's* ever-repeating, irritating cry. Nowadays, we call this repetition of sound "rhyming." But it had no name when I invented it.

When I was done, the lord ordered several retainers to memorize the poem. "I want to hear it over and over," she said. "What a splendid idea it is to make words ring against each other in this fashion! How striking the sound! How memorable! Between you and the traveling plumber, I will certainly be famous."

That night was spent like the first one, everyone except me feasting. I feigned indigestion and poured my drinks on the floor under the feasting table. The lord was tricky and liked winning. Who could say what she might order put in my cup or bowl, now that she had my poem?

When the last retainer fell over and began to snore, I got up and walked to the hall's main door. Sometime in the next day or so, the lord would discover that her wizard had lost a part to death and that one of her paperweights was missing. I did not want to be around when these discoveries were made.

Standing in the doorway, I considered looking for the treadmill. Maybe I could free the prisoners. They might be travelers like me, innocent victims of the lord's malice and envy and her desire for hot water on every floor. But there were likely to be guards around the treadmill, and the guards might be sober. I was only one goxhat. I could not save everyone. And the servant had said they were criminals.

I climbed the stairs quietly, gathered my belongings and the baby, and left through a window down a rope made of knotted sheets.

The sky was clear; the brilliant star we call Beacon stood above the high peaks, shedding so much light I had no trouble seeing my way. I set a rapid pace eastward. Toward morning, clouds moved in. The Beacon vanished. Snow began to fall, concealing my trail. The baby, nursing on the scout, made happy noises.

. . .

Two days later, I was out of the mountains, camped in a forest by an unfrozen stream. Water made a gentle sound, purling over pebbles. The trees on the banks were changers, a local variety that is blue in summer and yellow in winter. At the moment, their leaves were thick with snow. "Silver and gold," my poet murmured, looking up.

The scribe made a note.

A *wishik* clung to a branch above the poet and licked its wings. Whenever it shifted position, snow came down.

> "The *wishik* cleans wings
> As white as snow.
> Snow falls on me, white
> As a *wishik*,"

the poet said.

My scribe scribbled.

One of my cudgel-carriers began the discussion. "The Bane of Poets was entirely neuter. Fear of death made it crazy. Bent Foot was entirely male. Giving in to violence, he stole children from his neighbor. The last lord I encountered, the ruler of the heated keep, was female, malicious and unfair. Surely something can be learned from these encounters. A person should not be one sex entirely, but rather—as I am—a harmonious mixture of male, female, and neuter. But this child can't help but be a single sex."

"I owe the child a debt of gratitude," said my best scout firmly. "Without her, I would have had pain and humiliation, when the lord—a kind of lunatic—unrolled my testes, as she clearly planned to do. At best, I would have limped away from the keep in pain. At worst, I might have ended in the lord's treadmill, raising water from the depths to make her comfortable."

"The question is a good one," said my scribe. "How can a person who is only one sex avoid becoming a monster? The best combination is the one I have: male, female, and both kinds of neuter. But even two sexes provide a balance."

"Other people—besides these three—have consisted of one sex," my scout said stubbornly. "Not all became monsters. It isn't sex that has influenced these lords, but the stony fields and spiny mountains of Ibri, the land's cold winters and ferocious wildlife. My various parts can teach the child my different qualities: the valor of the cudgel-carriers, the coolness of poet and scribe, the female tenderness that the rest of me has. Then she will become a single harmony."

The scout paused. The rest of me looked dubious. The scout continued. "Many people lose parts of themselves through illness, accident, and war; and some of these live for years in a reduced condition. Yes, it's sad and disturbing, but it can't be called unnatural. Consider aging and the end of life. The old die body by body, till a single body remains. Granted, in many cases, the final body dies quickly. But not always. Every town of good size has a Gram or Gaffer who hobbles around in a single self.

"I will not give up an infant I have nursed with my own milk. Do I wish to be known as ungrateful or callous? I, who have pinned all my hope on honor and fame?"

I looked at myself with uncertain expressions. The *wishik* shook down more snow.

"Well, then," said my poet, who began to look preoccupied. Another poem coming, most likely. "I will take the child to a crèche and leave her there."

My scout scowled. "How well will she be cared for there, among healthy children, by tenders who are almost certain to be prejudiced against a mite so partial and incomplete? I will not give her up."

"Think of how much I travel," a cudgel-carrier said. "How can I take a child on my journeys?"

"Carefully and tenderly," the scout replied. "The way my ancestors who were nomads did. Remember the old stories! When they traveled, they took everything, even the washing pot. Surely their children were not left behind."

"I have bonded excessively to this child," said my scribe to the scout.

"Yes, I have. It's done and can't be undone. I love her soft baby-down, her four blue eyes, her feisty spirit. I will not give her up."

I conversed this way for some time. I didn't become angry at myself, maybe because I had been through so much danger recently. There is nothing like serious fear to put life into perspective. Now and then, when the conversation became especially difficult, a part of me got up and went into the darkness to kick the snow or to piss. When the part came back, he or she or it seemed better.

Finally I came to an agreement. I would keep the child and carry it on my journeys, though half of me remained unhappy with this decision.

How difficult it is to be of two minds! Still, it happens; and all but the insane survive such divisions. Only they forget the essential unity that underlies differences of opinion. Only they begin to believe in individuality.

The next morning, I continued into Ib.

The poem I composed for the lord of the warm keep became famous. Its form, known as "ringing praise," was taken up by other poets. From it, I gained some fame, enough to quiet my envy; and the fame led to some money, which provided for my later years.

Did I ever return to Ibri? No. The land was too bitter and dangerous;

and I didn't want to meet the lord of the warm keep a second time. Instead, I settled in Lesser Ib, buying a house on a bank of a river named It–Could–Be–Worse. This turned out to be an auspicious name. The house was cozy and my neighbors pleasant. The child played in my fenced-in garden, tended by my female parts. As for my neighbors, they watched with interest and refrained from mentioning the child's obvious disability.

> "Lip-presser on one side.
> Tongue-biter on t'other.
> Happy I live,
> Praising good neighbors."

I traveled less than previously, because of the child and increasing age. But I did make the festivals in Greater and Lesser Ib. This was easy traveling on level roads across wide plains. The Ibian lords, though sometimes eccentric, were nowhere near as crazy as the ones in Ibri and no danger to me or other poets. At one of the festivals, I met the famous plumber, who turned out to be a large and handsome, male and neuter goxhat. I won the festival crown for poetry, and he/it won the crown for ingenuity. Celebrating with egg wine, we became amorous and fell into each other's many arms.

It was a fine romance and ended without regret, as did all my other romances. As a group, we goxhat are happiest with ourselves. In addition, I could not forget the prisoners in the treadmill. Whether the plumber planned it or not, he/it had caused pain for others. Surely it was wrong—unjust—for some to toil in darkness, so that others had a warm bed and hot water from a pipe?

I have to say, at times I dreamed of that keep: the warm halls, the pipes of water, the heated bathing pool and the defecating throne that had—have I forgotten to mention this?—a padded seat.

> "Better to be here
> In my cozy cottage.
> Some comforts
> Have too high a cost."

I never laid any fertile eggs. My only child is Ap the Foundling, who is also known as Ap of One Body and Ap the Many-talented. As the last nickname suggests, the mite turned out well.

As for me, I became known as The Clanger and The *Wishit,* because of my famous rhyming poem. Other names were given to me as well: The Child Collector, The Nurturer, and The Poet Who Is Odd.

Bestselling author Neil Gaiman was the creator and writer of the monthly cult DC Comics horror-weird series, *Sandman,* which *The LA Times* described as "The greatest epic in the history of comic books" and "the best monthly comic book in the world." *Sandman #19* won the World Fantasy Award for best short story, making it the first comic ever to be awarded a literary award. His other graphic novels include *Death: The Time of Your Life, Mr. Punch, Alice Cooper's The Last Temptation, Violent Cases,* and *Black Orchid*.

His novels include *Good Omens* (with Terry Pratchett), *Signals to Noise* (with Dave McKean), *Neverwhere, The Day I Swapped My Dad for Two Goldfish* (with Dave McKean), *Stardust, American Gods,* and *The Wolves in the Walls* (with Dave McKean). His short stories can be found in his collections *Angels and Visitations: a Miscellany, The Wake, Smoke and Mirrors: Short Fictions and Illusions,* and *Adventures in the Dream Trade*.

Film . . .

Gaiman wrote the English language script for Miyazaki's record-breaking Japanese film *Mononoke Hime* (*Princess Mononoke*), which Miramax released in 1999. His script was praised by Roger Ebert and Janet Maslin and was nominated for a Nebula Award. *Sandman* and his three-part series *Death: The High Cost of Living* have been optioned by Warner Brothers, and the film rights to *Neverwhere* have been bought by Jim Henson Productions, in association with Denise Di-Novi. Gaiman has written the script for the film. *Good Omens* is under movie option to the Samuelson Brothers (*Wilde, Carrington*) and Terry Gilliam is contracted to write and direct it.

Awards . . .

Neil Gaiman has won the Bram Stoker Award (three times), the Defender of Liberty Award (for his work "defending First Amendment freedoms"), the Eagle Award (twice), the GLAAD Award, the Harvey Award (twice), the Hugo Award (three times), the International Horror Critics' Guild Award, the Lucca Best Writer Prize, the Mythopoetic Award, the Nebula Award (three times), and the World Fantasy Award. He has also won the MacMillian Silver Pen Award (UK), Prix Vienne (Austria), Haxtur Award (Spain), HQ Award (Brazil), Julia

Verlanger Award (France), Kemi Award (Finland), Max Und Moritz Award (Germany), Ricky Award (Canada), and the Sproing Award (Norway).

By way of this subtle introduction, you should have probably gotten the idea that Neil Gaiman is famous. Yet when asked *about* being famous, he said:

"Well, no, fame I can take or leave, really. I'm probably slightly more famous than I've been comfortable with. Famous enough to have my phone calls returned is about as famous as I want to be. But even so . . . You sign for perhaps 10,000 people on a book tour. That's not really all that many people. More people would see you if you were on an infomercial at four o'clock in the morning. So in any real terms, I'm not famous. The little ugly kid who played Bud Bundy (David Faustino) is much more famous than I am."

His Nebula Award–winning novella "Coraline" (which also won the Hugo and the Bram Stoker Awards) was published as a novel. With thanks to the author's publisher and agent, I am including an excerpt—the first three chapters—of Gaiman's brilliantly wrought story here.

CORALINE [EXCERPT]

NEIL GAIMAN

ONE

Coraline discovered the door a little while after they moved into the house.

It was a very old house—it had an attic under the roof and a cellar under the ground and an overgrown garden with huge old trees in it.

Coraline's family didn't own all of the house—it was too big for that. Instead they owned part of it.

There were other people who lived in the old house.

Miss Spink and Miss Forcible lived in the flat below Coraline's, on the ground floor. They were both old and round, and they lived in their flat with a number of ageing Highland terriers who had names like Hamish and Andrew and Jock. Once upon a time Miss Spink and Miss Forcible had been actresses, as Miss Spink told Coraline the first time she met her.

"You see, Caroline," Miss Spink said, getting Coraline's name wrong, "both myself and Miss Forcible were famous actresses, in our time. We trod the boards, luvvy. Oh, don't let Hamish eat the fruitcake, or he'll be up all night with his tummy."

"It's Coraline. Not Caroline. Coraline," said Coraline.

In the flat above Coraline's, under the roof, was a crazy old man with a big mustache. He told Coraline that he was training a mouse circus. He wouldn't let anyone see it.

"One day, little Caroline, when they are all ready, everyone in the whole world will see the wonders of my mouse circus. You ask me why you cannot see it now. Is that what you asked me?"

"No," said Coraline quietly, "I asked you not to call me Caroline. It's Coraline."

"The reason you cannot see the mouse circus," said the man upstairs, "is that the mice are not yet ready and rehearsed. Also, they refuse to play the songs I have written for them. All the songs I have written for the mice to play go *oompah oompah*. But the white mice will only play *toodle*

oodle, like that. I am thinking of trying them on different types of cheese."

Coraline didn't think there really was a mouse circus. She thought the old man was probably making it up.

The day after they moved in, Coraline went exploring.

She explored the garden. It was a big garden: at the very back was an old tennis court, but no one in the house played tennis and the fence around the court had holes in it and the net had mostly rotted away; there was an old rose garden, filled with stunted, flyblown rosebushes; there was a rockery that was all rocks; there was a fairy ring, made of squidgy brown toadstools which smelled dreadful if you accidentally trod on them.

There was also a well. On the first day Coraline's family moved in, Miss Spink and Miss Forcible made a point of telling Coraline how dangerous the well was, and they warned her to be sure she kept away from it. So Coraline set off to explore for it, so that she knew where it was, to keep away from it properly.

She found it on the third day, in an overgrown meadow beside the tennis court, behind a clump of trees—a low brick circle almost hidden in the high grass. The well had been covered up by wooden boards, to stop anyone falling in. There was a small knothole in one of the boards, and Coraline spent an afternoon dropping pebbles and acorns through the hole and waiting, and counting, until she heard the *plop* as they hit the water far below.

Coraline also explored for animals. She found a hedgehog, and a snake-skin (but no snake), and a rock that looked just like a frog, and a toad that looked just like a rock.

There was also a haughty black cat, who sat on walls and tree stumps and watched her but slipped away if ever she went over to try to play with it.

That was how she spent her first two weeks in the house—exploring the garden and the grounds.

Her mother made her come back inside for dinner and for lunch. And Coraline had to make sure she dressed up warm before she went out, for it was a very cold summer that year; but go out she did, exploring, every day until the day it rained, when Coraline had to stay inside.

"What should I do?" asked Coraline.

"Read a book," said her mother. "Watch a video. Play with your toys. Go and pester Miss Spink or Miss Forcible, or the crazy old man upstairs."

"No," said Coraline. "I don't want to do those things. I want to explore."

"I don't really mind what you do," said Coraline's mother, "as long as you don't make a mess."

Coraline went over to the window and watched the rain come down. It wasn't the kind of rain you could go out in—it was the other kind, the kind that threw itself down from the sky and splashed where it landed. It was rain that meant business, and currently its business was turning the garden into a muddy, wet soup.

Coraline had watched all the videos. She was bored with her toys, and she'd read all her books.

She turned on the television. She went from channel to channel to channel, but there was nothing on but men in suits talking about the stock market, and talk shows. Eventually, she found something to watch: it was the last half of a natural history program about something called protective coloration. She watched animals, birds, and insects which disguised themselves as leaves or twigs or other animals to escape from things that could hurt them. She enjoyed it, but it ended too soon and was followed by a program about a cake factory.

It was time to talk to her father.

Coraline's father was home. Both of her parents worked, doing things on computers, which meant that they were home a lot of the time. Each of them had their own study.

"Hello Coraline," he said when she came in, without turning round.

"Mmph," said Coraline. "It's raining."

"Yup," said her father. "It's bucketing down."

"No," said Coraline. "It's just raining. Can I go outside?"

"What does your mother say?"

"She says you're not going out in weather like that, Coraline Jones."

"Then, no."

"But I want to carry on exploring."

"Then explore the flat," suggested her father. "Look—here's a piece of paper and a pen. Count all the doors and windows. List everything blue. Mount an expedition to discover the hot water tank. And leave me alone to work."

"Can I go into the drawing room?" The drawing room was where the Joneses kept the expensive (and uncomfortable) furniture Coraline's grandmother had left them when she died. Coraline wasn't allowed in there. Nobody went in there. It was only for best.

"If you don't make a mess. And you don't touch anything."

Coraline considered this carefully, then she took the paper and pen and went off to explore the inside of the flat.

She discovered the hot water tank (it was in a cupboard in the kitchen).

She counted everything blue (153).

She counted the windows (21).

She counted the doors (14).

Of the doors that she found, thirteen opened and closed. The other—the big, carved, brown wooden door at the far corner of the drawing room—was locked.

She said to her mother, "Where does that door go?"

"Nowhere, dear."

"It has to go somewhere."

Her mother shook her head. "Look," she told Coraline.

She reached up and took a string of keys from the top of the kitchen doorframe. She sorted through them carefully, and selected the oldest, biggest, blackest, rustiest key. They went into the drawing room. She unlocked the door with the key.

The door swung open.

Her mother was right. The door didn't go anywhere. It opened onto a brick wall.

"When this place was just one house," said Coraline's mother, "that door went somewhere. When they turned the house into flats, they simply bricked it up. The other side is the empty flat on the other side of the house, the one that's still for sale."

She shut the door and put the string of keys back on top of the kitchen doorframe.

"You didn't lock it," said Coraline.

Her mother shrugged. "Why should I lock it?" she asked. "It doesn't go anywhere."

Coraline didn't say anything.

It was nearly dark outside now, and the rain was still coming down, pattering against the windows and blurring the lights of the cars in the street outside.

Coraline's father stopped working and made them all dinner.

Coraline was disgusted. "Daddy," she said, "you've made a *recipe* again."

"It's leek and potato stew with a tarragon garnish and melted Gruyère cheese," he admitted.

Coraline sighed. Then she went to the freezer and got out some microwave chips and a microwave minipizza.

"You know I don't like recipes," she told her father, while her dinner went around and around and the little red numbers on the microwave oven counted down to zero.

"If you tried it, maybe you'd like it," said Coraline's father, but she shook her head.

That night, Coraline lay awake in her bed. The rain had stopped, and she was almost asleep when something went *t-t-t-t-t-t*. She sat up in bed.

Something went k*reeee* . . .

. . . *aaaak*

Coraline got out of bed and looked down the hall, but saw nothing strange. She walked down the hall. From her parents' bedroom came a low snoring—that was her father—and an occasional sleeping mutter—that was her mother.

Coraline wondered if she'd dreamed it, whatever it was.

Something moved.

It was little more than a shadow, and it scuttled down the darkened hall fast, like a little patch of night.

She hoped it wasn't a spider. Spiders made Coraline intensely uncomfortable.

The black shape went into the drawing room, and Coraline followed it a little nervously.

The room was dark. The only light came from the hall, and Coraline, who was standing in the doorway, cast a huge and distorted shadow onto the drawing room carpet—she looked like a thin giant woman.

Coraline was just wondering whether or not she ought to turn on the lights when she saw the black shape edge slowly out from beneath the sofa. It paused, and then dashed silently across the carpet toward the farthest corner of the room.

There was no furniture in that corner of the room.

Coraline turned on the light.

There was nothing in the corner. Nothing but the old door that opened onto the brick wall.

She was sure that her mother had shut the door, but now it was ever so slightly open. Just a crack. Coraline went over to it and looked in. There was nothing there—just a wall, built of red bricks.

Coraline closed the old wooden door, turned out the light, and went to bed.

She dreamed of black shapes that slid from place to place, avoiding the light, until they were all gathered together under the moon. Little black shapes with little red eyes and sharp yellow teeth.

They started to sing,

> We are small but we are many
> We are many we are small
> We were here before you rose
> We will be here when you fall.

Their voices were high and whispering and slightly whiney. They made Coraline feel uncomfortable.

Then Coraline dreamed a few commercials, and after that she dreamed of nothing at all.

TWO

The next day it had stopped raining, but a thick white fog had lowered over the house.

"I'm going for a walk," said Coraline.

"Don't go too far," said her mother. "And dress up warmly."

Coraline put on her blue coat with a hood, her red scarf, and her yellow Wellington boots.

She went out.

Miss Spink was walking her dogs. "Hello, Caroline," said Miss Spink. "Rotten weather."

"Yes," said Coraline.

"I played Portia once," said Miss Spink. "Miss Forcible talks about her Ophelia, but it was my Portia they came to see. When we trod the boards."

Miss Spink was bundled up in pullovers and cardigans, so she seemed more small and circular than ever. She looked like a large, fluffy egg. She wore thick glasses that made her eyes seem huge.

"They used to send flowers to my dressing room. They *did*," she said.

"Who did?" asked Coraline.

Miss Spink looked around cautiously, looking over first one shoulder and then over the other, peering into the mists as though someone might be listening.

"*Men,*" she whispered. Then she tugged the dogs to heel and waddled off back toward the house.

Coraline continued her walk.

She was three quarters of the way around the house when she saw Miss Forcible, standing at the door to the flat she shared with Miss Spink.

"Have you seen Miss Spink, Caroline?"

Coraline told her that she had, and that Miss Spink was out walking the dogs.

"I do hope she doesn't get lost—it'll bring on her shingles if she does, you'll see," said Miss Forcible. "You'd have to be an explorer to find your way around in this fog."

"I'm an explorer," said Coraline.

"Of course you are, luvvy," said Miss Forcible. "Don't get lost, now."

Coraline continued walking through the gardens in the gray mist. She always kept in sight of the house. After about ten minutes of walking she found herself back where she had started.

The hair over her eyes was limp and wet, and her face felt damp.

"Ahoy! Caroline!" called the crazy old man upstairs.

"Oh, hullo," said Coraline.

She could hardly see the old man through the mist.

He walked down the steps on the outside of the house that led up past Coraline's front door to the door of his flat. He walked down very slowly. Coraline waited at the bottom of the stairs.

"The mice do not like the mist," he told her. "It makes their whiskers droop."

"I don't like the mist much, either," admitted Coraline.

The old man leaned down, so close that the bottoms of his mustache tickled Coraline's ear. "The mice have a message for you," he whispered.

Coraline didn't know what to say.

"The message is this. *Don't go through the door.*" He paused. "Does that mean anything to you?"

"No," said Coraline.

The old man shrugged. "They are funny, the mice. They get things wrong. They got your name wrong, you know. They kept saying Coraline. Not Caroline. Not Caroline at all."

He picked up a milk bottle from the bottom of the stairs and started back up to his attic flat.

Coraline went indoors. Her mother was working in her study. Her mother's study smelled of flowers.

"What shall I do?" asked Coraline.

"When do you go back to school?" asked her mother.

"Next week," said Coraline.

"Hmph," said her mother. "I suppose I shall have to get you new school clothes. Remind me, dear, or else I'll forget," and she went back to typing things on the computer screen.

"What shall I *do*?" repeated Coraline.

"Draw something," Her mother passed her a sheet of paper and a ball-point pen.

Coraline tried drawing the mist. After ten minutes of drawing she still had a white sheet of paper with

M   T
S
I

written on it in one corner in slightly wiggly letters. She grunted and passed it to her mother.

"Mm. Very modern, dear," said Coraline's mother.

Coraline crept into the drawing room and tried to open the old door in the corner. It was locked once more. She supposed her mother must have locked it again. She shrugged.

Coraline went to see her father.

He had his back to the door as he typed. "Go away," he said cheerfully as she walked in.

"I'm bored," she said.

"Learn how to tap-dance," he suggested, without turning around.

Coraline shook her head. "Why don't you play with me?" she asked.

"Busy," he said. "Working," he added. He still hadn't turned around to look at her. "Why don't you go and bother Miss Spink and Miss Forcible?"

Coraline put on her coat and pulled up her hood and went out of the house. She went downstairs. She rang the door of Miss Spink and Miss Forcible's flat. Coraline could hear a frenzied woofing as the Scottie dogs ran out into the hall. After a while Miss Spink opened the door.

"Oh, it's you, Caroline," she said. "Angus, Hamish, Bruce, down now, luvvies. It's only Caroline. Come in, dear. Would you like a cup of tea?"

The flat smelled of furniture polish and dogs.

"Yes, please," said Coraline. Miss Spink led her into a dusty little room, which she called the parlor. On the walls were black-and-white photographs of pretty women, and theater programs in frames. Miss Forcible was sitting in one of the armchairs, knitting hard.

They poured Coraline a cup of tea in a little pink bone china cup, with a saucer. They gave her a dry Garibaldi biscuit to go with it.

Miss Forcible looked at Miss Spink, picked up her knitting, and took a deep breath. "Anyway, April. As I was saying: you still have to admit, there's life in the old dog yet."

"Miriam, dear, neither of us is as young as we were."

"Madame Arcati," replied Miss Forcible. "The nurse in *Romeo.* Lady Bracknell. Character parts. They can't retire you from the stage."

"Now, Miriam, we *agreed,*" said Miss Spink. Coraline wondered if they'd forgotten she was there. They weren't making much sense; she decided they were having an argument as old and comfortable as an armchair, the kind of argument that no one ever really wins or loses but which can go on forever, if both parties are willing.

She sipped her tea.

"I'll read the leaves, if you want," said Miss Spink to Coraline.

"Sorry?" said Coraline.

"The tea leaves, dear. I'll read your future."

Coraline passed Miss Spink her cup. Miss Spink peered shortsightedly at the black tea leaves in the bottom. She pursed her lips.

"You know, Caroline," she said, after a while, "you are in terrible danger."

Miss Forcible snorted, and put down her knitting. "Don't be silly, April. Stop scaring the girl. Your eyes are going. Pass me that cup, child."

Coraline carried the cup over to Miss Forcible. Miss Forcible looked into it carefully, shook her head, and looked into it again.

"Oh dear," she said. "You were right, April. She *is* in danger."

"See, Miriam," said Miss Spink triumphantly. "My eyes are as good as they ever were. . . ."

"What am I in danger from?" asked Coraline.

Misses Spink and Forcible stared at her blankly. "It didn't say," said Miss Spink. "Tea leaves aren't reliable for that kind of thing. Not really. They're good for general, but not for specifics."

"What should I do then?" asked Coraline, who was slightly alarmed by this.

"Don't wear green in your dressing room," suggested Miss Spink.

"Or mention the Scottish play," added Miss Forcible.

Coraline wondered why so few of the adults she had met made any sense. She sometimes wondered who they thought they were talking to.

"And be very, very careful," said Miss Spink. She got up from the arm-chair and went over to the fireplace. On the mantelpiece was a small jar, and Miss Spink took off the top of the jar and began to pull things out of it. There was a tiny china duck, a thimble, a strange little brass coin, two paper clips and a stone with a hole in it.

She passed Coraline the stone with a hole in it.

"What's it for?" asked Coraline. The hole went all the way through the middle of the stone. She held it up to the window and looked through it.

"It might help," said Miss Spink. "They're good for bad things, some-times."

Coraline put on her coat, said good-bye to Misses Spink and Forcible and to the dogs, and went outside.

The mist hung like blindness around the house. She walked slowly to the stairs up to her family's flat, and then stopped and looked around.

In the mist, it was a ghost-world. *In danger?* thought Coraline to herself. It sounded exciting. It didn't sound like a bad thing. Not really.

Coraline went back upstairs, her fist closed tightly around her new stone.

THREE

The next day the sun shone, and Coraline's mother took her into the nearest large town to buy clothes for school. They dropped her father off at the railway station. He was going into London for the day to see some people.

Coraline waved him good-bye.

They went to the department store to buy the school clothes.

Coraline saw some Day-Glo green gloves she liked a lot. Her mother refused to buy them for her, preferring instead to buy white socks, navy blue school underpants, four gray blouses, and a dark gray skirt.

"But Mum, *everybody* at school's got gray blouses and everything. *Nobody's* got green gloves. I could be the only one."

Her mother ignored her; she was talking to the shop assistant. They were talking about which kind of sweater to get for Coraline, and were agreeing that the best thing to do would be to get one that was embarrassingly large and baggy, in the hopes that one day she might grow into it.

Coraline wandered off and looked at a display of Wellington boots shaped like frogs and ducks and rabbits.

Then she wandered back.

"Coraline? Oh, there you are. Where on earth were you?"

"I was kidnapped by aliens," said Coraline. "They came down from outer space with ray guns, but I fooled them by wearing a wig and laughing in a foreign accent, and I escaped."

"Yes, dear. Now, I think you could do with some more hair clips, don't you?"

"No."

"Well, let's say half a dozen, to be on the safe side," said her mother.

Coraline didn't say anything.

In the car on the way back home, Coraline said, "What's in the empty flat?"

"I don't know. Nothing, I expect. It probably looks like our flat before we moved in. Empty rooms."

"Do you think you could get into it from our flat?"

"Not unless you can walk through bricks, dear."

"Oh."

They got home around lunchtime. The sun was shining, although the day was cold. Coraline's mother looked in the fridge and found a sad little tomato and a piece of cheese with green stuff growing on it. There was only a crust in the bread bin.

"I'd better dash down to the shops and get some fish fingers or something," said her mother. "Do you want to come?"

"No," said Coraline.

"Suit yourself," said her mother, and left. Then she came back and got her purse and car keys and went out again.

Coraline was bored.

She flipped through a book her mother was reading about native people in a distant country; how every day they would take pieces of white silk and draw on them in wax, then dip the silks in dye, then draw on them more in wax and dye them some more, then boil the wax out in hot water, and then finally, throw the now-beautiful cloths on a fire and burn them to ashes.

It seemed particularly pointless to Coraline, but she hoped that the people enjoyed it.

She was still bored, and her mother wasn't yet home.

Coraline got a chair and pushed it over to the kitchen door. She climbed onto the chair and reached up. She got down, then got a broom from the broom cupboard. She climbed back on the chair again and reached up with the broom.

Chink.

She climbed down from the chair and picked up the keys. She smiled triumphantly. Then she leaned the broom against the wall and went into the drawing room.

The family did not use the drawing room. They had inherited the furniture from Coraline's grandmother, along with a wooden coffee table, a side table, a heavy glass ashtray, and the oil painting of a bowl of fruit. Coraline could never work out why anyone would want to paint a bowl of fruit. Other than that, the room was empty: there were no knickknacks on the mantelpiece, no statues or clocks; nothing that made it feel comfortable or lived-in.

The old black key felt colder than any of the others. She pushed it into the keyhole. It turned smoothly, with a satisfying *clunk*.

Coraline stopped and listened. She knew she was doing something wrong, and she was trying to listen for her mother coming back, but she heard nothing. Then Coraline put her hand on the doorknob and turned it; and, finally, she opened the door.

It opened on to a dark hallway. The bricks had gone as if they'd never been there. There was a cold, musty smell coming through the open doorway: it smelled like something very old and very slow.

Coraline went through the door.

She wondered what the empty flat would be like—if that was where the corridor led.

Coraline walked down the corridor uneasily. There was something very familiar about it.

The carpet beneath her feet was the same carpet they had in her flat. The wallpaper was the same wallpaper they had. The picture hanging in the hall was the same that they had hanging in their hallway at home.

She knew where she was: she was in her own home. She hadn't left.

She shook her head, confused.

She stared at the picture hanging on the wall: no, it wasn't exactly the same. The picture they had in their own hallway showed a boy in old-fashioned clothes staring at some bubbles. But now the expression on his face was different—he was looking at the bubbles as if he was planning to do something very nasty indeed to them. And there was something peculiar about his eyes.

Coraline stared at his eyes, trying to figure out what exactly was different. She almost had it when somebody said, "Coraline?"

It sounded like her mother. Coraline went into the kitchen, where the voice had come from. A woman stood in the kitchen with her back to Coraline. She looked a little like Coraline's mother. Only . . .

Only her skin was white as paper.

Only she was taller and thinner.

Only her fingers were too long, and they never stopped moving, and her dark red fingernails were curved and sharp.

"Coraline?" the woman said. "Is that you?"

And then she turned around. Her eyes were big black buttons.

"Lunchtime, Coraline," said the woman.

"Who are you?" asked Coraline.

"I'm your other mother," said the woman. "Go and tell your other father that lunch is ready." She opened the door of the oven. Suddenly Coraline realized how hungry she was. It smelled wonderful. "Well, go on."

Coraline went down the hall, to where her father's study was. She opened the door. There was a man in there, sitting at the keyboard, with his back to her. "Hello," said Coraline. "I—I mean, she said to say that lunch is ready."

The man turned around.

His eyes were buttons, big and black and shiny.

"Hello Coraline," he said. "I'm starving."

He got up and went with her into the kitchen. They sat at the kitchen table, and Coraline's other mother brought them lunch. A huge, golden-brown roasted chicken, fried potatoes, tiny green peas. Coraline shoveled the food into her mouth. It tasted wonderful.

"We've been waiting for you for a long time," said Coraline's other father.

"For me?"

"Yes," said the other mother. "It wasn't the same here without you. But we knew you'd arrive one day, and then we could be a proper family. Would you like some more chicken?"

It was the best chicken that Coraline had ever eaten. Her mother sometimes made chicken, but it was always out of packets or frozen, and was very dry, and it never tasted of anything. When Coraline's father cooked chicken he bought real chicken, but he did strange things to it, like stewing it in wine, or stuffing it with prunes, or baking it in pastry, and Coraline would always refuse to touch it on principle.

She took some more chicken.

"I didn't know I had another mother," said Coraline, cautiously.

"Of course you do. Everyone does," said the other mother, her black button eyes gleaming. "After lunch I thought you might like to play in your room with the rats."

"The rats?"

"From upstairs."

Coraline had never seen a rat, except on television. She was quite looking forward to it. This was turning out to be a very interesting day after all.

After lunch her other parents did the washing up, and Coraline went down the hall to her other bedroom.

It was different from her bedroom at home. For a start it was painted in an off-putting shade of green and a peculiar shade of pink.

Coraline decided that she wouldn't want to have to sleep in there, but that the color scheme was an awful lot more interesting than her own bedroom.

There were all sorts of remarkable things in there she'd never seen before: windup angels that fluttered around the bedroom like startled sparrows; books with pictures that writhed and crawled and shimmered; little dinosaur skulls that chattered their teeth as she passed. A whole toy box filled with wonderful toys.

This is more like it, thought Coraline. She looked out of the window. Outside, the view was the same one she saw from her own bedroom: trees, fields, and beyond them, on the horizon, distant purple hills.

Something black scurried across the floor and vanished under the bed. Coraline got down on her knees and looked under the bed. Fifty little red eyes stared back at her.

"Hello," said Coraline. "Are you the rats?"

They came out from under the bed, blinking their eyes in the light. They had short, soot-black fur, little red eyes, pink paws like tiny hands, and pink, hairless tails like long, smooth worms.

"Can you talk?" she asked.

The largest, blackest of the rats shook its head. It had an unpleasant sort of smile, Coraline thought.

"Well," asked Coraline, "what *do* you do?"

The rats formed a circle.

Then they began to climb on top of each other, carefully but swiftly, until they had formed a pyramid with the largest rat at the top.

The rats began to sing, in high, whispery voices,

We have teeth and we have tails
We have tails we have eyes
We were here before you fell
You will be here when we rise.

It wasn't a pretty song. Coraline was sure she'd heard it before, or something like it, although she was unable to remember exactly where.

Then the pyramid fell apart, and the rats scampered, fast and black, toward the door.

The other crazy old man upstairs was standing in the doorway, holding a tall black hat in his hands. The rats scampered up him, burrowing into his pockets, into his shirt, up his trouser legs, down his neck.

The largest rat climbed onto the old man's shoulders, swung up on the long gray mustache, past the big black button eyes, and onto the top of the man's head.

In seconds the only evidence that the rats were there at all were the restless lumps under the man's clothes, forever sliding from place to place across him; and there was still the largest rat, who stared down, with glittering red eyes, at Coraline from the man's head.

The old man put his hat on, and the last rat was gone.

"Hello Coraline," said the other old man upstairs. "I heard you were here. It is time for the rats to have their dinner. But you can come up with me, if you like, and watch them feed."

There was something hungry in the old man's button eyes that made Coraline feel uncomfortable. "No, thank you," she said. "I'm going outside to explore."

The old man nodded, very slowly. Coraline could hear the rats whispering to each other, although she could not tell what they were saying.

She was not certain that she wanted to know what they were saying.

Her other parents stood in the kitchen doorway as she walked down the corridor, smiling identical smiles, and waving slowly. "Have a nice time outside," said her other mother.

"We'll just wait here for you to come back," said her other father.

When Coraline got to the front door, she turned back and looked at them. They were still watching her, and waving, and smiling.

Coraline walked outside, and down the steps.

Karen Joy Fowler is the author of two story collections and four novels, including *Sarah Canary* and *The Sweetheart Season*. Her third novel, *Sister Noon,* was a finalist for the PEN/Faulkner award and her most recent novel, *The Jane Austen Book Club,* made *The New York Times* and other bestseller lists. She has taught creative writing at Stanford, the University of California at Davis, Cleveland State, Alabama University, and numerous summer workshops. She's a frequent instructor in the Michigan State Clarion workshop. Her short-story collection *Black Glass* won the World Fantasy Award in 1999; her first two novels were both *New York Times* notables in their year.

About her story, she writes:

"My own gorilla trail begins with Donna Haraway. A few years ago I read her assertion that, in 1921, Carl Akeley of the NY Museum of Natural History, took two women on safari in order to kill (and stuff) a mountain gorilla.

"His motivations for this, as described by Haraway, were startling to me. She says that he wished to undermine the public perception of gorillas as aggressive, dangerous, and therefore, good hunting. He hoped that, if mere women could kill one, men would come to feel that the sport was beneath them. Akeley wished to save the mountain gorillas while at the same time collecting a few specimens for a museum diorama.

"A few lines further along, I was startled again. One of the women chosen for this hunt turned out to be Mary Hastings Bradley. She took along her six-year-old daughter, Alice Bradley, who would grow up to be our own James Tiptree, Jr.

"This essay sent me next to Bradley's own account of the trip. Her memoir, *On the Gorilla Trail,* does not confirm Haraway's hypothesis as to the motive. It does, however, include some vivid photos of the kill. I began to put together a piece whose referents would be Mary Bradley's safari and James Tiptree's superlative 'The Women Men Don't See.'

"Both of these served merely as jumping off points. The safari I describe is not at all like Bradley's. My story is a response to rather than a rewrite of Tiptree's. In particular,

I wished to add two subsets I felt her story ignored—the women men do see and the men women don't. Meanwhile many other things came into the mix: primate studies, King Kong, Belgian Congo politics, Tarzan, harems, spiders, and perilous card games."

WHAT I DIDN'T SEE

KAREN JOY FOWLER

I saw Archibald Murray's obituary in the *Tribune* a couple of days ago. It was a long notice, because of all those furbelows he had after his name, and dredged up that old business of ours, which can't have pleased his children. I, myself, have never spoken up before, as I've always felt that nothing I saw sheds any light, but now I'm the last of us. Even Wilmet is gone, though I always picture him such a boy. And there is something to be said for having the last word, which I am surely having.

I still go to the jungle sometimes when I sleep. The sound of the clock turns to a million insects all chewing at once, water dripping onto leaves, the hum inside your head when you run a fever. Sooner or later Eddie comes, in his silly hat and boots up to his knees. He puts his arms around me in the way he did when he meant business and I wake up too hot, too old, and all alone.

You're never alone in the jungle. You can't see through the twist of roots and leaves and vines, the streakish, tricky light, but you've always got a sense of being seen. You make too much noise when you walk.

At the same time, you understand that you don't matter. You're small and stuck on the ground. The ghosts of paths weren't made for you. If you get bitten by a snake, it's your own damn fault, not the snake's, and if someone doesn't drag you out you'll turn to mulch just like anything else would and show up next as mold or moss, ferns, leeches, ants, millipedes, butterflies, beetles. The jungle is a jammed-alive place, which means that something is always dying there.

Eddie had this idea once that defects of character could be treated with doses of landscape: the ocean for the histrionic, mountains for the domineering, and so forth. I forget the desert, but the jungle was the place to send the self-centered.

We seven went into the jungle with guns in our hands and love in our hearts. I say so now when there is no one left to contradict me.

Archer organized us. He was working at the time for the Louisville Museum of Natural History and he had a stipend from Collections for skins and bones. The rest of us were amateur enthusiasts and paid our own way just for the adventure. Archer asked Eddie (arachnids) to go along and Russell MacNamara (chimps), and Trenton Cox (butterflies), who couldn't or wouldn't, and Wilmet Siebert (big game), and Merion Cowper (tropical medicine), and also Merion's wife, only he turned out to be between wives by the time we left, so he was the one who brought Beverly Kriss.

I came with Eddie to help with his nets, pooters, and kill jars. I was never the sort to scream over bugs, but if I had been, twenty-eight years of marriage to Eddie would have cured me. The more legs a creature had, the better Eddie thought of it. Up to point. Up to eight.

In fact Archer was anxious there be some women and had specially invited me, though Eddie didn't tell me so. This was smart; I would have suspected I was along to do the dishes (though of course there were the natives for this) and for nursing the sick, which we did end up at a bit, Beverly and I, when the matter was too small or too nasty for Merion. I might not have come at all if I'd known I was wanted. As it was, I learned to bake a passable bread on campfire coals with a native beer for yeast, but it was my own choice to do so and I ate as much of the bread myself as I wished.

I pass over the various boats on which we sailed, though these trips were not without incident. Wilmet turned out to have a nervous stomach; it started to trouble him on the ocean and then stuck around when we hit dry land again. Russell was a drinker, and not the good sort, unlucky and suspicious, a man who thought he loved a game of cards, but should have never been allowed to play. Beverly was a modern girl in 1928 and could chew gum, smoke, and wipe the lipstick off her mouth and onto yours all at the same time. She and Merion were frisky for Archer's taste and he tried to shift this off onto me, saying I was being made uncomfortable, when I didn't care one way or the other. I worried that it would be a pattern and every time one of the men was tired on the trail they'd say we had to stop on my account. I told Eddie right away I wouldn't like it if this was to happen. So by the time we were geared up and walking in, we already thought we knew each other pretty well and we didn't entirely like what we knew. Still, I guessed we'd get along fine when there was more to occupy us. Even during those long days it took to reach the mountains—the endless trains, motor cars, donkeys, mules, and finally our very own feet—things went smoothly enough.

By the time we reached the Lulenga Mission, we'd seen a fair bit of Africa—low and high, hot and cold, black and white. I've learned some things in the years since, so there's a strong temptation now to pretend that

I felt the things I should have felt, knew the things I might have known. The truth is otherwise. My attitudes toward the natives, in particular, were not what they might have been. The men who helped us interested me little and impressed me not at all. Many of them had their teeth filed and were only ten years or so from cannibalism, or so we were informed. No one, ourselves included, was clean, but Beverly and I would have tried, only we couldn't bathe without the nuisance of being spied on. Whether this was to see if we looked good or only good to eat, I did not wish to know.

The fathers at the mission told us that slaves used to be led through the villages in ropes so that people could draw on their bodies the cuts of meat they were buying before the slaves were butchered, and with that my mind was set. I never did acknowledge any beauty or kindness in the people we met, though Eddie saw much of both.

We spent three nights in Lulenga, which gave us each a bed, good food, and a chance to wash our hair and clothes in some privacy. Beverly and I shared a room, there not being sufficient number for her to have her own. She was quarreling with Merion at the time though I forget about what. They were a tempest, those two, always shouting, sulking, and then turning on the heat again. A tiresome sport for spectators, but surely invigorating for the players. So Eddie was bunked up with Russell, which put me out, because I liked to wake up with him.

We were joined at dinner the first night by a Belgian administrator who treated us to real wine and whose name I no longer remember though I can picture him yet—a bald, hefty man in his sixties with a white beard. I recall how he joked that his hair had migrated from his head to his chin and then settled in where the food was plentiful.

Eddie was in high spirits and talking more than usual. The spiders in Africa are exhilaratingly aggressive. Many of them have fangs and nocturnal habits. We'd already shipped home dozens of button spiders with red hourglasses on their backs, and some beautiful golden violin spiders with long delicate legs and dark chevrons underneath. But that evening Eddie was most excited about a small jumping spider, which seemed not to spin her own web, but to lurk instead in the web of another. She had no beautiful markings; when he'd first seen one, he'd thought she was a bit of dirt blown into the silken strands. Then she grew legs and, as we watched, stalked and killed the web's owner and all with a startling cunning.

"Working together, a thousand spiders can tie up a lion," the Belgian told us. Apparently it was a local saying. "But then they don't work together, do they? The blacks haven't noticed. Science is observation and Africa produces no scientists."

In those days all gorilla hunts began at Lulenga, so it took no great discernment to guess that the rest of our party was not after spiders. The Belgian told us that only six weeks past, a troupe of gorilla males had attacked a tribal village. The food stores had been broken into and a woman carried off. Her bracelets were found the next day, but she'd not yet returned and the Belgian feared she never would. It was such a sustained siege that the whole village had to be abandoned.

"The seizure of the woman I dismiss as superstition and exaggeration," Archer said. He had a formal way of speaking; you'd never guess he was from Kentucky. Not so grand to look at—inch-thick glasses that made his eyes pop, unkempt hair, filthy shirt cuffs. He poured more of the Belgian's wine around, and I recall his being especially generous to his own glass. Isn't it funny, the things you remember? "But the rest of your story interests me. If any gorilla was taken I'd pay for the skin, assuming it wasn't spoiled in the peeling."

The Belgian said he would inquire. And then he persisted with his main point, very serious and deliberate. "As to the woman, I've heard these tales too often to discard them so quickly as you. I've heard of native women subjected to degradations far worse than death. May I ask you as a favor then, in deference to my greater experience and longer time here, to leave your women at the mission when you go gorilla hunting?"

It was courteously done and obviously cost Archer to refuse. Yet he did, saying to my astonishment that it would defeat his whole purpose to leave me and Beverly behind. He then gave the Belgian his own thinking, which we seven had already heard over several repetitions—that gorillas were harmless and gentle, if oversized and overmuscled. Sweet-natured vegetarians. He based this entirely on the wear on their teeth; he'd read a paper on it from some university in London.

Archer then characterized the famous Du Chaillu description—glaring eyes, yellow incisors, hellish dream creatures—as a slick and dangerous form of self aggrandizement. It was an account tailored to bring big game hunters on the run and so had to be quickly countered for the gorillas' own protection. Archer was out to prove Du Chaillu wrong and he needed me and Beverly to help. "If one of the girls should bring down a large male," he said, "it will seem as exciting as shooting a cow. No man will cross a continent merely to do something a pair of girls has already done."

He never did ask us, because that wasn't his way. He just raised it as our Christian duty and then left us to worry it over in our minds.

Of course we were all carrying rifles. Eddie and I had practiced on bottles and such in preparation for the trip. On the way over I'd gotten pretty good at clay pigeons off the deck of our ship. But I wasn't eager to kill a gentle vegetarian—a nightmare from hell would have suited me a good deal better (if scared me a great deal more.) Beverly too, I'm guessing.

Not that she said anything about it that night. Wilmet, our youngest at twenty-five years and also shortest by a whole head—blond hair, pink cheeks, and little rat's eyes—had been lugging a tin of British biscuits about the whole trip and finishing every dinner by eating one while we watched. He was always explaining why they couldn't be shared when no one was asking. They kept his stomach settled; he couldn't afford to run out and so on; his very life might depend on them if he were sick and nothing else would stay down and so forth. We wouldn't have noticed if he hadn't persisted in bringing it up.

But suddenly he and Beverly had their heads close together, whispering, and he was giving her one of his precious biscuits. She took it without so much as a glance at Merion, even when he leaned in to say he'd like one, too. Wilmet answered that there were too few to share with everyone so Merion upset a water glass into the tin and spoiled all the biscuits that remained. Wilmet left the table and didn't return and the subject of the all-girl gorilla hunt passed by in the unpleasantness.

That night I woke under the gauze of the mosquito net in such a heat I thought I had malaria. Merion had given us all quinine and I meant to take it regularly, but I didn't always remember. There are worse fevers in the jungle, especially if you've been collecting spiders, so it was cheerful of me to fix on malaria. My skin was burning from the inside out, especially my hands and feet, and I was sweating like butter on a hot day. I thought to wake Beverly, but by the time I stood up the fit had already passed and anyway her bed was empty.

In the morning she was back. I planned to talk to her then, get her thoughts on gorilla hunting, but I woke early and she slept late.

I breakfasted alone and went for a stroll around the Mission grounds. It was cool with little noise beyond the wind and birds. To the west, a dark trio of mountains, two of which smoked. Furrowed fields below me, banana plantations, and trellises of roses, curving into archways that led to the church. How often we grow a garden around our houses of worship. We march ourselves through Eden to get to God.

Merion joined me in the graveyard where I'd just counted three deaths by lion, British names all. I was thinking how outlandish it was, how sadly unlikely that all the prams and nannies and public schools should come to this, and even the bodies pinned under stones so hyenas wouldn't come for them. I was hoping for a more modern sort of death myself, a death at home, a death from American causes, when Merion cleared his throat behind me.

He didn't look like my idea of a doctor, but I believe he was a good one. Well-paid, that's for sure and certain. As to appearances, he reminded me of the villain in some Lillian Gish film, meaty and needing a shave, but handsome enough when cleaned up. He swung his arms when he walked so he took up more space than he needed. There was something to this confidence I admired, though it irritated me on principle. I often liked him least of all and I'm betting he was sharp enough to know it. "I trust you slept well," he said. He looked at me slant-wise, looked away again. *I trust you slept well.* I trust you were in no way disturbed by Beverly sneaking out to meet me in the middle of the night.

Or maybe—I trust Beverly didn't sneak out last night.

Or maybe just I trust you slept well. It wasn't a question, which saved me the nuisance of figuring the answer.

"So," he said next, "what do you think of this gorilla scheme of Archer's?" and then gave me no time to respond. "The fathers tell me a party from Manchester went up just last month and brought back seventeen. Four of them youngsters—lovely little family group for the British museum. I only hope they left us a few." And then, lowering his voice, "I'm glad for the chance to discuss things with you privately."

There turned out to be a detail to the Belgian's story judged too delicate for the dinnertable, but Merion, being a doctor and maybe more of a man's man than Archer, a man who could be appealed to on behalf of women, had heard it. The woman carried away from the village had been menstruating. This at least the Belgian hoped, that we'd not go up the mountain with our female affliction in full flower.

And because he was a doctor I told Merion straight out that I'd been light and occasional; I credited this to the upset of travel. I thought to set his mind at ease, but I should have guessed I wasn't his first concern.

"Beverly's too headstrong to listen to me," he said. "Too young and reckless. She'll take her cue from you. A solid, sensible, mature woman like you could rein her in a bit. For her own good."

A woman unlikely to inflame the passions of jungle apes was what I heard. Even in my prime I'd never been the sort of woman poems are written about, but this seemed to place me low indeed. An hour later I saw the humor in it, and Eddie surely laughed at me quickly enough when I confessed it, but at the time I was sincerely insulted. How sensible, how mature was that?

I was further provoked by the way he expected me to give in. Archer was certain I'd agree to save the gorillas and Merion was certain I'd agree to save Beverly. I had a moment's outrage over these men who planned to run me by appealing to what they imagined was my weakness.

Merion more than Archer. How smug he was, and how I detested his calm acceptance of every advantage that came to him, as if it were no more than his due. No white woman in all the world had seen the wild gorillas yet—we were to be the first—but I was to step aside from it just because he asked me.

"I haven't walked all this way to miss out on the gorillas," I told him, as politely as I could. "The only question is whether I'm looking or shooting at them." And then I left him, because my own feelings were no credit to me and I didn't mean to have them anymore. I went to look for Eddie and spend the rest of the day emptying kill jars, pinning and labeling the occupants.

The next morning Beverly announced, in deference to Merion's wishes, that she'd be staying behind at the mission when we went on. Quick as could be, Wilmet said his stomach was in such an uproar that he would stay behind as well. This took us all by surprise as he was the only real hunter among us. And it put Merion in an awful bind—we'd more likely need a doctor on the mountain than at the mission, but I guessed he'd sooner see Beverly taken by gorillas than by Wilmet. He fussed and sweated over a bunch of details that didn't matter to anyone and all the while the day passed in secret conferences—Merion with Archer, Archer with Beverly, Russell with Wilmet, Eddie with Beverly. By dinnertime Beverly said she'd changed her mind and Wilmet had undergone a wonderful recovery. When we left next morning we were at full complement, but pretty tightly strung.

It took almost two hundred porters to get our little band of seven up Mount Mikeno. It was a hard track with no path, hoisting ourselves over roots, cutting and crawling our way through tightly woven bamboo. There were long slides of mud on which it was impossible to get a grip. And always sharp uphill. My heart and my lungs worked as hard or harder than my legs and though it wasn't hot I had to wipe my face and neck continually. As the altitude rose I gasped for breath like a fish in a net.

We women were placed in the middle of the pack with gun-bearers both ahead and behind. I slid back many times and had to be caught and set upright again. Eddie was in a torment over the webs we walked through with no pause as to architect and Russell over the bearers who, he guaranteed, would bolt with our guns at the first sign of danger. But we wouldn't make camp if we stopped for spiders and couldn't stay the course without our hands free. Soon Beverly sang out for a gorilla to come and carry her the rest of the way.

Then we were all too winded and climbed for hours without speaking, breaking whenever we came suddenly into the sun, sustaining ourselves with chocolate and crackers.

Still our mood was excellent. We saw elephant tracks, large, sunken bowls in the mud, half-filled with water. We saw glades of wild carrots and an extravagance of pink and purple orchids. Grasses in greens so delicate they seemed to be melting. I revised my notions of Eden, leaving the roses behind and choosing instead these remote forests where the gorillas lived—foggy rains, the crooked hagenia trees strung with vines, golden mosses, silver lichen; the rattle and buzz of flies and beetles; the smell of catnip as we stepped into it.

At last we stopped. Our porters set up which gave us a chance to rest. My feet were swollen and my knees stiffening, but I had a great appetite for dinner and a great weariness for bed; I was asleep before sundown. And then I was awake again. The temperature, which had been pleasant all day, plunged. Eddie and I wrapped ourselves in coats and sweaters and each other. He worried about our porters, who didn't have the blankets we had, although they were free to keep a fire up as high as they liked. At daybreak, they came complaining to Archer. He raised their pay a dime apiece since they had surely suffered during the night, but almost fifty of them left us anyway.

We spent that morning sitting around the camp, nursing our blisters and scrapes, some of us looking for spiders, some of us practicing our marksmanship. There was a stream about five minutes' walk away with a pool where Beverly and I dropped our feet. No mosquitoes, no sweat bees, no flies, and that alone made it paradise. But no sooner did I have this thought and a wave of malarial heat came on me, drenching the back of my shirt.

When I came to myself again, Beverly was in the middle of something and I hadn't heard the beginning. She might have told me Merion's former wife had been unfaithful to him. Later this seemed like something I'd once been told, but maybe only because it made sense. "Now he seems to think the apes will leave me alone if only I don't go tempting them," she said. "Lord!"

"He says they're drawn to menstrual blood."

"Then I've got no problem. Anyway Russell says that Burunga says we'll never see them, dressed as we're dressed. Our clothes make too much noise when we walk. He told Russell we must hunt them naked. I haven't passed that on to Merion yet. I'm saving it for a special occasion."

I had no idea who Burunga was. Not the cook and not our chief guide, which were the only names I'd bothered with. I was, at least (and I do see now, how very least it is) embarrassed to learn that Beverly had done otherwise. "Are you planning to shoot an ape?" I asked. It came over me all of sudden that I wanted a particular answer, but I couldn't unearth what answer that was.

"I'm not really a killer," she said. "More a sweet-natured vegetarian. Of the meat-eating variety. But Archer says he'll put my picture up in the museum. You know the sort of thing—rifle on shoulder, foot on body, eyes to the horizon. Wouldn't that be something to take the kiddies to?"

Eddie and I had no kiddies; Beverly might have realized it was a sore spot. And Archer had made no such representations to me. She sat in a spill of sunlight. Her hair was short and heavy and fell in a neat cap over her ears. Brown until the sun made it golden. She wasn't a pretty woman so much as she just drew your eye and kept it. "Merion keeps on about how he paid my way here. Like he hasn't gotten his money's worth." She kicked her feet and water beaded up on her bare legs. "You're so lucky. Eddie's the best."

Which he was, and any woman could see it. I never met a better man than my Eddie and in our whole forty-three years together there were only three times I wished I hadn't married him. I say this now, because we're coming up on one of those times. I wouldn't want someone thinking less of Eddie because of anything I said.

"You're still in love with him, aren't you?" Beverly asked. "After so many years of marriage."

I admitted as much.

Beverly shook her golden head. "Then you'd best keep with him," she told me.

Or did she? What did she say to me? I've been over the conversation so many times I no longer remember it at all.

In contrast, this next bit is perfectly clear. Beverly said she was tired and went to her tent to lie down. I found the men playing bridge, taking turns at watching. I was bullied into playing, because Russell didn't like his cards and thought to change his luck by putting some empty space between hands. So it was me and Wilmet opposite Eddie and Russell, with Merion and Archer in the vicinity, smoking and looking on. On the other side of the tents the laughter of our porters.

I would have liked to team with Eddie, but Russell said bridge was too dangerous a game when husbands and wives partnered up and there was a ready access to guns. He was joking, of course, but you couldn't have told by his face.

While we played Russell talked about chimpanzees and how they ran their lives. Back in those days no one had looked at chimps yet so it was all only guesswork. Topped by guessing that gorillas would be pretty much the same. There was a natural order to things, Russell said, and you could reason it out; it was simple Darwinism.

I didn't think you could reason out spiders; I didn't buy that you could reason out chimps. So I didn't listen. I played my cards and every so often a word would fall in. Male this, male that. Blah, blah, dominance. Survival of the fittest, blah, blah. Natural selection, nature red in tooth and claw. Blah and blah. There was an argument then as to whether by simple Darwinism we could expect a social arrangement of monogamous married couples or whether the males would all have harems. There were points to be made either way and I didn't care for any of those points.

Wilmet opened with one heart and soon we were up to three. I mentioned how Beverly had said she'd get her picture in the Louisville Museum if she killed an ape. "It's not entirely my decision," Archer said. "But, yes, part of my plan is that there will be pictures. And interviews. Possibly in magazines, certainly in the museum. The whole object is that people be told." And this began a discussion over whether, for the purposes of saving gorilla lives, it would work best if Beverly was to kill one or if it should be me. There was some general concern that the sight of Beverly in a pith helmet might be, somehow, stirring, whereas if I were the one, it wouldn't be cute in the least. If Archer really wished to put people off gorilla-hunting, then, the men agreed, I was his girl. Of course it was not as bald as that, but that was the gist.

Wilmet lost a trick he'd hoped to finesse. We were going down and I suddenly saw that he'd opened with only four hearts, which, though they were pretty enough, an ace and a king included, was a witless thing to do. I still think so.

"I expected more support," he said to me, "when you took us to two," as if it were my fault.

"Length is strength," I said right back and then I burst into tears, because he was so short it was an awful thing to say. It took me more by surprise than anyone and most surprising of all, I didn't seem to care about the crying. I got up from the table and walked off. I could hear Eddie apologizing behind me as if I was the one who'd opened with four hearts. "Change of life," I heard him saying. It was so like Eddie to know what was happening to me even before I did.

It was so unlike him to apologize for me. At that moment I hated him with all the rest. I went to our tent and fetched some water and my rifle. We weren't any of us to go into the jungle alone so no one imagined this was what I was doing.

The sky had begun to cloud up and soon the weather was colder. There was no clear track to follow, only antelope trails. Of course I got lost. I had thought to take every possible turn to the right and then reverse this coming back, but the plan didn't suit the landscape nor achieve the end desired. I had a whistle, but was angry enough not to use it. I counted on Eddie to find me eventually as he always did.

I believe I walked for more than four hours. Twice it rained, intensifying all the green smells of the jungle. Occasionally the sun was out and the mosses and leaves overlaid with silvered water. I saw a cat print that made me move my rifle off of safe to ready and then often had to set it aside as the track took me over roots and under hollow trees. The path was unstable and sometimes slid out from under me.

Once I put my hand on a spider's web. It was a domed web over an orb, intricate and a beautiful pale yellow in color. I never touched a silk so strong. The spider was big and black with yellow spots at the undersides of her legs and, judging by the corpses, she carried all her victims to the web's center before wrapping them. I would have brought her back, but I had nothing to keep her in. It seemed a betrayal of Eddie to let her be, but that sort of evened our score.

Next thing I put my hand on was a soft looking leaf. I pulled it away full of nettles.

Although the way back to camp was clearly downhill, I began to go up. I thought to find a vista, see the mountains, orient myself. I was less angry by now and suffered more from the climbing as a result. The rain began again and I picked out a sheltered spot to sit and tend my stinging hand.

I should have been cold and frightened, but I wasn't either. The pain in my hand was subsiding. The jungle was beautiful and the sound of rain a lullaby. I remember wishing that this was where I belonged, that I lived here. Then the heat came on me so hard I couldn't wish at all.

A noise brought me out of it—a crashing in the bamboo. Turning, I saw the movement of leaves and the backside of something rather like a large black bear. A gorilla has a strange way of walking—on the hind feet and the knuckles, but with arms so long their backs are hardly bent. I had one clear look and then the creature was gone. But I could still hear it and I was determined to see it again.

I knew I'd never have another chance; even if we did see one later the men would take it over. I was still too hot. My shirt was drenched from sweat and rain; my pants, too, and making a noise whenever I bent my knees. So I removed everything and put back only my socks and boots. I left the rest of my clothes folded on the spot where I'd been sitting, picked up my rifle, and went into the bamboo.

Around a rock, under a log, over a root, behind a tree was the prettiest open meadow you'd ever hope to see. Three gorillas were in it, one male, two female. It might have been a harem. It might have been a family—a father, mother and daughter. The sun came out. One female combed the other with her hands, the two of them blinking in the sun. The male was seated in a patch of wild carrots, pulling and eating them with no particular ardor. I could see his profile and the gray in his fur. He twitched his fingers a bit, like a man listening to music. There were flowers—pink and white—in concentric circles where some pond had been and now wasn't. One lone tree. I stood and looked for a good long time.

Then I raised the barrel of my gun. The movement brought the eyes of the male to me. He stood. He was bigger than I could ever have imagined. In the leather of his face I saw surprise, curiosity, caution. Something else, too. Something so human it made me feel like an old woman with no clothes on. I might have shot him just for that, but I knew it wasn't right—to kill him merely because he was more human than I anticipated. He thumped his chest, a rhythmic beat that made the women look to him. He showed me his teeth. Then he turned and took the women away.

I watched it all through the sight of my gun. I might have hit him several times—spared the women, freed the women. But I couldn't see that they wanted freeing and Eddie had told me never to shoot a gun angry. The gorillas faded from the meadow. I was cold then and I went for my clothes.

Russell had beaten me to them. He stood with two of our guides, staring down at my neatly folded pants. Nothing for it but to walk up beside him and pick them up, shake them for ants, put them on. He turned his back as I dressed and he couldn't manage a word. I was even more embarrassed. "Eddie must be frantic," I said to break the awkwardness.

"All of us, completely beside ourselves. Did you find any sign of her?" Which was how I learned that Beverly had disappeared.

We were closer to camp than I'd feared if farther than I'd hoped. While we walked I did my best to recount my final conversation with Beverly to Russell. I was, apparently, the last to have seen her. The card game had broken up soon after I left and the men gone their separate ways. A couple of hours later, Merion began looking for Beverly who was no longer in her tent. No one was alarmed, at first, but by now they were.

I was made to repeat everything she'd said again and again and questioned over it, too, though there was nothing useful in it and soon I began to feel I'd made up every word. Archer asked our guides to look over the ground about the pool and around her tent. He had some cowboy scene in his mind, I suppose, the primitive who can read a broken branch, a footprint, a bit of fur and piece it all together. Our guides looked with great seriousness, but found nothing. We searched and called and sent up signaling shots until night came over us.

"She was taken by the gorillas," Merion told us. "Just as I said she'd be." I tried to read his face in the red of the firelight, but couldn't. Nor catch his tone of voice.

"No prints," our chief guide repeated. "No sign."

That night our cook refused to make us dinner. The natives were talking a great deal amongst themselves, very quiet. To us they said as little as possible. Archer demanded an explanation, but got nothing but dodge and evasion.

"They're scared," Eddie said, but I didn't see this.

A night even more bitter than the last and Beverly not dressed for it. In the morning the porters came to Archer to say they were going back. No measure of arguing or threatening or bribing changed their minds. We could come or stay as we chose; it was clearly of no moment to them. I, of course, was given no choice, but was sent back to the mission with the rest of the gear excepting what the men kept behind.

At Lulenga one of the porters tried to speak with me. He had no English and I followed none of it except Beverly's name. I told him to wait while I fetched one of the fathers to translate, but he misunderstood or else he refused. When we returned he was gone and I never did see him again.

The men stayed eight more days on Mount Mikeno and never found so much as a bracelet.

Because I'm a woman I wasn't there for the parts you want most to hear. The waiting and the not-knowing were, in my view of things, as hard or harder than the searching, but you don't make stories out of that. Something happened to Beverly, but I can't tell you what. Something happened on the mountain after I left, something that brought Eddie back to me so altered in spirit I felt I hardly knew him, but I wasn't there to see what it was. Eddie and I departed Africa immediately and not in the company of the other men in our party. We didn't even pack up all our spiders.

For months after, I wished to talk about Beverly, to put together this possibility and that possibility and settle on something I could live with. I felt the need most strongly at night. But Eddie couldn't hear her name. He'd sunk so deep into himself, he rarely looked out. He stopped sleeping and wept from time to time and these were things he did his best to hide from me. I tried to talk to him about it, I tried to be patient and loving, I tried to be kind. I failed in all these things.

A year, two more passed, and he began to resemble himself again, but never in full. My full, true Eddie never did come back from the jungle.

Then one day, at breakfast, with nothing particular to prompt it, he told me there'd been a massacre. That after I left for Lulenga the men had spent the days hunting and killing gorillas. He didn't describe it to me at all, yet it sprang bright and terrible into my mind, my own little family group lying in their blood in the meadow.

Forty or more, Eddie said. Probably more. Over several days. Babies, too. They couldn't even bring the bodies back; it looked so bad to be collecting when Beverly was gone. They'd slaughtered the gorillas as if they were cows.

Eddie was dressed in his old plaid robe, his gray hair in uncombed bunches, crying into his fried eggs. I wasn't talking, but he put his hands over his ears in case I did. He was shaking all over from weeping, his head trembling on his neck. "It felt like murder," he said. "Just exactly like murder."

I took his hands down from his head and held on hard. "I expect it was mostly Merion."

"No," he said. "It was mostly me."

At first, Eddie told me, Merion was certain the gorillas had taken Beverly. But later, he began to comment on the strange behavior of the porters. How they wouldn't talk to us, but whispered to each other. How they left so quickly. "I was afraid," Eddie told me. "So upset about Beverly and then terribly afraid. Russell and Merion, they were so angry I could smell it. I thought at any moment one of them would say something that couldn't be unsaid, something that would get to the Belgians. And then I wouldn't be able to stop it anymore. So I kept us stuck on the gorillas. I kept us going after them. I kept us angry until we had killed so very many and were all so ashamed, there would be no way to turn and accuse someone new."

I still didn't quite understand. "Do you think one of the porters killed Beverly?" It was a possibility that had occurred to me, too; I admit it.

"No," said Eddie. "That's my point. But you saw how the blacks were treated back at Lulenga. You saw the chains and the beatings. I couldn't let them be suspected." His voice was so clogged I could hardly make out the words. "I need you to tell me I did the right thing."

So I told him. I told him he was the best man I ever knew. "Thank you," he said. And with that he shook off my hands, dried his eyes, and left the table.

That night I tried to talk to him again. I tried to say that there was nothing he could do that I wouldn't forgive. "You've always been too easy on me," he answered. And the next time I brought it up, "If you love me, we'll never talk about this again."

Eddie died three years later without another word on the subject passing between us. In the end, to be honest, I suppose I found that silence rather unforgivable. His death even more so. I have never liked being alone.

As every day I more surely am; it's the blessing of a long life. Just me left now, the first white woman to see the wild gorillas and the one who saw nothing else—not the chains, not the beatings, not the massacre. I can't help worrying over it all again, now I know Archer's dead and only me to tell it, though no way of telling puts it to rest.

Since my eyes went, a girl comes to read to me twice a week. For the longest time I wanted nothing to do with gorillas, but now I have her scouting out articles as we're finally starting to really see how they live. The thinking still seems to be harems, but with the females slipping off from time to time to be with whomever they wish.

And what I notice most in the articles is not the apes. My attention is caught instead by these young women who'd sooner live in the jungle with the chimpanzees or the orangutans or the great mountain gorillas. These women who freely choose it—the Goodalls and the Galdikas and the Fosseys. And I think to myself how there is nothing new under the sun, and maybe all those women carried off by gorillas in those old stories, maybe they all freely chose it.

When I am tired and have thought too much about it all, Beverly's last words come back to me. Mostly I put them straight out of my head, think about anything else. Who remembers what she said? Who knows what she meant?

But there are other times when I let them in. Turn them over. Then they become, not a threat as I originally heard them, but an invitation. On those days I can pretend that she's still there in the jungle, dipping her feet, eating wild carrots, and waiting for me. I can pretend that I'll be joining her whenever I wish and just as soon as I please.

In *The Encyclopedia of Science Fiction,* edited by John Clute and Peter Nicholls, author Brian Stableford refers to Barry N. Malzberg's writing as "unparalleled in its intensity and in its apocalyptic sensibility." He also writes that Malzberg "is a master of black humor, and is one of the few writers to have used SF's vocabulary of ideas extensively as apparatus in psychological landscapes, dramatizing relationships between the human mind and its social environment in an SF theatre of the absurd."

Malzberg profoundly understands that his fiction is but a metaphor for his life; and his life, as refracted through such brilliant novels as *Herovit's World,* becomes a metaphor for science fiction and the wider literature. It should come as no surprise that he has become known as the conscience of SF. Take a look at his postmodern history of the genre, *The Engines of the Night,* where fiction and autobiography seamlessly mesh. And take a look at the autobiographical essay that follows. It was published in the June 2003 issue of *The Magazine of Fantasy & Science Fiction:* a special Barry Malzberg issue.

Gordon Van Guilder, the editor and publisher of *F&SF,* writes:

"One of the great joys of alternate history stories lies in imagining the different paths reality might take. I find it relatively easy to imagine what might have happened if Barry Malzberg had become the editor of *The New York Times Book Review* (three intense years in which the publication broke all their own rules, followed by the ousting of Barry and fifteen years of editors attempting to undo what he had done) or if he had become a critic at large for *The New Yorker* (a position he'd still hold, having created a whole class of writers and musicians who would express both joy and dismay at having been "Malzberged"). Here is an essay that outlines a path Barry did take, one that leads us behind the scenes of one of the most important literary outposts of the past fifty years. . . ."

TRIPPING WITH THE ALCHEMIST

BARRY N. MALZBERG

As we began so must we end. As we die with the living, deep tip of the Hatlo Hat to Thomas Stearns Eliot and a wink to our own honorable Robert Silverberg, so we are born with the dead. (*Magazine of Fantasy & Science Fiction,* by the way: April 1974 issue.) Let us see if we can manage that ever-interesting phenomenon.

They speak, and as we age, their voices are ever more convincing, signatory than those of the living. Eventually, as one prepares to join the majority, they become the entire population.

Their voices are insistent; they carry truths which are, perhaps, not really understood for a long time. I scuttle through small and sudden land mines of understanding now: and every day I step on one which I had not known was there. It ignites.

This is, fortunately, a metaphor so far. Nonetheless, here are some results of that continuing ignition.

I have been in publishing for thirty-eight years now and mark the entrance into publishing as the onset of the real world. Almost everything I know today I learned there because almost everything I thought I knew to that point was wrong. So bid farewell for just a little while to the living and let us venture into that other and more richly populated land from which at least we travelers will for a time emerge.

I began work and adult life there on June 2, 1965. "There" was the Scott Meredith Literary Agency, then, according to the brochure it sent to all prospective fee clients and, in fact, to almost everyone else, the largest, most famous, and most successful literary agency in the country. Millions of copies of this brochure circulated from late 1967 after the agency had abandoned its twenty-year full-page ad in *Writer's Digest.* The brochure continued to circulate for a while after the death in February 1993 of Scott Meredith, a death which right up to the end had seemed impossible to him and was therefore utterly surprising. Death was by no means even remotely in his Directory of Operations. Would have been in the worst taste, you know.

I was then just short of twenty-six, six-feet-four-and-a-half inches then as now, a sullen and recriminative two hundred pounds with the foundation of a really promising practicing alcoholism (sixteen happy years of that lay ahead of me) and was, I thought, a fetchingly and romantically bitter, altogether enterprising lad. What I did not know and had to learn was that my bitterness was callow and although I thought I understood the situation, I did not. Now I do. Then I would have said that the bitterness could be allayed and the situation fixed; now I know that nothing could have truly changed the situation. Get the editors to pay attention to me, make a few decent sales, get work into the O. Henry Prize Stories, win the National Book Award. Like Phillip Roth had at twenty-six. Phillip Roth was happy, wasn't he? So why wouldn't this work for me? Editors had been miserable to me, their indifference was shocking, but this was only because I didn't have the right connections. Maybe Scott Meredith would give me the connections. He was selling Norman Mailer, wasn't he? If Scott could sell Norman Mailer for a million dollars, then he could certainly sell me for a few hundred and get me going. Of course I had been hired as a fee reader, not as Norman Mailer-manqué. But why couldn't I be both? In my last months on the graduate fellowship at Syracuse University I had queried Scott Meredith and had received a pitch for the fee department.

Twenty-five dollars to read and evaluate the novella I had described, The Barracks Rage. "You sound like just the kind of promising and ambitious writer in whom we are most interested," Scott Meredith wrote, "And I would be happy to work with you. Unfortunately and until you prove you can earn your keep on commission through steady sales, we must charge a modest fee to defray our expenses while we evaluate your work and, we hope, groom you for the major markets." Seemed reasonable to me. If I had had twenty-five dollars for such merriment I would have disbursed them and The Barracks Rage at once to Fifth Avenue. Unfortunately, my assets at that time, in March 1965, were a little less than $500, the Fellowship about to expire with the academic year paid $200 a month, and my wife, a CCNY graduate, had been deemed unemployable all around town "because she is married to a student and they quit all the time."

We were going to run out of money, we had determined in October 1964, by June of 1965 unless something in the way of money intervened. Nothing intervened and this proved to be one of the more accurate of my early opinions . . . far more accurate in any case than my evaluation of maiden claimers, three years old and up, at six furlongs had been at Aqueduct racetrack in South Ozone Park somewhat earlier that year. I had had to pass on the agency's offer but I wondered if I would not live to regret that. Would I allow twenty-five dollars to stand between me and Norman Mailer's agent? The harder fact is that I did not have twenty-five dollars' worth of faith in my work by then. I had, in fact, no faith at all. (Somewhat transmogrified, this remains the case.)

Ah those offices! The Scott Meredith Literary Agency might have been the largest and most famous of all successful literary agencies but its quarters, a loftlike sprawl, were unimposing and the room air conditioners barely worked. The place became utterly fetid in the July afternoons. Those offices were in the second building the agency had occupied, this in 1949, three years after its founding. In that summer of Summer Knowledge, they were at 580 Fifth Avenue, at 47th Street in Manhattan's diamond district. That district was magnificently if most malevolently described by that one-time employee in a very short story, "None So Blind," which was published in the pages of this magazine about forty years ago. Blind beggars and their dogs, keening voices, Orthodox Jews in full raiment staggering, their pockets bulging with diamonds. Huddled, hurried conferences on the sidewalk or in the street, the furtive exchange of jewels for money, the barking of the dogs, scuttle of tragic. The diamond district conflated greed and piety, fast commerce and duplicity; singular prayer and loss in a noisomely abrupt and jangled fashion.

Years later, a friend who had worked in the area confided that there had been a cathouse on the second floor of a building just west of Fifth Avenue where the dealers could clamber upstairs to jump the bones, their pockets atwinkle with diamonds. James Blish would surely have included that if he had known. For subsequent publication, he went to what was probably the original title, "Who's in Charge Here?" His answer, as mine in my own context was clear: not me, boss. The aliens disguised as blind beggars? Their dogs who were perhaps Masters of it all? Scott Meredith? Sidney Meredith? Pick a number as long as it wasn't mine. Sure wasn't mine.

All these years later, well more than half a lifetime, those early, stunned weeks at what I came to think of as the slaughterhouse are as vivid in recall as they were staggering through that brilliant, hard summer. Whatever had brought me for a walk-in role that turned into a spectacular if intermittent run as a supernumerary, it was an even richer and more variegated time in the life of the agency.

In fact, it was that summer which we know was pivotal for the nation, the end of the Great Society and the true launching of Vietnam, and it was a significant summer for the agency as well. Dynastic shifts were attempted, working methods became ever more empiric. In the hallway outside the office stood, somewhat sullenly, two agents from the FBI. The FBI was eager to meet with Scott, to have a discussion about his supply service. The agency, under another corporate name, had been an underground railroad for manuscript pornography published by Greenleaf Publications in California and Hoover's boys were determinedly on the case, dedicated to preserving the union from graphic (not too graphic, however) descriptions of the act of generation.

Unfortunately for Hoover, although certainly good if temporary news to Greenleaf's eventually indicted publisher and editor-in-chief, no photograph of Scott Meredith had ever been published. Therefore, he was able to whisk through the less public of the agency's two entrances (PACKAGE DELIVERY ONLY) without notice. Staff were instructed to say, "Mr. Meredith is on a very extended selling tour through the capitals of Europe and we have no idea when he will return." After a couple of months of this form of unaudited Home Relief, Hoover's men were withdrawn and the inquiry refocused upon demand rather than supply . . . much like, come to think of it, the War on Drugs so many decades later.

Meanwhile, Scott and his brother, known to all as Sidney although there were rumors that this was not his name, were engaged in a continuing series of negotiations to sell the agency to someone, anyone, please. At the right price, please. Scott had at that time been in business for nineteen years, was forty-two years old, perhaps felt that the parade was passing him by although he engaged not at all in the more conventional acting-out of the bored or entrapped middle-aged male.

The brothers, always it seemed deeply engaged in anguished conversation, would stalk from the office somewhere toward midday with expressions of expectancy; they always returned looking sullen. Some wit, on one afternoon of extended absence, drew a crude picture of an ocean liner, the sea to the top of its smokestacks, the caption GOOD SHIP SMLA. The ship be sinking.

But that simply wasn't so. The ship wasn't sinking, regardless of Hoover's machinations; heedless of Scott's boredom, indifferent to the morale of its interchangeable employees, the agency then and for several years had been a consequence which ran well on magic, reflex, and iron ritual, whatever the state of employee morale. Kemelman was on the bestseller list, Hunter's "87th precinct" was flourishing, Mailer was turning to nonfiction. And fee business was excellent, about ninety scripts a week for a two-man fee department which very quickly became three, then four, and by 1968 had reached five. In the late 1970s and early 1980s there were as many as eight full-time fee men, each accountable for about thirty scripts a week. The scripts ran the full range of fiction and nonfiction, long and short, ambitious and cowardly, proficient to laughably inept (inept dominated). It was vox populi in its purest yet most variegate form and each of those scripts was accompanied with a check: ten dollars then for the magazine pieces, thirty-five dollars for the novels. At the time, submissions of short stories and articles ran at a ratio of five to one to books; later, of course, as the market shifted, that ratio shifted and by the early 1980s five to one was in favor of the novels.

The people who wrote the reports (Scott Meredith always signed them, the reports bore no other signature until the day after his death: continuity, repression of identity, no fee writer would ever be given the kind of exposure which might lead him to set up a competitive business) received roughly twenty percent of the take. "Capitalism in its purest, most open form," one fee writer noted quizzically. "You know what they are paying, you see what you are getting. They send thirty-five dollars with a novel, you get ten dollars for doing all of the work. Pay seventy percent of your income for desk space and a letterhead. And quit or stay, you are swamped by the system."

Very early in my employment, the later-day fetidity of the offices neatly externalizing my mental state and the state of the manuscripts I was evaluating, I came to the irresistible notion of a novel based on the fee department. Probably in epistolary format, back-and-forth between a range of fee clients and the wretches responding to them, my novel would partake of the collision of gullibility and indifference, intensity and disdain, all of it as systematized as an assembly line, the authors of the responses as indifferent to the meaning and central absurdity of the situation as swallows in a cathedral. All that human need, ten- and thirty-five-dollar checks tremblingly enclosed, the rage, power fantasies, sexual speculations, unified gravity theories, and texts on the Apocalypse skimmed by the underpaid Youth of America, the reports synchronically indulgent and dismissive. Ah, that slaughterhouse! The purity and folly of pseudo-gemeinschaft in a country whose devices were far overtaking the capacity of most people to deal with them.

"So why don't you write it?" Victor Levine, the other fee guy, said when I told him of my own human need. "I bet there would be a lot of people interested."

"I'll tell you why I can't," I said. "Because every time I think of writing that novel, I see another novel sitting like a big rock in the middle of the road: Nathanael West's novel, *Miss Lonelyhearts.* And I can't drive around it."

The protagonist of *Miss Lonelyhearts* is a newspaper reporter detailed to the advice column; the queries from the lonely, the mad, the deformed, drive him crazy. "The letters weren't funny. They weren't funny any more." Miss Lonelyhearts—we never know him by any other name—finally driven crazy by the letters and by his own helplessness, assaults his ungiving editor Shrike and disappears into the vessel of his own need just as the fee reader, juxtaposed against the shattered, the unsculptured, the desperate voices, could, were contempt and self-mockery to fail, himself fall into the abyss of his contempt. Many did.

I might have also mentioned West's other famous novel, *The Day of the Locust,* in which the dispossessed, the anonymous, and infuriated who had come to California to die, knowing that they could go no further, that they had run out of Continent, riot at a Hollywood movie premiere and bring to life the dream-canvas of its protagonist, "the Burning of Los Angeles."

But I did not think of *The Day of the Locust* then; *Miss Lonelyhearts* was just about as far as I could go in that first post-graduate summer. And although I found a few objective-correlatives for the fee department (most notably in my epistolary short story "Agony Column" where the guy, an outraged resident of Manhattan's West Side, cannot get the politicians or magazine editors to send him in response to his outrage or his creation anything other than form rejections getting his name wrong), I never wrote the novel.

Others did, at least their own version. Mark David Chapman and John Hinckley, in what we (and they) laughingly call "real-life" did enact manuscript submission with a bullet as the writing and a gun as the delivery system. Lennon down in the courtyard, Reagan in the ambulance, now *that* was getting the editors' attention. So, complete with the alleged assassin's diary, a fee script if ever one existed, did Arthur Bremer, nemesis of George Wallace. The novel itself was written by that ex-employee Norman Spinrad in 1967 but *The Children of Hamelin,* after running serially in *The Los Angeles Free Press,* failed to find a book publisher. Only in 1993 did the novel obtain some limited visibility: a lone publishing entrepreneur in Texas sent out a scanty small press edition.

Donald Westlake's savage novel, *Adios Scheherezade,* based on the Greenleaf underground railroad, was, when you thought about it, a paradigm of the fee business and Westlake's riotous chapter of a fake literary agent in *Dancing Aztecs* is quite good but *Fee,* my working title for the novel which never quite worked, languished entire. Too late now and the culture has changed; it would have to be a historical novel: the Internet has completely reconfigured the situation. So this poisoned kiss and abrazzo appearing in *Fantasy & Science Fiction* almost exactly thirty-five years after my first contribution "Final War" (4/68 as by K. M. O'Donnell), is about as close as I am likely to get in or out of this lifetime.

Call the hot months of 1965 the Summer of the Fee, the alienation effect turning into swift and comedic commerce under my very eyes. "So this is the way it works," I mused, "I wonder if it's this way everywhere, if *The Hudson Review* or Curtis Brown are like this." Well, I learned, sometimes but probably not sufficiently; Scott Meredith's fee department was the default mode of writing itself, there was nothing so pure, nothing which so frankly exposed the situation.

But the summer embraced for the agency and the great Out There far more: it was the summer Evan Hunter's *Paper Dragon,* a novel of plagiarism, came in on contract (with a long internal monologue which owed a little more to Molly Bloom than perhaps it should), the summer that Mailer was struggling with *Why Are We in Vietnam?,* a novel he hated, but which he owed contractually to Putnam, written in three or four weeks to get Walter Minton to go away. (In another summer twenty years later, Mailer would perform the same stunt with *Tough Guys Don't Dance,* this time to escape from a commitment to Little Brown.) It was the summer that Harry Kemelman's *Friday the Rabbi Slept Late,* a thousand dollar first mystery novel published by a virtually unknown fifty-seven-year-old mystery short story writer and essayist on Orthodox Judaism, went in its paperback edition to the top of the bestseller lists, certainly not the agency's first bestseller but maybe its most successful commercial work to that time. Mailer's *An American Dream* had had the press, but Mailer never sold to his reputation, a conclusion which publisher after publisher grimly came to understand in the decades to follow.

It was the summer that George Lincoln Rockwell, founder and chief officer of the Nazi Party of America, was gunned to death in a Virginia parking lot by a disgruntled party member who felt that Rockwell was insufficiently committed to the cause. It was the second and last summer for the extravagantly disastrous and underattended New York World's Fair, brought to the city through the special courtesy of Robert Moses, and a bankruptcy petition like most of Moses's bigger ideas. In 1964, the Fair had run as a double feature with the Harlem riots, of which in its conclusive, public demonstration of the soaring indifference of the city's politicians to the real lives of more than half New York's population, it had been partially the cause.

And it was notably the summer—this was early July and it came live from the White House—in which Lyndon Baines Johnson announced the first massive increase in troops, the expansion of the draft calls while at the same time speaking of his reluctance to have "the flower of American youth" wasted in Vietnam. He'd find the courage, however. Nothing too difficult for this President. Found in time for the Tet offensive and the New Hampshire primary, too.

It was the summer that Scott went international, big plans for an agency whose rolling concourse would someday embrace Editions Gallimard and the ruins of Athens. He and Sidney, his faithful companion, four years older but known by all as the water-carrier, flew to London to open the new branch. Tomorrow the world. It was the summer that Scott and Sidney, en famille, traveled to Caesar's Palace in Las Vegas where, according to the literature mailed prospective fee clients, Scott, that big player, gambled all again and again on a roll of the dice.

It was not meant to be an eventful summer. My gambling days were over, I insisted, excluding the racetrack which was metaphysical. The Schubert Foundation Playwriting Fellow at Syracuse University had given it up after an exciting year of unceasing rejection and encroaching poverty; at the end, the Playwriting Fellow and his spouse had $200 in savings and a 1960 Dodge worth approximately the same and $750 worth of debt to the New York State Student Loan Fund. Drowning in rejection and overwhelmed by self-pity, or at least an absence of self-regard, the Playwriting Fellow declined an even larger Fellowship which would have given him another academic year, $3500 plus tuition and the opportunity to receive many more teasing letters of rejection from C. Michael Curtis of *The Atlantic Monthly,* and with his spouse (who reclaimed her old job) returned to New York City. "You say you like to read and write," the lady at Career Blazers said. "Well, here is a job at a literary agency where you read all the time. You should like that." Ninety dollars a week. And an employment agency's fee of $290, deducted over the first seven weeks, from my salary. Blaze that career!

So I reported to 580 Fifth Avenue, 13th Floor, Suite 706. There I was handed the famous "Rattlesnake Cave" test paper. This was an appalling Western short story of that title by one "Ray D. Lester," the name of the author an ancient agency in-joke; the story had been written in the late 1940s by Milton Lesser (who later became the mystery writer Stephen Marlowe) and given the byline as a jab at his coworker, Lester del Rey. The story mirthlessly described courtship hijinks narrated in dialect by an old-timer, and I aced it. ("The bosses really liked what you did," Richard Curtis said.) *Finnegans Wake, Hamlet, Macbeth, Pale Fire* have nothing on "Rattlesnake Cave," which for forty-seven years acted as a kind of keeper of all the keys. The finest minds of several generations were brought to notes and commentary: Dialect doesn't work well in the contemporary markets, Mr. Lester, and the frame device is also not much liked by contemporary editors. You should approach your material directly. Not in dialect. Find a sympathetic lead character. Present that sympathetic lead with an insuperable problem. Find a meaningful resolution which comes inevitably from the character's efforts to solve that problem. Make sure that the lead solves the problem unless you are writing that graduate student quality lit stuff but if you are, remember that it's not going to get you into *Ranch Romances* or *The Saturday Evening Post*. Maybe once in a while *Alfred Hitchcock's Mystery Magazine,* but you better be damned careful.

Ah, tempora! Ah mores! O lost and by the wind grieved! There I was, shortly ensconced at an IBM in that large, open, poorly air-conditioned office, no partitions, the doorways of the bosses' offices shut against the madding crowd, selected to write ENCOURAGING, HELPFUL, PLEASANT (capitals on the test sheet explaining the demands made of the prospective critic) letters to fee clients who were availing themselves of the evaluative and (they hoped) marketing services of the world's leading literary agent. ENCOURAGING, HELPFUL, PLEASANT letters nonetheless in the defined and irreversible negative turned out to be my signal talent; like the man with the chicken, I discovered within myself predilection and abilities I could not have measured. The Playwriting Fellow could really turn out those letters. Within three weeks he was making a piecework $260 a week writing ENCOURAGING, HELPFUL letters on fifteen to twenty novels and twenty to thirty short stories and astonishing the bosses every day of the week.

There had been remarkable fee men (the job historically filled 98 out of 100 vacancies and turnover with men; "fee women," of whom there had been one or two, simply could not or would not stand up to the brute demands of the job) in the past and there were more to come in the future but I had solved the system in a way that no one to that point had managed.

I was making a living wage at a job not construed to offer a living wage. "This man is a treasure," Sidney Meredith whispered to Richard Curtis on my fourth day of employment when I had delivered seven acceptable fee reports before two P.M. Scott Meredith, an equal opportunity exploiter (as long as you were white and male), certainly knew what to do with a treasure.

In the reminiscent introduction to *The Best of Malzberg* (Pocket Books, 1976), I referred to myself as the Golden Eagle and oh, my friends and ah, my foes, how the feathers flew!

And so flew, against all wiser counsel, against all the experience of the graduate year, that fierce and dark bird, ambition. Hello darkness, my old friend. Ambition fluttered its battered wings that summer, peeped feebly in the cage, scratched a few seeds, nibbled at the bars. Gothics weren't for me, nor Westerns, but mysteries and science fiction were possibilities. Science fiction looked particularly interesting. The agency represented an entire range of science fiction writers from Arthur C. Clarke and Poul Anderson through the middle ranges—Reynolds, Anvil, Philip Kindred Dick, who was then struggling to make $5000 a year on small paperback advances and penny-a-word serial rights from *Worlds of Tomorrow*—and down to what the charitable Damon Knight had in a letter called the "dung beetles" . . . people like X or Y who had sold through the big magazine markets of the 1950s and then had mirrored the collapse of those markets but were still being carried by Scott who, that fan, was sentimental about broken-down science fiction writers in a way he never was of his mysterists, confession writers, Western writers and (just two or three here) literary writers. (There also existed a good number of prominent science fiction writers who had, through the years, been represented by or quit the agency, but this was not to concern me for a while. The agency was contemptuous of its client list.)

"These guys are selling," I thought, looking at the manuscripts of the middle-to-bottom range. "If they can do it, maybe I can. After all, I used to read a lot of this stuff. I can start off being modest. *Galaxy* is paying three cents a word; *Worlds of If* a penny a word, *Analog* five cents. Not to forget the big money at Belmont or Lancer: fifteen hundred dollars for a novel. Avon and NAL might pay even more than that. This sure beats *The Hudson Review,* which isn't buying me anyway."

I decided to be cunning. I had indeed read a lot of this stuff. The newsstand 6/51 *Astounding* was the first sf publication I had encountered, and soon enough I found in Horace Gold's *Galaxy* of early 1952, that Year of the Jackpot, the true and the real: *Demolished Man,* "Command Performance," and a little later *Gravy Planet,* "Delay in Transit," "Baby Is Three," an astonishing run then as it would be now . . . I had been a stone science fiction fan, perhaps as fiercely devoted as any (although with no knowledge then of an organized or unorganized fandom) in those glowing years. Then came high school, however, and a sudden acquaintance with Thomas Wolfe

and a sense that it was time to put away childish things, go for the gonfalon.
"I wanted to be Thomas Wolfe, write furiously, get laid, drink a lot and die
young," I wrote in a reminiscent piece much later of that time and thus began a cyclical course. I alternated between periods of renunciation of science fiction and furious reading; I accumulated magazines and sold them
repeatedly, I was and was not a science fiction fan and finally walked away
from all of it in my freshman year at Syracuse, determined as never before
to be serious, to write fiercely, drink brutally, get laid, and die young.

I took care of the drinking part efficiently, showing real promise. I did
not show equal gifts for the other parts, although I tried and in the Schubert
Foundation year tried very hard indeed to be Philip Roth or at least Evan S.
Connell, Jr. But by the time I had staggered away from Syracuse and into the
odorous loft of Suite 706, I was certainly ready to try something else. Anvil
and Reynolds seemed to be selling this stuff, why not me? Philip K. Dick
was publishing work like "Cantata 140" and "Oh to Be a Blobel!" At two
and three cents a word: why not me? It was time to remember that my very
first rejection slip in 1951 had come from *Amazing Stories*.

Selah: I might have been detached from science fiction at this time,
hadn't read it in a while, had all those quality lit ambitions (Richard Wilson
had been in a playwriting course with me earlier that year and it was only
years later that I made the connection between that unpromising play-
wright and the crack science fiction writer and Futurian, so detached was I)
but maybe, just maybe I could slip through some of this stuff as well.
Charles Fontenay and Winston K. Marks had sold between them over a
hundred short stories (Fontenay had sold a couple of Ace Doubles as well);
if they could do it, why not me? "Ambition has been the undoing of better
men than you and me," Bill Pronzini and I were to come to counsel one
another in much later summers, but in 1965, all against my will, ambition
was the only factor which stood between me and a career of HELPFUL
ENCOURAGING letters, and slowly over the next year, as the Summer of
Love held its breath and came toward us, as LBJ got increasingly sullen in
his recently revealed conversations with Richard Russell about those
Kennedy bastards who had put him into this Vietnam thing, as Scott summoned his entire staff into his office on the night of the Great New York
Blackout of 11/65 and shakily insisted that they keep him company by
candlelight . . . as all of this and so much else was happening I was teaching
myself in the most painful way to write salable science fiction.

Broke-down literary palace that I might have been, I was densely shrewd
enough to sense that science fiction offered a market. Of my further adventures much has been recorded in *Engines of the Night* and various introductions and essays scattered here and there and I will relent on the catalog.

I worked at the agency continuously from 6/65 until 11/67 when I
was fired for reasons never made clear ("You're obviously smarter than me

but you make me uncomfortable," Scott said) and went off to become briefly Managing Editor of the doomed men's magazine, *Escapade.* (I had already been fired in 5/66 very late in my wife's first pregnancy but that firing was rescinded, possibly because I told Sidney when he did it that his timing was abominable: surely now the brothers should have waited until my wife was in the labor room with the infant half-delivered and then drop the hammer.) After *Escapade*'s collapse I was in and out of the agency's fee department as a not-quite member of staff until 8/27/71 when I looked at an IBM typewriter which stared back at me, the two of us saying in alternating lines, "I cannot do this any more, I cannot write another fee report, I have reached the end of the line here," and offered two weeks' notice. "Don't worry about notice," I was told, "Just get the hell out of here now. Go please. Just go."

Which I did for ten years, embarking upon what I suppose could be called a full-time freelancing career ("Writing is not a full-time occupation," Big Ernie had said and Big Ernie had it right, all the way up to Big Rifle on Big Morning in Big Ketchum . . . but he had a solution for the problem). Many, many millions of words and much angst later I came to my Perfect Storm of epiphany in March of 1981: if I kept on attempting to do what I could barely do anymore it was going to destroy me and this was no metaphor, no figure of speech. "Need a fee man?" I wrote Sidney Meredith. The next day was the day that Hinckley submitted his bullet without a covering letter, sending Reagan into many weeks of considered editorial response. It was very clear that my internal chaos, reflected in the larger situation, would indeed drag me swiftly to the end of days without intervention, and a few days after that I had my reenlistment interview. "We have to know that you won't leave us in a couple of weeks," Sidney said, "That you'll be able to give us at least a year." "I'll give you a year," I said, "In fact I'll sign a statement giving you two." I figured two years would be all I needed to figure out my next move and a way back to writing's swamp.

Twelve years later, in the calamitous afterwash of Scott's death, I realized that I was still trying to figure out my next move. Eight years after that when the Agency's dwindled aftermath moved to new and tiny quarters which left me without desk space, I decided that I was just on the verge of finding my next move, just polishing it up, boss, a condition which, back at home, continues. Finding a way back, folks.

But the agency suspires in memory. While I continued to ponder my next move, the agency overtakes in memory. It had become a most remarkable, almost inimitable machine so staggeringly efficient that it could transcend its own frequent incompetence which grips. As John Campbell was

Astounding and for a long time science fiction itself, so was the Scott Mere-dith Literary Agency, charnel house and empirical majesty Scott Feldman. Scott Feldman as Scott Meredith was among the most significant and sig-natory of all the jumped-up fans of his active generation, the founders, those architects of First Fandom, the Futurians, the Hydra Club, the early World Science Fiction Conventions beginning in 1939. The Futurians and their friends were a pool from which many soon prominent in science fic-tion were extracted, but Scott Meredith was unusual in that he became prominent outside of science fiction, detached himself from it utterly. X. J. Kennedy, the poet, and perhaps Jack Speer, the Congressman from Wash-ington State, were the only figures comparable to have emerged from sci-ence fiction fanac to public careers . . . and had through the course of those careers suppressed the linkage to science fiction.

"I owe Scott everything," Norman Spinrad, who had worked at the agency from 1962 to 1964, once said to me. "He taught me what I needed to know. I hated it but it was the most valuable thing that ever happened to me as a writer. Scott taught me publishing! Scott showed me early what a cesspool it was, what shit it was, I never had to be disillusioned after that."

Of course that is the kind of insight which can be well expanded. It was not only publishing which could be regarded as a cesspool. No one who spent more than a few months at Scott Meredith was ever to be sur-prised by any of the revelations of Watergate. Watergate as a demonstration of the methodology of concealment, the institutionalization of lying, was the Scott Meredith Agency written much larger. And much less effective.

And no writer ever employed by that agency—Lawrence Block, Don-ald E. Westlake, James Blish, Damon Knight, Phil Klass (briefly), Laurence M. Janifer, James Jerrold Mundis, Richard Curtis, Stephen Marlowe, Evan Hunter—would have said any different. From the proselytizing, EN-COURAGING HELPFUL fee department at one end to the peregrina-tions of Mailer or Wodehouse or Drew Pearson or Meyer Levin or Gerald Green or Arthur Clarke, Irving Shulman, and later, Carl Sagan, the triumph of Grub Street and its processes was never in question. The machinery of the agency, its institutionalization of misdirection, seemed initially complex to the uninformed, but it proclaimed itself—as Spinrad came to attest—in utter simplicity. The agency both refracted and celebrated the corruption of publishing as that corruption, thanks to conglomeratization, the margin-alization of "serious" writing, the centrality of exploitative writing overtook publishing through the decades.

Over and again in the collected works of Larry Block, Donald E. West-lake, Damon Knight—fee men all—occurs what I came to identify as the Meredith Moment: the protagonist stares across a desk or over a car seat or from a barstool at his companion and senses for the first time the full and awful corruption of that other person; a corruption which until then had

been concealed or misdirected but now, in a triggered incident of antago-
nism, reveals itself full and clear. That moment is in Westlake's first mystery,
The Mercenaries, when the protégé of a mobster suddenly understands what
a mobster really does. It appears many times in Larry Block's Matthew
Scudder novels when his alcoholic, broken ex-cop sees evil entire and real-
izes that he must be as evil to vanquish that source. It is there again and
again in Hunter's "87th Precinct" novels, it is there in Damon Knight's
1950s short story in the strange art machine which created freehand masterpieces: disassembled it is empty; little shafts of light cutting through its
dark space. Norman Spinrad's novel, *The Mind Game,* is ostensibly a roman
à clef on Scientology, but Spinrad's smug and obdurate guru owes more to
the man for whom Spinrad had worked closely in the early 1960s than it
does to L. Ron Hubbard, whom Spinrad had never met.

Was Scott really that way? Or were these miserably treated and uniformly underpaid employees magnifying Scott because their resentment itself was enormous? Great recrimination demands a large subject, will
invent one if it does not exist. This is a difficult call. The real Scott Meredith was elusive. "Who is the real Scott Meredith?" a young editor, Melinda
Kaplan, asked the table at an after-hours social.

("Maybe there is no real Scott Meredith," I said. "Or maybe the 'real'
Scott Meredith is exactly he who we construct." Hard to know.) This man
was elusive and not only to the FBI; his first name is still in dispute. Isaac
Asimov recalls him as "Scott Feldman" in *In Memory Yet Green,* but some
fans believe that he was really named *Sidney,* that he took the more upscale
"Scott" in early childhood and then, just as he had saddled his brother Sidney with the grubbier clerical details of the agency, so he had given his
brother his own first name, pushing Sid's real first name, whatever that had
been, off the deck into the briny blue. No definitive version ever emerged.

It would seem that the agency had been founded incontestably upon a
paradigm of deceit. Always, from the start, those letters written in Scott's
name were not of his authorship, the manuscripts allegedly read by Scott
were not. (The work of the entire client list was read by Scott's editors.
Scott, by the late 1950s, read the work of no client, not Hunter, not Mailer,
not Kemelman who in Kemelman's fixation on Orthodox Judaism, clearly
made Scott, that very secular Jew, uncomfortable. The letters were signed
by him, however, and the work of the important clients was read for detailed written synopsis to be given Scott so that he could fake his way
through any conversation.) A man of mystery who in his last ten years
would interact only with his three senior editors and secretaries, who
would pass men in the hallway who had worked for him for years and not
even acknowledge them, Scott Meredith was not to be easily understood.
Through the course of my own time in his employ, I recall four or five conversations, none of them longer than five minutes, and maybe fifty nods in

the hallway in passing. Over all the years. And I had to have been, through sheer accumulation of years, at least dimly recognizable.

And yet all of this is only part and a lesser part of the centrality and significance of the agency. Touch it anywhere and it slips away; it is elusive, a mystery, it is one of those religious parables dealing with the unknowable name of the True God. As with ambition, better men than I have battered themselves against the edifice in search of the unreplicatable truth—but there is here, I believe, an answer, that One True Thing which explains if not all, enough. We are getting there. We are, as Mailer would write, prowling the terrain, we have the beast in view; we are in difficult land, glimpsing the beast in odd, shuddering views; given time and the courage to continue our little patrol, we will securely trap that beast although we will never bring it home whole. It will, however, be in our possession.

But only if we observe the rules of the prowl; only in a difficult way, only in time. Here now: In 1968, a little after RFK's assassination and in the bowels of a summer which was uncompromisingly apocalyptic to us Lefties, I sent a preoccupied memo to Scott (he would communicate primarily in this way, and his notes elicited a pseudo-gemeinschaft available in person only to Mailer/Hunter/Sagan and of course senior editors) musing on the horror of it all and the effect it would have on publishing. "Forget the large picture," he wrote. "You can take care of the large picture, I just want to keep this agency going now like a big machine, right through to the end." I was reminded of a famous line of Walt Disney's in an interview toward the end of his life: What had made him proudest? "That I kept this thing together," he said, "That I was able to make it work and keep it working all the way." That Disney managed and so did Scott: the agency was a son of a bitch of a machine, had the aspect of the upper offices of a slaughterhouse: whatever unthinkable events were occurring below, only a faint smell and the bills of lading reached the penthouse.

And even as the country seemed to be coming apart, as Robert Kennedy's funeral train hit some people standing on the tracks and killed them, as George Wallace called for the elimination of all the pointy-heads, as Nixon scuttled from one airless television studio to another mumbling of his secret plan to end the Vietnam War, even then and more than ever, the agency was a big machine, felt like a big machine, get out of the way, here it comes.

Staring at or through that office in the spring and summer of 1968 when the place was perhaps at the height of its efficiency and reach, Mailer's *Steps of the Pentagon* running in Harper's then and Clarke/Kubrick's *2001* opening, it seemed beyond shattering, immutable, shaped for a kind of shapeless and eternal flux like the air itself. Everything worked; the stuff which wasn't working, detailed so savagely in the Mailer essays, was merely another aspect of the agency's penetration. Oh this is the place to be, I thought, this is set to

Nielsen's Fourth Symphony, the "Inextinguishable," running like the blood itself. That part which can never be destroyed.

Ah Scott, ah mores! Because the agency—one way to look at this—was in an intricate and brilliant fashion the Slan Shack of a science fiction fan and abscondant treasurer, Scott Feldman. The League of whose proceeds he had been master had become the world itself.

Was that perhaps then the answer? The elusive, perhaps unbearable answer against which Westlake's and Block's tormented principals had battered themselves? The answer, the secret: the agency was Scott's revenge, the revenge of an anonymous but, like so many, arrogant and driven fan upon his distant masters by engendering and propitiating a magnificent system which in turn reduced the writers to anonymity? Surely a van Vogt ploy. "This is the race which will rule the Sevagram." The Sevagram was the balance maintained by the fee department, and Scott was the ultimate Player in the World of Null A.

What a concept! What a thought! It was to stagger the bedraggled Golden Eagle, then at the true beginning of his science fiction career, "Final War" recently published in this magazine, "Death to the Keeper" scheduled to run in August. Big plans after all, the rising and furious river of ambition, an ambition not much different in kind and degree than that which might have seized Scott Feldman in 1938. The Lensmen (later the Players of Null A) take over the world or at least that part, publishing! Grab the fan club proceeds and the process! Even then vague intimation, distant rumbling: Scott had it all, the fee department, the devices which would protect and distance; he had all the money too . . . but I just might have the last word. Not only by virtue of chronology—that is an accident, living longer is not in itself the last word—but because I was, perhaps, going to become the science fiction writer Scott had wanted to be. Could such be?

It computes, Spock!

Is that the gift then? The last word on Kimball Kinnison in the canyons of New York publishing? Could it ever be that simple? If it were, if anything could be so reduced, then it was the agency and the arc of its circumstance which had to be measured.

Through the forty-seven years from its founding to Scott's death, the arc of its circumstance might be seen as paralleling, refracting the arc and accelerating corruption of publishing in this country over that period. The Lensmen aged, the magic adaptors did not, in the end, work: Roddenberry and Lucas and their highly advanced warriors took what they needed from the Lensmen and blasted out the worst, left wreckage and atomization.

That is clearly a working position. Hang an essay on it certainly. But does it credit too greatly an aging Scott Feldman who years before the end had become a retracted, a diminished figure, less a man of central mystery than a symbol of the clutter and detritus of publishing which the conglomerates, the video games, the computer had outmoded? Was Time-Warner Luke Sky-walker now to Scott's Kimball Kinnison? *Writing to Sell,* its plot-skeleton, Scott's fee department model was clear culture lag: it refracted the pulp market and pulp requisites of the 1930s, that decade which framed Scott. Clenched-jaw heroes with insuperable problems and terrific methodology were beginning to look pretty silly even before Lucas, before Roddenberry, before Moorcock's New Wave and Lawrence Block's tortured private eyes moved in.

Surely Scott institutionalized and propounded as no one ever had before the agency scams and the pulp ethic of the 1930s, but he was as time-bound a creature as A. L. Fierst, Ben Hibbs, Horace Gold: it just took longer for him to be so revealed. The agency, that savage machine, was in the end utterly disassembled. There is no last word because the only one who might speak it is Scott and Scott is gone. That remarkable, infuriating, troubled figure, infuriating and troubled in many ways like his client John W. Campbell, Scott Feldman staggered from the poverty of Brooklyn's Williamsburg a stone science fiction fan in search of the Way Out. He was only distantly pendant to the Futurians, but it was he who became richer than any of them and probably more influential too.

For here was the secret which was not so much a secret: it has been put in print by Moskowitz after Scott's death but was told me in his lifetime by Harry Harrison, who had served in the Queens Science Fiction League with Scott: Feldman had appropriated the treasury in 1940 and had fled, only to emerge after the war in sudden, vulpine business on Broadway and 57th Street in a one-room literary agency with his brother running blocking back. Out of the mists of what might have been Theodore Sturgeon's literary agency came Scott Meredith.

Out of the mists with him came Sturgeon's small client list: Arthur C. Clarke, Judith Merril, Sturgeon himself, Phil Klass. Out of the mists, Scott now Meredith went to the second postwar World Science Fiction Convention in Philadelphia (John W. Campbell, Guest of Honor) and recruited every science fiction writer he could, beginning with Lester del Rey. And his other inheritance from the mists were a bedraggled band of pulp Western writers, a scattering of pulp mysterists.

And from the start—before in fact Kimball had a Destructor Beam—there was that fee department.

In 1948, Richard Prather, twenty-five, had emerged: the fee for a novel then $25. Scott sold the first of the Shell Scott mysteries to Gold Medal Books for $2,500, an astonishing advance for an unknown writer at the time and the first of a stunningly successful series. John Farris's *Harrison High* came in the 1950s; later there were science fiction, Westerns, an Edgar Award-winning mystery. Bruce D. Reeves's $35 fee novel from 1965, *The Night Action:* $13,500 from New American Library, $75,000 from Warner

Pictures. (Never made.) Those successes, the Reeves savagely publicized, filled the brochure with the pure, lofting smell of hope.

Convincing as was the brochure, an even more interesting list could be compiled of writers who sought representation through the fee department and whose works were declined or, in one case, unsuccessfully marketed: try Stephen King, Evan S. Connell, Jr., then a war veteran and Columbia undergraduate (Connell was that singular case), John Barth, Raymond Carver, Robert Parker.

Talk of Joe Gould's never published (and as known at last unwritten) *History of the Twentieth Century!* The underside of the fee department represents a story more compelling than that commonly acknowledged.

Prather broke not only the fee department but the agency through, however, the first truly successful client. A few years later, employee Evan Hunter, who started by scrambling (under his birth name, Salvatore Lombino) in the second-level science fiction and mystery markets, wrote *The Blackboard Jungle* (expansion of a short story, "To Break a Wall," first published in *Discovery*) and the agency sold it to Simon & Schuster, for an ordinary $1,500; shortly after its publication, *The Ladies' Home Journal* bought second serial rights for $10,000 and MGM the movie rights for a hundred and that was the agent of transmogrification, not just for Hunter but the agency itself which was suddenly more than broker for a concatenation of pulp writers. Then Scott arrived at the behest of his cousin Cy Rembar, the agency's new attorney, and *An American Dream*. Oh, Scott had a good time through those decades. The best part of the day was the arrival at 10 A.M. to the mail neatly arranged on his desk and opening the envelopes with checks. He would glow, observers recall, sometimes with pure laughter.

What vindication!

So, then, if all is not certain, it can at least be speculated: the narrative of the agency is the narrative of a science fiction fan's revenge as he advanced through levels of contemporary publishing. "You can't call him 'Dr. Asimov,'" Scott said to me angrily as he threw back on his desk a letter I had drafted in Scott's name, asking a favor. "I grew up with this guy, we were practically having sex on the same bed at the same time, although not with each other. He's Isaac! Isaac! Isaac! Call him that!"

That Isaac was a landsman seemed true; years later when the agency took over the *Fantastic Voyage II* contractual disorder, and when Scott convinced Asimov to write a sequel to a novel he had said he would never sequelize, the two sauntered like the Brothers Karamazov from Scott's office to the exit, whisking by the fee department alcove, laughing merrily. $300,000 advance. A good score for the boys from Williamsburg and Brownsville, products both of the public education system. And a long way from the Queens Science Fiction League, from the 1947 Philadelphia Convention, from the blooming years of the plot-skeleton and the Blish/Knight fee department which produced not only "Tiger Ride" (*Astounding Science Fiction,* 1948), but *In Search of Wonder* and *The Issue at Hand.*

One had to consider also, I did, the corrupting effect of the fee department itself upon those employees who entertained writing ambitions. Fee work itself taught precision, taught structure but—

Some were successful, others much less so but fee work—all of that need! All of that anonymity of the fee clients! All of that crazed and glacial detachment of the fee writer which was the necessary technique, just as Miss Lonelyhearts had had to laugh at his correspondents to do his job at all . . . all of this had a certain effect, turned some (maybe to a degree all) cold, even cruel. What came from fee employment was a sense of the arbitrary and interchangeable mode of circumstance; the line between fee client and fee reader was chance: both were struggling within and serving a system and both functioned within a necessary mutual delusion: one that held this: power could also be the possession of the powerless.

Everything, after all, could be seen as a fee script; everyone was a fee client. "I want to write a novel," someone said in the alcove, "in which the fee clients take over the world." "Fool," David Schiller said, putting down a manuscript, "they already have. What do you think Reagan, Bush, Meese, the whole bunch of them are . . . jumped-up fee clients who got lucky and are living their fantasies." If Scott Meredith was a jumped-up fan and club treasurer, dreamer of the Lensmen, hiding behind a persona of power, then surely the same could be said of Reagan. Vox populi with a smile and grand bearing, dumped into the White House. (In fact, a former Reagan speechwriter sent in a few fee short stories in the late '90s. They were just about what Schiller would have expected, even though he was gone to Book of the Month by then and they were read by me.)

Confronted by the sheer volume of vox populi's manuscripts, the seriousness, the weight, and the hopelessness, it was all too easy for a fee reader to give up his own ambition. Many did through the years; the department was a filter through which the strongest crawled in their Nietzschean way, but many blooming novelists came to grief. Turnover in the fee department—and everywhere else there—was severe; the fixtures stayed, all right, but the history of the agency is rich in new employees, both clerical and editorial, who went out for a long lunch on their first or fifth day and never returned. Or were requested not to return. Capitalism, again, in its rawest form.

So, to an ineluctable extent, then, the story of that agency is that of a science fiction fan's advance through first the underside and then the more celebrated precincts of American publishing. John Lahr saw this in his 1971 novel *The Autograph Hound* and Nathanael West of course in his description of that film premiere, the fan-as-assassin, the crowd of adulators turned murderers. Was this then the heart of the artichoke? Scott had turned all of them into fee clients—the big-name professionals whose manuscripts were read by the underlings, the other clients who received letters signed by him but whom he never saw and with whom he had no involvement, the fee clients who were not people at all but abstraction. Each population served the others, the professionals functioned as bait for the fee clients, the fee clients paid all the agency overhead, the employees who stayed or left endured the exploitation and carried the legend. It was, certainly from the mid-1950s onward, that gleaming, deadly machine which I had so admired in 1968; that immutable device.

Sure it faded. Most things do. The Great Society, The Roosevelt Coalition, the White Man's Burden, even the Sermon on the Mount. Why should the agency, which was, after all, founded upon recrimination and in the world to wreak a fan's revenge, be exempt from the general condition? "My name is Ozymandias, King of Kings; look upon my works, ye mighty, and despair," and within months after his death, Scott's Agency had utterly atomized, its senior agents fleeing with the client list, his widow, huddled weeping with her carnivorous "advisors" and panicking to sell the remains of the agency and its backlist at what would have been a tenth of its valuation a year earlier. The finish, after the long seasons of Scott's dying, was as abrupt as an earthquake and it all went under sea level. "Scott Meredith" for those in publishing under forty evokes little association, and that which was his agency is a letterhead now and a collection box.

Still, oh the times we had! The places we went to become what one beholds and in the end, perhaps, to know of no distinction.

Dreaming, more dream than occurrence, only dream in fact like Kimball Kinnison and the Martian Odyssey, those long twilight afternoons in the late 1960s with Revolution on the office Muzak and the furious fee man doing heroin in the men's room, taking a break in mid-report to share supplies and anecdotes. Mailer and Gerald Green and Harry Kemelman prancing through the offices, Alfred Chester, not important enough to be permitted to see Scott, breaking past the receptionist in a run and scrambling into Scott's office where (when they were invited in ten minutes later) staff found the bald expatriate from Brooklyn and a sunny if very tense Scott Meredith giggling over glasses of wine.

The writer who felt G. P. Putnam had destroyed his work, calling Scott (not getting through, of course, so settling for me) to say, "Just want to tell you that I'm coming into the city with a gun to kill Walter Minton. You tell that bearded fuck he better watch out for me." The fee man who locked himself into a cubicle in the toilet, denuded himself and grimly masturbated several times a day, "because I can't stand reading this shit anymore and writing them as if they were sane. As if I were sane."

As if he were sane.

Finally: in the funeral home on Long Island on Valentine's Day, 1993,

I sat half an hour before the funeral in the chapel with the closed coffin. Scott's other book, *George S. Kaufman and His Friends,* had been published to moderate success in 1974; he had spent years on it (a semi-sequel, *Louis B. Mayer and His Enemies,* was contracted by Doubleday but never delivered), and it was the spirit of Kaufman which I felt in that room.

"Goddamn," I thought, echoing one of Kaufman's most famous lines, spoken about a bridge partner who had left for the men's room. "For the first time, I know exactly what the son of a bitch is doing." "I know what you're doing, finally," I said to the occupant of the box, but of course this was, properly speaking, not so. None of us ever know what the others, particularly the dead, are doing.

I had another thought looking at that box, a thought I had had looking at my Uncle Herbert on his deathbed and at a fetching sprite of a parakeet lying after long agony on the floor of her cage . . . I had never realized that they were so small. He was so much smaller in that box than I remembered, no longer subject but object, and as I looked at the impermeable service it was as if, receding, he had already gone. "He won't grow in memory, he will only diminish," I had thought in my times of fury at Scott, but now it was not anger but sadness which overtook.

Gone. All gone. Those months of swift atomization lay ahead but they already seemed in the bleak light to have occurred and it was not Scott nor his body nor his agency but only the shriveled memory which I confronted. And soon that to be extinguished: the Queens Science Fiction League, First Fandom, the Futurians. The Great Globe Itself.

Gone. Gone as the Great Society, as Shawn's *New Yorker,* as the Algonquin Round Table and George S. Kaufman's Broadway. Gone as Tailgunner Joe and Joseph Welch and the hearings and Douglas MacArthur and all of the other faded old soldiers. Gone like Gernsback's Science Club and Tremaine's Thought Variants. Gone like Gnome and Shasta and FPCI.

And only I to tell the tale? Certainly not. But perhaps only I on this distant precipice at such great distance to make it worth the telling.

What say, folks? Light the pyre; hold it high, let us sit upon the ground and tell sad stories of the death of Kings. The long day has closed; the Captains and the Kings depart.

But the Word and those who, living, die through it remain.

—for Ben Cheever and Gordon Van Gelder
New Jersey: June 2002

Charles L. Harness was honored at the 2004 Nebula Awards as Author Emeritus.

Michael Moorcock has called him "a writer of intellect and power," James Blish said that he was "the best exponent of the extensively recomplicated plot," and Brian Aldiss wrote that his novel *The Paradox Men* "must come close to anybody's idea of one kind of pure science fiction: the wild and imaginative kind which juggles amusedly with many scientific concepts."

Harness is a master of the genre, and his wildly extrapolative, ornately plotted short novel "The Rose" had a profound effect on an entire generation of writers. (And that includes your editor.) It might sound odd to characterize an SF story as being ahead of its time—the time was 1953—but "The Rose" *was* ahead of its time! Harness is also the author of *The Ring of Ritornel, Wolfhead, Firebird, The Catalyst, The Venetian Court, Redworld, Krono, Lurid Dreams, Lunar Justice,* and *Cybele, With Bluebonnets.* His collections include *The Rose* and *An Ornament to His Profession.* His story "An Ornament to His Profession," which draws on his experience as a successful patent attorney, is a classic of the genre.

To quote Brian Stableford, again in *The Encyclopedia of Science Fiction*: "Charles L. Harness is an original, stylish, and imaginatively audacious writer whose relative neglect is difficult to understand."

I must confess, *I* can't understand why Harness has been so neglected over the years, but SFWA deserves kudos for making the first move to right a wrong.

John W. Campbell Award–winning author George Zebrowski discusses the work of Charles L. Harness. Zebrowski is the author of more than forty books, which include *Macrolife, Stranger Suns, The Sunspacers Trilogy, The Omega Point Trilogy, Brute Orbits, Cave of Stars, The Killing Star* (with Charles Pellegrino), and the short story collections *The Monadic Universe, Swift Thoughts,* and the forthcoming *Black Pockets.*

In addition to the essay that follows, I am pleased to include a story by Charles L. Harness.

AUTHOR EMERITUS CHARLES L. HARNESS: WIELDER OF LIGHT

GEORGE ZEBROWSKI

Born in 1915, Charles L. Harness, who earned degrees in chemistry and law and worked as a patent attorney before retiring, is still in the midst of a period of productivity that resumed in the 1970s, with a new novel and stories appearing every two years. He belongs to a select group of writers, among them William Tenn, James Gunn, Ward Moore, Chad Oliver, and others who began to publish in the 1940s, and whose accomplishments easily rank with the masters of SF, even while the vagaries of publishing have made it difficult for these talents to find their audiences, much less to make these audiences grow.

Two of Harness's later novels, *Krono* (1988) and *Lurid Dreams* (1990), were highly praised by publications as diverse as *Locus* and *The New York Times,* and yet were neglected by his publishers, even as the chorus of praise for his entire body of work (begun in the 1950s and 1960s by Damon Knight, Judith Merril, Arthur C. Clarke, James Blish, Michael Moorcock, and Brian W. Aldiss, to name a few of the most prominent voices in that chorus) became louder and more articulate.

The Paradox Men, one of the most unusual science fiction novels ever published, first saw print in the May 1949 *Startling Stories* magazine under the title *Flight Into Yesterday*. In 1953, a badly edited, poorly proofread and printed hardcover of the expanded version was published under the same title. Ace Double Novels published the book in 1955 as *The Paradox Men,* the title under which the book is known today; the flip side of this format presented Jack Williamson's *Dome Around America*. Although the novel's colorful ideas, energy and unusual conviction were recognized (it draws on the author's deeps of personal remembrance, trauma, and love), the book went out of print in the United States.

Following Michael Moorcock's reprinting of Harness's early stories in *New Worlds* during the mid-1960s, there was a renewed interest in his work. A new edition of *The Paradox Men,* with an appreciative introduction by

Brian W. Aldiss, was published by Faber. A British science fiction book club edition followed in 1966, with paperback editions in 1967. In 1976 Brian W. Aldiss and Harry Harrison reintroduced the novel to British readers in the SF Masters Series from New English Library, but there was no new American edition.

Harness's best known work, a short novel entitled *The Rose,* had been ignored by American publishers, and had finally appeared in the British magazine *Authentic Science Fiction Monthly* in March 1953; but it was not until 1966 that there was a book edition, which also included two stories, "The New Reality" and "The Chessplayers." It was published, through the efforts of Michael Moorcock, by Compact Books, which was also the publisher of *New Worlds.* Strangely enough, but typically for Harness, this paperback edition was followed by a Sidgwick & Jackson hardcover in 1968. An American paperback finally appeared from Berkley in 1969, possibly because Harness had been published in Damon Knight's *Orbit* series of original anthologies from the same house, where Knight had been an editorial consultant. Panther did a paperback in Britain in the same year, and reprinted it in 1970 and 1981.

But throughout this period there was still no new edition of *The Paradox Men.* Brian Aldiss intrigued new readers by reprinting a chapter in his anthology *Space Opera* (Doubleday, 1974). A number of critics, reviewers, and editors whetted readers' appetites by citing this now legendary novel. Robert Silverberg, in his editorial note to "Time Trap" in *Alpha One* (1970), described *The Paradox Men* as a "dizzyingly intricate novel, which repays close study by anyone wishing to master the craft of plotting." A decade later there was still no new edition. Collectors knew that this was a novel not to be missed, if they could only find a copy. Harness continued to grow as a writer, with *two* legendary books to his name, yet still there was no new edition of *The Paradox Men.*

In 1979, as Harness began his current period of sustained creativity, *The Science Fiction Encyclopedia,* edited by Peter Nicholls, described him as "a highly imaginative writer whose relative neglect in his own country is difficult to understand." The newest edition of this reference work repeats the same statement, word for word.

In 1984, I included the novel in my ten-volume set for Crown, *Classics of Modern Science Fiction;* all the volumes sold out, but were not kept in print. I learned from Harness at that time that his original title for this novel was *Toynbee Twenty-Two,* which refers to the British historian's numbering of civilizations that have come and gone. T-21 is the future civilization in the story, which is struggling to avoid the decline predicted by Arnold Toynbee's theory of history. The Toynbean philosophers in Harness's story hope that space travel, by means of a faster-than-light starship, the T-22, will serve as a bridge to a new culture. In our world, Arthur C. Clarke and others have expressed the hope that the opening of space will liberate human creativity and spark a new renaissance, as we move beyond a planet of limited economic horizons and power struggles.

I also learned that *Flight Into Yesterday,* both the magazine and first hardcover title of this same novel, was the title chosen by Sam Merwin, then editor of *Startling Stories.* Donald A. Wollheim, the editor of Ace Books at the time, changed the title to *The Paradox Men,* which is perhaps the most intriguing of the novel's three titles, because it accurately describes the ambiguous predicament of the story's major characters. For this reason, and to avoid confusion among readers and bibliographers, the author finally chose to keep the title of the novel's largest edition; but he retained his original title as the title of Chapter 22.

In preparing the Crown edition, the author and I gave the novel a careful line-by-line reading, correcting dropped punctuation, typos, and wrong words. Harness took the opportunity to expand overly compressed scenes, and made important details more lucid through a judicious updating of terms, as well as improving the general movement of the story. The purely mechanical defects of previous editions had been a needless obstacle for readers. In effect, the Crown edition was given the normal book editing that was not always available in the science fiction field of the 1940s and 1950s. Crown's edition, with some 3500 words of restored and revised material, was the first definitive version of a genuine SF classic, replacing the previous editions. The Easton Press Masterpieces of Science Fiction leatherbound edition of 1992 corrected the typos of the Crown edition, and included a newly revised afterword by the author, as well as a revised introduction by me.

Reactions to the novel's first book publication were mixed. Groff Conklin seemed baffled in his January 1954 *Galaxy* review, but found the novel "pretty astonishing, if only because of the cauldronful of ideas and fantasies that are mixed up in it." P. Schuyler Miller's review in the April 1954 *Astounding* described the novel as an "action entertainment," but he failed to notice the story's compulsive, dreamlike power and treatment of serious issues. Anthony Boucher's review in *The Magazine of Fantasy & Science Fiction* for September 1953 found the book to be a "fine swashbuckling adventure of space-and-time travel, the politics of tyranny, and the identity problems of an amnesiac superman . . ." and compared the work to A. E. van Vogt's two Weapons Shop novels; however, Boucher also found the story to be too intricate and its science confusing and perhaps mistaken. In this last criticism he was wrong, since there are solutions to equations involving travel near and beyond light speed that permit the result that Harness elects to have in his novel; whether this is physically true or not is irrelevant to the use of this result for dramatic "what if" purposes. Harness's use of both science and technology follows Arthur C. Clarke's Third Law—"that any sufficiently advanced technology is indistinguishable from magic." Harness is aware of what it might take to have the effects he wants, but he does not always elaborate on the details or dwell on them. A good example of this kind of fictional use of stylized science and technology is Clarke's *Against the Fall of Night* (1953).

When Harness's novel came out in paperback three years later as *The Paradox Men,* Damon Knight, the most influential science fiction reviewer of the time, hailed it (in *Infinity Science Fiction,* February 1956) as "the brilliant peak of Charles L. Harness's published work," and described it as being "symmetrically arranged, the loose ends tucked in, and every last outrageous twist of the plot justified in science and logic," and "you can trust Harness to wind up this whole ultracomplicated structure, somehow, symmetrically and without fakery. Finally, when it's all done, the story means something." He used similar words in his review of Alfred Bester's *The Stars My Destination,* 1956. Knight goes on to conclude that "Harness's theme is the triumph of the spirit over flesh. . . . This is the rock under all Harness's hypnotic cat's cradle of invention—faith in the spirit, the denial of pain, and the affirmation of eternal life."

Manipulated by a player whose identity is hidden from both the protagonist and the reader, Alar the Thief survives a series of life-threatening encounters, each of which develops his concealed nature further and moves him closer toward death and transfiguration, all in the cause of breaking humanity out of its cul-de-sac of cyclical history.

One of Harness's major concerns in his fiction is with the unsatisfactory state of human nature, which many of his protagonists seek to transcend. It is this theme that gives his stories their mythic character, while the scientific and technological details weave a poetic fabric of glittering plausibility. That we could be different, that our societies could be different, that our histories might have been otherwise, that creative change is possible—these are the siren songs of science fiction, whether heard in an extravagant mood or with the hope that genuine possibilities wait only for our will and hand. In *The Paradox Men* a casual reader will find epic poetry, an ecstasy of ideas, and a critical view of his own humanity. The deep currents of personal history out of which Harness writes, together with his background in patent law and chemistry, make for a powerful melodrama that is compelling and enigmatic even after several readings.

Michael Moorcock, in his 1968 introduction to *The Rose,* emphasizes that "Harness chose to write SF in the magazine style popular at the time (although he is, as 'The Chessplayers' shows, quite happy to write in a more 'sophisticated' style if it suits him) and at first glance most of his work appears to be nothing more than good, baroque SF adventure fiction. A closer look shows nuances and throw away ideas revealing a serious mind operating at a much deeper and broader level than its contemporaries in the

SF field. Behind all the extravagance, and making full use of it, is Harness's mind, reasoning (where normally the SF writer rationalizes or reacts) and concerned (where much SF rejects) with the fundamental issues of human existence. That sounds pompous—but *The Rose* is never pompous, never pretentious, and this, too, gives it an edge over a lot of better-known SF novels."

An admirer of A. E. van Vogt, Harness built on that author's dreamlike scenarios and wheels-within-wheels plotting, and achieved what James Blish called "the extensively recomplicated plot." *The Paradox Men* is comparable to Alfred Bester's *The Demolished Man* (1953) and *The Stars My Destination* (1956) in its sweep and color, especially in the ethereal beauty of Harness's closing pages. *The Rose* and *The Paradox Men* stand in relation to Harness's short fiction as do Bester's two novels to his short fiction. All four draw resourcefully on genre materials and visual possibilities; and while Bester may have the purely stylish edge, Harness has both style and substance.

The Stars My Destination does seem to owe to Harness's novel; and there is more than a bit of Harness and van Vogt in Kurt Vonnegut's *The Sirens of Titan* (1959). Gully Foyle and Winston Niles Rumfoord are kindred to Alar the Thief, who is kin to Gilbert Gosseyn in van Vogt's *The World of Null-A* (1948). Like his brother heroes, Alar is scattered in agony across a swath of space-time, but is striving to learn more about himself and to reform a recalcitrant human nature, although Alar seems more ethical than the nihilists Foyle and Rumfoord and the confused Gosseyn, and is finally more effective than all of them.

In his introduction to the first British hardcover edition, Brian W. Aldiss wrote: "Of all the types of science fiction story, my favorite is the wine-dark patch in which we find Charles Harness's novel, *The Paradox Men*. Here we find tales that challenge us with their wildness, only to sweep us away into belief on a tide of excitement and convincing detail. Though their themes may be unified, they are built from a number of strange and unexpected things. They combine madness and logic, beauty and fear. They are not fantasy, nor are they scientific fiction. These pure science fiction novels may be categorized as Widescreen Baroque. They like a wide screen, with space and possibly time travel as props, and at least the whole solar system as their setting." Aldiss adds that "for all its slam-bang action, *The Paradox Men* holds a particular enchantment. I have likened it to novels I admire, *The Stars My Destination* and *The Sirens of Titan*; but they lack the tenderness for humanity that gives the present book its freshness and its last scenes their conviction. Unlike the science fiction being written in England, America, and Russia, the values here are not purely materialistic."

To this I can only add that no SF hero ever remade human history as flamboyantly, as thoroughly, or as movingly as Alar the Thief: he steals the way to human progress. The full meaning of this is for the reader to discover, but I promise that you'll want to make the trip more than once. I have long suspected that readers who admire Philip K. Dick's works might also enjoy those of Harness; what both authors have in common is a "tenderness for humanity" and a dazzling "wildness" of ideas and action.

Praise for Harness's work became even more vocal in the 1980s and 1990s, with critics and fans calling for more intelligent publishing support of his work. In the last twenty years *The Rose* and *The Paradox Men* have appeared on lists of all-time best SF novels, and together with his short fiction have been highly praised in every reference work. The consensus today is that the already high opinion of Harness's work can only increase.

And, finally, Charles Harness was able to publish his first volume of collected short fiction when NESFA Press brought out *An Ornament to His Profession* in 1998, covering five decades of creativity paralleling the author as novelist, and followed it with a collection of novels, *Rings,* in 1999, which included an original novel. Both volumes are still in print. We might have had such a collection decades ago, except for the excuses of publishing economies, which look at past sales records with no regard for what goes on between an author and his readers or with any faith in the author's future. As with illicit love affairs, the publisher is always the last to know! The myth of sales records deserves to be exploded, since it is clear that in a statistical sense publishers would do just as well to be guided by merit alone as by commerce; they might even do better to let the "free market" of taste do its work instead of trying to fix the horse race. An obvious contradiction thus exists at the heart of the business machine, which prattles about "free enterprise" but in truth skews the outcomes.

When I wrote these words, I had just talked with the author and learned that new stories are to be published in the near future, new novels await a publisher, and from the vigor in his voice I know that Charlie Harness is a mere youth *following* the unstoppable ninety-year-old Jack Williamson, who is still writing. When I asked Harness whether he had any favorites in his fictions, he said, "George, I liked them all equally well when I was writing them!" And when I asked him what about his overly modest statement which he likes to make, that he did it for the money, he hems and haws—and I know the truth: he just couldn't help being Charles L. Harness, with his intelligence and talent, and he was unable to keep from growing and developing his skills and doing as well as he did, and he can't hide the love that sings from his stories.

The author writes:

"This is my historical period. My bemused ancestors fought on both sides during the Civil War. West Virginia (where we came from) seceded from Virginia and joined the Union, but one of my distant Harness uncles organized and outfitted a company with his own money and joined up with General Lee. The Harness house on Route 220 near Moorefield, West Virginia, still stands, with rifle ports in the basement. And George Washington actually did spend the night there on his way to fiasco at what is now Pittsburgh."

CHARLES L. HARNESS

General Lee." A statement. A greeting. A question. "General" with a hard "g," and each syllable precisely enunciated. And something odd about the accent. More like "Gaynayral Lay."

The two officers in gray jackets stared down from their horses at the stranger who stood by his own mount, a beautiful bay. The soft radiance of the paschal moon revealed a man in uniform, but the jacket and trousers were neither blue nor gray. The newcomer was dressed in black. From his bearing, clearly a soldier. Rank uncertain.

The stranger saluted the tall officer with the white beard. "General Lee. I am Oberst Karl von Mainz, of the Army of West Germany."

If General Lee was puzzled, he concealed it well. He returned the salute and nodded toward his companion. "Colonel von Mainz, my aide, Major Potter." He studied the visitor a moment. "I presume you are a military attaché from His Majesty, King William of Prussia. Welcome, sir. We haven't had an attaché since the British Colonel Freemantle rode with us to Gettysburg. You must have overcome incredible hardships to join me here at Appomattox Court House, and quite possibly to no purpose." He peered through the semi-light. "I don't remember you in Richmond. How did you get through? The roads are jammed with Union troops."

"I used . . . a different approach, Herr General."

"Ah? Well, no matter. Major, would you please extend our hospitality to the colonel?"

His aide sighed. "It's parched corn and creek water, sir. No coffee. No tea. No brandy."

Robert Lee thought back. A Richmond lady had entertained him in her parlor a few months ago. She had given him a cup of real tea, made from what were probably the last genuine tea leaves in the doomed city. She had drunk her own cup of "tea," which he knew to be dark water from the James River. He had never let on. She had sipped, and she had smiled.

A true Southern lady. All this was passing away. He said. "By your leave, Colonel, I will now retire. There will be action tomorrow morning that decides whether the war is over or whether it continues."

"Herr General, I know all about that. The Army of Northern Virginia now consists of two small infantry corps—Gordon and Longstreet—and a little cavalry. And you are in a tight box. On your east is General Meade, with the Second and Sixth Corps. To the west is Custer and most of the Union cavalry. To the south is Sheridan's cavalry. That's the bottom of the box, and that's where the Union lines are weakest. You propose to break out through Sheridan, move rapidly south on the Lynchburg Road, join up with General Johnston in North Carolina, and drag the war out until the North is willing to negotiate an honorable peace. But it won't work, Herr General."

General Lee looked at the German for a long time. "Sir, you seem to know a great deal about the tactical situation. So tell me, why can't I break out through the south?"

"Because, Herr General, history has already written the dénouement of this, your last campaign." He did not look at Major Potter. "May we discuss this in private, Herr General?"

Lee shrugged. "Very well." He dismounted and gave the reins to his aide. "Oh, it's perfectly all right, Potter. We'll be in the tent."

A stump of candle was already burning on the cracker box when they went inside. The Confederate officer motioned to the camp chair, then eased himself down on the cot. "I think we can push through Sheridan," he said.

The other nodded. "True, in the dawn fighting you will push back Sheridan's dismounted cavalry. Your boys will cheer. But that's the end of it. General Ord's Fifth Corps arrives just in time to reinforce Sheridan. The great game is over. You send out a rider with a white flag. At eleven tomorrow morning, Palm Sunday, you will send General Grant notice that you would like to meet him to discuss surrender terms. You will accept his demand for unconditional surrender. Tomorrow afternoon, except for a little scattered action in other theatres, the war will be over."

Lee was silent.

Von Mainz shrugged. "You think I am insane? I am not insane, General Lee. I know many events that lie in your future."

"How is this possible?"

"You think of me as a loyal subject of King William of Prussia and an officer of the Prussian army, in this year eighteen hundred five and sixty. Not exactly, General. I am not what you suppose. There are two very basic facts that you must accept. If you can accept these two facts and all that they imply, then you can understand everything you need to know about me. Fact number one, I am from your future. I was born in the year two thousand and thirty. I am thirty-five years old. I left the American Sector of Berlin this morning, April 8, in the year two thousand five and sixty, almost exactly two hundred years in your future. I am indeed a colonel, but not in the Prussian army. I am a colonel in the Neues Schutz-Staffeln—the 'NSS'—an underground paramilitary organization devoted to reuniting West and East Germany." He waited. "You don't believe me? Not just yet? No matter. I assure you, I can provide proof."

"West Germany . . . East Germany?" said Lee. "I don't understand."

"Never mind. It's a long story. With the general's permission, I'd like to state the second fact."

"Proceed. What is your second fact?"

"The second fact is that you can win the war. Not merely the impending battle. You can win the whole war."

Lee looked at him sharply. "How?"

"With a new weapon."

The older man smiled faintly. "Which you brought with you, of course, from your twenty-first century?"

"Of course. And please do not smile, General. It does not become you; nor is it fitting to the occasion."

Lee stood up. "Now, you really must excuse me, Colonel. Tomorrow will be a difficult day." He walked to the tent door. "There's Potter over there, by the napoleon. He'll find a place for you to sleep."

Colonel von Mainz joined him at the tent door and peered out into the moonlight. "A napoleon. Hah! The deadliest cannon of the war. Favored by both sides. Range, one mile. With canister at two hundred yards, wipes out an entire platoon. Like a giant sawed-off shotgun. The difficulty is, Grant has three times as many as you have, as well as plenty of powder and skilled gun crews. But you can even the odds, my General." The stranger flashed black eyes at his reluctant host. "May I demonstrate?"

"Go ahead."

Von Mainz smiled, then held a finger up. "On the other hand, General, it would be more convincing if you performed the experiment yourself."

"Really, Colonel—"

"Would the general please pull out the weapon from my rifle boot."

Lee walked over to von Mainz's horse, pushed the saddle bags aside, and tugged at what appeared to be a plain rifle stock. The thing came out with a long squeak. Lee carried it into a patch of moonlight for a better look. He frowned. "It's not a rifle . . . ?"

"Not exactly. Now then, shall I retire with your Major Potter, or do you want me to tell you about this . . . instrument?"

"Hm. It's a weapon, you said?"

"It is, indeed." The visitor smiled and crossed his arms over his chest.

"What does it fire?" asked Lee.

"Something in the nature of an electric charge."

"Electricity? For heaven's sake! But to what effect?"

"See for yourself. First, ask the good Major Potter to move a few meters away from the napoleon."

"Very well." Lee called out, "Major—move away to your left a bit. There. That's fine."

"Now," said the visitor, "take it to your shoulder and hook your finger around the trigger, just as you would a rifle. Aim it at the cannon barrel."

"What's this on the barrel?" muttered Lee. "A telescopic sight? No— what in the name of heaven! I can see everything, plain as day!"

"A snooperscope," explained von Mainz. "It senses infrared radiation."

"Whatever *that is,*" said Lee. He began to perspire.

"A gentle squeeze on the trigger," prompted the German.

Lee felt a faint click as he closed the trigger.

The cannon seemed to vanish. The great Confederate first squinted; then his eyes opened very wide. Something was still there. Dust. Metallic dust glinting in the soft moonlight. Now beginning to settle. And a clatter as the wooden wheel spokes and undercarriage collapsed.

Lee hurried out to the shambles, followed by von Mainz. The general poked into the dust clumps with a boot toe. He bent over, picked up a handful, and smelled it cautiously. A faint odor—something like the residue of a lightning strike. He tossed the dust aside.

Major Potter ran over to Lee. "General! Are you all right? What happened?"

Lee stared first at his aide, then at the German colonel. "Potter, everything's fine. Excuse us, please. The colonel and I still have somewhat to discuss." He handed the strange weapon gingerly to von Mainz and motioned him back into the tent. The candle sputtered at the sudden draft.

"There are five more such weapons in my saddle bags," said von Mainz. "They merely require assembly. So. What do you think? Do you believe me now?"

"I believe," said Lee, "that I have seen a remarkable thing." He sat on the cot and motioned to the chair again. "How does it work?"

"I'm not a technical man—but I think I can give you the basic theory. You've heard of atoms, of course?"

"Yes."

"Atoms are made up mostly of even smaller particles called protons and neutrons. These in turn consist of sub-particles called quarks. These quarks are held together by a thing called the strong force, or color force. It is also called 'gluon,' because it functions like glue in holding the quarks together." He peered over at the tired gray face. "Do you follow me, General?"

"No, I'm afraid not."

"Well, I'm sorry. Shall I go on?"

"Please do."

"Very well, then. It appears that quarks have at least five flavors: up, down, strange, charm, and bottom. But we'll skip all that. The point is, General, that in my birth year, two thousand and thirty, a means was discovered to de-sensitize the gluon associated with the so-called *down* quark, which exists in neutrons of the structural metals. Since neutrons are made of one up-quark and two down-quarks, the consequence was that such metals could readily be caused to disintegrate. Your napoleon is—was—brass, an alloy of copper and zinc. Brass is quite susceptible. But so are musket barrels, swords, all the iron and steel instruments of war. Even the harmless things yield to it: belt buckles, buttons, stirrups, mess kits, telegraph keys, telescope barrels, spectacle rims . . ."

The general patted his jacket pocket uncertainly.

Von Mainz laughed. "Your glasses are safe, General. The weapon never backfires."

Lee studied his visitor in silence. Finally he said, "The demonstration was indeed a success. Quite remarkable. I accept it as proof that you are from another time and place. But *that* simply raises additional questions. How did you get here from the future? What is it to you whether the South wins or loses? Why did you select me for your presentation?"

"Not so fast, dear General. Good questions, all valid, and there are answers. Why *you?* You are the commander-in-chief of all the armies of the Confederacy, and your army has a very pressing need for the weapon. You were therefore the logical choice.

"Now then, how did I get here? Not quite so easy to answer, but I can try. There is a device—really an entire cellar room—in Berlin. It is associated with an immense power source, all very accurately calibrated. In the center of the room is a sort of plate, a machine, actually, very cleverly constructed. A person stands on that plate, together with certain things he may wish to bring along, even including a horse. Then the dials are set to a specific time and place in the past, a compatriot pulls a switch, and the plate is empty. If the warp is accurate, the person in the chair moves from Berlin twenty sixty-five to . . . wherever, whenever . . ."

"I . . . see," murmured the general. "I think I see." He put his fingers to his forehead. "So here you are. But why? What difference does the outcome of this war make to you . . . to the NSS . . . to the Germany of the twenty-first century?"

"*Why?* Because I—my group—we want to change the past, and hence the future fate of the German people. You and I together can do this."

"Go on."

"I'm sure you realize, General, that in the history about to be written the South loses the war. The Union is reestablished. The United States spreads across the continent 'from sea to shining sea,' as your hymn says. Very quickly America becomes rich and populous. But she is not done with war. There will be a great war in nineteen fourteen to nineteen eighteen: at the start, Germany against England, France, and Russia. We would have won this war, except that America came in against us. Germany rose from the ashes and in nineteen thirty-nine tried again, against almost the same enemies. Again, we almost made it. Our armies lay on the outskirts of Leningrad— oh, St. Petersburg to you. We could see the church spires of Moscow. But once more America came in against us. America sent Russia immense quantities of war materials: shipload after shipload through the Persian Gulf, and in the north by Murmansk. These weapons you would find quite incredible. Self-propelled cannons with iron plating, called 'tanks.' Machines that flew through the air, capable of dropping terrible bombs. And big horseless carriages for moving troops rapidly. Our German armies had these things too, of course, but in nowhere near the numbers the Americans were able to furnish our Russian enemies." He sighed and took a deep breath. "In nineteen hundred three and forty the Russians began a general counterattack across the entire eastern front—some twelve hundred miles long. For us it was the beginning of the end. We gave up two years later."

"But you speak of history. All that will happen whether the South wins or loses."

"No, we think not. Our forecasters have made a number of studies on great machines called computers. The results agree as to several essential points. If America exists in two countries, North and South, neither would possess the industrial and manpower resources to make a difference in the war of nineteen fourteen to nineteen eighteen. Germany would have won. The German emperor—the kaiser—would have stayed in power, and there would have been no need for the war of nineteen thirty-nine to forty-five. Stalingrad . . . Lend Lease . . . our Führer committing suicide in a bunker in Berlin . . . all moot . . . will never happen."

"You are telling me, sir," mused the general, "if the South wins now, in eighteen sixty-five, Germany wins in nineteen eighteen."

"Exactly." The visitor smiled crookedly. "And more than that. The world wins. For twenty million people are scheduled to die in the war of nineteen thirty-nine to forty-five. They would live. And that's not all. America develops a bomb capable of destroying all humanity all over the globe. If the South wins in eighteen sixty-five, that bomb would not be available in nineteen forty-five."

"Interesting. And very curious. I can see that science is due to make immense strides in the decades ahead. But tell me—this present weapon— this strange rifle—what do you call it?"

"Dis. Short for disintegrator."

"Was it—perhaps I should say *will* it—be used in one of your future wars?"

"No, General. Happily—or unhappily—the radiation is readily nulli-fied by insulating the metal with a certain coating."

"Suppose the North discovers this defensive coating?"

"They won't. It requires an alloy that won't be available for a hundred and fifty years." He looked at the general expectantly. "Well, sir?"

Lee seemed lost in thought. Finally he said, "No, I cannot accept the weapon."

Von Mainz was astonished. "But *why?*"

"Colonel, I can say a thing to you, a total stranger, that I cannot say to Mr. Davis, or to any of my own officers, or even to my wife."

"Sir?"

Lee's voice dropped. He said quietly, "I believe that the Almighty wills that the South shall lose."

The man from the future stared at him.

Lee said, almost sadly, "I am convinced at last that God has been trying to give me a message these past four years. I could have won at Sharpsburg in '62, except that one of my officers used my battle plan as a cigar wrapper, and it fell into McClellan's hands. And I would have won at Gettysburg if Stonewall Jackson had been there. But he had been shot at Chancellorsville by his own picket—another freak accident. And last year, in the battle of The Wilderness, victory was within our grasp. Longstreet was reaching out to take it—when he was shot by his own men. Another ghastly and impos-sible mistake. And that's not the end of it. Last year in his march to Rich-mond, Grant split his army to cross the North Anna River—Warren on the right, Hancock on the left. I moved in between them, and I could have smashed first one and then the other, except that I fell ill. If we had won on any of these occasions—Sharpsburg or Gettysburg or The Wilderness or on the North Anna—Britain and France would have recognized the South as a new nation. The North would have had to lift the blockade. Money, arms, food, everything would have poured in. We could have negotiated an easy peace with Washington, and we would have remained in permanent fact the Confederate States of America. But Providence intervened. Always at the critical place, the critical hour. I believe it to be the will of the Almighty."

"The will of the Almighty?" Von Mainz's jaw dropped. "Is childish su-perstition to decide this great struggle? *Gott in Himmel!* Is the strain finally too much?" He peered in hard suspicion at the man on the cot. "Let us face the realities, Herr General. Look at the facts! Lincoln has already carved your beloved state in two. The western section he calls West Virginia. The federals hold your plantation at Arlington. Your wife is an invalid in Rich-mond, and the city is burning. Are these calamities the will of God? Your son Fitzhugh rots in a federal prison. The war has already killed his wife and two children. And your own daughter Annie. Do you see in this a di-vine plan, General? Your army is starving. No rations in two days. You are finished. When this is over, General, the best that life can offer you is presidency of a tiny southern college with an enrollment of forty-five students."

"All that you say is true, and it is tragic," said Lee. "But some day the country will be great once again. Lincoln will see to that. He will not permit the South to be ground down like a conquered province."

Von Mainz laughed softly. "Lincoln dies one week from today. He will be assassinated while attending a play at Ford's Theatre in Washington."

The candle flame shuddered as Lee's head jerked up. "No!"

"Yes. History, dear General. And to your beloved South, terrible things are done by Lincoln's successors."

Lee groaned. "But the common people . . . we are of one blood . . . we are brothers."

Von Mainz shrugged.

Lee leaned over, stuffed a loose trouser leg back into a Wellington boot top, then tried to get up. His mouth twisted with pain.

His visitor leaned forward, concerned, but the older man waved him back. "Rheumatism, Colonel. I'm an old man. My joints . . ." He was up. "I cannot take your weapons, Colonel. I will take my chances on breaking out tomorrow. I think it pointless for you to remain any longer. How will you return to your time?"

"No problem, General. I step out into the darkness. There's a sort of gate, near where my horse is tethered. I go through with my weapons, and you never see me again. I'll leave the bay behind. He's yours, if you want him. Remind General Grant that in your army, the horses belong to the men personally, not to the Confederate government."

"If it should come to that."

"It will." The colonel looked overhead at the full moon. "Perhaps it's all for the best. You've heard of Jules Verne?"

"The French science writer? I've heard of him. Never read any of his books, though I understand *Five Weeks in a Balloon* was quite popular with our young people."

"Yes. And this year, *From Earth to the Moon*."

"Wild fantasy, Colonel."

"Is it? Your great *United* States of America will launch a manned ship from Cape Canaveral and it will land on the Moon, following which it will safely return to Earth. It will do that in just about one hundred years from now. And I have seen the return of the first *interstellar* ship. The ion engine was designed in Washington and Lee University."

"'Ion' engine? All after my time. And I don't believe I know the institution. Any connection with the Lees of Virginia?"

"Very close, General." His guest smiled wryly. "The starship, incidently, was named the *Robert E. Lee. Auf Wiedersehen,* Herr General." He saluted, and disappeared through the tent flap.

The old soldier stared after him. Over a quarter million Southern lads dead in this war. It had lain within his power to make good their sacrifice, and he had thrust it aside. What would Stonewall Jackson think? And Jeb Stuart, and A.P. Hill? Were they all whirling in their graves?

Was he a secret Unionist at heart? Did he see this bountiful land stretching in a single golden band from Atlantic to Pacific, and from New Orleans to the Canadian border? Did he secretly think all men should be free? He had never owned a slave, except briefly, when he inherited a few from his mother-in-law. He had promptly emancipated them.

How much humiliation lay ahead for him, and for the army?

It was morning, and he was looking toward the south with fieldglasses.

"We got through Sheridan," he muttered. "But that's the end of it." He handed the glasses to his aide. "That's Ord coming up, isn't it?"

"Ord? Can't make out the regimentals, sir. Yes, I'm afraid so. A corps, at least."

"Row on row of blue," murmured Lee.

"Sir?"

"Never mind. The war's over, Potter. Signal General Gordon. He knows what to do."

"But—"

"Get on with it, Potter."

Wilmer McLean had a horrid sinking feeling in his gut. He knew now that the Almighty had had his eye on him in this war, from start to finish. On July 21, 1861, General Beauregard had requisitioned McLean's fine farmhouse near Manassas, and had just sat down to dinner, when a cannonball crashed into the dining room fireplace, thereby announcing that the federals were on their way to Richmond. So Wilmer McLean had sold out and moved south and west, to the village of Appomattox Court House, and here had built an even finer house, where by all logic he should have been to farm in peace and quiet, out of the path of armies.

But Fate had decreed otherwise. For just now his carriage circle and his front yard and his porch and his parlor swarmed with more generals and lesser officers—of both sides—than there were bees in his blossoming apple trees.

They all stopped talking a moment and made a path for an unkempt, slouched-over officer in a mud-spattered blue uniform. "Is General Lee up?" he asked. Somebody said yes, and he walked up on the porch and into Wilmer McLean's house.

"The rest is easy, General Lee," said General Gordon. "Our troops just march off down that road there, stack arms in the field at the right, and then they go home."

"There's a line of Yankees along the roadside," said Major Potter uneasily.

"Don't worry, Potter," said Lee. "That's Chamberlain's brigade. Just to keep order. Decent chap, Chamberlain. Used to be a college professor."

"There go my boys," said Gordon. "I'd better get out there with them."

"Yes, of course," said Lee. "Go on."

The officer cantered away.

From somewhere ahead a bugle shrilled. It echoed and re-echoed down the road. Then General Lee and his aide heard a hoarse shout, repeated up and down the blue line along the road, then the slapping of thousands of rifles on hardened palms.

Major Potter stood up in his stirrups. "My God, sir! What——!"

"It's all right, Major," said Lee quietly. "General Chamberlain has just given his Yanks the order for 'carry arms.' It's the 'marching salute'—the highest honor fighting men can give other fighting men." His eyes began to glow. "And look at Gordon. He's standing his horse up. His sword is out, and he's ordering . . . our boys to return . . . the salute." He coughed softly. "Dusty hereabouts, Potter."

"Yes, sir."

The *United* States, thought Lee. Both sides are going to try. We've got the future. It's all ahead of us. There for the taking. Science, that's what we need. Math. Chemistry. Physics. That's the road for our young people. And we need a vision. This fellow Verne has a vision. Get his books.

Potter was trying to ask him something. "What now, sir?"

Back to earth. "Where do you live, Major?"

"Florida, sir. My folks have a little farm on the Atlantic side."

"I was there in '61, trying to strengthen the forts. Where is your farm, Potter?"

"You probably never heard of it, sir, a place called Cape Canaveral."

"Oh, but I have, Potter."

"Really, sir?" The ex-officer looked at the man in gray with pleasure and astonishment, but no explanation was given him.

"Let's go home, Potter." Lee wheeled his horse and cantered off toward Richmond.

Adam-Troy Castro made his first professional sale to *Spy Magazine* in 1987 and has sold more than seventy short stories since then to magazines and anthologies such as *Science Fiction Age*, *Adventures In the Twilight Zone*, *Pulphouse*, *Analog Science Fiction and Fact*, *The Magazine of Fantasy & Science Fiction*, and *Urban Nightmares*. He is the author of *An Alien Darkness*, *A Desperate Decaying Darkness*, *Vossoff and Nimmitz*, *With Stars In Their Eyes* (with Jerry Oltion), and four Spider-Man novels. Some of his short stories can be found in his collections *Lost In Booth Nine* and *Tangled Strings*.

He writes:

"This is my 9/11 story, I'm afraid.

"As a New York native who moved to Florida in 1995, my immediate reaction on that day the towers fell was an irrational, but no less overwhelming, regret that I wasn't there to bear witness. I wasn't foolish enough to believe that I could have done anything to ameliorate the tragedy, but I couldn't shake the feeling that my fealty to the city I loved demanded more from me than the limited degree of horror I was capable of sharing from a safe distance.

"In the days that followed, I encountered several reasonable folks who told me they'd never want to go to New York, now. They didn't want to be in the line of fire during further attacks. Contrasting that with my own craving to walk Manhattan's streets as soon as possible made me think of all the people, all over the world, who feel deep connection to their respective homelands, and fight the very idea of leaving, even when the charms of those storied places are regularly broken by spasms of sudden, violent bloodshed.

"People like the Israelis. The Palestinians. The Irish. The Czechs. The exact ratio varies, but like my heroine Caralys, they all find one day of hell a fair price for nine days of home.

"So where's my fictional country, Enysbourg? It's a place of light and miracles, most of the time. It's also a code for the place that's always home even if I live elsewhere. E for Empire, NY for New York, S for State, Bourg for Burg, or City. New York, New York."

OF A SWEET SLOW DANCE IN THE WAKE OF TEMPORARY DOGS

ADAM-TROY CASTRO

Before

ONE

On the last night before the end of everything, the stars shine like a fortune in jewels, enriching all who walk the quaint cobble-stoned streets of Enysbourg. It is a celebration night, like most nights in the capital city. The courtyard below my balcony is alive with light and music. Young people drink and laugh and dance. Gypsies in silk finery play bouncy tunes on harmonicas and mandolins. Many wave at me, shouting invitations to join them. One muscular young man with impossibly long legs and a face equipped with a permanent grin takes it upon himself to sprint the length of the courtyard only to somersault over the glittering fountain at its center. For a heartbeat out of time he seems to float, enchanted, over the water. Then I join his friends in applause as he bellyflops, drenching himself and the long-haired girls wading at the fountain's other rim. The girls are not upset but delighted. Their giggles tinkle like wind chimes as they splash across the fountain themselves, flinging curtains of silver water as their shiny black hair bobs back and forth in the night.

TWO

Intoxicated from a mixture of the excellent local wine and the even better local weed, I consider joining them, perhaps the boring way via the stairs and perhaps via a great daredevil leap from the balcony. I am, after all, stripped to the waist. The ridiculous boxers I brought on the ship here could double as a bathing suit, and the way I feel right now I could not only make the fountain but also sail to the moon. But after a moment's consideration I decide not. That's the kind of grand theatrical gesture visitors to

Enysbourg make on their first night, when they're still overwhelmed by its magic. I have been here nine nights. I have known the festivals that make every night in the capital city a fresh adventure. I have explored the hanging gardens, with all their deceptive challenges. I have climbed the towers of pearl just down the coast. I have ridden stallions across Enysbourg's downs, and plunged at midnight into the warm waters of the eastern sea. I have tasted a hundred pleasures, and wallowed in a hundred more, and though far from sick of them, feel ready to take them at a more relaxed pace, partaking not as a starving man but as a connoisseur. I want to be less a stranger driven by lust, more a lover driven by passion.

So I just take a deep breath and bask in the air that wafts over the slanting tiled roofs: a perfume composed of equal parts sex and spice and the tang of the nearby ocean, all the more precious for being part of the last night before the end of everything. It occurs to me, not for the first time, that this might be the best moment of my life: a life that, back home, with its fast pace and its anonymous workplaces and climate-controlled, gleaming plastic everything, was so impoverished that it's amazing I have any remaining ability to recognize joy and transcendence at all. In Enysbourg such epiphanies seem to come several times a minute. The place seems determined to make me a poet, and if I don't watch out I might hunt down paper and pen and scrawl a few lines, struggling to capture the inexpressible in a cage of fool amateurish June-moon-and-spoon.

THREE

The curtains behind me rustle, and a familiar presence leaves my darkened hotel room to join me on the balcony. I don't turn to greet her, but instead close my eyes as she wraps me in two soft arms redolent of wine and perfume and sex. Her hands meet at the center of my chest. She rests a chin on my shoulder and murmurs my name in the musical accent that marks every word spoken by every citizen of Enysbourg.

"Robert," she says, and there's something a little petulant about the way she stresses the first syllable, something adorable and mocking in the way she chides me for not paying enough attention to her.

By the time I register the feel of her bare breasts against my bare back, and realize in my besotted way that she's mad, she's insane, she's come out on the balcony in full view of everybody without first throwing on something to cover herself, the youths frolicking in the fountain have already spotted her and begun to serenade us with a chorus of delighted cheers. "Kiss her!" shouts a boy. "Come on!" begs a girl. "Let us see!" yells a third. "Don't go inside! Make love out here!" When I turn to kiss the woman behind me, I am cheered like a conqueror leading a triumphant army into Rome.

Her name is Caralys, and she is of course one of the flowers of Enys-bourg: a rare beauty indeed, even in a country where beauty is everywhere. She is tall and lush, with dark eyes, skin the color of caramel, and a smile that seems to hint at secrets propriety won't let her mention. Her shiny black hair cascades down her back in waves, reflecting light even when everything around her seems to be dark.

I met her the day after my arrival, when I was just a dazed and exhausted tourist sitting alone in a café redolent of rich ground coffee. I wasn't just off the boat then, not really. I'd already enjoyed a long awkward night being swept up by one celebration after another, accepting embraces from strangers determined to become friends, and hearing my name, once given, become a chant of hearty congratulation from those applauding my successful escape from the land of everyday life. I had danced the whole night, cheered at the fires of dawn, wept for reasons that puzzled me still, and stumbled to bed, where I enjoyed the dreamless bliss that comes from exhaustion. It was the best night I'd known in a long time. But I was a visitor still, reluctant to sur-render even the invisible chains that shackled me; and even as I'd jerked my-self awake with caffeine, I'd felt tired, surfeited, at odds.

I was so adrift that when Caralys sauntered in, her hair still tousled and cheeks still shining from the celebrations of the night before, her dress of many patches rustling about her ankles in a riot of multiple colors, I almost failed to notice her. But then she'd sat down opposite me and declared in the sternest of all possible tones that even foreigners, with all their worries, weren't allowed to wear grimaces like mine in Enysbourg. I blinked, almost believing her, be-cause I'd heard words just like those the previous night, from a pair of fellow visitors who had caught me lost in a moment of similar repose. Then she tit-tered, first beneath her breath and then with unguarded amusement, not un-derstanding my resistance to Enysbourg's charms, but still intrigued, she explained much later, by the great passion she saw imprisoned behind my gray, civilized mien. "You are my project," she said, in one expansive moment. "I am going to take a tamed man and make him a native of Enysbourg."

She may well succeed, for we have been in love since that first day, both with each other and with the land whose wonders she has been showing me ever since.

FOUR

We have fought only once, just yesterday, when in a thoughtless lapse I suggested that she return with me on the ship home. Her eyes flashed the exasperation she always showed at my moments of thoughtless naïveté: an irritation so grand that it bordered on contempt. She told me it was an arrogant idea, the kind only a foreigner could have.

Why would she leave this place that has given her life? And why would I think so much of her to believe that she would? Was that all she was to me? A prize to be taken home, like a souvenir to impress my friends with my trip abroad? Didn't I see how diminished she would be, if I ever did that to her? "Would you blind me?" she demanded. "Would you amputate my limbs? Would you peel strips off my skin, slicing off piece after piece until there was nothing left of me but the parts that remained convenient to you? This is my country, Robert. My blood." And she was right, for she embodies Enysbourg, as much as the buildings themselves, and for her to abandon it would be a crime against both person and place. Both would be diminished, as much as I'll be diminished if I have to leave her behind.

FIVE

We leave the balcony and go back inside, where, for a moment in the warm and sweet-smelling room, we come close to collapsing on the bed again, for what seems the thousandth time since we woke sore but passionate this morning. But this is the last night before the end of everything, when Enysbourg's wonders emerge in their sharpest relief. They are not to be missed just so we can keep to ourselves. And so she touches a finger to the tip of my nose and commands that it's time to go back into the world. I obey.

We dress. I wear an open vest over baggy trousers, with a great swooping slouch hat glorious in its vivid testimony to Enysbourg's power to make me play the willing fool. She wears a fringed blouse and another ankle-length skirt of many patches, slit to midthigh to expose a magnificent expanse of leg. Dozens of carved wooden bracelets, all loose enough to shift when she moves, clack like maracas along her forearms. Her lips are red, her flowered hair aglow with reflected light. Two curling locks meet in the center of her forehead, right above her eyes, like mischievous parentheses. Somewhere she wears bells.

Laughing, she leads me from the room, and down the narrow stairs, chattering away at our fellow guests as they march in twos and threes toward their own celebrations of this last night. We pass a man festooned with parrots, a woman with a face painted like an Italian landscape, a fire-eater, a juggler in a suit of carnival color, a cavorting clown-faced monkey who hands me a grape and accepts a small coin in payment. Lovers of all possible, and some impossible, gender combinations flash inebriated grins as they surrender their passions in darkened alcoves. Almost everybody we pass is singing or dancing or sharing dizzy, disbelieving embraces. Every time I pause in sheer amazement at something I see, Caralys chuckles at my saucer-eyed disbelief, and pulls me along, whispering that none of this would be half as marvelous without me there to witness it.

Even the two fellow tourists we jostle, as we pass through the arched entranceway and into the raucous excitement of the street, become part of the excitement, because I know them. They are the ones I met on that first lost day before Caralys, before I learned that Enysbourg was not just a vacation destination offered as brief reward for earning enough to redeem a year of dullness and conformity, but the repository of everything I'd ever missed in my flavorless excuse for a life. Jerry and Dee Martel are gray retirees from some awful industrial place where Dee had done something or other with decorating and Jerry had managed a firm that molded the plastic shells other companies used to enclose the guts of useful kitchen appliances. When they talk about their jobs now, as they did when they found me that first night, they shudder with the realization that such things swallowed so many years of finite lives. They were delivered when they vacationed in Enysbourg, choosing it at random among all the other oases of tamed exoticism the modern world maintains to make people forget how sterile and homogenous things have become. On arriving they'd discovered that it was not a tourist trap, not an overdeveloped sham, not a fraud, and not an excuse to sell plastic souvenirs that testify to nothing but the inane gullibility of the people who buy them, but the real thing, the special place, the haven that made them the people they had always been meant to be. They'd emigrated, in what Jerry said with a wink was their "alternative to senility."

"Was it a sacrifice for us?" Jerry asked, when we met. "Did it mean abandoning our security? Did it even mean embracing some hardships? Of course it did. It meant all those things and more. You may not think so, but then you're a baby; you haven't even been in Enysbourg long enough to know. But our lives back home were empty. They were nothing. At least here, life has a flavor. At least here, life is something to be treasured."

Living seven years later as natives, spending half their time in the capital and half their time out in the country exploring caves and fording rivers and performing songs they make up on the spot, they look thirty years younger than their mere calendar ages: with Jerry lean and robust and tanned, Dee shorter and brighter and interested in everything. They remember me from nine days ago and embrace me like a son, exclaiming how marvelous I look, how relaxed I seem in comparison with the timid creature they met then. They want to know if this means I'm going to stay. I blush and admit I don't know. I introduce them to Caralys and they say it seems an easy choice to them. The women hit it off. Jerry suggests a local inn where we can hear a guitarist he knows, and before long we're there, claiming a corner table between dances, listening to his friend: another old man, an ancient man really, with twinkling eyes and spotted scalp and a wispy comic-opera mustache that, dangling to his collarbone, looks like a boomerang covered with lint.

SIX

It's not that I hate my country," Jerry says, when the women have left together, in the way that women have. His eyes shine and his voice slurs from the effects of too much drink. "I can't. I know my history. I know the things she's accomplished, the principles she's stood for, the challenges she's faced. I've even been around for more of it than I care to remember. But coming here was not abandoning her. It was abandoning what she'd become. It was abandoning the drive-throughs and the ATMs and the talking heads who pretend they have the answers but would be lucky to remember how to tie their shoes. It was remembering what life was supposed to be all about, and seizing it with both hands while we still had a few good years still left in us. It was victory, Robert; an act of sheer moral victory. Do you see, Robert? Do you see?"

I tell him I see.

"You think you do. But you still have a ticket out, day after tomorrow. Sundown, right? Ach. You're still a tourist. You're still too scared to take the leap. But stay here a few more weeks and then tell me that you see."

I might just do that, I say. I might stay here the rest of my life.

He dismisses me with a wave of his hand. "Sure you say that. You say that now. You say that because you think it's so easy to say that. You haven't even begun to imagine the commitment it takes."

But I love Caralys.

"Of course you do. But will you be fair to her, in the end? Will you? You're not her first tourist, you know."

SEVEN

Jerry has become too intense for me, in a way utterly at odds with the usual flavor of life in Enysbourg. If he presses on, I might have to tell him to stop.

But I am rescued. The man with the wispy mustache returns from the bar with a fresh mug of beer, sets it beside him on a three-legged stool, picks up a stringed instrument a lot like a misshapen guitar, and begins to sing a ballad in a language I don't understand. It's one of Enysbourg's many dialects, a tongue distinguished by deep rolling consonants and rich sensual tones, so expressive in the way it cavorts the length of an average sentence that I don't need a translation to know that he's singing a hymn to lost love long remembered.

When he closes his eyes I can almost imagine him as the fresh-faced young boy staring with earnest panic at the eyes of the fresh-faced young woman whose beauty first made him want to sing such songs. He sings of pain, a sense of loss, a longing for something denied to him. But there is also wonder, a sense of amazement at all the dreams he's ever managed to fulfill.

Or maybe that's just my head, making the song mean what I want it to mean. In either event, the music is slow and heartfelt until some kind of mid-verse epiphany sends its tempo flying. And all of a sudden the drum beats and the hands clap and the darkened room bursts with men and women rising from the shadows to meet on the dance floor in an explosion of flailing hair and whirling bodies. There are children on shoulders and babies on backs and a hundred voices united in the chorus of the mustached man's song, which seems to fill our veins with fire. Jerry has already slid away, his rant of a few moments before forgotten in the urgency of the moment. I recognize nobody around me but nevertheless see no strangers. As I decide to stay in Enysbourg, to spend the rest of my life with Caralys, to raise a family with her, to keep turning pages in this book I've just begun to write, the natives seem to recognize the difference in me. I am handed a baby, which I kiss to the sound of cheers. I hand it back and am handed another. Then another. The music grows louder, more insistent. A wisp of smoke drifts by. Clove, tobacco, hashish, or something else; it is there and then it is gone.

I blink and catch a glimpse of Caralys, cut off by the crowd. She is trying to get to me, her eyes wide, her face shining, her need urgent. She knows I have decided. She can tell. She is as radiant as I have ever seen her, and though jostled by the mob she is determined to make her way to my side. She too has something to say, something that needs to be spoken, through shattered teeth and a mouth filled with blood.

During

EIGHT

There is no sunlight. The skies are too sullied by the smoke of burning buildings to admit the existence of dawn. What arrives instead are gray and sickly shadows, over a moonscape so marked with craters and shattered rubble that in most places it's hard to tell where the buildings stood in the first place. Every few seconds, the soot above us brightens, becomes as blinding as a parody of the light it's usurped, and rocks the city with flame and thunder. Debris pelts everything below. A starving dog cowering in a hollow formed by two shattered walls bolts, seeking better haven in a honeycomb of fallen masonry fifty meters of sheer hell away. But even before it can round the first twisted corpse, a solid wall of shrapnel reduces the animal to a scarlet mist falling on torn flesh.

I witness its death from the site of my own. I am already dead. I still happen to be breathing, but that's a pure accident. Location is all. The little girl who'd been racing along two paces ahead of me, mad with fear, forced to rip off her flaming clothes to reveal the bubbling black scar the chemical burns have made of her back, is now a corpse. She's a pair of legs protruding from a mound of fallen brick. Her left foot still bears a shoe. Her right is pale, naked, moon-white perfect, unbloodied. I, who had been racing along right behind her, am not so fortunate. The same concussion wave that put her out of her misery sent me flying. Runaway stones have torn deep furrows in my legs, my belly, my face, my chest. I have one seeping gash across my abdomen and another across one cheek; both painful, but nothing next to the greater damage done by the cornice that landed on my right knee, splintering the bone and crushing my leg as close to flat as a leg can get without bursting free of its cradling flesh. The stone tumbled on as soon as it did its work, settling in a pile of similar rocks; it looks like any other, but I still think I can identify it from over here, using the marks it left along the filthy ground.

I have landed in a carpet of broken glass a meter or so from what, for a standing person, would be a ragged waist-high remnant of wall. It is good fortune, I suppose; judging from the steady tattoo of shrapnel and rifle fire impacting against the other side, it's that wall which for the moment spares me the fate of the little girl and the dog. Chance has also favored me by letting me land within sight of a irregular gap in that wall, affording me a view of what used to be the street but which right now is just a narrow negotiable path between craters and mounds of smoking debris. My field of vision is not large, but it was enough to show me what happened to the dog. If I'm to survive this, it must also allow me to see rescue workers, refugees, even soldiers capable of dragging me to wherever the wounded are brought.

But so far there has been no help to be seen. Most of the time even my fragmentary view is obscured by smoke of varying colors: white, which though steaming hot is also thin and endurable, passing over me without permanent damage; black, which sickens me with its mingled flavors of burning rubber and bubbling flesh; and the caustic yellow, which burns my eyes and leaves me gagging with the need to void a stomach already long empty. I lick my lips, which are dry and cracked and pitted, and recognize both hunger and thirst in the way the world pales before me. It is the last detail. Everything I consumed yesterday, when Enysbourg was paradise, is gone; it, and everything I had for several days before. Suddenly, I'm starving to death.

NINE

There is another great burst of sound and light, so close parts of me shake apart. I try to scream, but my throat is dry, my voice a mere wisp, my mouth a sewer sickening from the mingled tastes of blood and ash and things turned rotten inside me. I see a dark shape, a man, Jerry Martel in fact, move fast past the gap in the wall. I hear automatic fire and I hear his brief cry as he hits the dirt in a crunch of flesh and gravel. He is not quite dead at first, and though he does not know I am here, just out of sight, a collaborator in his helplessness, he cries out to me anyway: a bubbling, childish cry, aware that it's about to be cut off but hoping in this instant that it reaches a listener willing to care. I can't offer the compassion Jerry craves, because I hate him too much for bringing fresh dangers so close to the place where I already lie broken. I want him gone.

A second later fate obliges me with another burst of automatic weapons fire. Brick chips fill the air like angry bees, digging more miniature craters; one big one strikes my ravaged knee and I spasm, grimacing as my bowels let loose, knowing it won't matter because I released everything I had inside me long ago. I feel relief. He was my friend, but I'm safer with him gone.

TEN

I smell more smoke. I taste mud. I hear taunts in languages I don't recognize, cries and curses in the tongues spoken in Enysbourg. A wave of heat somewhere near me alerts me that a fire has broken out. I drag myself across ragged stones and broken glass closer to the gap in the wall, entertaining vainglorious ambitions of perhaps crawling through and making it untouched through the carnage to someplace where people can fix me. But the pain is too much, and I collapse, bleeding now from a dozen fresher wounds, having accomplished nothing but to provide myself a better view.

I see the elderly musician with the huge mustache stumble on by, his eyes closed, his face a sheen of blood, his arms dangling blistered and lifeless at his sides, each blackened and swollen to four times its natural size. I see a woman, half-mad, her mouth ajar in an unending silent scream, clutching a tightly wrapped but still ragged bundle in a flannel blanket, unwilling to notice that whatever it held is now just a glistening smear across her chest. I see a tall and robust and athletic man stumble on by, his eyes vacant, his expression insane, his jaw ripped free and dangling from his face by a braided ribbon of flesh. I see all that and I hear more explosions and I watch as some of the fleeing people fall either whole or in pieces and I listen as some are released by death and, more important, as others are not.

Something moving at insane speed whistles through the sky above, passing so near that its slipstream tugs at my skin. I almost imagine it pulling me off the ground, lifting me into the air, allowing me a brief moment of flight behind it before it strikes and obliterates its target. For a moment I wish it would; even that end would be better than a deathbed of shattered rock and slivered glass. Then comes the brightest burst of light and most deafening wave of thunder yet, and for a time I become blind and deaf, with everything around me reduced to a field of pure white.

ELEVEN

When the world comes back, not at all improved, it is easy to see the four young men in identical uniforms who huddle in a little alcove some twenty meters away. There is not much to them, these young men: they all carry rifles, they all wear heavy packs, they're all little more than boys, and their baggy uniforms testify to a long time gone without decent food. When one turns my way, facing me and perhaps even seeing me, but not registering me as a living inhabitant of the corpse-strewn landscape, his eyes look sunken, haunted, unimaginably ancient. He is, I realize, as mad as the most pitiful among the wounded—a reasonable response to his environment, and one I would share if I could divest the damnable sanity that forces me to keep reacting to the horror. He turns back to his comrades and says something; then he looks over them, at something beyond my own limited field of vision, and his smile is enough to make me crave death all over again. His comrades look where he's looking and smile the same way: all four of them showing their teeth.

The three additional soldiers picking their way through the rubble bear a woman between them. It is Caralys. Two stand to either side of her, holding her arms. A third stands behind her, holding a serrated knife to her throat with one hand and holding a tight grip on her hair with the other. That soldier keeps jabbing his knee into the small of her back to keep her going. He has to; she's struggling with every ounce of strength available to her, pulling from side to side, digging her feet into the ground, cursing them to a thousand hells every time they jerk her off her feet and force her onward.

She is magnificent, my Caralys. She is stronger, more vibrant, than any one of them. In any fair fight she would be the only one left standing. But she is held by three, and while she could find an opportunity to escape three, the soldiers from the alcove, who now rush to help their comrades, bring the total all the way up to seven. There is no hope with seven. I know this even as I drag myself toward her from the place where I lie broken. I know this even as she struggles to drive her tormentors away with furious kicks. But these boys are too experienced with such things. They take her by the ankles, lift her off the ground, and bear her squirming and struggling form across the ravaged pavement to a clear place in the rubble, where they pin her to the ground, each one taking a limb. They must struggle to keep her motionless. The soldier with the darkest eyes unslings his rifle, weighs it in his arms, and smashes its butt across her jaw. The bottom half of her face crumples like shattered pottery.

There is nothing I can do but continue to crawl toward her, toward them.

Caralys coughs out a bubble of fresh blood. Fragments of teeth, driven from her mouth, cling to what's left of her chin. She shrieks and convulses and tries to kick. Her legs remain held. The same soldier who just smashed her face now sees that his job is not yet done. He raises his rifle above his head and drives the stock, hard, into her belly. She wheezes and chokes. She tries to curl into a ball of helpless misery, seeking escape within herself. But the soldiers won't even permit that. Another blow, this one to her forehead, takes what little fight is left. Her eyes turn to blackened smears. Her nose blows pink bubbles which burst and dribble down her cheeks in rivulets. She murmurs an animal noise. The soldier responsible for making her manageable makes a joke in a language I don't know, which can't possibly be funny, but still makes the others laugh. They rip off her filthy dress and spread her legs farther apart. The leader steps away, props his rifle against a fragment of wall, and returns, dropping his pants. As he gives his swollen penis a lascivious little waggle, I observe something wrong with it, something I can see from a distance; it looks green, diseased, half-rotted. But he descends, forcing himself into her, cursing her with every thrust, his cruel animal grunts matched by her own bubbling exhalations, less gasps of pain or protests at her violation than the involuntary noises made as her diaphragm is compressed again and again and again. It doesn't last long, but by the time he pulls out, shakes himself off, and pulls his pants back up, the glimpse I catch of her face is enough to confirm that she's no longer here.

Caralys is alive, all right. I can see her labored breath. I can feel the outrage almost as much as she does. But she's not in this place and time. Her mind has abandoned this particular battlefield for another, inside her head, which might not provide any comfort but nevertheless belongs only to her. What's left in this killing ground doesn't even seem to notice as one of the other soldiers releases his grip on her right arm, takes his position, and commences a fresh rape.

TWELVE

There are no words sufficient for the hate I feel. I am a human being with a human being's dimensions, but the hate is bigger than my capacity to contain it. It doesn't just fill me. It replaces me. It becomes everything I am. I want to claw at them and snap at them and spew hatred at them and rip out their throats with my teeth. I want to leave them blackened corpses and I want to go back to wherever they came from and make rotting flesh of their own wives and mothers. I want to bathe in their blood. I want to die killing them. I want to scar the earth where they were born. I want to salt the farmland so nothing ever grows there again. If hatred alone lent strength, I would rend the world itself. But I cry out without a voice, and I crawl forward without quite managing to move, and I make some pathetic little sound or another, and it carries across the smoky distance between me and them and it accomplishes nothing but advise the enemy that I'm here.

In a single spasm of readiness, they all release Caralys, grab their weapons, scan the rubble-field for the source of the fresh sound. The one using her at the moment needs only an extra second to disengage, but he pulls free in such a panicked spasm that he tumbles backward, slamming his pantless buttocks into a puddle of something too colored by rainbows to qualify as water. The leader sees me. He rolls his eyes, pulls a serrated blade from its sheath at his hip, and covers the distance between us in three seconds.

The determined hatred I felt a heartbeat ago disappears. I know that he's the end of me and that I can't fight him and I pray that I can bargain with him instead, that I can barter Caralys for mercy or medical attention or even an easier death. I think all this, betraying her, and it makes me hate myself. That's the worst, this moment of seeing myself plain, this illustration of the foul bargains I'd be willing to make in exchange for a few added seconds of life. It doesn't matter that there aren't any bargains. I shouldn't have wanted any.

I grope for his knife as it descends but it just opens the palms of my hands and christens my face and chest with blood soon matched by that which flows when he guts me from crotch to rib cage. My colon spills out in thick ropes, steaming in the morning air. I feel cold. The agony tears at me. I can't even hope for death. I want more than death. I want more than oblivion. I want erasure. I want a retroactive ending. I want to wipe out my whole life, starting from my conception. Nothing, not even the happy moments, is worth even a few seconds of this. It would be better if I'd never lived.

But I don't die yet.

THIRTEEN

don't die when he walks away, or when he and his fellow soldiers return to their fun with Caralys. I don't die when they abandon her and leave in her place a broken thing that spends the next hours choking on its own blood. I don't even die when the explosions start again, and the dust salts my wounds with little burning embers. I don't die when the ground against my back shakes like a prehistoric beast about to tear itself apart with rage. I don't even die when the rats come to me, to enjoy a fresh meal. I want to die, but maybe that release is more than I deserve. So I lie on my back beneath a cloudscape of smoke and ash, and I listen to Caralys choke, and I listen to the gunfire and I curse that sociopathic monster God and I do nothing, nothing, when the flies come to lay their eggs.

After

FOURTEEN

wake on a bed of freshly mowed grass. The air is cool and refreshing, the sky as blue as a dream, the breeze a delicious mixture of scents ranging from sea salt to the sweatier perfume of passing horses. From the light, I know it can't be too long after dawn, but I can tell I'm not the first one up. I can hear songbirds, the sounds of laughing children, barking dogs, music played at low volumes from little radios.

Unwilling to trust the sensations of peace, I resist getting up long enough to first grab a fistful of grass, luxuriating in the feel of the long thin blades as they bunch up between my fingers. They're miraculous. They're alive. I'm alive.

I turn my head and see where I am: one of the city's many small parks, a place lined with trees and decorated with orchid gardens. The buildings visible past the treeline are uncratered and intact. I'm intact. The other bodies I see, scattered here and there across the lawn, are not corpses, but sleepers, still snoring away after a long lazy evening beneath the stars. There are many couples, even a few families with children, all peaceful, all unworried about predators either animal or human. Even the terror, the trauma, the soul-withering hate, the easy savagery that subsumes all powerless victims, all the emotional scars that had ripped me apart, have faded. And the only nearby smoke comes from a sandpit not far upwind, where a jolly bearded man in colorful suspenders has begun to cook himself an outdoor breakfast.

FIFTEEN

I rise, unscarred and unbroken, clad in comfortable native clothing: baggy shorts, a vest, a jaunty feathered hat. I even have a wine bottle, three-quarters empty, and a pleasant taste in my mouth to go with it. I drink the rest and smile at the pleasant buzz. The thirst remains, but for something nonalcoholic. I need water. Itch from the stray blades of grass peppering my exposed calves and forearms, I contort my back, feeling the vertebrae pop. It feels good. I stretch to get my circulation going. I luxuriate in the tingle of the morning air. Across the meadow, a little girl points at me and smiles. She is the same little girl I saw crushed by masonry yesterday. It takes me a second to smile back and wave, a second spent wondering if she recognizes me, if she finds me an unpleasant reminder. If so, there is no way to tell from the way she bears herself. She betrays no trauma at all. Rather, she looks as blessed as any other creature of Enysbourg.

The inevitable comparison to Caralys assigns me my first mission for the day. I have to find her, hold her, confirm that she too has emerged un-scathed from the madness of the day before. She must have, given the rules here, but the protective instincts of the human male still need to be respected. So I wander from the park, into the streets of a capitol city just starting to bustle with life; past the gondolas taking lovers down the canals; past the merchants hawking vegetables swollen with flavor; past a juggler in a coat of carnival color who has put down his flaming batons and begun to toss delighted children instead. I see a hundred faces I know, all of whom nod with the greatest possible warmth upon seeing me, perhaps recognizing in my distracted expression the look of a foreigner who has just experienced his first taste of Enysbourg's greatest miracle.

Nobody looks haunted. Nobody looks terrorized. Nobody looks like the survivors of madness. They have shaken off the firebombings that reduced them to screaming torches, the bayonets that jabbed through their hearts, the tiny rooms where they were tortured at inhuman length for information they did not have. They have shrugged away the hopelessness and the rampant disease and the mass graves where they were tossed beside their bullet-riddled neighbors while still breathing themselves. They remember it all, as I remember it all, but that was yesterday, not today, and this is Enysbourg, a land where it never happened, a land which will know nothing but joy until the end of everything comes again, ten days from now.

SIXTEEN

On my way back to the hotel I pass the inn where Caralys and I went dancing the night before the end of everything. The scents that waft through the open door are enough to make me swoon. I almost pass by, determined to find Caralys before worrying about my base animal needs, but then I hear deep braying laughter from inside, laughter I recognize as Jerry Martel's. I should go inside. He has been in Enysbourg for years and may know the best ways to find loved ones after the end of everything. The hunger is a consideration, too. Stopping to eat now, before finding Caralys, might seem like a selfish act, but I won't do either one of us any good unless I do something to keep up my strength. Guilt wars with the needs of an empty stomach. My mouth waters. Caralys will understand. I go inside.

The place is dim and nearly empty. The old man with the enormous mustache is onstage, playing something inconsequential. Jerry, who seems to be the only patron, is at a corner table waiting for me. He waves me over, asks me if I'm all right, urges me to sit down, and waits for me to tell him how it was.

My words halting, I tell him it doesn't feel real anymore.

He claps me on the back. He says he's proud of me. He says he wasn't sure about me in the beginning. He says he had me figured for the kind of person who wouldn't be able to handle it, but look at me now, refreshed, invigorated, ready to handle everything. He says I remind him of himself. He beams and expects me to take that as a compliment. I give him a weak nod. He punches me in the shoulder and says that it's going to be fun having me around from now on: a new person, he says, to guide around the best of Enysbourg, who doesn't yet know all the sights, the sounds, the tastes, the joys and adventures. There are parts of Enysbourg, both in and outside the capital, that even most of those who live here don't know. He says it's enough to fill lifetimes. He says that the other stuff, the nasty stuff, the stuff we endure as the price of admission, is just a reason to cherish everything else. He says that the whole country is a treasure trove of experience for people willing to take the leap, and he says I look like one of those people.

And of course, he says, punching my arm again, there's Caralys: sweet, wanton Caralys, whom he has already seen taking her morning swim by the sea. Caralys, who will be so happy to see me again. He says I should remember what Caralys is like when she's delighted. He says that now that I know I can handle it I would have to be a fool to let her go. He chuckles, then says, tell you what, stay right here, I'll go find her, I'm sure the two of you have a lot to talk about. And then he disappears, all before I have said anything at all.

Onstage, the man with the enormous mustache starts another song, playing this time not the misshapen guitar-thing from two nights ago, but something else, a U-shaped device with two rows of strings forming a criss-cross between ends and base. Its music is clear and resonant, with a wobbly quality that only adds to its emotional impact. The song is a slow one: a relief to me, since the raucous energy of Enysbourg's nights might be a bit much for me right now. I nod at the old man. He recognizes me. His grin broadens and his eyes slit with amusement. There's no telling whether he has some special affection for me as a person, or just appreciates the arrival of any audience at all. Either way, his warmth is genuine. He is grateful to me for being here. But he does not stop playing just to greet me. The song continues. The lyrics, once again in a language unknown to me, are once again still easy to comprehend. Whatever the particulars, this song is impossible to mistake as anything but a tribute to being alive. When the song ends, I toss him a coin, and he tosses it back, not insulted, just not interested. He is interested in the music for music's sake alone, in celebration, because celebration is the whole point.

SEVENTEEN

I think hard on the strange cycle of life in Enysbourg, dictated by law, respected as a philosophical principle, and rendered possible by all the technological genius the modern world can provide: this endless cycle which always follows nine days of sheer exuberance with one day of sheer Hell on Earth.

It would be so much easier if exposure to that Tenth Day were not the price of admission.

It would be so much better if we could be permitted to sail in on the Day After and sail out on the Night Before, enjoying those nine days of sweet abandon without any obligation to endure the unmitigated savagery of the tenth. The weekly exodus wouldn't be a tide of refugees; it would be a simple fact of life. If such a choice were possible, I would make it. Of course, I would also have to make Caralys come with me each time, for even if she was determined to remain behind and support her nation's principles, I could never feel at peace standing on the deck of some distant ship, watching Enysbourg's beautiful shoreline erupt in smoke and fire, aware that I was safe but knowing that she was somewhere in that no-man's-land being brutalized and killed. And there is no way she would ever come with me to such a weekly safe haven, when her land was a smoking ruin behind her. She would know the destruction temporary the same way I know it temporary, but she would regard her escape from the regular interval of terror an act of unforgivable treason against her home. It is as she said that time I almost lost her by proposing that she come back home with me, a suggestion I made not because home is such a great place, but because home would be easier. She said that leaving would be cowardice. She said that leaving would be betrayal. She said that leaving would be the end of her. And she said that the same went for any other attempt to circumvent the way things were here, including my own, which is why she'd despise me forever if I tried. The Tenth Day, she said, is the whole point of Enysbourg. It's the main reason the ships come and go only on the Day After. Nobody, not the natives like Caralys, and not the visitors like myself, is allowed their time in paradise unless they also pay the price. The question that faces everybody, on that Day After, is the same question that faces me now: whether life in Enysbourg is worth it.

I think of all the countries, my own included, that never know the magic Enysbourg enjoys nine days out of ten, that have become not societies but efficient machines, where life is all about keeping that machine in motion. Those nations know peace, and they know prosperity, but do they know life the way Enysbourg knows life, nine days out of every ten? I come from such a place and I suffocated in such a place—maybe because I was too much a part of the machine to recognize the consolations available to me, maybe because they weren't available to be found. Either way I know that I've never been happy, not before I came here. Here I found my love of being alive—but only nine days out of ten.

And is that Tenth Day really too much to endure, anyway? I think about all the countries that know that Tenth Day, not at safe predictable intervals, but for long stretches lasting months or years or centuries. I think about all the countries that have never known anything else. I think about all the terrorized generations who have lived and died and turned to bones with nothing but that Tenth Day to color their days and nights. For all those people, millions of them, Enysbourg, with that Tenth Day always lurking in recent memory and always building in the near future, is still a paradise beyond comprehension. Bring all those people here and they'd find this choice easy, almost laughable. They'd leap at the chance, knowing that their lives would only be better, most of the time.

It's only the comfortable, the complacent, the spoiled, who would even find the question an issue for internal debate. The rest would despise me for showing such reluctance to stay, and they'd be right. I've seen enough, and experienced enough, to know that they'd be right. But I don't know if I have what it takes to be right with them. I might prefer to be wrong and afraid and suffering their disdain at a safe distance, in a place untouched by times like Enysbourg's Tenth Day.

EIGHTEEN

I remember a certain moment, when we had been together for three days. Caralys had led me to a gorge, a few hours from the capital, a place she called a secret, and which actually seemed to be, as there were no legions of camera-toting tourists climbing up and down the few safe routes to the sparkling river below. The way down was not a well-worn path, carved by the weight of human feet. It was a series of compromises with what otherwise would have been a straight vertical drop—places where it became possible to slide down dirt grades, or descend from one rock ledge to another. Much of the way down was overgrown, with plants so thick that only her unerring sense of direction kept us descending on the correct route, and not via a sudden, fatal, bone-shattering plunge from a height. She moved through it all with a grace unlike any I had ever seen, and also with an urgency I could not understand, but which was nevertheless intense enough to keep me from complaining through my hoarse breath and aching bones. Every once in a while she turned, to smile and call me her adventurer. And every time she did, the special flavor she gave the word was enough to keep me going, determined to rush anyplace she wanted me to follow.

The grade grew gentler the closer we came to the river at the gorge bottom. It became a mild slope, dim beneath thick forest canopy, surrounded on all sides by the rustling of a thousand leaves and the chittering of a thousand birds. Once the water itself grew audible, there was nothing but a wall of sound all around us. She picked up speed and began to run, tearing off her clothes as she went. I ran after her, gasping, almost breaking my neck a dozen times as I tripped over this root, that half-buried rock. By the time I emerged in daylight at a waterfront of multicolored polished stones, she was well ahead of me. I was hopping on one leg to remove my boots and pants and she was already naked and up to her waist in midriver, her perfect skin shiny from wet and glowing from the sun.

She had led us directly to a spot just below one of the grandest waterfalls I had ever seen with my own eyes. It was an unbroken wall of rushing silver, descending from a flat rock ledge some fifty meters above us. The grotto at its base was bowl-shaped and just wide enough to collect the up-river rapids in a pool of relative calm. The water was so cold that I emitted an involuntary yelp, but Caralys just laughed at me, enjoying my reaction. I dove in, feeling the temperature shock in every pore, then stood up, dripping, exuberant, wanting nothing in this moment but to be with her.

She caught my wrist before I could touch her. "No."

I stopped, confused. No? Why no? Wasn't this what she wanted, in this perfect place she'd found for us?

She released my arm and headed toward the wall of water, splashing through the river as it grew deeper around her, swallowing first her hips and then her breasts and then her shoulders, finally requiring her to swim. Her urgency was almost frightening now. I thought of how easy it might be to drown here, for someone who allowed herself to get caught beneath that raging wall of water, and I said, "Hey," rushing after her, not enjoying the cold quite as much anymore. I don't know what fed that river, but it was numbing enough to be glacial runoff. Thoughts of hypothermia struck for the first time, and I felt the first stab of actual fear just as she disappeared beneath the wall.

The moment I passed through, with sheets of freezing water assaulting my head and shoulders, was one of the loudest I'd ever known. It was a roaring, rumbling, bubbling cacophony, so intense that it drowned out all the other sounds that filled this place. The birds, the wind, the softer bubbling of the water downstream, they were wiped out, eliminated by this one all-encompassing noise. I almost turned around. But I kept going, right through the wall.

On the other side I found air and a dark dank place. Caralys had pulled herself onto a mossy ledge just above the waterline, set against a great stone wall. There she sat with her back to the stone, hugging her legs, her knees tucked tight beneath her chin. Her eyes were white circles reflecting the light passing through the water now behind me. I waded toward her, found an empty spot on the ledge beside her, and pulled myself up too. The stone, I found without much surprise, was like ice, not a place I wanted to stay for long. But I joined her in contemplating the daylight as it prismed through a portal of plummeting water. It seemed brilliant out there: a lot like another world, seen through an enchanted gateway.

"It's beautiful," I said.

She said nothing, so I turned to see if she was all right. She was still staring at the water. She was in shadow, and a trick of the light had shrouded most of her profile in darkness, reducing her outline to a dimly lit crescent. The droplets balancing on the tip of her nose were like little glistening pearls. I saw, too, that she was trembling, though at the time I attributed that to the cold alone. She said, "Listen."

I listened. And heard only the sound of the waterfall, less deafening now that we'd passed some distance beyond it. And something else: her teeth, chattering.

She said, "The silence."

It took me a second to realize that this was the miracle she'd brought me here to witness: the way the waterfall, in all its harmless fury, now insulated us from all the sounds we had been hearing all morning. It was as if none of what we'd heard out there, all the time it had taken us to hike to this place she knew so well, now existed at all. None of it was there. None of it could touch us.

It seemed important to her.

At that moment, I could not understand why.

NINETEEN

I am in the little restaurant, thinking all this, when a soft voice calls my name. I look up, and of course it's Caralys: sweet, beautiful Caralys, who has found me in the place where we prefer to think we saw each other last. She is, of course, unmarked and unwounded, all the insults inflicted by the soldiers either healed or wiped away like bad rumors. She looks exactly like she did the night before last, complete with fringed blouse and patchy dress and two curling strands of hair that meet in the center of her forehead. If there is any difference in her, it lies in what I now recognize was there all along: the storm clouds of memory roiling behind her piercing black eyes. She's not insane, or hard, the way she should be after enduring what she's endured; Enysbourg always wipes away all scars, physical and psychological both. But it does not wipe away the knowledge. And her smile, always so guileless in its radiance, now seems to hold a dark challenge. I can see that she has always held me and my naïveté in the deepest possible contempt. She couldn't have felt any other way, in the presence of any man who had never known the Tenth Day. I had been an infant by Enysbourg's standards, a man who could not understand her or the forces that shaped her. I must have seemed bland, dull, and in my own comfortable way, even retarded.

I find to my surprise that I feel contempt as well. Part of me is indignant at her effrontery at looking down at me. After all, she has had other tourists. She has undertaken other Projects with other men, from other places, trying time and time again to make outsiders into natives of her perverse little theme park to savagery. What does she expect from me, in the end? Who am I to her? If I leave, won't she just find another tourist to play with for ten days? And why should I stay, when I should just see her as the easy vacation tramp, always eager to go with the first man who comes off the boat?

It's hard not to be repulsed by her.

But that hate pales beside the awareness that in all my days only she has made me feel alive.

And her own contempt, great as it is, seems drowned by her love, shining at me with such intensity that for a moment I almost forget the fresh secrets now filling the space between us. I stand and fall into her arms. We close our eyes and taste each other's tears. She whispers, "It is all right, Robert. I understand. It is all right. I want you to stay, but won't hate you if you go."

She is lying, of course. She will despise me even more if I go. She will know for certain that Enysbourg has taught me nothing. But her love will be just as sincere if I stay.

It's the entire reason she seeks out tourists. She loathes our naïveté. But it's also the one thing she can't provide for herself.

TWENTY

Jerry Martel stands nearby, beaming and self-congratulatory. Dee has joined him, approving, cooing, maternal. Maybe they hope we'll pay attention to them again. Or maybe we're just a new flavor for them, a novelty for the expatriates living in Enysbourg.

Either way, I ignore them and pull Caralys close, taking in the scent of her, the sheer absolute ideal of her, laughing and weeping and unable to figure out which is which. She makes sounds that could be either, murmuring words that could be balms for my pain or laments for her own. She tells me again that it's going to be all right, and I don't know whether she's telling the truth. I don't even know whether she's all that sure herself. I just know that, if I take that trip home, I will lose everything she gave me, and be left with nothing but the gray dullness of my everyday life. And if I stay, deciding to pay the price of that Tenth Day in exchange for the illusion of Eden, we'll never be able to acknowledge the Tenth Day on the other days, when everything seems to be all right. We won't mention the times spent suffocating beneath rubble, or spurting blood from severed limbs, or choking out our lungs from poison gas. I will never know how many hells she's known, and how many times she's cried out for merciful death. I'll never be able to ask if what I witnessed yesterday was typical, worse than average, or even an unusually good day, considering. She'll never ask about any of the horrors that happen to me. These are not things discussed during peacetime in Enysbourg. We won't even talk about them if I stay, and if we remain in love, and if we marry and have children, and if they grow up bright and beautiful and filled with wonder; and if every ten days we find ourselves obliged to watch them ground beneath tank treads, or worse. In Enysbourg such things are not the stuff of words. In Enysbourg a certain silence is just the price of being alive.

And a small price it is, in light of how blessed those who live here have always been.

Just about all Caralys can do, as the two of us begin to sway together in a sweet slow dance, is continue to murmur reassurances. Just about all I can do is rest my head against her chest, and close my eyes to the sound of her beating heart. Just about all we can do together is stay in this moment, putting off the next one as long as possible, and try not to remember the dogs, the hateful snarling dogs, caged for now but always thirsty for a fresh taste of blood.

"The mere absence of war is not peace."
—PRESIDENT JOHN F. KENNEDY

For J.H.

The Rhysling Awards are named after the Blind Singer of the Spaceways featured in Robert A. Heinlein's "The Green Hills of Earth." They are given each year by members of the Science Fiction Poetry Association in two categories, best long poem and best short poem.

Charles Saplak and Mike Allen's "Epochs in Exile: A Fantasy Trilogy" tied with Sonya Taaffe's "Matlacihuatl's Gift" for the 2004 Rhysling Award for Best Long Poem. Mike Allen works as a newspaper reporter in Roanoke, Virginia. He edits the biannual poetry journal *Mythic Delirium*, and his poems have sold to such places as *Asimov's, Strange Horizons,* and *Weird Tales*. A book of poetry, *Descent into Light,* is forthcoming from DNA Publications.

Charles Saplak also lives in Roanoke and is the author of the fiction collection *Forgotten Gods and Slighted Soldiers,* published by DNA Books.

Allen describes how he and Saplak wrote "Epochs in Exile":

"This poem, the third of four we've written together, began as Charles Saplak's idea, but he generously invited me along. We constructed the narrative backward, writing the final part first. I remember brainstorming sessions, multiple drafts and one final working-over in Charlie's family room, haggling over every line and line break, as we shaped Kaetzal's lonely journey."

Sonya Taaffe, author of "Matlacihuatl's Gift," has had a long-standing interest in mythology and folklore. Her short fiction and poetry have appeared in various magazines and anthologies, including *Not One of Us, Star★Line, Realms of Fantasy, Mythic Delirium, City Slab, Mercy of Tides,* and *Blowing Kisses*. She is currently pursuing a Ph.D. in Classics at Yale University.

She writes:

"I wrote 'Matlacihuatl's Gift' under the influence of several literature and folklore classes, but the catalyst was Lewis Hyde's *Trickster Makes This World,* in which I first found mention of Matlacihuatl, the Mujer enredadora—Entangling Woman—of the Chiapas Highlands of Mexico.

Her liminal character, her nature that turns strangers' assumptions and physical certainties upside down and inside out, fascinated me. The spaces in between always have. Luis Yglesias, Peter Gould, Alison McGurrin: thank you. *Contraria sunt complementa.*"

The 2004 Rhysling Award for Short Poem went to Ruth Berman for "Potherb Gardening." Her short fiction has appeared in magazines such as *Analog, The Magazine of Fantasy & Science Fiction, New Worlds, Asimov's, Jewish Frontier, Shofar,* and many literary and small press magazines and anthologies. Her poetry has been published in many magazines and anthologies, which include *Asimov's, Amazing, Analog, Weird Tales, Starshore, Star*Line, Saturday Review, Toronto Life, Jewish Currents, Reconstructionist, Kansas Quarterly, Amanuensis, Green's Magazine, Inlet, Spectrum,* and *Southern Humanities Review.*

She writes:

"Reading Harrison Ainsworth's clunky but absorbing *The Lancashire Witches* (based on a historical witch-hunt), set me musing on the superstitious fear of women reflected in the popular figure of the Wicked Witch. One result was this poem, when it further occurred to me that a poison-garden (a popular image in versions as wildly different as Hawthorne's 'Rappaccini's Daughter' or the *Star Trek* episode of 'The Way to Eden') is necessarily also a medicines-garden—and it takes on a different, less spooky, less romantic aspect when seen from the point of view of the gardener. For many years, the university I attended had a poison-garden (carefully fenced) growing outside the pharmacy school building. The building is still there, but it no longer houses the pharmacy school, and the garden has been paved over. I used to pause whenever I went by there to stare—spooked and admiring—at the poison-flowers."

RUTH BERMAN

Now a garden for the craft,
Said the witch,
Needs fertilizing, same's you would
Your roses or your kitchengarden–
Same, I mean, except, of course,
You want special dung for special gardens.

Unicorn-soil gets rid of poisons
Spreading from your upas tree.
It also discourages rabbits and tent-worms.

Mermaid-soil's good for marshes.

Roc-soil will encourage your aconite
And cloudberry or yellowrocket or wingwort–
Anything you plan to stir in flying potions.
Griffin-soil's good, too,
Phoenix if you can get it,
But it's pricey,
And if it's offered in a catalogue,
It's probably not the real thing, anyhow,
I don't care how old and established and rellable.

Don't use dragon-soil–
It'll bum the roots
Even of fireweed and flame trees.

Fairies, now, say they don't produce
And no use asking–
They're too ethereal
Too above that sort of thing.
Where they've been dancing, though,
You get good mushrooms.

CHARLES SAPLAK and MIKE ALLEN

ONE: REFLECTIONS ON A FAR SHORE

I, Kaetzal, Claw of Drakhoun, walk this far shore, alone.
Baleful sun fires the horizon of the quiet sea; one moon,
Alone, silvers the jungle at my back. Starfarer no more.
Here will I go insane. The exile pod floats beside me,
Distortion waves shimmering off the gravity shifter. It can
Take me anywhere, but would shatter were I to challenge this
Sky. It cannot be reprogrammed. Disruptor, exoskeleton,
Metabolic batteries, resonator—I've enough tools to name
Myself King—of this forsaken dustspeck of a world.
A serpent glides through the slime at my feet, jeweled back
Sparkling in moonlight. I see myself, three thousand years
Hence: a belly crawler, naked and unthinking, a taster of
Mud. I finger my disruptor. Shall I Kill this serpent,
Punish it for mocking me? Shall I teach it who is King?
A shorebird circles the surf, hunting, silhouetted on the
Smooth blue moon. Should I Kill all? I could cleanse
This world, were I so inclined. But why should any be
Allowed to die before I do? The Elders locked within my
Code a new template—eggs, sperm, rebirthing rhythm—
I am now a self-replicator, like a fungus.
This they called Mercy . . .

What shade the Drakhoun sky tonight? What pattern the five
Moons? What tale throbs through The Dreamsong, now that
Kaetzal, lone voice of discord, has been silenced? Angry, I
Shed the exoskeleton, drop it into the mud. Why wear
Another prison? Before two steps I collapse to my hands and
Knees, crawl in circles, humiliated, my punishment complete.
A crude chorus trips my resonator—one could hardly call
These minds at all. I strain to peer into the jungle.
Tribes of mangy apes—no, not so pure as apes—another
Thing—*human*. I reach for the disruptor, to reduce them
All to sand—but no. Instead I show them a little trick
I've learned, a quirk of this oxygen-rich world.
I breathe fire.

Scurrying, they leave a ghost in my resonator—a serpent
God, shedding skin, breathing fire. Laughing, I place my
Exoskeleton and disruptor in the pod, send them over the sea
To shatter, fire announcing a new legend, lord, and exile.
Earth's Sole Dragon, I set forth. My tiny universe beckons.

TWO: WETBORN IN WINTER

I ache for the Sun. I will not see the Spring.
Every century or so, I've learned, Winter smashes these
Mountains, and snow falls for weeks. This is such a storm.
The cave mouth has iced over. I'm so still and cold, the
Ice could be within my bones. I groan, and moist,
Warm breath creates a spiral aperture in the ice disc
Closing me in, a crystalline iris which shifts and swirls.
Through this I peer, hoping to glimpse a starry sky
Beyond this blizzard. Is it right to long for home,
After so many centuries? Is it good to ache for my bright,
Warm life, on The Homeworld, so many galaxies away?
There is too much time to think in winter.
And this winter is different: Another is here.

Time, heavy as miles of ice. Though I'm chilled, Another is
Warm, swaddled in my beating heart, shifting and wriggling
In my clean blood. When I was my mother, did I resent
Myself so? Excruciating destroyer, ignorant, selfish.
I writhe around my cave, bleating and bellowing. My cries
Shatter ice, hurl avalanches through chasms.
Do grannies in the village below soothe babies with whispers
Of Old Tseng Chen, whose cries echo around the moon?
There is no time to think. One has awakened.
I don't know that a claw is slicing through my chest
Until I look down and see it. Paralyzed, I watch
My body split, my blood pool on the cave floor.
A jeweled serpent, fifteen feet long, splashes free.

Its scales harden as it licks my blood from the floor.
Panting, I wish to scream, but hold my breath for fear
I'd burn the exquisite murderer. It finds my open chest,

Gnaws there, moves to my throat. I stare at the cave mouth,
Unfeeling, and fancy distant stars. Soon it eats
Through my eye. It gnaws through the socket, and for only a
Moment, the pain is fabulous. Then it is upon my brain.
Darkness, and sleep, until I awaken, eating this bloody gray
Bread. I look to the cave mouth and wonder: What are stars?

I return to this strange feast, this mountain of icy flesh.
I breathe fire, slink between blackened bones like a cage
Of the past. Days and nights pass—I know, I remember:
Someday the ice will break, and I will see the Spring.

THREE: THOUGHTS BEFORE THE SLAYER

Marvelous and tiny, yet another approaches. Wasn't it just
A decade ago when the last ventured here? Or was it a
Century? These things blur together. Regardless, another
Approaches, his heart throbbing, daunting my ancient ears,
Hand-hammered armor clanking and creaking, brittle iron
Sword held aloft, resonating in the wind.
        And me?
Too weary to tell him of my legends, memories really.
Learned not at a granny's knee, but gnawed from the inside
Of my dead mother's skull when I was wet-born, as she had
Gnawed them from her mother's, and so on, seventy times on
This earth, beneath this sun.

He stops; kneels; a prayer to whisper, his pious words
Whipped away by the wind.

I slide along the rock ledge before my cave, wish for more
Sun—how I've always loved this sun. Should I interrupt
His prayer to talk about this sun, or talk of cool blue suns
I remember? Or great red suns which fill strange skies, cast
Shadows on castles which were old when his race was young?

He continues to pray, this creature come to kill me. My
Teeth hurt. I cannot bear the thought of eating. Some days

I can't breathe fire, and my own smoke chokes me. My heart
Hisses within my chest, and worst—there are no eggs.
I Welcome him, this tiny knight, but also want to tell of my
Line, how one thousand, seven hundred, and sixty-three lives
Ago my First arrived, sent his starship to the ocean floor.
How I've watched since then, seen these tiny unscaled ones
Stand up from the ape, construct cathedrals. How when first
I saw a war I could have scoured this Earth clean, set fire
To the sky. How when first I heard a lullaby cooed in a
Cold cave, I knew this race would prevail. . . .

His prayers are done. What name his god? Or should I ask
His name—Saint George, Glooscap, Sigurd? Or ask which of
A thousand names he calls me—Nidhogg, Draconis, Hydra?

He arises, steps forward, sword drawn, fear and courage in
His eyes. I roll over in the warm sun, on this world grown
Too small for legends. He targets my breast, pale and
Penetrable, while I wonder what will be said, when his
Descendants meet my ancestors, out among the stars.

SONYA TAAFFE

Be wary when you kiss her: which mouth
you choose to press your lips against
when you meet her in the highlands
where she walks alone. By roadsides,
by moonlight, sway of hair falling dark
down her sinuous back, her steps hold
the grace of shadows, panthers,
and under your touch her skin breathes
like a flower. Be careful when you approach her
as she awaits you in the dark,
when you slide one hand beneath
her riverbed hair, whispering the words
that lovers and liars always use:
por favor, querida, nunca más and siempre,
calling on time and all eternity
to hold fast your love as you lay her down
silent where her arms wind around
your back, where her mouth fits to yours,
where you cannot resist her and she never
says no. Her beauty burns the mind.
Printed with your kisses—lip and cheekbone,
throat and palm, vulnerable nape of the neck
when you push her hair aside to taste
the second mouth she hides there,
flowerlike, no more a mouth than what
she keeps between her earth-warm thighs—
moving on you like the tide, she holds you
tight so that you cannot see, as you cry out
into the hollow of her tawny throat,
what smile her face wears in the aftershock.
No time for wariness or regret
when you have left her, under trees' shadows
at the roadside, when you have kissed
both her mouths and burst stars within her
and lied your love to her in the dark:
down in the cities again, you wonder
what made her laugh as you walked away,
why she folded your hand over the coins

you tried to press into her palm, freeing
your fingers with a gesture that almost
pulled you back. Did she foresee
this nausea in the morning, these twinges
in your belly as though a salt sea
shifted within you, while you check
your weight and frown, resolve to drink
less beer and work out more—and you want
to eat the oddest things—does she know how
you never dream her face except smiling,
close-mouthed and confident, sideways
step over what you thought you knew?
Her coin is reversal; she inverts
the mirror, pays you out
in the shadow side of common knowledge
until you no longer recognize where she began,
where you end, until you understand
what she gave you when you took from her,
in nine months' time, to overturn your world.

The *Washington Post Book World* called Harlan Ellison "one of the great living American short story writers," and *The Los Angeles Times* said: "It's long past time for Harlan Ellison to be awarded the title: 20th century Lewis Carroll." And though we've now slipped into the 21st, if this *most* unusual Nebula finalist for short story is any indication, Harlan is *still* pursuing the vision dangerous and antic.

He's written or edited seventy-six books; more than seventeen hundred stories, essays, articles, and newspaper columns; two dozen teleplays, for which he received the Writers Guild of America most outstanding teleplay award for solo work an unprecedented four times; and a dozen movies. He won the Mystery Writers of America Edgar Allan Poe award twice, the Horror Writers Association Bram Stoker award six times (including The Lifetime Achievement Award in 1996), the Nebula three times, and the Hugo eight (and a half times, don't ask), and received the Silver Pen for Journalism from P.E.N. He has also won the World Fantasy Award, the British Fantasy Award, the American Mystery Award, two Audie Awards, the Ray Bradbury Award, and a Grammy nomination for Spoken Word recordings. In 1990, he was honored by P.E.N. for his continuing commitment to artistic freedom and the battle against censorship.

His books include the novels *Web of the City, The Sound of a Scythe, Spider Kiss*; the graphic novels *Demon With a Glass Hand, Night and the Enemy, Vic and Blood: the Chronicles of a Boy and His Dog, Harlan Ellison's Dream Corridor*; and the short story collections (to name but a few) *Troublemakers, Slippage, Angry Candy, Stalking the Nightmare, Shatterday, Strange Wine, Deathbird Stories, Love Ain't Nothing but Sex Misspelled, Paingod and Other Delusions, I Have No Mouth & I Must Scream*, and *Mind Fields* (in collaboration with the Polish Surrealist Jacek Yerka). His nonfiction includes *Memos From Purgatory, The Glass Teat* and *The Other Glass Teat, Harlan Ellison's Watching*, and *An Edge in My Voice*. He is also the editor of the groundbreaking collections *Dangerous Visions*—"What we mean when we say an important book," wrote *The New York Times*—and *Again, Dangerous Visions.*

He worked as a consultant and host for the radio series *2000X,* a series of twenty-six one-hour dramatized radio adaptations of famous SF stories for *The Hollywood Theater of the Ear,* for which, in 2002, SFWA gave him the Ray Bradbury Award for Drama Series: For Program Host & Creative Consultant: NPR Presentation of 2000X. He has created scripts for *The Twilight Zone* (including Danny Kaye's final performance) and *The Outer Limits*; and has signed to develop his award-winning *Outer Limits* script, "Demon With a Glass Hand," for Miramax's Dimension Films as a theatrical feature.

Harlan Ellison writes about his story "Goodbye to All That" with his usual panache and razor-sharp wit:

"Before Michael Chabon and Dave Eggers bought this story for *McSweeney's,* I honored a longstanding request for a submission from Francis Ford Coppola's *Zoetrope All-Story* by sending 'Goodbye to All That.' It was scheduled soon to be published in the Wesleyan University Press original anthology *Envisioning the Future,* edited by Prof. Marleen Barr, but the First Periodical Rights were free, and I liked 'Goodbye . . .' so much I thought it would fit right into the 'Utopia' issue of *Zoetrope.* Synchronicity.

"So I sent it off to the managing editor, Justine Cook, a lovely and gracious woman who had steadily *nuhdzed* me for a story for almost a year. Well, she only *loved* it, she told me, and she wanted it, and she was going to submit it to the 'staff of editors,' she told me, who made group decisions about what went into the magazine. I confess my blood ran cold when I learned that the Sanhedrin of *Zoetrope All-Story* was something like thirteen white women, most of whom had graduated from the Seven Sisters schools. It is nearly impossible to get thirteen Jews to agree on anything, much less thirteen *shiksas.*

"But I bided my time for several weeks till her call.

"Yes, the Cultural Council of Coppola Critics, each one the very incarnation of Calliope, *adored* the story. Yes, they wanted very much to publish it. Yes, they would pay a larger fee if I would sign the *Zoetrope* contract giving them first option on the film/tv rights. But first, if I didn't mind answering a couple of questions about the story? Blood runs cold; but I agreed to do my best to unsnarl their skein.

"The first question: 'Mr. Ellison, is this story supposed to be, like, *funny*?'

"Say *whaaat*?! Surely the part about the yak left no doubt that this was an antic absurdist, *funny* story.

"I replied that I did indeed hope the telling of the tale would bring a chuckle or two, particularly the part about the yak; and the menu listing. 'Uh-huh,' she said.

"The second question, from another woman: 'Why did you put the Cleveland Indians in this story? Does it have reference to some archetypal image?'

"I replied that I put the 1948 Indians in the story because I was very fond of the 1948 Indians. 'I see,' she said.

"The third question, from yet another Calliope: 'What is this story supposed to be? How are we to think of it?'

"I replied exactly thus: 'Well, let me see. If, say, James Hilton had written, instead of *Lost Horizon*, say, Eugene Ionesco's *Rhinoceros* . . . it would be this story. Or, no, wait; let me put it this way. If, instead of having written *The Razor's Edge*, Somerset Maugham had written, for instance, Samuel Beckett's *Waiting for Godot* . . . it would be this story.'

"There was silence. A trio of silence.

" 'It's absurdist,' I said, struggling for rapprochement. 'Dickens, as written by Donald Westlake.'

" 'Who is Donald Westlake?' one of them asked.

"*Oh, dear*, I thought.

"But then yet came the Final Question: 'Can you tell us what the punchline means?'

"I paused only a nanosecond. 'It means, uh, nothing,' I said. 'It is what it is. The ultimate punchline. It stands alone.'

"They were trigonally taciturn. That went on for a while. Then I sighed, because I really did like Ms. Cook, and I knew she was trying to do me a solid, and I felt sorry for her, as well as for the other young women. And I said, 'You're not Jewish, are you?' I meant no disrespect. Truly.

"And they asked, with only a smidge of 'tude, 'Why would you ask that?' And I asked it again, politely; and they all averred that they were not, to be sure, of a Semitic persuasion. So I said, 'I'm afraid I can't let you publish my story.' Goodness, what a lot of air bubbles and *fumfuh*'ing.

" 'Why not?!?'

" 'Because you don't understand it, and I'm afraid you never will, and it's somehow wrong to sell a story as close to the heart as this one is, even to nice people who just don't *get* it. So I'd appreciate it if you'd just send it back, and I'll try to write something else for you another time.'

"The letter from Justine Cook that accompanied return of the manuscript began like this: 'Dear Harlan, As I hope you realize, I am disappointed not to have "Goodbye to All That" in our Utopia issue. Unfortunately, I was not only constrained in the end by our contract . . . but you would have had to revise your story, and I know that you do not accept editing of your work.' Etcetera. Nice letter, actually. Wanted *another* story as quickly as I could offer one. (She was wrong about me rejecting editorial suggestions out of hand, however. All I require is that the editor be smarter and more knowledgeable than I. At least about the story in question.)

"As it turns out, it isn't a matter of Jewishness or Gentileness. Because Silverberg didn't get it, either, and Gene Wolfe laughed his ass off.

"It is, I suspect, a matter of being a little loopy in the head. People who think 'a sense of humor' and 'wit' are the same thing, probably won't like it. People who never heard the old joke that ends, 'Life *isn't* a fountain?' also will scratch their heads. I am not, repeat *not,* saying with some arrogant elitist hubris that people who don't like this story are any less beautiful, cogent, well-dressed, righteous, or intellectually expansive than those who do. All I'm saying humbly, abjectly, is that this is a *great* short story, written by a humble, abject journeyman on the road to the mountaintop whereat reside Kafka, Borges, Dali and Antonin Artaud.

"The rest is up to you. I'm watching."

HARLAN ELLISON®

"Like a Prime Number, the Ultimate Punchline stands alone."
Daniel Manus Pinkwater

He knew he was approaching The Core of Unquenchable Perfection, because the Baskin-Robbins "flavor of the month" was tunafish-chocolate. If memory served (served, *indeed!* if only! but, no, it did nothing of the sort . . . it just lay about, eating chocolate truffles, whimpering to be waited on, hand and foot) he was now in Nepal. Or Bhutan. Possibly Tannu Touva.

He had spent the previous night at a less-than-opulent b&b in the tiny, forlorn village of Moth's Breath—which had turned out to be, in fact, not a hostelry, but the local abattoir—and he was as yet, even this late in the next day, unable to rid his nostrils of the stultifying memory of formaldehyde. His yak had collapsed on the infinitely upwardly spiraling canyon path leading to the foothills that nuzzled themselves against the flanks of the lower mountains timorously raising their sophomore bulks toward the towering ancient massif of the thousand-peaked Mother of the Earth, *Chomolungma,* the pillar of the sky upon which rested the mantle of the frozen heavens. Snow lay treacherously thick and deep and placid on that celestial vastness; snow blew in ragged curtains as dense as swag draperies across the summits and chasms and falls and curved scimitar-blade sweeps of icefields; snow held imperial sway up here, high so high up here on this sacred monolith of the Himalayas that the natives called the Mother-Goddess of the Earth, *Chomolungma.*

Colman suffered from poriomania. Dromomania was his curse. From agromania, from parateresiomania, from ecdemonomania, from each and all of these he suffered. But mostly dromomania.

Compulsive traveling. Wanderlust.

Fifty United States before the age of twenty-one. All of South America before twenty-seven. Europe and most of Africa by his thirtieth birthday.

Australia, New Zealand, the Antarctic, much of the subcontinent by thirty-three. And all of Asia but this frozen nowhere as his thirty-ninth birthday loomed large but a week hence. Colman, helpless planomaniac, now climbed toward The Nidus of Ineluctable Reality (which he knew he was nearing, for his wafer-thin, solar-powered, internet-linked laptop advised him that Ben & Jerry had just introduced a new specialty flavor, Sea Monkey—which was actually only brine shrimp-flavored sorbet) bearing with him the certain knowledge that if the arcane tomes he had perused were to be believed, then somewhere above him, somewhere above the frozen blood of the Himalayan ice-falls, he would reach The Corpus of Nocturnal Perception. Or The Abyss of Oracular Aurochs. Possibly The Core of Absolute Discretion.

There had been a lot of books, just a *lot* of books. And no two agreed. Each had a different appellation for the Ultimate. One referred to it as The Core of Absolute Discretion, another The Intellectual Center of the Universe, yet a third fell to the impenetrable logodædalia of: The Foci of Conjunctive Simultaneity. Perhaps there had been too *many* books. But shining clearly through the thicket of rodomontade there was always the ineluctable, the inescapable truth: there *was* a place at the center of it all. Whether Shangri-la or Utopia, paradisaical Eden or the Elysian Fields, whether The Redpath of Nominative Hyperbole or The Last and Most Porous Membrane of Cathexian Belief, there was a valley, a greensward, a hill or summit, a body of water or a field of grain whence it all came.

A place where Colman could travel to, a place that was the confluence of the winds of Earth, where the sound of the swaying universe in its cradle of antiquity melded with the promise of destiny.

But where it might be, was the puzzle.

Nepal, Katmandu, Bhutan, Mongolia, Tibet, The Tuva Republic, Khembulung . . . it *had* to be up here, somewhere. He'd tried everywhere else. He'd narrowed the scope of the search to a fine channel, five by five, and at the end he would penetrate that light and reach, at last, The Corpus of Nocturnal Perception, or *whatever;* and then, perhaps only then, would his mad unending need to wander the Earth reach satiation.

Then, so prayed Colman deep in the cathedral of his loneliness, then he might begin to lead a life. Home, family, friends, purpose beyond *this* purpose . . . and perhaps no purpose at all, save to exist as an untormented traveler.

His yak had died, there on the trail; he presumed from sheer fright at the prospect of having to schlep him up that great divide, into the killing snowfields. The yak was widely known to be a beast of really terrific insight and excellent, well at least pretty good, instincts.

Death before dishonor was not an unknown concept to the noble yak.

Colman had tried several simple, specific, and sovereign remedies to resuscitate the imperial beast: liquor from toads boiled in oil to help reduce the fever; leaves of holly mixed with honey, burned to ash in oast ovens and rendered into syrup; the force-feeding of a live lizard tongue, swallowed whole in one gulp (very difficult, as the yak was thoroughly dead); tea made from tansy; tea made from vervain.

Absolutely no help. The yak was dead. Colman was afoot in the killing icefields. On his way to Utopia, to Shangri-la or, at least, The Infinitely Replenishing Fountain of Mythic Supposition. There had been just a *lot* of books.

He reconciled the thought: *I'll never make it with all this gear.* Then, the inevitable follow-up: *I'll never make it* without *all this gear.* He unshipped the dead noble beast and began, there on the slope, to separate the goods into two piles, seeing his chances of survival diminishing with every item added to the heap on his right. He lifted his tinted goggles onto his forehead and stared with naked eye at the massif looming above him. There were more than a few hysterical flurries of snow. Naturally: there was a storm coming.

He knew he was nearing The Heart of Irredeemable Authenticity because the happily-buzzing laptop informed him that not only had geomancy been declared the official state religion of Austria, but that Montevideo had been renamed Happy Acres. An investment banker in Montreal had been found dismembered, parts of his body deposited in a variety of public trash bins and dumpsters, but Colman didn't think that had anything of the significant omen about it.

The storm had broken over him, sweeping down from the pinnacles less than two hours after he had crossed the great divide, broached the slope, and begun his ascent toward the summit now hidden by thunderheads. Abrading ground-glass flurries erupted out of crevasses; and the swirling lacelike curtains of ice and snow were cruelly driven by a demented wind. He thought he had never known cold before, no matter how cold he had ever been, never anything like this. His body moaned.

And he kept climbing. There was no alternative. He would either reach The Corporeality of the Impossible Metaphor, or he would be discovered eons hence, when this would all be swampy lowland, by whatever species had inherited the planet after the poles shifted.

Hours were spent by Colman coldly contemplating the possible positions his centuries-frozen (but perfectly flash-frozen) corpse might assume. He recalled a Rodin sculpture in a small park in Paris, he thought it was an *hommage* to Maupassant or Balzac, one or the other, and remembered the right hand, the way it curled, and the position of the fingers. He envisioned himself entombed in just that way, sculptural hand with spread fingers protruding from the ages of ice. And so, hours were spent trudging with ice-axe in hand, up the killing icefields, dreaming in white of death tableaux.

Until he fell forward and lay still, as the storm raged over him. There was silence only in that unfrozen inner place beyond the residence of the soul.

When he awoke, *not* having frozen to death at all, which eventually struck him as fairly miraculous (but, in fact, easily explained by the storm having blown itself out quickly, and the escarpment just above him providing just enough shelter), he got to his feet, pulled the staff loose from the snow pack, and looked toward the summit.

High above him, blazing gloriously in the last pools of sunlight whose opposite incarnations were fields of blue shadow, he beheld the goal toward which he had climbed, that ultimate utopian goal he had sought across entire continents, through years of wandering. There it was, as the books had promised: The Singular Scheme of Cosmic Clarity. The center, the core, the hub, the place where all answers reside. He had found lost Shangri-la, whatever its real name might be. He saw above him, in the clearness of the storm-scoured waning day, what appeared to be a golden structure rising from the summit, its shape a reassuring and infinitely calming sweep of dual archlike parabolas. He thought that was what the shapes were called: parabolas.

Now there was no exhaustion. No world-weariness. He was not even aware that inside his three pairs of thermal socks, inside his crampon'd boots, all the toes of his left foot and three of his right had gone black from frostbite.

Mad with joy, he climbed toward those shining golden shapes, joyfully mad to enter into, at last, The Sepulchre of Revealed Truths. There may have been a great many books but, oh frabjous day, they were all, every last one of them, absolutely dead on the money. The Node of Limitless Revealment. Whatever.

It was very clean inside. Sparkling, in fact. The tiles underfoot were spotless, reflective, and calming. The walls were pristine, in hues of pastel solicitude that soothed and beckoned. There were tables and chairs throughout, and at one end a counter of some magnificent gleaming metal that showed Colman his ravaged reflection, silvered and extruded, but clearly wan and near total exhaustion. Patches of snowburned flesh had peeled away on both cheeks, chin, nose. The eyes somewhat unfocused as if coated with albumin. The Sanctum of Coalesced Revelations was brightly lit, scintillant surfaces leading the eye toward the shining bar of the magic metal counter. Colman shambled forward, dropping his ice staff; he was a thing drawn off the mountain barely alive, into this oasis of repose and cleanliness, light and succor.

There was a man in his late thirties standing behind the gleaming metal counter. He smiled brightly at Colman. He had a nice face. "Hi! Welcome to The Fountainhead of Necessary Perplexity. May I take your order, please?"

Colman stood rooted and wordless. He knew precisely what was required of him—each and every one of the arcane tomes had made it clear there was a verbal sigil, a password, a phrase that need be spoken to gain access to the holiest of holies—but he had no idea what that *open sesame* might be. The Gardyloo of Ecstatic Entrance. Wordless, Colman looked beseechingly at the counterman.

He may have said, "Uh . . ."

"Please make your selection from the menu," said the man behind the counter, who wore a classic saffron robe and a small squared-off cardboard hat. Colman remembered a film clip of The Andrews Sisters singing "Boogie Woogie Bugle Boy," wearing just such "garrison caps." The counterman pointed to the black-on-yellow signage suspended above the gleaming deck. Colman pondered the choices:

THE OXEN ARE SLOW, BUT THE EARTH IS PATIENT

CHANCE FAVORS THE PREPARED MIND

IT TAKES A HEAP O' LIVIN' TO MAKE A HOUSE A HOME

DEATH COMES WITHOUT THE THUMPING OF DRUMS

I LIKE YOUR ENERGY

THE AVALANCHE HAS ALREADY STARTED; IT'S TOO
LATE FOR THE PEBBLES TO VOTE

EVERY CLOUD HAS A SILVER LINING

DON'T LOOK BACK. SOMETHING MAY BE GAINING ON YOU.

YES, LIFE IS HARD; BUT IF IT WERE EASY, EVERYBODY
WOULD BE DOING IT

LIFE IS A FOUNTAIN

TRUST IN ALLAH, BUT TIE YOUR CAMEL

THE BARKING DOG DOES NO HARM TO THE MOON

THE MAN WHO BURNS HIS MOUTH ON HOT MILK BLOWS ON
HIS ICE CREAM

NO ONE GETS OUT OF CHILDHOOD ALIVE

SO NEAR, AND YET SO FAR

MAN IS COAGULATED SMOKE FORMED BY HUMAN
PREDESTINATION . . . DUE TO RETURN TO THAT STATE
FROM WHICH IT ORIGINATED

French Fries are à la carte.

Colman drew a deep, painful breath. To get to this point, and to blow it because of a few words . . . unthinkable. His mind raced. There were deep thoughts he could call up from a philosophy base on the laptop, the aphorisms and rubrics of six thousand years of human existence, but it was only one of them, only one—like a prime number—that would stand alone and open to him the portals of wisdom; only one that would be accepted by this gatekeeper of *Universal* Oneness; only one unknown core jot of heartmeat that would serve at this moment.

He tried to buy himself a caesura: he said to the saffron-robed counterman, "Uh . . . one of those . . . 'Life is a Fountain'? I know that one; you've got to be kidding, right? 'Life is a fountain . . . '?"

The counterman looked at him with shock. "Life *isn't* a fountain?"

Colman stared at him. He wasn't amused.

"Just fooling," the counterman said, with a huge smile. "We always toss in an old gag, just to mix it up with the Eternal Verities. Life should be a bit of a giggle, a little vaudeville, whaddaya think?"

Colman was nonplussed. He was devoid of plus. He tried to buy another moment: "So, uh, what's your name?"

"I'll be serving you. My name's Lou."

"Lou. What are you, a holy man, a monk from some nearby lamasery? You look a little familiar to me."

Lou chuckled softly again, as if he were long used to the notoriety and had come to grips with it. "Oh, heck no, I'm not a holy man; you probably recognize me from my bubble gum card. I used to play a little ball. Last name's Boudreau." Colman asked him how to spell that, and he did, and Colman went to his rucksack, dropped on one of the tables, and he pulled out the laptop and did a Google search for the name *Lou Boudreau*.

He read what came up on the screen.

He looked at what he had read on the screen for a long time. Then he went back to the counter.

"You were the player-manager of the World Champion 1948 Cleveland Indians. Shortstop. 152 games, 560 at bats, 199 hits, 116 runs. You were the all-time franchise leader with a .355 batting average, slugging and on-base percentages and a .987 OPS! What are you doing here, for gawdsakes?!"

Boudreau removed the little paper hat, scratched at his hair for a moment, sighed, and said, "Rhadamanthus carries a grudge."

Colman stared dumbly. Zeus had three sons. One of them was Rhadamanthus, originally a judge in the afterlife, assigned the venue of the Elysian Plain, which was considered a very nice neighborhood. But sometime between Homer and Virgil, flame-haired Rhadamanthus got reassigned to Tartarus, listed in all the auto club triptychs as Hell. Strict judge of the dead. No sin goes unpunished. From which the word "rhadaman-thine" bespeaks inflexibility.

"What did you do to honk him off?"

"I went with Bearden instead of Bob Lemon in the first game of the series against the Boston Braves. We lost one to nothing. Apparently he had a wad down on the game."

A slim black man, quite young, wearing a saffron robe and a card-board garrison cap, came out of the back. Lou aimed a thumb at him. "Larry Doby, center fielder. First Negro to play in the American League." Doby smiled, gave a little salute, and said to Colman, "Figure it out yet?"

Colman shook his head.

"Well, good luck." Then, in Latin, he added, "*Difficilia quae pulchra.*" Colman had no idea what that meant, but Doby seemed to wish him well with the words. He said thank you.

Lou pointed toward the rear. "That's our drive-thru attendant, Joe Gordon, great second baseman. Third baseman Ken Keltner on the grill with our catcher, Jim Hegan; Bob Feller's working maintenance just till his arm gets right again, but Lemon and Steve Gromek'll be handling the night shift. And our fry guy is none other than the legendary Leroy 'Satchel' Paige . . . hey, Satch, say hello to the new kid!"

Lifting the metal lattice basket out of the deep fryer filled with siz-zling vegetable oil, Satchel Paige knocked the basket half-full of potatoes against the edge of the tub to shake away excess drippings, and grinned hugely at Colman. "You see mine up there?" he said, cocking his head to-ward the signage of wise sayings. Colman nodded and smiled back.

"Well," said Lou Boudreau, saffron-robed counterman shortstop manager of the 1948 World Series champion Cleveland Indians, who had apparently really pissed off Rhadamanthus, "are you ready to or-der?"

Time had run out. Colman knew this was it. Whatever he said next would be either the gate pass or the bum's rush. He considered the choices on the menu, trying to pick one that spoke to his gut. It had to be *one* of them.

His mind raced. It *had* to be one of them.

He paused. It was the moment of the cortical-thalamic pause. *Why* did it have to be one of them?

Life *wasn't* a fountain.

There was only one thing to say to God, if one were at the Gate. At the Core, the Nexus, the Center, the Eternal Portal. Only one thing that made sense, whether this was God or just a minimum-wage, part-time employee. Colman straightened, unfurrowed his brow, and spoke the only words that would provide entrance if one were confronting God. He said to Lou Boudreau:

"Let me talk to the Head Jew."

The peppy little shortstop grinned and nodded and said, "May I super-size that for you?"

Elizabeth Moon holds degrees in history and biology and served in the US Marine Corps. Her novels include the *Deed of Paksenarrion* series; *Sassinak* and *Generation Warriors* (with Anne McCaffrey); the *Legacy of Gird* series; the *Serrano Legacy* series; *Trading In Danger*; *Remnant Population*; and *Marque and Reprisal*. Some of her stories can be found in her collections *Lunar Activity* and *Phases*, as well as in a number of anthologies, most recently *Masters of Fantasy* and *The Dragon Quintet*. Her novel *The Speed of Dark* won this year's Nebula Award. *The Midwest Book Review* called it "an incredible novel that captures the essences of an intelligent autistic person struggling to independently survive in a constantly changing world . . . This strong tale with powerful characters will remind the audience of *Flowers for Algernon* and *Rain Man* as Elizabeth Moon takes the reader inside the soul of the hero."

The author has kindly allowed us to see how she came to write *The Speed of Dark*. An excerpt from the novel follows her poignant and informative memoir.

THE STORY BEHIND THE BOOK: A PERSONAL VIEW

ELIZABETH MOON

any years ago, when my husband was in medical school, I thought
neurology was the dullest of the organ-system segments. It seemed
that neurologists did nothing much but stick pins into people to
see where they flinched. Computed tomography was beginning to open up
new possibilities for neurologists, and MRI and PET scanning would soon
follow, but right then I knew nothing about them. My interests lay outdoors,
in wildlife management, habitat restoration, and so on.

If someone had asked me, before we had a child, if I would consider
spending the next twenty years learning about developmental neurology,
cognition, sensory integration, and so on, and take on the care of an autistic child, I would have said no, loudly, explaining (over my shoulder, as I fled
back to field biology and rural medicine) that I didn't have the right background for that. Not me, never me.

You can almost hear the Cosmos chuckling wickedly. Best laid plans
and all that.

We adopted our son as an infant in 1983. My first reaction to our son's
developmental problems was the typical mix of panic and grief. Was it my
fault? Could it be fixed, whatever it was? I redoubled my efforts to do
everything every child development book recommended, to no avail. We
had no diagnosis early on (and no accurate diagnosis for some years).

As adoptive parents, we weren't faced with the worry of whose genes
were at fault. Still, plenty of people were sure it had to be "the mom,"
though they had no clue what was wrong. Of course my writing (and science fiction at that!) had to be the problem. "If you'd just quit writing that
stuff, he'd be normal," someone said. Luckily, his medical team didn't agree.

On our first visit to the pediatric neurologist, the possibilities offered
ranged from reassuring ("He may grow out of it") to dire ("or he may be
showing the signs of a neurodegenerative disease and you must face the
possibility that he may regress to a vegetative state and die before he's ten").

I clearly remember the specialist saying "Well, at least we're sure he's not autistic," because he clung to me and cried when the resident tried to pick him up.

In the next couple of years, his diagnosis changed from "severe global developmental delay, unspecified" through "expressive language disorder" to "pervasive developmental delay," as he showed more unmistakable signs of autism. Doctors then—twenty years ago—were very reluctant to call any developmental delay autism if they could help it. Autism was considered such a devastating diagnosis, presenting parents with so hopeless a future, that no one wanted to say the word. Now it almost seems that autism is the diagnosis du jour; you see articles on it almost every day. By the time we heard "autism," it came as a relief. It meant he wasn't going to die in a few years.

In the meantime, I had discovered that by the irony of life, everything I had ever done—from tutoring math to animal behavior analysis, from programming computers to playing the piano, etc.—was relevant to parenting an autistic child. All of it helped me in the effort to help him grow into an adult who could survive—and enjoy—the world as it is.

Our experience as parents of an autistic boy has been both like and unlike that of other parents we read about and talk to. "Challenging but rewarding" is probably the shortest way to describe it. The long-form description fills pages, notebooks, boxes, file cabinets. The usual milestones of childhood—first word, first two-syllable utterance, first two-word sentence, first question—arrived years late. There were months when we saw no progress, or (very scary) regression, months and years with snail-like progress, before others began to realize what a nifty kid he is. I have pages of language analysis, notes on specific behaviors, and of course a shelf of books (actually two shelves now) from popular to highly technical, all with marginal notes. ("Yes!!" and "Idiot!!" and "Well, maybe . . .")

Parenting is always partly luck, and in our case we were lucky to have had such varied education and experience, because at the time the information available to parents ranged from insufficient to erroneous. I mention these things here not to brag, but to encourage other parents in similar situations to look for the relevance of their experience to the current problem, whatever it is. The unlikeliest things turn out to be useful.

A good basic education taught me to absorb a lot of technical material rapidly and to evaluate sources. I had enough background in biology and medicine to dive straight into the professional literature. It's amazing how fast you can learn a new field when you have a compelling reason to do so. Critical skills developed for scholarly pursuits translate readily into evaluation of sources in the new field.

Working with second- and third-generation computers while in the military had given me a good mental model of information processing.

That let me evaluate psychological theories of autism and cognition from a fresh angle. There's a lot more to cognition than the brain equivalent of the central processor. I could look at our son's neurological apparatus as a collection of modules: the I/O or senses, a bus, some buffers, and so on. I knew how a mismatch of data transmission rates could cause trouble.

In graduate school, working toward a career in wildlife management, I'd taken a course in animal behavior, partly because I'd been fascinated by Jane Goodall's work with chimpanzees.

Wildlife biologists were far ahead of child psychologists of the day in fine-grained observation of behavior, I discovered. We were taught that all behavior has meaning—it all communicates something to the careful, thoughtful observer. Attention reflects sensory sensitivity and discrimination: what an organism pays attention to tells the observer much about its sensory processing. Stress often emerges as patterned activity ("stimming," in human terms) or withdrawal and unresponsiveness ("shutting down" or "zoning out"). The physical precursors of these more obvious stress reactions—tension in certain muscle groups, yawning, deviation of gaze—are similar across a variety of mammalian species.

Over the years, starting in high school, I had worked with children in various ways—babysitter, church nursery school volunteer, and tutor of both "normal" and retarded children. I'd read Montessori's books while in college the first time, thinking ahead to having children of my own, and later I'd read John Holt's books on education. All this gave me a feel for how different children learn, how different children approach problem-solving, and honed my skills at devising creative teaching methods for each individual.

I'd also read Karen Pryor's book *Lads Before the Wind* while in graduate school; it was my first exposure to the creative use of behavior shaping by positive reinforcement. I'd used those methods in retraining animals. Later, I found her book *Don't Shoot the Dog,* with its very handy (and witty) explication of the eight basic training strategies.

All these—and many other—varied lumps of knowledge or skill turned out to be useful. The supportive members of the family and friends (some weren't supportive) were also important. My husband, though working very long hours during our son's childhood, was a warm and loving presence, not withdrawing from a disabled son the way many men do. My mother was particularly supportive. She had been an engineer and was also a gifted seamstress and needleworker in general. She made him special clothes (it was then very hard to find diapers in larger sizes) and designed and made incredible fabric educational aids that used color and texture and shape. Several friends accepted our son's differences, and met me for lunch once a week, even helping us both learn to ice-skate, which he wanted to do.

I realized very soon that most of what was known or thought about autism up to the mid-1980s was nonsense, and the interventions then recommended were, most of them, appalling (some were abusive, in my opinion) and ineffective—we were told that 90 percent of the children like our son ended up in institutions, forever isolated from the world. That negative prognosis actually helped, because it freed me from the fear that trying something different would necessarily do harm. If the therapies suggested mostly didn't work . . . and the knowledge base mostly wasn't there . . . then making my own observations and experimenting could hardly do worse.

I looked at our son, who was—when not screaming loudly—a happy toddler, and decided that I could do better than that. If he could laugh and smile as an infant and small child, then the capacity for joy was there—and I would support it. I started with careful, detailed observation of his behavior, going beyond the normal v. deviant dichotomy most texts then employed. What could he do? What were his sensory channels responding to? Was the response time slow or fast? How slow?

Simple observations proved that the "central processor error" theory was false, at least for our son. His learning was flawless in some areas (these were labeled "splinter skills" by some therapists, and considered useless) and severely impaired in others. He learned letters, numbers, and geometric figures easily; he had great difficulty interpreting photographs, images on the television screen, and cartoons. He could recognize a horse, cow, donkey, or sheep in a field (we drove past such fields daily) but could not recognize a picture of one of these animals in a book. He recognized some sounds with great precision but others made no impression. He showed empathy (which shot down the famed "theory of mind" approach as well).

It was fascinating to map all his abilities and inabilities, to build a clear picture of what worked and what didn't. From that map, I could then try to guess what approach might work. All the previous experience came into play, with observations evaluated in light of computers and animal behavior. It was scary at first, since I had no formal credentials in this area, but also exhilarating, a great intellectual challenge. No parent would want a child to be disabled so the parent could have a learning experience, but once we had the child with the problem, that intellectual challenge kept me from the emotional sinkhole that swallows so many parents of autistic kids.

For years, I thought of writing another parent-experience book to help other parents realize the possibilities, but by the time I could clear a space in my schedule, somewhere around 1997–98, the field had caught up with me. Autism was recognized as a neurologic condition, not a mental illness; vastly better early and school-age interventions were available (many of them looked like what I'd done, though I still found the professional discussions too rigid and unimaginative).

That's when the idea of a novel first tickled my brain. I'd read Oliver

Sacks's many books, including those which touched on, or were about, autism, but the two which most affected me were *A Leg to Stand On,* about his experiences as a patient, and *Seeing Voices,* about the Deaf community and its struggle to be accepted as a legitimate community. Both these books clarified issues about identity and disability (whether temporary or permanent) and society's attitude towards defined disabilities.

The controversy among the deaf about cochlear implants struck me particularly. Most parents equate "making normal" with "healing"; they consider not-normal to be pathologic, and they search for the magic treatment or pill that will make their child normal. Deaf parents who oppose cochlear implants for children born deaf argue that being deaf is not a flaw, and "making them normal" is not healing. Some autistic people I met online felt the same way—they did not consider their autism to be the problem, but instead believed the problem was society's reaction to their difference. They wanted to be accepted as they were, rather than being forced or at least pressured to be like everyone else.

Slowly, hesitantly, a soft-spoken youngish man began talking in my head. He named himself Lou; he began showing me the world through his eyes. Rather than trust me (as many characters do) to tell his story, he insisted he wanted to tell it himself. First person, present tense, grammatical oddities and all. We argued about it, in that crazy way novelists talk to their characters. I leaned on my experience and argued for third person; Lou was patient but inexorable. His story, his voice, his choice.

Living with Lou for that year or so was similar to moving to a foreign country I had only visited before. Yet Lou was—is—utterly and completely human. He struggled with his identity as most of us struggle with ours, pressured as we all are by our culture to reshape ourselves to a better fit, and by internal forces to respond to experience with growth.

Many of us carry labels of pathology pasted on us by someone in authority: underachiever, overachiever, addictive personality, enabler, depressive personality, hyper, lazy, and so on. Some of us have taken these labels in and acted on them; we become what we're told we are, and we wonder if we had to be that way. There's nothing alien about wondering who you are, why you are who you are, and who you may become. How much is inborn? How much is social pressure? How much is the interaction of both with sheer random accident? Many questions, few answers.

As with all my books so far, the actual story began with a character in a quandary. I worried, for the first week or so, that Lou might be too much like our son, but Lou had enough self-determination to eject those fragments of our son which I accidentally put in. Lou is older and more mature, quieter, more thoughtful, less exuberant, more intelligent, a little sadder. His preferences in color, food, and hobbies are all different.

The actual writing required me to stay in Lou's viewpoint for days at a time. It was the hardest writing, in the technical sense, I've ever done. First-person writing is hard anyway, and first-person viewpoint of someone not at all like the writer is much more difficult. To hold the focus on Lou's mental processes, to think myself into his mind, I had to become him at some level. Toward the end, I caught myself "being" Lou with other people. Sometimes they gave me very odd looks. It was even hard to escape that persona when I was starting the next book.

I've been asked if this book "romanticizes" autism because it is not uniformly bleak. It doesn't. No parent of an autistic child has any romantic illusions about autism or the difficulties involved in parenting an autistic child. I wouldn't want to relive the relentless grind of those early years when progress was so slow. Yet the situation for autistic persons now is not all bleak; the reality is that autistic children can and do grow out of the most difficult stage, and both children and adults can enjoy life and can form healthy relationships. Our son's preschool teacher remarked that when he was happy he could light up the whole room—the trick was helping him "find happy" as he put it. He is still (at twenty now, as I write this) a remarkably happy and gentle young adult, though clearly and obviously not "normal."

"I chose the particular passage of *The Speed of Dark* given here, Chapter 2, because all the major players are on stage as seen through Lou's eyes. His world—his job, his apartment, his hobby, his routines, the people he interacts with—are all there. The main issues he will wrestle with are just visible; decisions—his and those of others—are shadowy mountains on the horizon."

ELIZABETH MOON

Mr. Crenshaw is the new senior manager. Mr. Aldrin, our boss, took him around that first day. I didn't like him much—Crenshaw, that is—because he had the same false-hearty voice as the boys' PE teacher in my junior high school, the one who wanted to be a football coach at a high school. Coach Jerry, we had to call him. He thought the special-needs class was stupid, and we all hated him. I don't hate Mr. Crenshaw, but I don't like him, either.

Today on the way to work I wait at a red light, where the street crosses the interstate. The car in front of me is a midnight-blue minivan with out-of-state plates, Georgia. It has a fuzzy bear with little rubber suckers stuck to the back window. The bear grins at me with a foolish expression. I'm glad it's a toy; I hate it when there's a dog in the back of a car, looking at me. Usually they bark at me.

The light changes, and the minivan shoots ahead. Before I can think, No, don't! two cars running a red light speed through, a beige pickup with a brown stripe and an orange watercooler in the back and a brown sedan, and the truck hits the van broadside. The noise is appalling, shriek/crash/squeal/crunch all together, and the van and truck spin, spraying arcs of glittering glass. . . . I want to vanish inside myself as the grotesque shapes spin nearer. I shut my eyes.

Silence comes back slowly, punctuated by the honking horns of those who don't know why traffic stopped. I open my eyes. The light is green. People have gotten out of their cars; the drivers of the wrecked cars are moving, talking.

The driving code says that any person involved in an accident should not leave the scene. The driving code says stop and render assistance. But I was not involved, because nothing but a few bits of broken glass touched my car. And there are lots of other people to give assistance. I am not trained to give assistance.

I look carefully behind me and slowly, carefully, edge past the wreck. People look at me angrily. But I didn't do anything wrong; I wasn't in the accident. If I stayed, I would be late for work. And I would have to talk to policemen. I am afraid of policemen.

I feel shaky when I get to work, so instead of going into my office I go to the gym first. I put on the "Polka and Fugue" from *Schwanda the Bagpiper,* because I need to do big bounces and big swinging movements. I am a little calmer with bouncing by the time Mr. Crenshaw shows up, his face glistening an ugly shade of reddish beige.

"Well now, Lou," he says. The tone is clouded, as if he wanted to sound jovial but was really angry. Coach Jerry used to sound like that. "Do you like the gym a lot, then?"

The long answer is always more interesting than the short one. I know that most people want the short uninteresting answer rather than the long interesting one, so I try to remember that when they ask me questions that could have long answers if they only understood them. Mr. Crenshaw only wants to know if I like the gym room. He doesn't want to know how much.

"It's fine," I tell him.

"Do you need anything that isn't here?"

"No." I need many things that aren't here, including food, water, and a place to sleep, but he means do I need anything in this room for the purpose it is designed for that isn't in this room.

"Do you need that music?"

That music. Laura taught me that when people say "that" in front of a noun it implies an attitude about the content of the noun. I am trying to think what attitude Mr. Crenshaw has about that music when he goes on, as people often do, before I can answer.

"It's so difficult," he says. "Trying to keep all that music on hand. The recordings wear out. . . . It would be easier if we could just turn on the radio."

The radio here has loud banging noises or that whining singing, not music. And commercials, even louder, every few minutes. There is no rhythm to it, not one I could use for relaxing.

"The radio won't work," I say. I know that is too abrupt by the hardening in his face. I have to say more, not the short answer, but the long one. "The music has to go through me," I say. "It needs to be the right music to have the right effect, and it needs to be music, not talking or singing. It's the same for each of us. We need our own music, the music that works for us."

"It would be nice," Mr. Crenshaw says in a voice that has more overtones of anger, "if we could each have the music we like best. But most people—" He says "most people" in the tone that means "real people, normal people." "Most people have to listen to what's available."

"I understand," I say, though I don't actually. Everyone could bring in a player and their own music and wear earphones while they work, as we do. "But for us—" For us, the autistic, the incomplete. "It needs to be the right music."

Now he looks really angry, the muscles bunching in his cheeks, his face redder and shinier. I can see the tightness in his shoulders, his shirt stretched across them.

"Very well," he says. He does not mean that it is very well. He means he has to let us play the right music, but he would change it if he could. I wonder if the words on paper in our contract are strong enough to prevent him from changing it. I think about asking Mr. Aldrin.

It takes me another fifteen minutes to calm down enough to go to my office. I am soaked with sweat. I smell bad. I grab my spare clothes and go take a shower. When I finally sit down to work, it is an hour and forty-seven minutes after the time to start work; I will work late tonight to make up for that.

Mr. Crenshaw comes by again at closing time, when I am still working. He opens my door without knocking. I don't know how long he was there before I noticed him, but I am sure he did not knock. I jump when he says. "Lou!" and turn around.

"What are you doing?" he asks.

"Working," I say. What did he think? What else would I be doing in my office, at my workstation?

"Let me see," he says, and comes over to my workstation. He comes up behind me; I feel my nerves rucking up under my skin like a kicked throw rug. I hate it when someone is behind me. "What is that?" He points to a line of symbols separated from the mass above and below by a blank line. I have been tinkering with that line all day, trying to make it do what I want it to do.

"It will be the . . . the link between this"—I point to the blocks above—"and this." I point to the blocks below.

"And what are they?" he asks.

Does he really not know? Or is this what the books call instructional discourse, as when teachers ask questions whose answers they know to find out if the students know? If he really doesn't know, then whatever I say will make no sense. If he really does know, he will be angry when he finds out I think he does not.

It would be simpler if people said what they meant.

"This is the layer-three system for synthesis," I say. That is a right answer, though it is a short one.

"Oh, I see," he says. His voice smirks. Does he think I am lying? I can see a blurry, distorted reflection of his face in the shiny ball on my desk. It is hard to tell what its expression is.

"The layer-three system will be embedded into the production codes," I say, trying very hard to stay calm. "This ensures that the end user will be able to define the production parameters but cannot change them to something harmful."

"And you understand this?" he says.

Which this is this? I understand what I am doing. I do not always understand why it is to be done. I opt for the easy short answer.

"Yes," I say.

"Good," he says. It sounds as false as it did in the morning. "You started late today," he says.

"I'm staying late tonight," I say. "I was one hour and forty-seven minutes late. I worked through lunch, that is thirty minutes. I will stay one hour and seventeen minutes late."

"You're honest," he says, clearly surprised.

"Yes," I say. I do not turn to look at him. I do not want to see his face. After seven seconds, he turns to leave. From the door he has a last word.

"Things cannot go on like this, Lou. Change happens."

Nine words. Nine words that make me shiver after the door is closed.

I turn on the fan, and my office fills with twinkling, whirling reflections. I work on, one hour and seventeen minutes. Tonight I am not tempted to work any longer than that. It is Wednesday night, and I have things to do.

Outside it is mild, a little humid. I am very careful driving back to my place, where I change into T-shirt and shorts and eat a slice of cold pizza.

Among the things I never tell Dr. Fornum about is my sex life. She doesn't think I have a sex life because when she asks if I have a sex partner, a girlfriend or boyfriend, I just say no. She doesn't ask more than that. That is fine with me, because I do not want to talk about it with her. She is not attractive to me, and my parents said the only reason to talk about sex was to find out how to please your partner and be pleased by your partner. Or if something went wrong, you would talk to a doctor.

Nothing has ever gone wrong with me. Some things were wrong from the beginning, but that's different. I think about Marjory while I finish my pizza. Marjory is not my sex partner, but I wish she were my girlfriend. I met Marjory at fencing class, not at any of the social events for disabled people that Dr. Fornum thinks I should go to. I don't tell Dr. Fornum about fencing because she would worry about violent tendencies. If laser rag was enough to bother her, long pointed swords would send her into a panic. I don't tell Dr. Fornum about Marjory because she would ask questions I don't want to answer. So that makes two big secrets, swords and Marjory.

When I've eaten, I drive over to my fencing class, at Tom and Lucia's. Marjory will be there. I want to close my eyes, thinking of Marjory, but

I am driving and it is not safe. I think of music instead, of the chorale of Bach's *Cantata no. 39*.

Tom and Lucia have a large house with a big fenced backyard. They have no children, even though they are older than I am. At first I thought this was because Lucia liked working with clients so much that she did not want to stay home with children, but I heard her tell someone else that she and Tom could not have children. They have many friends, and eight or nine usually show up for fencing practice. I don't know if Lucia has told anyone at the hospital that she fences or that she sometimes invites clients to come learn fencing. I think the hospital would not approve. I am not the only person under psychiatric supervision who comes to Tom and Lucia's to learn to fight with swords. I asked her once, and she just laughed and said, "What they don't know won't scare them."

I have been fencing here for five years. I helped Tom put down the new surface on the fencing area, stuff that's usually used for tennis courts. I helped Tom build the rack in the back room where we store our blades. I do not want to have my blades in my car or in my apartment, because I know that it would scare some people. Tom warned me about it. It is important not to scare people. So I leave all my fencing gear at Tom and Lucia's, and everyone knows that the left-hand-but-two slot is mine and so is the left-hand-but-two peg on the other wall and my mask has its own pigeonhole in the mask storage.

First I do my stretches. I am careful to do all the stretches; Lucia says I am an example to the others. Don, for instance, rarely does all his stretches, and he is always putting his back out or pulling a muscle. Then he sits on the side and complains. I am not as good as he is, but I do not get hurt because I neglect the rules. I wish he would follow the rules because I am sad when a friend gets hurt.

When I have stretched my arms, my shoulders, my back, my legs, my feet, I go to the back room and put on my leather jacket with the sleeves cut off at the elbow and my steel gorget. The weight of the gorget around my neck feels good. I take down my mask, with my gloves folded inside, and put the gloves in my pocket for now. My épée and rapier are in the rack; I tuck the mask under one arm and take them out carefully.

Don comes in, rushed and sweating as usual, his face red. "Hi, Lou," he says. I say hi and step back so he can get his blade from the rack. He is normal and could carry his épée in his car if he wanted without scaring people, but he forgets things. He was always having to borrow someone else's, and finally Tom told him to leave his own here.

I go outside. Marjory isn't here yet. Cindy and Lucia are lining up with épées; Max is putting on his steel helmet. I don't think I would like the steel helmet; it would be too loud when someone hit it. Max laughed when I told him that and said I could always wear earplugs, but I hate earplugs.

They make me feel as if I have a bad cold. It's strange, because I actually like wearing a blindfold. I used to wear one a lot when I was younger, pretending I was blind. I could understand voices a little better that way. But feeling my ears stuffed up doesn't help me see better.

Don swaggers out, épée tucked under his arm, buttoning his fancy leather doublet. Sometimes I wish I had one like that, but I think I do better with plain things.

"Did you stretch?" Lucia asks him.

He shrugs. "Enough."

She shrugs back. "Your pain," she says. She and Cindy start fencing. I like to watch them and try to figure out what they're doing. It's all so fast I have trouble following it, but so do normal people.

"Hi, Lou," Marjory says, from behind me. I feel warm and light, as if there were less gravity. For a moment I squeeze my eyes shut. She is beautiful, but it is hard to look at her.

"Hi, Marjory," I say, and turn around. She is smiling at me. Her face is shiny. That used to bother me, when people were very happy and their faces got shiny, because angry people also get shiny faces and I could not be sure which it was. My parents tried to show me the difference, with the position of eyebrows and so on, but I finally figured out that the best way to tell was the outside corners of the eyes. Marjory's shiny face is a happy face. She is happy to see me, and I am happy to see her.

I worry about a lot of things, though, when I think about Marjory. Is autism contagious? Can she catch it from me? She won't like it if she does. I know it's not supposed to be catching, but they say if you hang around with a group of people, you'll start thinking like them. If she hangs around me, will she think like me? I don't want that to happen to her. If she were born like me it would be fine, but someone like her shouldn't become like me. I don't think it will happen, but I would feel guilty if it did. Sometimes this makes me want to stay away from her, but mostly I want to be with her more than I am.

"Hi, Marj," Don says. His face is even shinier now. He thinks she is pretty, too. I know that what I feel is called jealousy; I read it in a book. It is a bad feeling, and it means that I am too controlling. I step back, trying not to be too controlling, and Don steps forward. Marjory is looking at me, not at Don.

"Want to play?" Don says, nudging me with his elbow. He means do I want to fence with him. I did not understand that at first. Now I do. I nod, silently, and we go to find a place where we can line up.

Don does a little flick with his wrist, the way he starts every bout, and I counter it automatically. We circle each other, feinting and parrying, and then I see his arm droop from the shoulder. Is this another feint? It's an opening, at least, and I lunge, catching him on the chest.

"Got me," he says. "My arm's really sore."

"I'm sorry," I say. He works his shoulder, then suddenly leaps forward and strikes at my foot. He's done this before; I move back quickly and he doesn't get me. After I get him three more times, he heaves a great sigh and says he's tired. That's fine with me; I would rather talk to Marjory. Max and Tom move out to the space we were using. Lucia has stopped to rest; Cindy is lined up with Susan.

Marjory is sitting beside Lucia now; Lucia is showing her some pictures. One of Lucia's hobbies is photography. I take off my mask and watch them. Marjory's face is broader than Lucia's. Don gets between me and Marjory and starts talking.

"You're interrupting," Lucia says.

"Oh, sorry," Don says, but he still stands there, blocking my view.

"And you're right in the middle," Lucia says. "Please get out from between people." She flicks a glance at me. I am not doing anything wrong or she would tell me. More than anyone I know who isn't like me, she says very clearly what she wants.

Don glances back, huffs, and shifts sideways. "I didn't see Lou," he says.

"I did," Lucia says. She turns back to Marjory. "Now here, this is where we stayed on the fourth night. I took this from inside—what about that view!"

"Lovely," Marjory says. I can't see the picture she's looking at, but I can see the happiness on her face. I watch her instead of listening to Lucia as she talks about the rest of the pictures. Don interrupts with comments from time to time. When they've looked at the pictures, Lucia folds the case of the portable viewer and puts it under her chair.

"Come on, Don," she says. "Let's see how you do with me." She puts her gloves and mask back on and picks up her épée. Don shrugs and follows her out to an open space.

"Have a seat," Marjory says. I sit down, feeling the slight warmth from Lucia in the chair she just left. "How was your day?" Marjory asks.

"I almost was in a wreck," I tell her. She doesn't ask questions; she just lets me talk. It is hard to say it all; now it seems less acceptable that I just drove away, but I was worried about getting to work and about the police.

"That sounds scary," she says. Her voice is warm, soothing. Not a professional soothing, but just gentle on my ears.

I want to tell her about Mr. Crenshaw, but now Tom comes back and asks me if I want to fight. I like to fight Tom. Tom is almost as tall as I am, and even though he is older, he is very fit. And he's the best fencer in the group.

"I saw you fight Don," he says. "You handle his tricks very well. But he's not improving—in fact, he's let his training slide—so be sure you fight some of the better fencers each week. Me, Lucia, Cindy, Max. At least two of us, okay?"

At least means "not less than." "Okay," I say. We each have two long blades, épée and rapier. When I first tried to use a second blade, I was always banging one into the other. Then I tried to hold them parallel. That way they didn't cross each other, but Tom could sweep them both aside. Now I know to hold them at different heights and angles.

We circle, first one way, then the other. I try to remember everything Tom has taught me: how to place my feet, how to hold the blades, which moves counter which moves. He throws a shot; my arm rises to parry it with my left blade; at the same time I throw a shot and he counters. It is like a dance: step-step-thrust-parry-step. Tom talks about the need to vary the pattern, to be unpredictable, but last time I watched him fight someone else, I thought I saw a pattern in his nonpattern. If I can just hold him off long enough, maybe I can find it again.

Suddenly I hear the music of Prokofiev's *Romeo and Juliet,* the stately dance. It fills my head, and I move into that rhythm, slowing from the faster movements. Tom slows as I slow. Now I can see it, that long pattern he has devised because no one can be utterly random. Moving with it, in my personal music, I'm able to stay with him, blocking every thrust, testing his parries. And then I know what he will do, and without thought my arm swings around and I strike with a *punta riversa* to the side of his head. I feel the blow in my hand, in my arm.

"Good!" he says. The music stops. "Wow!" he says, shaking his head.

"It was too hard I am sorry," I say.

"No, no, that's fine. A good clean shot, right through my guard. I didn't even come close to a parry on it." He is grinning through his mask. "I told you you were getting better. Let's go again."

I do not want to hurt anyone. When I first started, they could not get me to actually touch anyone with the blade, not hard enough to feel. I still don't like it. What I like is learning patterns and then remaking them so that I am in the pattern, too.

Light flashes down Tom's blades as he lifts them both in salute. For a moment I'm struck by a dazzle, by the speed of the light's dance.

Then I move again, in the darkness beyond the light. How fast is dark? Shadow can be no faster than what casts it, but not all darkness is shadow. Is it? This time I hear no music but see a pattern of light and shadow, shifting, twirling, arcs and helices of light against a background of dark.

I am dancing at the tip of the light, but beyond it, and suddenly feel that jarring pressure on my hand. This time I also feel the hard thump of Tom's blade on my chest. I say, "Good," just as he does, and we both step back, acknowledging the double kill.

"Owwww!" I look away from Tom and see Don leaning over with a hand to his back. He hobbles toward the chairs, but Lucia gets there first and sits beside Marjory again. I have a strange feeling: that I noticed and that I cared. Don has stopped, still bent over. There are no spare chairs now, as other fencers have arrived. Don lowers himself to the flagstones finally, grunting and groaning all the way.

"I'm going to have to quit this," he says. "I'm getting too old."

"You're not old," Lucia says. "You're lazy." I do not understand why Lucia is being so mean to Don. He is a friend, it is not nice to call friends names except in teasing. Don doesn't like to do the stretches and he complains a lot, but that does not make him not a friend.

"Come on, Lou," Tom says. "You killed me; we killed each other; I want a chance to get you back." The words could be angry, but the voice is friendly and he is smiling. I lift my blades again.

This time Tom does what he never does and charges. I have no time to remember what he says is the right thing to do if someone charges; I step back and pivot, pushing his off-hand blade aside with mine and trying for a thrust to his head with the rapier. But he is moving too fast; I miss, and his rapier arm swings over his own head and gives me a whack on the top of the head.

"Gotcha!" he says.

"You did that how?" I ask, and then quickly reorder the words. "How did you do that?"

"It's my secret tournament shot," Tom says, pushing his mask back. "Someone did it to me twelve years ago, and I came home and practiced until I could do it to a stump . . . and normally I use it only in competition. But you're ready to learn it. There's only one trick." He was grinning, his face streaked with sweat.

"Hey!" Don yells across the yard. "I didn't see that. Do it again, huh?"

"What is the trick?" I ask.

"You have to figure out how to do it for yourself. You're welcome to my stump, but you've just had all the demonstration you're going to get. I will mention that if you don't get it exactly right, you're dead meat to an opponent who doesn't panic. You saw how easy it was to parry the off-hand weapon."

"Tom, you haven't showed me that one—do it again," Don says.

"You're not ready," Tom says. "You have to earn it." He sounds angry now, just as Lucia did. What has Don done to make them angry? He hasn't stretched and gets tired really fast, but is that a good reason? I can't ask now, but I will ask later.

I take my mask off and walk over to stand near Marjory. From above I can see the lights reflecting from her shiny dark hair. If I move back and forth, the lights run up and down her hair, as the light ran up and down Tom's blades. I wonder what her hair would feel like.

"Have my seat," Lucia says, standing up. "I'm going to fight again."

I sit down, very conscious of Marjory beside me. "Are you going to fence tonight?" I ask.

"Not tonight. I have to leave early. My friend Karen's coming in at the airport, and I promised to pick her up. I just stopped by to see . . . people."

I want to tell her I'm glad she did, but the words stick in my mouth. I feel stiff and awkward. "Karen is coming from where?" I finally say.

"Chicago. She was visiting her parents." Marjory stretches her legs out in front of her. "She was going to leave her car at the airport, but she had a flat the morning she left. That's why I have to pick her up." She turns to look at me; I glance down, unable to bear the heat of her gaze. "Are you going to stay long tonight?"

"Not that long," I say. If Marjory is leaving and Don is staying, I will go home.

"Want to ride out to the airport with me? I could bring you back by here to pick up your car. Of course, it'll make you late getting home; her plane won't be in until ten-fifteen."

Ride with Marjory? I am so surprised/happy that I can't move for a long moment. "Yes," I say. "Yes." I can feel my face getting hot.

On the way to the airport, I look out the window. I feel light, as if I could float up into the air. "Being happy makes it feel like less than normal gravity," I say.

I feel Marjory's glance. "Light as a feather," she says. "Is that what you mean?"

"Maybe not a feather. I feel more like a balloon," I say.

"I know that feeling," Marjory says. She doesn't say she feels like that now. I don't know how she feels. Normal people would know how she feels, but I can't tell. The more I know her, the more things I don't know about her. I don't know why Tom and Lucia were being mean to Don, either.

"Tom and Lucia both sounded angry with Don," I say. She gives me a quick sideways glance. I think I am supposed to understand it, but I don't know what it means. It makes me want to look away; I feel funny inside.

"Don can be a real heel," she says.

Don is not a heel; he is a person. Normal people say things like this, changing the meaning of words without warning, and they understand it. I know, because someone told me years ago, that *heel* is a slang word for "bad person." But he couldn't tell me why, and I still wonder about it. If someone is a bad person and you want to say that he is a bad person, why not just say it? Why say "heel" or "jerk" or something? And adding "real" to it only makes it worse. If you say something is real, it should be real.

But I want to know why Tom and Lucia are angry with Don more than I want to explain to Marjory about why it's wrong to say Don is a real heel. "Is it because he doesn't do enough stretches?"

"No." Marjory sounds a little angry now, and I feel my stomach tightening. What have I done? "He's just . . . just mean, sometimes, Lou. He makes jokes about people that aren't funny."

I wonder if it is the jokes or the people that aren't funny. I know about jokes that most people don't think are funny, because I have made some. I still don't understand why some jokes are funny and why mine aren't, but I know it is true.

"He made jokes about you," Marjory says, a block later, in a low voice. "And we didn't like it."

I don't know what to say. Don makes jokes about everybody, even Marjory. I didn't like those jokes, but I didn't do anything about it. Should I have? Marjory glances at me again. This time I think she wants me to say something. I can't think of anything. Finally I do.

"My parents said acting mad at people didn't make them act better."

Marjory makes a funny noise. I don't know what it means. "Lou, sometimes I think you're a philosopher."

"No," I say. "I'm not smart enough to be a philosopher."

Marjory makes the noise again. I look out the window; we are almost to the airport. The airport at night has different-colored lights laid out along the runways and taxiways. Amber, blue, green, red. I wish they had purple ones. Marjory parks in the short-term section of the parking garage, and we walk across the bus lanes into the terminal.

When I'm traveling alone, I like to watch the automatic doors open and close. Tonight, I walk on beside Marjory, pretending I don't care about the doors. She stops to look at the video display of departures and arrivals. I have already spotted the flight it must be: the right airline, from Chicago, landing at 10:15 P.M., on time, Gate Seventeen. It takes her longer; it always takes normal people longer.

At the security gate for "Arrivals," I feel my stomach tightening again. I know how to do this; my parents taught me, and I have done it before. Take everything metallic out of your pockets and put it in the little basket. Wait your turn. Walk through the arch. If nobody asks me any questions, it's easy. But if they ask, I don't always hear them exactly: it's too noisy, with too many echoes off the hard surfaces. I can feel myself tensing up.

Marjory goes first: her purse onto the conveyor belt, her keys in the little basket. I see her walk through; no one asks her anything. I put my keys, my wallet, my change into the little basket and walk through. No buzz, no bleep. The man in uniform stares at me as I pick up my keys, my wallet, my change and put them back in my pockets. I turn away, toward Marjory waiting a few yards away. Then he speaks.

"May I see your ticket, please? And some ID?"

I feel cold all over. He hasn't asked anyone else—not the man with the long braided hair who pushed past me to get his briefcase off the conveyor belt, not Marjory—and I haven't done anything wrong. You don't have to have a ticket to go through security for arrivals; you just have to know the flight number you're meeting. People who are meeting people don't have tickets because they aren't traveling. Security for departures requires a ticket.

"I don't have a ticket," I say. Beyond him, I can see Marjory shift her weight, but she doesn't come closer. I don't think she can hear what he is saying, and I don't want to yell in a public place.

"ID?" he says. His face is focused on me and starting to get shiny. I pull out my wallet and open it to my ID. He looks at it, then back at me. "If you don't have a ticket, what are you doing here?" he asks.

I can feel my heart racing, sweat springing out on my neck. "I'm . . . I'm . . . I'm . . ."

"Spit it out," he says, frowning. "Or do you stutter like that all the time?"

I nod. I know I can't say anything now, not for a few minutes. I reach into my shirt pocket and take out the little card I keep there. I offer it to him; he glances at it.

"Autistic, huh? But you were talking; you answered me a second ago. Who are you meeting?"

Marjory moves, coming up behind him. "Anything wrong, Lou?"

"Stand back, lady," the man says. He doesn't look at her.

"He's my friend," Marjory says. "We're meeting a friend of mine on Flight Three-eighty-two, Gate Seventeen. I didn't hear the buzzer go off. . . ." There is an edge of anger to her tone.

Now the man turns his head just enough to see her. He relaxes a little. "He's with you?"

"Yes. Was there a problem?"

"No, ma'am. He just looked a little odd. I guess this"—he still has my card in his hand—"explains it. As long as you're with him . . ."

"I'm not his keeper," Marjory says, in the same tone that she used when she said Don was a real heel. "Lou is my friend."

The man's eyebrows go up, then down. He hands me back my card and turns away. I walk away, beside Marjory, who is headed off in a fast walk that must be stretching her legs. We say nothing until after we arrive at the secured waiting area for Gates Fifteen through Thirty. On the other side of the glass wall, people with tickets, on the departures side, sit in rows; the seatframes are shiny metal and the seats are dark blue. We don't have seats in arrivals because we are not supposed to come more than ten minutes before the flight's scheduled arrival.

This is not the way it used to be. I don't remember that, of course—I was born at the turn of the century—but my parents told me about being able to just walk right up to the gates to meet people arriving. Then after the 2001 disasters, only departing passengers could go to the gates. That was so awkward for people who needed help, and so many people asked for special passes, that the government designed these arrival lounges instead, with separate security lines. By the time my parents took me on an airplane for the first time, when I was nine, all large airports had separated arriving and departing passengers.

I look out the big windows. Lights everywhere. Red and green lights on the tips of the airplanes' wings. Rows of dim square lights along the planes, showing where the windows are. Headlights on the little vehicles that pull baggage carts. Steady lights and blinking lights.

"Can you talk now?" Marjory asks while I'm still looking out at the lights.

"Yes." I can feel her warmth; she is standing very close beside me. I close my eyes a moment. "I just . . . I can get confused." I point to an airplane coming toward a gate. "Is that the one?"

"I think so." She moves around me and turns to face me. "Are you all right?"

"Yes. It just . . . happens that way sometimes." I am embarrassed that it happened tonight, the first time I have ever been alone with Marjory. I remember in high school wanting to talk to girls who didn't want to talk to me. Will she go away, too? I could get a taxi back to Tom and Lucia's, but I don't have a lot of money with me.

"I'm glad you're okay," Marjory says, and then the door opens and people start coming off the plane. She is watching for Karen, and I am watching her. Karen turns out to be an older woman, gray-haired. Soon we are all back outside and then on the way to Karen's apartment. I sit quietly in the backseat, listening to Marjory and Karen talk. Their voices flow and ripple like swift water over rocks. I can't quite follow what they're talking about. They go too fast for me, and I don't know the people or places they speak of. It's all right, though, because I can watch Marjory without having to talk at the same time.

When we get back to Tom and Lucia's, where my car is, Don has gone and the last of the fencing group are packing things in their car. I remember that I did not put my blades and mask away and go outside to collect them, but Tom has picked them up, he says. He wasn't sure what time we would get back; he didn't want to leave them out in the dark.

I say good-bye to Tom and Lucia and Marjory and drive home in the swift dark.

Jeffrey Ford is the author of the novels *The Physiognomy, Memoranda, The Beyond,* and *The Portrait of Mrs. Charbuque.* He has published more than fifty short stories in various magazines and anthologies including *The Magazine of Fantasy & Science Fiction, Sci Fiction, Argosy, The Year's Best Fantasy & Horror, Polyphony, The Dark, Year's Best Fantasy #3, Fantasy: The Best of 2002,* and *The Thackery T. Lambshead Disease Guide.* Some of his stories can be found in his collection, *The Fantasy Writer's Assistant.* A new story collection, *The Empire of Ice Cream,* is forthcoming.

He writes:

"I still do most of my writing late at night when everyone is asleep, even though I have to be up by 6:30 a.m. to take the kids to school. Those dark, quiet hours are a beautiful time of the day. When I get too tired to stay awake, I hear voices in my ears, and very often they speak pieces of stories to me. Sometimes I remember them and write them down. When I write, I have the feeling that the stories and novels already exist somewhere in my head, or out there somewhere in another dimension, and the process of writing them is the process of merely discovering them."

Ford has won the World Fantasy Award three times for best novel, best collection, and best short story. And he won the Nebula award for this breathtaking story about the doubling joys and sorrows of synesthesia. . . .

THE EMPIRE OF ICE CREAM

JEFFREY FORD

Are you familiar with the scent of extinguished birthday candles? For me, their aroma is superceded by a sound like the drawing of a bow across the bass string of a violin. This note carries all of the melancholic joy I have been told the scent engenders—the loss of another year, the promise of accrued wisdom. Likewise, the notes of an acoustic guitar appear before my eyes as a golden rain, falling from a height just above my head only to vanish at the level of my solar plexus. There is a certain imported Swiss cheese I am fond of that is all triangles, whereas the feel of silk against my fingers rests on my tongue with the flavor and consistency of lemon meringue. These perceptions are not merely thoughts, but concrete physical experiences. Depending upon how you see it, I, like approximately nine out of every million individuals, am either cursed or blessed with a condition known as synesthesia.

It has only recently come to light that the process of synesthesia takes place in the hippocampus, part of the ancient limbic system where remembered perceptions—triggered in diverse geographical regions of the brain as the result of an external stimulus—come together. It is believed that everyone, at a point somewhere below consciousness, experiences this coinciding of sensory association, yet in most it is filtered out, and only a single sense is given predominance in one's waking world. For we lucky few, the filter is broken or perfected, and what is usually subconscious becomes conscious. Perhaps, at some distant point in history, our early ancestors were completely synesthetic, and touched, heard, smelled, tasted, and saw all at once—each specific incident mixing sensoric memory along with the perceived sense without affording precedence to the findings of one of the five portals through which "reality" invades us. The scientific explanations, as far as I can follow them, seem to make sense now, but when I was young and told my parents about the whisper of vinyl, the stench of purple, the spinning blue gyres of the church bell, they feared I was defective and that my mind was brimming with hallucinations like an abandoned house choked with ghosts.

As an only child, I wasn't afforded the luxury of being anomalous. My parents were well on in years—my mother nearly forty, my father already forty-five—when I arrived after a long parade of failed pregnancies. The fact that, at age five, I heard what I described as an angel crying whenever I touched velvet would never be allowed to stand, but was seen as an illness to be cured by whatever methods were available. Money was no object in the pursuit of perfect normalcy. And so my younger years were a torment of hours spent in the waiting rooms of psychologists, psychiatrists and therapists. I can't find words to describe the depths of medical quackery I was subjected to by a veritable army of so-called professionals who diagnosed me with everything from schizophrenia to bipolar depression to low IQ caused by muddled potty training. Being a child, I was completely honest with them about what I experienced, and this, my first mistake, resulted in blood tests, brain scans, special diets and the forced consumption of a demon's pharmacopoeia of mind-deadening drugs that diminished my will but not the vanilla scent of slanting golden sunlight on late autumn afternoons.

My only-child status, along with the added complication of my "condition," as they called it, led my parents to perceive me as fragile. For this reason, I was kept fairly isolated from other children. Part of it, I'm sure, had to do with the way my abnormal perceptions and utterances would reflect upon my mother and father, for they were the type of people who could not bear to be thought of as having been responsible for the production of defective goods. I was tutored at home by my mother instead of being allowed to attend school. She was actually a fine teacher, having a Ph.D. in History and a firm grasp of classical literature. My father, an actuary, taught me Math, and in this subject I proved to be an unquestionable failure until I reached college age. Although x=y might have been a suitable metaphor for the phenomenon of synesthesia, it made no sense on paper. The number 8, by the way, reeks of withered flowers.

What I was good at was music. Every Thursday at 3:00 in the afternoon, Mrs. Brithnic would arrive at the house to give me a piano lesson. She was a kind old lady with thinning white hair and the most beautiful fingers—long and smooth as if they belonged to a graceful young giantess. Although something less than a virtuoso at the keys, she was a veritable genius at teaching me to allow myself to enjoy the sounds I produced. Enjoy them I did, and when I wasn't being dragged hither and yon in the pursuit of losing my affliction, home base for me was the piano bench. In my imposed isolation from the world, music became a window of escape I crawled through as often as possible.

When I'd play, I could see the notes before me like a fireworks display of colors and shapes. By my twelfth year, I was writing my own compositions, and my notation on the pages accompanying the notes of a piece referred to the visual displays that coincided with them. In actuality, when I played, I was really painting—in mid-air, before my eyes—great abstract works in the tradition of Kandinsky. Many times, I planned a composition on a blank piece of paper using the crayon set of 64 colors I'd had since early childhood. The only difficulty in this was with colors like magenta and cobalt blue, which I perceive primarily as tastes, and so would have to write them down in pencil as licorice and tapioca on my colorfully scribbled drawing where they would appear in the music.

My punishment for having excelled at the piano was to lose my only real friend, Mrs. Brithnic. I remember distinctly the day my mother let her go. She calmly nodded, smiling, understanding that I had already surpassed her abilities. Still, though I knew this was the case, I cried when she hugged me good-bye. When her face was next to mine, she whispered into my ear, "Seeing is believing," and in that moment, I knew that she had completely understood my plight. Her lilac perfume, the sound of one nearly inaudible B-flat played by an oboe, still hung about me as I watched her walk down the path and out of my life for good.

I believe it was the loss of Mrs. Brithnic that made me rebel. I became desultory and despondent. Then one day, soon after my thirteenth birthday, instead of obeying my mother, who had just told me to finish reading a textbook chapter while she showered, I went to her pocketbook, took five dollars and left the house. As I walked along beneath the sunlight and blue sky, the world around me seemed brimming with life. What I wanted more than anything else was to meet other young people my own age. I remembered an ice-cream shop in town where, when passing by in the car returning from whatever doctor's office we had been to, there always seemed to be kids hanging around. I headed directly for that spot while wondering if my mother would catch up to me before I made it. When I pictured her drying her hair, I broke into a run.

Upon reaching the row of stores that contained The Empire of Ice Cream, I was out of breath as much from the sheer exhilaration of freedom as from the half-mile sprint. Peering through the glass of the front door was like looking through a portal into an exotic other world. Here were young people, my age, gathered in groups at tables, talking, laughing, eating ice cream—not by night, after dinner—but in the middle of broad daylight. I opened the door and plunged in. The magic of the place seemed to brush by me on its way out as I entered, for the conversation instantly died away. I stood in the momentary silence as all heads turned to stare at me.

"Hello," I said, smiling, and raised my hand in greeting, but I was too late. They had already turned away, the conversation resumed, as if they had merely afforded a grudging glimpse to see the door open and close at the behest of the wind. I was paralyzed by my inability to make an impression, the realization that finding friends was going to take some real work.

"What'll it be?" said a large man behind the counter.

I broke from my trance and stepped up to order. Before me, beneath a bubble dome of glass, lay the Empire of Ice Cream. I'd never seen so much of the stuff in so many colors and incarnations—with nuts and fruit, cookie and candy bits, mystical swirls the sight of which sounded to me like a distant siren. There were deep vats of it set in neat rows totaling thirty flavors. My diet had never allowed for the consumption of confections or desserts of any type, and rare were the times I had so much as a thimbleful of vanilla ice cream after dinner. Certain doctors had told my parents that my eating these treats might seriously exacerbate my condition. With this in mind, I ordered a large bowl of coffee ice cream. My choice of coffee stemmed from the fact that that beverage was another item on the list of things I should never taste.

After paying, I took my bowl and spoon and found a seat in the corner of the place from which I could survey all the other tables. I admit that I had some trepidations about digging right in, since I'd been warned against it for so long by so many adults. Instead, I scanned the shop, watching the other kids talking, trying to overhear snatches of conversation. I made eye contact with a boy my own age two tables away. I smiled and waved to him. He saw me and then leaned over and whispered something to the other fellows he was with. All four of them turned, looked at me, and then broke into laughter. It was a certainty they were making fun of me, but I basked in the victory of merely being noticed. With this, I took a large spoonful of ice cream and put it in my mouth.

There is an attendant phenomenon of the synesthetic experience I've yet to mention. Of course I had no term for it at this point in my life, but when one is in the throes of the remarkable transference of senses, it is accompanied by a feeling of "epiphany," a "eureka" of contentment that researchers of the anomalous condition would later term *noetic*, borrowing from William James. That first taste of coffee ice cream elicited a deeper noetic response than I'd ever before felt, and along with it came the appearance of a girl. She coalesced out of thin air and stood before me, obscuring my sight of the group that was still laughing. Never before had I seen through tasting, hearing, touching, smelling, something other than simple abstract shapes and colors.

She was turned somewhat to the side and hunched over, wearing a plaid skirt and a white blouse. Her hair was the same dark brown as my own, but long and gathered in the back with a green rubber band. There was a sudden shaking of her hand, and it became clear to me that she was putting out a match. Smoke swirled away from her. I could see now that she had been lighting a cigarette. I got the impression that she was wary of being caught in the act of smoking. When she turned her head sharply to look back over her shoulder, I dropped the spoon on the table. Her look instantly enchanted me.

As the ice cream melted away down my throat, she began to vanish, and I quickly lifted the spoon to restoke my vision, but it never reached my lips. She suddenly went out like a light when I felt something land softly upon my left shoulder. I heard the incomprehensible murmur of recrimination, and knew it as my mother's touch. She had found me. A great wave of laughter accompanied my removal from The Empire of Ice Cream. Later I would remember the incident with embarrassment, but for the moment, even as I spoke words of apology to my mother, I could think only of what I'd seen.

The ice-cream incident—followed hard by the discovery of the cigar box of pills I hid in my closet, all of the medication that I'd supposedly swallowed for the past six months—led my parents to believe that heaped upon my condition was now a tendency toward delinquency that would grow, if unchecked, in geometrical proportion with the passing of years. It was decided that I should see yet another specialist to deal with my behavior, a therapist my father had read about who would prompt me to talk my willfulness into submission. I was informed of this in a solemn meeting with my parents. What else was there to do but acquiesce? I knew that my mother and father wanted, in their pedestrian way, what they believed was best for me. Whenever the situation would infuriate me, I'd go to the piano and play, sometimes for three or four hours at a time.

Dr. Stullin's office was in a ramshackle Victorian house on the other side of town. My father accompanied me on the first visit, and, when he pulled up in front of the sorry old structure, he checked the address at least twice to make sure we'd come to the right place. The doctor, a round little man with a white beard and glasses with small circular lenses, met us at the front door. Why he laughed when we shook hands at the introductions, I hadn't a clue, but he was altogether jolly, like a pint-size Santa Claus dressed in a wrinkled brown suit one size too small. He swept out his arm to usher me into his house, but when my father tried to enter, the doctor held up his hand and said, "You will return in one hour and five minutes."

My father gave some weak protest and said that he thought he might be needed to help discuss my history to this point. Here the doctor's demeanor instantly changed. He became serious, official, almost commanding.

"I'm being paid to treat the boy. You'll have to find your own therapist."

My father was obviously at a loss. He looked as if he was about to object, but the doctor said, "One hour and five minutes." Following me inside, he quickly shut the door behind him.

As he led me through a series of unkempt rooms lined with crammed bookshelves, and one in which piles of paper covered the tops of tables and desks, he said, laughing, "Parents: so essential, yet sometimes like something you've stepped in and cannot get off your shoe. What else is there but to love them?"

We wound up in a room at the back of the house made from a skeleton of thin steel girders and paneled with glass panes. The sunlight poured in, and surrounding us, at the edges of the place, also hanging from some of the girders, were green plants. There was a small table on which sat a teapot and two cups and saucers. As I took the seat he motioned for me to sit in, I looked out through the glass and saw that the backyard was one large, magnificent garden, blooming with all manner of colorful flowers.

After he poured me a cup of tea, the questioning began. I'd had it in my mind to be as recalcitrant as possible, but there was something in the manner in which he had put my father off that I admired about him. Also, he was unlike other therapists I'd been to, who would listen to my answers with complete reservation of emotion or response. When he asked why I was here, and I told him it was because I'd escaped in order to go to the ice-cream shop, he scowled and said, "Patently ridiculous." I was unsure if he meant me or my mother's response to what I'd done. I told him about playing the piano, and he smiled warmly and nodded. "That's a good thing," he said.

After he asked me about my daily routine and my home life, he sat back and said, "So, what's the problem? Your father has told me that you hallucinate. Can you explain?"

No matter how ingratiating he'd been, I had already decided that I would no longer divulge any of my perceptions to anyone. Then he did something unexpected.

"Do you mind?" he asked as he took out a pack of cigarettes.

Before I could shake my head no, he had one out of the pack and lit. Something about this, perhaps because I'd never seen a doctor smoke in front of a patient before, perhaps because it reminded me of the girl who had appeared before me in the ice-cream shop, weakened my resolve to say nothing. When he flicked his ashes into his half-empty teacup, I started talking. I told him about the taste of silk, the various corresponding colors for the notes of the piano, the nauseating stench of purple.

I laid the whole thing out for him and then sat back in my chair, now somewhat regretting my weakness, for he was smiling, and the smoke was leaking out of the corners of his mouth. He exhaled, and in that cloud came the word that would validate me, define me and haunt me for the rest of my life—*synesthesia.*

By the time I left Stullin's office that day, I was a new person. The doctor spoke to my father and explained the phenomenon to him. He cited historical cases and gave him the same general overview of the neurological workings of the condition. He also added that most synesthetes don't experience the condition in such a variety of senses as I did, although it was not unheard of. My father nodded every now and then but was obviously perplexed at the fact that my long-suffered *condition* had, in an instant, vanished.

"There's nothing wrong with the boy," said Stullin, "except for the fact that he is, in a way, exceptional. Think of it as a gift, an original way of sensing the world. These perceptions are as real for him as are your own to you."

Stullin's term for my condition was like a magic incantation from a fairy tale, for through its power I was released from the spell of my parents' control. In fact, their reaction to it was to almost completely relinquish interest in me, as if after all of their intensive care I'd been found out to be an imposter now unworthy of their attention. When it became clear that I would have the ability to go about my life as any normal child might, I relished the concept of freedom. The sad fact was, though, that I didn't know how to. I lacked all experience at being part of society. My uncertainty made me shy, and my first year in public school was a disaster. What I wanted was a friend my own age, and this goal continued to elude me until I was well out of high school and in college. My desperation to connect made me ultimately nervous, causing me to act and speak without reserve. This was the early 1960s, and if anything was important in high school social circles at the time, it was remaining *cool*. I was the furthest thing from cool you might imagine.

For protection, I retreated into my music and spent hours working out compositions with my crayons and pens, trying to corral the sounds and resultant visual pyrotechnics, odors and tastes into cohesive scores. All along, I continued practicing and improving my abilities at the keyboard, but I had no desire to become a performer. Quite a few of my teachers through the years had it in their minds that they could shape me into a brilliant concert pianist. I would not allow it, and when they insisted, I'd drop them and move on. Nothing frightened me more than the thought of sitting in front of a crowd of onlookers. The weight of judgment lurking behind even one set of those imagined eyes was too much for me to bear. I'd stayed on with Stullin, visiting once a month, and no matter his persistent proclamations as to my relative normalcy, it was impossible for me, after years of my parents' insisting otherwise, to erase the fact that I was, in my own mind, a freak.

My greatest pleasure away from the piano at this time was to take the train into the nearby city and attend concerts given by the local orchestra or small chamber groups that would perform in more intimate venues. Rock and roll was all the rage, but my training at the piano and the fact that calm solitude as opposed to raucous socializing was the expected milieu of the symphony drew me in the direction of classical music. It was a relief that most of those who attended the concerts I did were adults who paid no attention to my presence. From the performances I witnessed, from the stereo I goaded my parents into buying for me, and my own reading, I, with few of the normal distractions of the typical teenager, gathered an immense knowledge of my field.

My hero was J. S. Bach. It was from his works that I came to understand mathematics . . . and, through a greater understanding of math, came to a greater understanding of Bach—the golden ratio, the rise of complexity through the reiteration of simple elements, the presence of the cosmic in the common. Whereas others simply heard his work, I could also feel it, taste it, smell it, visualize it, and in doing so was certain I was witnessing the process by which all of Nature had moved from a single cell to a virulent, diverse forest. Perhaps part of my admiration for the good cantor of Leipzig was his genius with counterpoint, a practice where two or more distinct melodic lines delicately join at certain points to form a singularly cohesive listening experience. I saw in this technique an analogy to my desire that some day my own unique personality might join with that of another's and form a friendship. Soon after hearing the fugue pieces that are part of *The Well-Tempered Clavier*, I decided I wanted to become a composer.

Of course, during these years, both dreadful for my being a laughing-stock in school and delightful for their musical revelations, I couldn't forget the image of the girl who momentarily appeared before me during my escape to The Empire of Ice Cream. The minute that Dr. Stullin pronounced me sane, I made plans to return and attempt to conjure her again. The irony of the situation was that just that single first taste of coffee ice cream had ended up making me ill, either because I'd been sheltered from rich desserts my whole life or because my system actually was inherently delicate. Once my freedom came, I found I didn't have the stomach for all of those gastronomic luxuries I had at one time so desired. Still, I was willing to chance the stomachache in order to rediscover her.

On my second trip to The Empire, after taking a heaping spoonful of coffee ice cream and experiencing again that deep noetic response, she appeared as before, her image forming in the empty space between me and the front window of the shop. This time she seemed to be sitting at the end of a couch situated in a living room or parlor, reading a book. Only her immediate surroundings, within a foot or two of her body, were clear to me. As my eyes moved away from her central figure, the rest of the couch, and the table beside her, holding a lamp, became increasingly ghostlike; images from the parking lot outside the shop window showed through. At the edges of the phenomenon, there was nothing but the merest wrinkling of the atmosphere. She turned the page, and I was drawn back to her. I quickly fed myself another bit of ice cream and marveled at her beauty. Her hair was down, and I could see that it came well past her shoulders. Bright green eyes, a small, perfect nose, smooth skin, and full lips that silently moved with each word of the text she was scanning. She was wearing some kind of very sheer, powder blue pajama top, and I could see the presence of her breasts beneath it.

I took two spoonfuls of ice cream in a row, and, because my desire had tightened my throat and I couldn't swallow, their cold burned my tongue. In the time it took for the mouthful of ice cream to melt and trickle down my throat, I simply watched her chest subtly heave with each breath, her lips move, and I was enchanted. The last thing I noticed before she disappeared was the odd title of the book she was reading—*The Centrifugal Rickshaw Dancer.* I'd have taken another spoonful, but a massive headache had blossomed behind my eyes, and I could feel my stomach beginning to revolt against the ice cream. I got up and quickly left the shop. Out in the open air, I walked for over an hour, trying to clear my head of the pain while at the same time trying to retain her image in my memory. I stopped three times along my meandering course, positive I was going to vomit, but I never did.

My resistance to the physical side effects of the ice cream never improved, but I returned to the shop again and again, like a binge drinker to the bottle, hangover be damned, whenever I was feeling most alone. Granted, there was something of a voyeuristic thrill underlying the whole thing, especially when the ice cream would bring her to me in various states of undress—in the shower, in her bedroom. But you must believe me when I say that there was much more to it than that. I wanted to know everything about her. I studied her as assiduously as I did *The Goldberg Variations* or Schoenberg's serialism. She was, in many ways, an even more intriguing mystery, and the process of investigation was like constructing a jigsaw puzzle, reconfiguring a blasted mosaic.

I learned that her name was Anna. I saw it written on one of her sketch pads. Yes, she was an artist, and I believe had great aspirations in this direction, as I did in music. I spent so many spoonfuls of coffee ice cream, initiated so many headaches, just watching her draw. She never lifted a paintbrush or pastel, but was tied to the simple tools of pencil and paper. I never witnessed her using a model or photograph as a guide. Instead, she would place the sketch pad flat on a table and hunker over it. The tip of her tongue would show itself from the right corner of her lips when she was in deepest concentration. Every so often, she'd take a drag on a cigarette that burned in an ashtray to her left. The results of her work, the few times I was lucky enough to catch a glimpse, were astonishing. Sometimes she was obviously drawing from life, the portraits of people whom she must've known. At other times she'd conjure strange creatures or mandalalike designs of exotic blossoms. The shading was incredible, giving weight and depth to her creations. All of this from the tip of a graphite pencil one might use to work a calculation or jot a memo. If I did not adore her, I might've envied her innate talent.

To an ancillary degree, I was able to catch brief glimpses of her surroundings, and this was fascinating for the fact that she seemed to move through a complete, separate world of her own, some kind of *other* reality that was very much like ours. I'd garnered enough to know that she lived in a large old house with many rooms, the windows covered with long drapes to block out the light. Her work area was chaotic, stacks of her drawings covering the tops of tables and pushed to the sides of her desk. A black-and-white cat was always prowling in and out of the tableau. She was very fond of flowers and often worked in some sun-drenched park or garden, creating painstaking portraits of amaryllis or pansies, and although the rain would be falling outside my own window, there the skies were bottomless blue.

Although over the course of years I'd told Stullin much about myself, revealed my ambitions and most secret desires, I had never mentioned Anna. It was only after I graduated high school and was set to go off to study at Gelsbeth Conservatory in the nearby city that I decided to reveal her existence to him. The doctor had been a good friend to me, albeit a remunerated one, and was always most congenial and understanding when I'd give vent to my frustrations. He persistently argued the optimistic viewpoint for me when all was as inky black as the aroma of my father's aftershave. My time with him never resulted in a palpable difference in my ability to attract friends or feel more comfortable in public, but I enjoyed his company. At the same time, I was somewhat relieved to be severing all ties to my troubled past and escaping my childhood once and for all. I was willing to jettison Stullin's partial good to be rid of the rest.

We sat in the small sunroom at the back of his house, and he was questioning me about what interests I would pursue in my forthcoming classes. He had a good working knowledge of classical music and had told me at one of our earliest meetings that he'd studied the piano when he was younger. He had a weakness for the Romantics, but I didn't hold it against him. Somewhere in the midst of our discussion I simply blurted out the details of my experiences with coffee ice cream and the resultant appearances of Anna. He was obviously taken aback. He leaned forward in his chair and slowly went through the procedure of lighting a cigarette.

"You know," he said, releasing a cascade of smoke, the aroma of which always manifested itself for me in the faint sound of a mosquito, "that is quite unusual. I don't believe there has ever been a case of a synesthetic vision achieving a figurative resemblance. They are always abstract. Shapes, colors, yes, but never an image of an object, not to mention a person."

"I know it's the synesthesia," I said. "I can feel it. The exact same experience as when I summon colors from my keyboard."

"And you say she always appears in relation to your eating ice cream?" he asked, squinting.

"Coffee ice cream," I said.

This made him laugh briefly, but his smile soon diminished, and he brought his free hand up to stroke his beard. I knew this action to be a sign of his concern. "What you are describing to me would be, considering the current medical literature, a hallucination."

I shrugged.

"Still," he went on, "the fact that it is always related to your tasting the ice cream, and that you can identify an associated noetic feeling, I'd have to agree with you that it seems related to your condition."

"I knew it was unusual," I said. "I was afraid to mention it."

"No, no, it's good that you did. The only thing troubling me about it is that I am too aware of your desire to connect with another person your age. To be honest, it has all of the earmarks of a wish fulfillment that points back to a kind of hallucination. Look, you don't need this distraction now. You're beginning your life, you are moving on, and there is every indication that you'll be successful in your art. When the other students at the Conservatory understand your abilities, you'll make friends, believe me. It won't be like high school. Chasing this insubstantial image could impede your progress. Let it go."

And so, not without a large measure of regret, I did. To an extent, Stullin was right about Gelsbeth. It wasn't like high school, and I did make the acquaintance of quite a few like-minded people with whom I could at least connect on the subject of music. I wasn't the only odd fish in that pond, believe me. To be a young person with an overriding interest in Bach or Mozart or Scriabin was its own eccentricity for those times. The place was extremely competitive, and I took the challenge. My fledgling musical compositions were greeted with great interest by the faculty, and I garnered a degree of notoriety when one day a fellow student discovered me composing a chamber piece for violins and cello using my set of crayons. I would always work in my corresponding synesthetic colors and then transpose the work, scoring it in normal musical notation.

The years flew by, and I believe they were the most rewarding of my entire life. I rarely went home to visit, save on holidays when the school was closed, even though it was only a brief train ride from the city. The professors were excellent but unforgiving of laziness and error. It wasn't a labor for me to meet their expectations. For the first time in my life, I felt what it meant to play, an activity I'd never experienced in childhood. The immersion in great music, the intricate analysis of its soul, kept me constantly engaged, filled with a sense of wonder.

Then, in my last year, I became eligible to participate in a competition for composers. There was a large cash prize, and the winner's work would be performed at a concert in the city's symphony hall by a well-known musician. The difficulty of being a composer was always the near-impossibility of getting one's work performed by competent musicians in a public venue. The opportunity presented by the competition was one I couldn't let slip away. More important than the money or the accolades would be a kind of recognition that would bring me to the attention of potential patrons who might commission a work. I knew that it was time to finally compose the fugue I'd had in mind for so many years. The utter complexity of the form, I believed, would be the best way to showcase all of my talents.

When it came time to begin the composition of the fugue, I took the money I'd made tutoring young musicians on the weekends and put it toward renting a beach house out on Varion Island for two weeks. In the summers the place was a bustling tourist spot for the wealthy, with a small central town that could be termed quaint. In those months, I wouldn't have been able to touch the price of the lowliest dwelling for a single day's rent. It was the heart of winter, though, when I took a leave from the school, along with crayons, books, and a small tape player, and fled by way of bus and cab to my secret getaway.

The house I came to wasn't one of the grand wooden mansions on stilts that lined the road along the causeway, but instead a small bungalow, much like a concrete bunker. It was painted an off-putting yellow that tasted to me for all the world like cauliflower. It sat atop a small rise, and its front window faced the ocean, giving me a sublime view of the dunes and beach. What's more, it was within walking distance of the tiny village. There was sufficient heat, a telephone, a television, a kitchen with all the appliances, and I instantly felt as at home there as I had anywhere in my life. The island itself was deserted. On my first day, I walked down to the ocean and along the shore the mile and a half to the eastern point and then back by way of the main road, passing empty houses, and I saw no one. I'd been told over the phone by the realtor that the diner in town and a small shop that sold cigarettes and newspapers stayed open through the winter. Thankfully, she was right, for without the diner, I would have starved.

The setting of the little bungalow was deliciously melancholic, and for my sensibilities that meant conducive to work. I could hear the distant breaking of waves and, above that, the winter wind blowing sand against the window glass, but these were not distractions. Instead, they were the components of a silence that invited one to dream wide awake, to let the imagination open, and so I dove into the work straightaway. On the first afternoon, I began recording in my notebook my overall plan for the fugue. I'd decided that it would have only two voices. Of course, some had been composed with as many as eight, but I did not want to be ostentatious. Showing reserve is as important a trait of technical mastery as is that of complexity.

I already had the melodic line of the subject, which had been a castoff from another project I'd worked on earlier in the year. Even though I decided it was not right for the earlier piece, I couldn't forget it and kept revising it here and there, playing it over and over. In the structure of a fugue, one posits the melodic line or subject, and then there is an answer (counterpoint), a reiteration of that line with differing degrees of variation, so that what the listener hears is like a dialogue (or a voice and its echo) of increasing complexity. After each of the voices has entered the piece, there is an episode that leads to the reentry of the voices and given answers, now in different keys. I had planned to use a technique called *stretto,* in which the answers, as they are introduced, overlap somewhat the original subject lines. This allows for a weaving of the voices so as to create an intricate tapestry of sound.

All this would be difficult to compose but nothing outlandishly original. It was my design, though, to impress the judges by trying something new. Once the fugue had reached its greatest state of complication, I wanted the piece to slowly, almost logically at first, but then without rhyme or meter, crumble into chaos. At the very end, from that chaotic cacophony, there would emerge one note, drawn out to great length, which would eventually diminish into nothing.

For the first week, the work went well. I took a little time off every morning and evening for a walk on the beach. At night I would go to the diner and then return to the bungalow to listen to Bach's *Art of the Fugue* or *Toccata and Fugue in D Minor,* some Brahms, Haydn, Mozart, and then pieces from the inception of the form by composers like Sweelinck and Froberger. I employed the crayons on a large piece of good drawing paper, and although to anyone else it would not look like musical notation, I knew exactly how it would sound when I viewed it. Somewhere after the first week, though, I started to slow down, and by Saturday night my work came to a grinding halt. What I'd begun with such a clear sense of direction had me trapped. I was lost in my own complexity. The truth was, I was exhausted and could no longer pick apart the threads of the piece—the subject, the answer, the counter-subject snarled like a ball of yarn.

I was thoroughly weary and knew I needed rest, but even though I went to bed and closed my eyes, I couldn't sleep. All day Sunday, I sat in a chair and surveyed the beach through the front window. I was too tired to work but too frustrated about not working to sleep. That evening, after having done nothing all day, I stumbled down to the diner and took my usual seat. The place was empty save for one old man sitting in the far corner, reading a book while eating his dinner. This solitary character looked somewhat like Stullin for his white beard, and at first glance, had I not known better, I could've sworn the book he was reading was *The Centrifugal Rickshaw Dancer.* I didn't want to get close enough to find out for fear he might strike up a conversation.

The waitress came and took my order. When she was finished writing on her pad, she said, "You look exhausted tonight."

I nodded.

"You need to sleep," she said.

"I have work to do," I told her.

"Well, then, let me bring you some coffee."

I laughed. "You know, I've never had a cup of coffee in my life," I said.

"Impossible," she said. "It looks to me like tonight might be a good time to start."

"I'll give it a try," I told her, and this seemed to make her happy.

While I ate, I glanced through my notebook and tried to reestablish for myself the architecture of the fugue. As always, when I looked at my notes, everything was crystal clear, but when it came time to continue on the score, every potential further step seemed the wrong way to go. Somewhere in the midst of my musing, I pushed my plate away and drew toward me the cup and saucer. My usual drink was tea, and I'd forgotten I had changed my order. I took a sip, and the dark, bitter taste of black coffee startled me. I looked up, and there was Anna, staring at me, having just lowered a cup away from her lips. In her eyes I saw a glint of recognition, as if she were actually seeing me, and I'm sure she saw the same in mine.

I whispered, "I see you."

She smiled. "I see you too," she said.

I would have been less surprised if a dog had spoken to me. Sitting dumbfounded, I reached slowly out toward where she seemed to sit across from me in the booth. As my hand approached, she leaned back away from it.

"I've been watching you for years," she said.

"The coffee?" I said.

She nodded. "You are a synesthete, am I right?"

"Yes," I said. "But you're a figment of my imagination, a product of a neurological anomaly."

Here she laughed out loud. "No," she said, "you are."

After our initial exchange, neither of us spoke. I was in a mild state of shock, I believe. "This can't be," I kept repeating in my mind, but there she was, and I could hear her breathing. Her image appeared even sharper than it had previously under the influence of the coffee ice cream. And now, with the taste that elicited her presence uncompromised by cream and sugar and the cold, she remained without dissipating for a good few minutes before beginning to mist at the edges and I had to take another sip to sharpen the focus. When I brought my cup up to drink, she also did at the same exact time, as if she were a reflection, as if I were her reflection, and we both smiled.

"I can't speak to you where I am. They'll think I've lost my mind," I whispered.

"I'm in the same situation," she said.

"Give me a half hour and then have another cup of coffee, and I'll be able to speak to you in private."

She nodded in agreement and watched as I called for the check.

By the time the waitress arrived at my booth, Anna had dissolved into a vague cloud, like the exhalation of a smoker. It didn't matter, as I knew she couldn't be seen by anyone else. As my bill was being tallied, I ordered three cups of coffee to go.

"That coffee is something, isn't it?" said the waitress. "I swear by it. Amazing you've never had any up to this point. My blood is three-quarters coffee, I drink so much of it," she said.

"Wonderful stuff," I agreed.

Wonderful it was, for it had awakened my senses, and I walked through the freezing, windy night, carrying in a box my containers of elixir, with all the joy of a child leaving school on Friday afternoon. The absurdity of the whole affair didn't escape me, and I laughed out loud remembering my whispered plan to wait a half hour and then drink another cup. The conspiratorial nature of it excited me, and I realized for the first time since seeing her that Anna had matured and grown more beautiful in the years I had forsaken her.

Back at the bungalow, I put the first of the large Styrofoam containers into the microwave in the kitchen and heated it for no more than thirty seconds. I began to worry that perhaps in Anna's existence time was altogether different and a half hour for me might be two or three or a day for her. The instant the bell sounded on the appliance, I took the cup out, seated myself at the small kitchen table and drank a long draught of the dark potion. Before I could put the cup down, she was there, sitting in the seat opposite me.

"I know your name is Anna," I said to her. "I saw it on one of your drawing pads."

She flipped her hair behind her ear on the left side and asked, "What's yours?"

"William," I said. Then I told her about the coffee ice cream and the first time I encountered her image.

"I remember," she said, "when I was a child of nine, I snuck a sip of my father's coffee he had left in the living room, and I saw you sitting at a piano. I thought you were a ghost. I ran to get my mother to show her, but when I returned you'd vanished. She thought little of it since the synesthesia was always prompting me to describe things that made no sense to her."

"When did you realize it was the coffee?" I asked.

"Oh, some time later. I again was given a taste of it at breakfast one morning, and there you were, sitting at our dining room table, looking rather forlorn. It took every ounce of restraint not to blurt out that you were there. Then it started to make sense to me. After that, I would try to see you as much as possible. You were often very sad when you were younger. I know that."

The look on her face, one of true concern for me, almost brought tears to my eyes. She was a witness to my life. I hadn't been as alone as I had always thought.

"You're a terrific artist," I said.

She smiled. "I'm great with a pencil, but my professors are demanding a piece in color. That's what I'm working on now."

Intermittently in the conversation we'd stop and take sips of coffee to keep the connection vital. As it turned out, she too had escaped her normal routine and taken a place in order to work on a project for her final portfolio review. We discovered all manner of synchronicities between our lives. She admitted to me that she'd also been a loner as a child and that her parents had a hard time dealing with her synesthetic condition. As she put it, "Until we discovered the reality of it, I think they thought I was crazy." She laughed, but I could tell by the look in her eyes how deeply it had affected her.

"Have you ever told anyone about me?" I asked.

"Only my therapist," she said. "I was relieved when he told me he'd heard of rare cases like mine."

This revelation brought me up short, for Stullin had told me he had never encountered anything of the sort in the literature. The implications of this inconsistency momentarily reminded me that she was not real, but I quickly shoved the notion from my thoughts and continued the conversation.

That night, by parsing out the coffee I had, and she doing the same, we stayed together until two in the morning, telling each other about our lives, our creative ideas, our dreams for the future. We found that our synesthetic experiences were similar and that our sense impressions were often transposed with the same results. For instance, for both her and me, the aroma of new-mown grass was circular and the sound of a car horn tasted of citrus. She told me that her father was an amateur musician who loved the piano and classical music. In the middle of my recounting for her the intricacies of the fugue I was planning, she suddenly looked up from her cup and said, "Oh no, I'm out of coffee." I looked down at my own cup and realized I'd just taken the last sip.

"Tomorrow at noon," she said as her image weakened.

"Yes," I yelled, afraid she wouldn't hear me.

Then she became a phantom, a miasma, a notion, and I was left staring at the wall of the kitchen. With her gone, I could not sit still for long. All the coffee I'd drunk was coursing through me, and because my frail system had never before known the stimulant, my hands literally shook from it. I knew sleep was out of the question, so after walking around the small rooms of the bungalow for an hour, I sat down to my fugue to see what I could do.

Immediately, I picked up the trail of where I had been headed before Saturday's mental block had set in. Everything was piercingly clear to me, and I could hear the music I was noting in various colors as if there were a tape of the piece I was creating playing as I created it. I worked like a demon, quickly, unerringly, and the ease with which the answers to the musical

problems presented themselves gave me great confidence and made my decisions ingenious. Finally, around eight in the morning (I hadn't noticed the
sunrise), the coffee took its toll on me, and I became violently ill. The stomach pains, the headache, were excruciating. At ten, I vomited, and that relieved the symptoms somewhat. At eleven A.M., I was at the diner, buying
another four cups of coffee.

The waitress tried to interest me in breakfast, but I said I wasn't hungry.
She told me I didn't look well, and I tried to laugh off her concern. When
she pressed the matter, I made some surly comment to her that I can't now
remember, and she understood I was interested in nothing but the coffee. I
took my hoard and went directly to the beach. The temperature was milder
that day, and the fresh air cleared my head. I sat in the shelter of a deep hollow amidst the dunes to block the wind, drank, and watched Anna at work,
wherever she was, on her project—a large, colorful abstract drawing. After
spying on her for a few minutes, I realized that the composition of the
piece, its arrangement of color, presented itself to me as the melodic line of
Symphony no. 8 in B Minor, by Franz Schubert. This amused me at first, to
think that my own musical knowledge was inherent in the existence of her
world, that my imagination was its essence. What was also interesting was
that such a minor interest of mine, Schubert, should manifest itself. I supposed that any aspect of my life, no matter how minor, was fodder for this
imaginative process. It struck me just as quickly, though, that I didn't want
this to be so. I wanted her to be apart from me, her own separate entity, for
without that, what would her friendship mean? I physically shook my head
to rid myself of the idea. When at noon she appeared next to me in my nest
among the dunes, I'd already managed to forget this worm in the apple.

We spent the morning together talking and laughing, strolling along the
edge of the ocean, climbing on the rocks at the point. When the coffee ran
low around three, we returned to the diner for me to get more. I asked them
to make me two whole pots and just pour them into large, plastic take-out
containers. The waitress said nothing but shook her head. In the time I was
on my errand, Anna, in her own world, brewed another vat of it.

We met up back at my bungalow, and as evening came on, we took out
our respective projects and worked together, across from each other at the
kitchen table. In her presence, my musical imagination was on fire, and she
admitted to me that she saw for the first time the overarching structure of
her drawing and where she was headed with it. At one point, I became so
immersed in the work, I reached out and picked up what I thought would
be one of my crayons but instead turned out to be a violet pastel. I didn't
own pastels, Anna did.

"Look," I said to her, and at that moment felt a wave of dizziness pass
over me. A headache was beginning behind my eyes.

She lifted her gaze from her work and saw me holding the violet stick.

We both sat quietly, in awe of its implications. Slowly, she put her hand out across the table toward me. I dropped the pastel and reached toward her. Our hands met, and I swear I could feel her fingers entangled with mine.

"What does this mean, William?" she said with a note of fear in her voice and let go of me.

As I stood up, I lost my balance and needed to support myself by clutching the back of the chair. She also stood, and as I approached her, she backed away. "No, this isn't right," she said.

"Don't worry," I whispered. "It's me." I took two wobbly steps and drew so close to her I could smell her perfume. She cringed but did not try to get away. I put my arms around her and attempted to kiss her.

"No," she cried. Then I felt the force of both her hands against my chest, and I stumbled backward onto the floor. "I don't want this. It's not real," she said and began to hurriedly gather her things.

"Wait, I'm sorry," I said. I tried to scrabble to my feet, and that's when the sum total of my lack of sleep, the gallons of caffeine, the fraying of my nerves, came together like the twining voices in a fugue and struck me in the head as if I had been kicked by a horse. My body was shaking, my vision grew hazy, and I could feel myself phasing in and out of consciousness. I managed to watch Anna turn and walk away as if passing through the living room. Somehow I got to my feet and followed her, using the furniture as support. The last thing I remember was flinging open the front door of the small house and screaming her name.

I was found the next morning, lying on the beach, unconscious. It was the old man with the white beard from the diner, who, on his daily early-morning beachcombing expedition, came across me. The police were summoned. An ambulance was called. I came to in a hospital bed the next day, the warm sun, smelling of antique rose, streaming through a window onto me.

They kept me at the small shore hospital two days for psychological observation. A psychiatrist visited me, and I managed to convince him that I'd been working too hard on a project for school. Apparently the waitress at the diner had told the police that I'd been consuming ridiculous amounts of coffee and going without sleep. Word of this had gotten back to the doctor who attended to me. When I told him it was the first time I had tried coffee and that I'd gotten carried away, he warned me to stay off it, telling me they found me in a puddle of my own vomit. "It obviously disagrees with your system. You could've choked to death when you passed out." I thanked him for his advice and promised him I'd stay well away from it in the future.

In the days I was at the hospital, I tried to process what had happened with Anna. Obviously, my bold advance had frightened her. It crossed my mind that it might be better to leave her alone in the future. The very fact that I was sure I'd made physical contact with her was, in retrospect, unsettling. I wondered if perhaps Stullin was right, and what I perceived to be a result of synesthesia was actually a psychotic hallucination. I left it an open issue in my mind as to whether I would seek her out again. One more meeting might be called for, I thought, at least to simply apologize for my mawkish behavior.

I asked the nurse if my things from the beach house had been brought to the hospital, and she told me they had. I spent the entirety of my last day there dressed and waiting to get the okay for my release. That afternoon, they brought me my belongings. I went carefully through everything, but it became obvious to me that my crayon score for the fugue was missing. Everything else was accounted for, but there was no large sheet of drawing paper. I asked the nurse, who was very kind, actually reminding me somewhat of Mrs. Brithnic, to double-check and see if everything had been brought to me. She did and told me there was nothing else. I called the Varion Island police on the pretense of thanking them and asked if they had seen the drawing. My fugue had vanished. I knew a grave depression would descend upon me soon due to its disappearance, but for the moment I was numb and slightly pleased to merely be alive.

I decided to return to my parents' house for a few days and rest up before returning to the conservatory in order to continue my studies. In the bus station near the hospital, while I was waiting, I went to the small newspaper stand in order to get a pack of gum and a paper with which to pass the time. As I perused the candy rack, my sight lighted upon something that made me feel the way Eve must have when she first saw the apple, for there was a bag of Thompson's Coffee-Flavored Hard Candy. The moment I read the words on the bag, I reached for them. There was a spark in my solar plexus, and my palms grew damp. *No Caffeine* the package read, and I was hard-pressed to believe my good fortune. I looked nervously over my shoulder while purchasing three bags of them, and when, on the bus, I tore a bag open, I did so with such violence, a handful of them scattered across the seat and into the aisle.

I arrived by cab at my parents' house and had to let myself in. Their car was gone, and I supposed they were out for the day. I hadn't seen them in some months and almost missed their presence. When night descended and they didn't return, I thought it odd but surmised they were on one of the short vacations they often took. It didn't matter. I sat at my old home base on the piano bench and sucked on coffee-flavored hard candies until I grew too weary to sit up. Then I got into my childhood bed, turned to face the wall as I always had when I was little, and fell asleep.

The next day, after breakfast, I resumed my vigil that had begun on the long bus trip home. By that afternoon my suspicions as to what had become of my fugue were confirmed. The candy did not bring as clear a view of Anna as did the ice cream, let alone the black coffee, but it was focused enough for me to follow her through her day. I was there when she submitted my crayon score as her art project for the end-of-the-semester review. How she was able to appropriate it, I have no idea. It defied logic. In the fleeting glimpses I got of the work, I tried to piece together how I'd gone about weaving the subjects and their answers. The second I would see it, the music would begin to sound for me, but I never got a good-enough look at it to sort out the complex structure of the piece. The two things I was certain of were that the fugue had been completed right up to the point where it was supposed to fall into chaos, and that Anna did quite well with her review because of it.

By late afternoon, I'd come to the end of my Thompson's candies and had but one left. Holding it in my hand, I decided it would be the last time I would conjure a vision of Anna. I came to the conclusion that her theft of my work had cancelled out my untoward advance, and we were now even, so to speak. I would leave her behind as I had before, but this time for good. With my decision made, I opened the last of the hard confections and placed it on my tongue. That dark, amber taste slowly spread through my mouth, and, as it did, a cloudy image formed and crystallized into focus. She had the cup to her mouth, and her eyes widened as she saw me seeing her.

"William," she said. "I was hoping to see you one more time."

"I'm sure," I said, trying to seem diffident, but just hearing her voice made me weak.

"Are you feeling better?" she asked. "I saw what happened to you. I was with you on the beach all that long night but could not reach you."

"My fugue," I said. "You took it."

She smiled. "It's not yours. Let's not kid ourselves; you know you are merely a projection of my synesthetic process."

"Who is a projection of whose?" I asked.

"You're nothing more than my muse," she said.

I wanted to contradict her, but I didn't have the meanness to subvert her belief in her own reality. Of course, I could have brought up the fact that she was told that figurative synesthesia was a known version of the disease. This was obviously not true. Also, there was the fact that her failed drawing, the one she'd abandoned for mine, was based on Schubert's Eighth, a product of my own knowledge working through her. How could I convince her she wasn't real? She must've seen the doubt in my eyes, because she became defensive in her attitude. "I'll not see you again," she said. "My therapist has given me a pill he says will eradicate my synesthesia. We have that here, in the true reality. It's already begun to work. I no longer hear my cigarette smoke as the sound of a faucet dripping. Green no longer tastes of lemon. The ring of the telephone doesn't feel like burlap."

This pill was the final piece of evidence. A pill to cure synesthesia? "You may be harming yourself," I said, "by taking that drug. If you cut yourself off from me, you may cease to exist. Perhaps we are meant to be together." I felt a certain panic at the idea that she would lose her special perception, and I would lose the only friend I had ever had who understood my true nature.

"Dr. Stullin says it will not harm me, and I will be like everyone else. Good-bye, William," she said and pushed the coffee cup away from her.

"Stullin," I said. "What do you mean, Stullin?"

"My therapist," she said, and although I could still see her before me, I could tell I had vanished from her view. As I continued to watch, she lowered her face into her hands and appeared to be crying. Then my candy turned from the thinnest sliver into nothing but saliva, and I swallowed. A few seconds more, and she was completely gone.

It was three in the afternoon when I put my coat on and started across town to Stullin's place. I had a million questions, and foremost was whether or not he treated a young woman named Anna. My thoughts were so taken by my last conversation with her that when I arrived in front of the doctor's walkway, I realized I had not noticed the sun go down. It was as if I had walked in my sleep and awakened at his address. The street was completely empty of people or cars, reminding me of Varion Island. I took the steps up to his front door and knocked. It was dark inside except for a light on the second floor, but the door was slightly ajar, which I thought odd, given it was the middle of the winter. Normally, I would have turned around and gone home after my third attempt to get his attention, but there was too much I needed to discuss.

I stepped inside, closing the door behind me. "Dr. Stullin," I called. There was no answer. "Doctor?" I tried again and then made my way through the foyer to the room where the tables were stacked with paper. In the meager light coming in through the window, I found a lamp and turned it on. I continued to call out as I went from room to room, turning on lights, heading for the sunroom at the back of the place where we always had our meetings. When I reached that room, I stepped inside, and my foot came down on something alive. There was a sudden screech that nearly made my heart stop, and then I saw the black-and-white cat, whose tail I had trod upon, race off into another room.

It was something of a comfort to be again in that plant-filled room. The sight of it brought back memories of it as the single safe place in the world when I was younger. Oddly enough, there was a cigarette going in the ashtray on the table between the two chairs that faced each other. Lying next to it, opened to the middle and turned down on its pages, was a copy of *The Centrifugal Rickshaw Dancer*. I'd have preferred to see a ghost to that book. The sight of it chilled me. I sat down in my old seat and watched the smoke from the cigarette twirl up toward the glass panes. Almost instantly, a great weariness seized me, and I closed my eyes.

That was days ago. When I found the next morning I could not open the doors to leave, that I could not even break the glass in order to crawl out, it became clear to me what was happening. At first I was frantic, but then a certain calm descended upon me, and I learned to accept my fate. Those stacks of paper in that room on the way to the sunroom—each sheet held a beautiful pencil drawing. I explored the upstairs, and there, on the second floor, found a piano and the sheet music for Bach's *Grosse Fugue*. There was a black-and-white photograph of Mrs. Brithnic in the upstairs hallway and one of my parents standing with Anna as a child.

That hallway, those rooms, are gone, vanished. Another room has disappeared each day I have been trapped here. I sit in Stullin's chair now, in the only room still remaining (this one will be gone before tonight), and compose this tale—in a way, my fugue. The black-and-white cat sits across from me, having fled from the dissipation of the house as it closes in around us. Outside, the garden, the trees, the sky, have all lost their color and now appear as if rendered in graphite—wonderfully shaded to give them an appearance of weight and depth. So too with the room around us: the floor, the glass panels, the chairs, the plants, even the cat's tail and my shoes and legs have lost their life and become the shaded grey of a sketch. I imagine Anna will soon be free of her condition. As for me, who always believed himself to be unwanted, unloved, misunderstood, I will surpass being a mere artist and become instead a work of art that will endure. The cat meows loudly, and I feel the sound as a hand upon my shoulder.

I wouldn't normally cite resource material for a story, but in the writing of "The Empire of Ice Cream" I was dealing with concepts I was not readily very familiar with. For information on the condition of synesthesia, I turned to The Man Who Tasted Shapes, *by Richard E. Cytowic.* The Art of Fugue, *by Alfred Mann, was a great help in understanding the history and architecture of this unusual musical form. I first came across the condition of figurative synesthesia in Thackery T. Lambshead's* Guide to Eccentric and Discredited Diseases.

Throughout every calendar year, the members of the Science Fiction and Fantasy Writers of America read and recommend novels and stories for the annual Nebula Awards. The editor of the "Nebula Awards Report" collects the recommendations and publishes them in the SFWA Forum. Near the end of the year, the NAR editor tallies the endorsements, draws up the preliminary ballot, and sends it to all active SFWA members. Under the current rules, each novel and story enjoys a one-year eligibility period from its date of publication. If the work fails to make the preliminary ballot during that interval, it is dropped from further Nebula consideration.

The NAR editor processes the results of the preliminary ballot and then compiles a final ballot listing the five most popular novels, novellas, novelettes, and short stories. For purposes of the Nebula Award, a novel is 40,000 words or more; a novella is 17,500 to 39,999 words; a novelette is 7,500 to 17,499 words; and a short story is 7,499 words or fewer. At the present time, SFWA impanels both a novel jury and a short-fiction jury to oversee the voting process and, in cases where a presumably worthy title was neglected by the membership at large, to supplement the five nominees with a sixth choice. Thus, the appearance of extra finalists in any category bespeaks two distinct professes: jury discretion and ties.

Founded in 1965 by Damon Knight, the Science Fiction Writers of America began with a charter membership of seventy-eight authors. Today it boasts over a thousand members and an augmented name. Early in his tenure, Lloyd Biggle Jr., SFWA's first secretary-treasurer, proposed that the organization periodically select and publish the year's best stories. This notion quickly evolved into the elaborate balloting process, an annual awards banquet, and a series of Nebula anthologies. Judith Ann Lawrence designed the trophy from a sketch by Kate Wilhelm. It is a block of Lucite containing a rock crystal and a spiral nebula made of metallic glitter. The prize is handmade, and no two are exactly alike.

The Damon Knight Grand Master Nebula Award goes to a living author for a lifetime of achievement in science fiction and/or fantasy. In accordance with SFWA's bylaws, the president nominates a candidate, normally after consulting with previous presidents and the board of directors. This nomination then goes before the officers; if a majority approves, the candidate becomes a Grand Master. Past recipients include Robert A. Heinlein (1974), Jack Williamson (1975), Clifford D. Simak (1976), L. Sprague de Camp (1978), Fritz Leiber (1980), Andre Norton (1983), Arthur C. Clarke (1985), Isaac Asimov (1986), Alfred Bester (1987), Ray Bradbury (1988), Lester del Rey (1990), Frederik Pohl (1992), Damon Knight (1994), A. E. van Vogt (1995), Jack Vance (1996), Poul Anderson (1997), Hal Clement (Harry Stubbs) (1998), Brian W. Aldiss (1999), Philip José Farmer (2000), Ursula K. Le Guin (2002), and Robert Silverberg (2003).

The thirty-ninth annual Nebula Awards banquet was held at the Weston Seattle Hotel in Seattle, Washington, on April 17, 2004, where Nebula Awards were given in the categories of novel, novella, novelette, short story, script, and lifetime achievement (Grand Master). As part of a program to recognize and appreciate senior writers who have made significant contributions to our field but who are no longer active or whose excellent work may no longer be as widely known as it once was, Charles L. Harness was honored as SFWA's Author Emeritus. Previous Author Emeritii include Emil Petaja (1995), Wilson Tucker (1996), Judith Merril (1997), Nelson Bond (1998), William Tenn (Phillip Klass) (1999), Daniel Keyes (2000), Robert Sheckley (2001), and Katherine MacLean (2003).

SELECTED TITLES FROM THE 2004 PRELIMINARY NEBULA BALLOT

NOVELS

The Mount by Carol Emshwiller (Small Beer Press)
Fitcher's Brides by Gregory Frost (Tor)
A Scattering of Jades by Alexander C. Irvine (Tor)
Maximum Ice by Kay Kenyon (Bantam)
The Scar by China Miéville (Del Rey)
Fallen Host by Lyda Morehouse (Roc)
The Return of Santiago by Mike Resnick (Tor)
Humans by Robert J. Sawyer (Tor)
Ruled Britannia by Harry Turtledove (New American Library)
Red Thunder by John Varley (Ace)

SHORT STORIES

"The Rose in Twelve Petals" by Theodora Goss
  (*Realms of Fantasy*, April 2002)
"Taste of Summer" by Ellen Klages
  (*Black Gate*, February 2002)
"The Tale of the Golden Eagle" by David D. Levine
  (*The Magazine of Fantasy & Science Fiction*, June 2003)
"Will You Be an Astronaut?" by Greg van Eekhout
  (*The Magazine of Fantasy & Science Fiction*, September 2002)

1965

Best Novel: *Dune* by Frank Herbert
Best Novella: "The Saliva Tree" by Brian W. Aldiss ‖ "He Who Shapes" by Roger Zelazny (tie)
Best Novelette: "The Doors of His Face, the Lamps of His Mouth" by Roger Zelazny
Best Short Story: "'Repent, Harlequin!' Said the Ticktockman" by Harlan Ellison

1966

Best Novel (tie): *Flowers for Algernon* by Daniel Keyes ‖ *Babel-17* by Samuel R. Delany
Best Novella: "The Last Castle" by Jack Vance
Best Novelette: "Call Him Lord" by Gordon R. Dickson
Best Short Story: "The Secret Place" by Richard McKenna

1967

Best Novel: *The Einstein Intersection* by Samuel R. Delany
Best Novella: "Behold the Man" by Michael Moorcock
Best Novelette: "Gonna Roll the Bones" by Fritz Leiber
Best Short Story: "Aye, and Gomorrah" by Samuel R. Delany

1968

Best Novel: *Rite of Passage* by Alexei Panshin
Best Novella: "Dragonrider" by Anne McCaffrey
Best Novelette: "Mother to the World" by Richard Wilson
Best Short Story: "The Planners" by Kate Wilhelm

1969

Best Novel: *The Left Hand of Darkness* by Ursula K. Le Guin
Best Novella: "A Boy and His Dog" by Harlan Ellison
Best Novelette: "Time Considered as a Helix of Semi-Precious Stones" by Samuel R. Delany
Best Short Story: "Passengers" by Robert Silverberg

1970

Best Novel: *Ringworld* by Larry Niven
Best Novella: "Ill Met in Lankhmar" by Fritz Leiber
Best Novelette: "Slow Sculpture" by Theodore Sturgeon
Best Short Story: No Award

1971

Best Novel: *A Time of Changes* by Robert Silverberg
Best Novella: "The Missing Man" by Katherine MacLean
Best Novelette: "The Queen of Air and Darkness" by Poul Anderson
Best Short Story: "Good News from the Vatican" by Robert Silverberg

1972

Best Novel: *The Gods Themselves* by Isaac Asimov
Best Novella: "A Meeting with Medusa" by Arthur C. Clarke
Best Novelette: "Goat Song" by Poul Anderson
Best Short Story: "When It Changed" by Joanna Russ

1973

Best Novel: *Rendezvous with Rama* by Arthur C. Clarke
Best Novella: "The Death of Doctor Island" by Gene Wolfe
Best Novelette: "Of Mist, and Grass, and Sand" by Vonda N. McIntyre
Best Short Story: "Love Is the Plan, the Plan Is Death" by James Tiptree, Jr.
Best Dramatic Presentation: *Soylent Green*
  Stanley R. Greenberg for Screenplay (based on the novel *Make Room! Make Room!*), Harry Harrison for *Make Room! Make Room!*

1974

Best Novel: *The Dispossessed* by Ursula K. Le Guin
Best Novella: "Born with the Dead" by Robert Silverberg
Best Novelette: "If the Stars Are Gods" by Gordon Eklund and Gregory Benford

Best Short Story: "The Day Before the Revolution" by Ursula K. Le Guin

Best Dramatic Presentation: *Sleeper* by Woody Allen

Grand Master: Robert A. Heinlein

1975

Best Novel: *The Forever War* by Joe Haldeman

Best Novella: "Home Is the Hangman" by Roger Zelazny

Best Novelette: "San Diego Lightfoot Sue" by Tom Reamy

Best Short Story: "Catch that Zeppelin!" by Fritz Leiber

Best Dramatic Writing: Mel Brooks and Gene Wilder for *Young Frankenstein*

Other Awards & Honors:
Grand Master: Jack Williamson

1976

Best Novel: *Man Plus* by Frederik Pohl

Best Novella: "Houston, Houston, Do You Read?" by James Tiptree, Jr.

Best Novelette: "The Bicentennial Man" by Isaac Asimov

Best Short Story: "A Crowd of Shadows" by Charles L. Grant

Other Awards & Honors:
Grand Master: Clifford D. Simak

1977

Best Novel: *Gateway* by Frederik Pohl

Best Novella: "Stardance" by Spider and Jeanne Robinson

Best Novelette: "The Screwfly Solution" by Raccoona Sheldon

Best Short Story: "Jeffty Is Five" by Harlan Ellison

Other Awards & Honors:
Special Award: *Star Wars*

1978

Best Novel: *Dreamsnake* by Vonda N. McIntyre

Best Novella: "The Persistence of Vision" by John Varley

Best Novelette: "A Glow of Candles, a Unicorn's Eye" by Charles L. Grant

Best Short Story: "Stone" by Edward Bryant

Other Awards & Honors:
Grand Master: L. Sprague de Camp

1979

Best Novel: *The Fountains of Paradise* by Arthur C. Clarke
Best Novella: "Enemy Mine" by Barry Longyear
Best Novelette: "Sandkings" by George R. R. Martin
Best Short Story: "giANTS" by Edward Bryant

1980

Best Novel: *Timescape* by Gregory Benford
Best Novella: "The Unicorn Tapestry" by Suzy McKee Charnas
Best Novelette: "The Ugly Chickens" by Howard Waldrop
Best Short Story: "Grotto of the Dancing Deer" by Clifford D. Simak

Other Awards & Honors:
Grand Master: Fritz Leiber

1981

Best Novel: *The Claw of the Conciliator* by Gene Wolfe
Best Novella: "The Saturn Game" by Poul Anderson
Best Novelette: "The Quickening" by Michael Bishop
Best Short Story: "The Bone Flute" by Lisa Tuttle
   (This Nebula Award was declined by the author.)

1982

Best Novel: *No Enemy but Time* by Michael Bishop
Best Novella: "Another Orphan" by John Kessel
Best Novelette: "Fire Watch" by Connie Willis
Best Short Story: "A Letter from the Clearys" by Connie Willis

1983

Best Novel: *Startide Rising* by David Brin
Best Novella: "Hardfought" by Greg Bear
Best Novelette: "Blood Music" by Greg Bear
Best Short Story: "The Peacemaker" by Gardner Dozois

Other Awards & Honors:
Grand Master: Andre Norton

1984

Best Novel: *Neuromancer* by William Gibson
Best Novella: "PRESS ENTER□" by John Varley
Best Novelette: "Bloodchild" by Octavia E. Butler
Best Short Story: "Morning Child" by Gardner Dozois

1985

Best Novel: *Ender's Game* by Orson Scott Card
Best Novella: "Sailing to Byzantium" by Robert Silverberg
Best Novelette: "Portraits of His Children" by George R.R. Martin
Best Short Story: "Out of All Them Bright Stars" by Nancy Kress

Other Awards & Honors:
Grand Master: Arthur C. Clarke

1986

Best Novel: *Speaker for the Dead* by Orson Scott Card
Best Novella: "R & R" by Lucius Shepard
Best Novelette: "The Girl Who Fell into the Sky" by Kate Wilhelm
Best Short Story: "Tangents" by Greg Bear

Other Awards & Honors:
Grand Master: Isaac Asimov

1987

Best Novel: *The Falling Woman* by Pat Murphy
Best Novella: "The Blind Geometer" by Kim Stanley Robinson
Best Novelette: "Rachel in Love" by Pat Murphy
Best Short Story: "Forever Yours, Anna" by Kate Wilhelm

Other Awards & Honors:
Grand Master: Alfred Bester

1988

Best Novel: *Falling Free* by Lois McMaster Bujold
Best Novella: "The Last of the Winnebagos" by Connie Willis
Best Novelette: "Schrodinger's Kitten" by George Alec Effinger
Best Short Story: "Bible Stories for Adults, No. 17: The Deluge" by
    James Morrow

Other Awards & Honors:
Grand Master: Ray Bradbury

1989

Best Novel: *The Healer's War* by Elizabeth Ann Scarborough
Best Novella: "The Mountains of Mourning" by Lois McMaster
    Bujold
Best Novelette: "At the Rialto" by Connie Willis
Best Short Story: "Ripples in the Dirac Sea" by Geoffrey A. Landis

1990

Best Novel: *Tehanu: The Last Book of Earthsea* by Ursula K. Le Guin
Best Novella: "The Hemingway Hoax" by Joe Haldeman
Best Novelette: "Tower of Babylon" by Ted Chiang
Best Short Story: "Bears Discover Fire" by Terry Bisson

Other Awards & Honors:
Grand Master: Lester del Rey

1991

Best Novel: *Stations of the Tide* by Michael Swanwick
Best Novella: "Beggars in Spain" by Nancy Kress
Best Novelette: "Guide Dog" by Mike Conner
Best Short Story: "Ma Qui" by Alan Brennert

1992

Best Novel: *Doomsday Book* by Connie Willis
Best Novella: "City of Truth" by James Morrow
Best Novelette: "Danny Goes to Mars" by Pamela Sargent
Best Short Story: "Even the Queen" by Connie Willis

Other Awards & Honors:
Grand Master: Frederik Pohl

1993

Best Novel: *Red Mars* by Kim Stanley Robinson
Best Novella: "The Night We Buried Road Dog" by Jack Cady
Best Novelette: "Georgia on My Mind" by Charles Sheffield
Best Short Story: "Graves" by Joe Haldeman

1994

Best Novel: *Moving Mars* by Greg Bear
Best Novella: "Seven Views of Olduvai Gorge" by Mike Resnick
Best Novelette: "The Martian Child" by David Gerrold
Best Short Story: "A Defense of the Social Contracts" by Martha
   Soukup

Other Awards & Honors:
Grand Master: Damon Knight
Author Emeritus: Emil Petaja

1995

Best Novel: *The Terminal Experiment* by Robert J. Sawyer
Best Novella: "Last Summer at Mars Hill" by Elizabeth Hand

Best Novelette: "Solitude" by Ursula K. Le Guin
Best Short Story: "Death and the Librarian" by Esther Friesner

Other Awards & Honors:
Grand Master: A. E. van Vogt
Author Emeritus: Wilson "Bob" Tucker

1996
Best Novel: *Slow River* by Nicola Griffith
Best Novella: "Da Vinci Rising" by Jack Dann
Best Novelette: "Lifeboat on a Burning Sea" by Bruce Holland Rogers
Best Short Story: "A Birthday" by Esther M. Friesner

Other Awards & Honors:
Grand Master: Jack Vance
Author Emeritus: Judith Merril

1997
Best Novel: *The Moon and the Sun* by Vonda N. McIntyre
Best Novella: "Abandon in Place" by Jerry Oltion
Best Novelette: "The Flowers of Aulit Prison" by Nancy Kress
Best Short Story: "Sister Emily's Lightship" by Jane Yolen

Other Awards & Honors:
Grand Master: Poul Anderson
Author Emeritus: Nelson Slade Bond

1998
Best Novel: *Forever Peace* by Joe Haldeman
Best Novella: "Reading the Bones" by Sheila Finch
Best Novelette: "Lost Girls" by Jane Yolen
Best Short Story: "Thirteen Ways to Water" by Bruce Holland Rogers

Other Awards & Honors:
Grand Master: Hal Clement (Harry Stubbs)
Bradbury Award: J. Michael Straczynski
Author Emeritus: William Tenn (Philip Klass)

1999
Best Novel: *Parable of the Talents* by Octavia E. Butler
Best Novella: "Story of Your Life" by Ted Chiang
Best Novelette: "Mars Is No Place for Children" by Mary A. Turzillo

Best Short Story: "The Cost of Doing Business" by Leslie What
Best Script: *The Sixth Sense* by M. Night Shyamalan

Other Awards & Honors:
Grand Master: Brian W. Aldiss
Author Emeritus: Daniel Keyes

2000

Best Novel: *Darwin's Radio* by Greg Bear
Best Novella: "Goddesses" by Linda Nagata
Best Novelette: "Daddy's World" by Walter Jon Williams
Best Short Story: "macs" by Terry Bisson
Best Script: *Galaxy Quest* by Robert Gordon and David Howard

Other Awards & Honors:
Grand Master: Philip José Farmer
Bradbury Award: Yuri Rasovsky and Harlan Ellison
Author Emeritus: Robert Sheckley

2001

Best Novel: *The Quantum Rose* by Catherine Asaro
Best Novella: "The Ultimate Earth" by Jack Williamson
Best Novelette: "Louise's Ghost" by Kelly Link
Best Short Story: "The Cure for Everything" by Severna Park
Best Script: *Crouching Tiger, Hidden Dragon* by James Schamus, Kuo
    Jung Tsai, and Hui-Ling Wang; from the book by Du Lu Wang

Other Awards & Honors:
President's Award: Betty Ballantine

2002

Best Novel: *American Gods* by Neil Gaiman
Best Novella: "Bronte's Egg" by Richard Chwedyk
Best Novelette: "Hell Is the Absence of God" by Ted Chiang
Best Short Story: "Creature" by Carol Emshwiller
Best Script: *The Lord of the Rings: The Fellowship of the Ring* by Fran
    Walsh and Philippa Boyens and Peter Jackson; based on *The Lord of
    the Rings* by J.R.R. Tolkien

Other Awards & Honors:
Grand Master: Ursula K. Le Guin
Author Emeritus: Katherine MacLean

2003

Best Novel: *The Speed of Dark* by Elizabeth Moon

Best Novella: "Coraline" by Neil Gaiman

Best Novelette: "The Empire of Ice Cream" by Jeffrey Ford

Best Short Story: "What I Didn't See" by Karen Joy Fowler

Best Script: *The Lord of the Rings: The Two Towers* by Fran Walsh & Philippa Boyens and Stephen Sinclair and Peter Jackson; based on *The Lord of the Rings* by J.R.R. Tolkien

Other Awards & Honors:

Grand Master: Robert Silverberg

Author Emeritus: Charles L. Harness

The Science Fiction and Fantasy Writers of America, Incorporated, includes among its members most of the active writers of science fiction and fantasy. According to the bylaws of the organization, its purpose "shall be to promote the furtherance of the writing of science fiction, fantasy, and related genres as a profession." SFWA informs writers on professional matters, protects their interests, and helps them in dealings with agents, editors, anthologists, and producers of non-print media. It also strives to encourage public interest in and appreciation of science fiction and fantasy.

Anyone may become an active member of SFWA after the acceptance of and payment for one professionally published novel, one professionally produced dramatic script, or three professionally published pieces of short fiction. Only science fiction, fantasy, and other prose fiction of a related genre, in English, shall be considered as qualifying for active membership. Beginning writers who do not yet qualify for active membership may join as associate members; other classes of membership include illustrator members (artists), affiliate members (editors, agents, reviewers, and anthologists), estate members (representatives of the estates of active members who have died), and institutional members (high schools, colleges, universities, libraries, broadcasters, film producers, futurist groups, and individuals associated with such institutions).

Anyone who is not a member of SFWA may subscribe to *The Bulletin of the Science Fiction and Fantasy Writers of America*. The magazine is published quarterly, and contains articles by well-known writers on all aspects of their profession. Subscriptions are $18.00 a year or $31.00 for two years. For information on how to subscribe to the *Bulletin,* or for more information about SFWA, write to:

SFWA, Inc.
P. O. Box 877
Chestertown, MD 21620
USA

Readers are also invited to visit the SFWA site on the World Wide Web at the following address:

http://www.sfwa.org